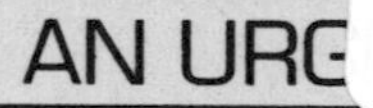

AN URG

"I'll have to put the matter to the Amalgamated Worlds Administration on Earth before we can discuss this further," Sumitral was saying. "In the meantime, I am glad to see we continue with the spirit of cooperation that has characterized this world of Rraladoon for over thirty years."

"Pardon me," Todd said, edging adroitly between the two diplomats, "I see little evidence of cooperation in your faces but a lot of wariness. Speaker Hrrto, would you like to know what the Gringg asked for in our talks?"

"Reeve, no!" Markudian cried, outraged.

"Markudian, yes!" Todd said, rounding on him. "I see this as a real test of Rraladoonan integrity, not Hayuman/Hrruban competition. Consider this," he went on urgently, looking around the circle. "One of the reasons the Gringg thought we were a single species was the way we worked together. I was delighted by that because it showed we'd learned to trust each other. But the first stir of the pot from outside, and we separate into distrustful—and greedy—strangers." Todd stared at each one in turn, his glance gliding over Greene's smug expression. "So let's reinstate the honesty we have always used in dealings on Rraladoon."

Ace Books by Anne McCaffrey

THE ROWAN
DAMIA
DAMIA'S CHILDREN

Books by Anne McCaffrey and Jody Lynn Nye

THE DEATH OF SLEEP
CRISIS ON DOONA
TREATY AT DOONA

ANNE McCAFFREY
AND
JODY LYNN NYE

ACE BOOKS, NEW YORK

This book is an Ace original edition,
and has never been previously published.

TREATY AT DOONA

An Ace Book / published by arrangement with
Bill Fawcett & Associates

PRINTING HISTORY
Ace edition/September 1994

ISBN: 0-441-00089-4

ACE®
Ace Books are published by The Berkley Publishing Group,
200 Madison Avenue, New York, NY 10016.
ACE and the "A" design are trademarks
belonging to Charter Communications, Inc.

PRINTED IN THE UNITED STATES OF AMERICA

10 9 8 7 6 5 4 3 2 1

TREATY
AT
DOONA

CHAPTER 1

THROUGH THE VOID THE SMALL BLUE-WHITE STAR twinkled enticingly, promising light and heat in generous measure. Those aboard the massive, matte-black spaceship approaching that star system on an elliptical angle had been drawn to investigate it by the various communication signals emanating from the third planet of that star. The planet, a blue and green globe around which three pocked moons circled, was also ringed by orbiting drones and several spaceships of considerably less mass than the newcomer. Such vehicles were considered by the passengers of the enormous spaceship to be as worthy of investigation as the broadcasts, for both phenomena indicated the presence of sentient beings and advanced technology.

The visiting vessel, which had no insignia or identifiable markings on its kilometer-long, irregularly cylindrical hull, sailed boldly toward this so-intriguing star system. Even as those aboard contained their initial elation of discovery and began to record this event, sensors at the system perimeter were spotted, their messages and internal composition examined by probes, the mechanisms briefly prevented from performing the function for which they had been designed. Excitement grew to a feverish pitch as specialists and consultants eagerly inspected the diagrams of the sophisticated warning systems. Everything pointed to the amazing fact that the inhabitants of this star system had created and nurtured a civilization sufficiently advanced to be worth the strangers' complete and immediate attention.

At the door of the Council Chamber, Todd Reeve, Human colony leader of Doonarrala, bowed and shook hands with arriving delegates, hopefully dissembling his most uneasy and ambivalent feelings about this wretched conference. He'd never imagined the idea of turning the Treaty Island subcontinent into a free trade and spaceport facility would come this far. The slim margin by which the colony referendum had passed vindicated his position, but the "yeas" had barely outnumbered the "nays," and the measure had passed. So he had been forced to take the next step—this meeting of Hrruban and Hayuman officials.

Beside him in the receiving line was his best friend, Hrriss, their twenty-seven-year friendship badly strained by their current, disparate views on the subject of a free port. Todd found it very hard to understand how Hrriss should pursue a course which, so obviously to Todd, abrogated both the Decision and Treaty by which this unusual mixed colony had been promulgated.

Right now, being greeted by smiles and affability, none of the delegates would have suspected that the almost legendary friendship of Hayuman and Hrruban was under considerable stress. For the first time, they had agreed to disagree.

The visiting delegates entered the room one by one, exchanging pleasantries with each of the Doonarralan dignitaries. Todd was impatient to get past the preliminaries and plunge into the problem, which might relieve the tension that twisted his nerves and tightened his neck and shoulders. His wife, Kelly, had done her best to knead out the worst of the kinks, silently supporting her husband throughout his campaign to defeat the proposal. Despite their mutual respect and deep attachment to this planet and all it stood for, Todd wasn't sure if Kelly totally agreed with him on this matter. She'd said all the proper things and had accompanied him and his father on their trips to all the Villages where the pros and cons were argued in open debate. But somehow, the feeling niggled at him that she was not as dead set against a free-trade port as he was.

Todd's father, Ken Reeve, had worked tirelessly for a "nay" verdict on the referendum, for the situation represented his worst nightmare come true for Doona: an insidious expansion that defeated the initial purpose of the colony—for both species. Doona could cease to be the pastoral paradise it was if suddenly plunged into rapid commercial development.

Somehow, Todd must make that fear so real to the delegates that today's conference would be the end of the matter. Otherwise, he might be forced to resign his position as the Hayuman colony leader, since he could not wholeheartedly accept such a change in Doonarrala.

The fact that the idea for a trade and spaceport facility originated with the Hrruban half of the colony did nothing to placate Todd's anxieties. The original premise, hammered into the Decision—and later the Treaty—would, he argued, be invalidated if part of the planet were to be commercialized. Ironic that this whole wretched idea had come from his suggestion that they name the western subcontinent "The Hrrunatan" after the late First Speaker, as a mark of the respect and love in which all Doonarralans, Hayuman and Hrruban, had held Hrruna.

Todd and the old First Speaker had had a most unusual relationship, despite their differences of species, culture, and age. It was therefore doubly ironic that what had been meant as a sincere tribute to Hrruna was rebounding against those he had so subtly protected during the colony's early stages.

Todd almost welcomed the discomfort of the formal, tailored tunic which rubbed his neck raw as the receiving line continued. It kept distracting him from his troubles. His thick black hair was newly cut and neatly brushed and he knew he looked well in the formal tunic, despite its constriction. He had good shoulders, a deep chest, and was tall, even for a Hayuman. Todd had never stood on ceremony but, as Kelly had said at their mostly silent breakfast, ceremony could be used to advantage. As he hoped to use it today. That didn't keep his collar from binding his neck.

He took some consolation in seeing that Hrriss was likewise chafed by Hrruban ceremonial gear, surreptitiously tugging at the jewelled straps that crisscrossed his tawny-furred torso under the loose red robe he wore for such a formal occasion. On other, less-charged occasions Hrriss would have glanced up at Todd, a hand-span taller than he, and rolled his large green eyes ceilingward, flattening back his tufted ears to express his discomfort. But today they were opponents—still friendly, still hoping for a way out of the dilemma which obsessed both—so their normal exchanges were constrained.

Beyond Hrriss was his father, Hrrestan, Hrruban co-leader with Todd, who was as staunchly in favor of the proposed alteration of Doonarrala's function as Todd and his father were opposed to it.

The veteran diplomat was currently chatting to the Hrruban Space Arm representative, Prrid. An old Stripe, the Senior Space Commandant stood with his hands clasped behind him, rocking back and forth, his tail tip held at a relaxed angle. Beside him, his aide, a mature and seasoned explorer, Mrrunda, stood on one foot and then the other, trying not to appear impatient for the proceedings to begin. He seemed to feel exactly the way Todd did. For all the times when, as a small boy, Todd had wished for a tail, he was glad now that he didn't have one, for it would have been lashing nervously. On the other hand, Hrrestan's caudal appendage was curved slightly, showing that he was at ease. The rest of the Hrruban Space Arm party were already standing near the conference table: three more officers, each with pouches stuffed with documentation.

"Admiral Barnstable," Todd said, calling himself to order as he greeted a tall, white-haired man in uniform who resembled the very portrait of an ancient sea captain. In a face of weather-beaten red, surprising in a man who had never been out on the seas of any planet, he had sharp blue eyes with which he now studied Todd. Hoping he passed muster, Todd smiled and bowed.

"Welcome to the Treaty Island of Doonarrala, sir. May I present Leader Hrrestan, Senior Commandant Prrid, and his aide, Captain Mrrunda?"

Everett Cabot Barnstable, representing Spacedep, was one of the more important delegates to the conference. There had been a lot of jockeying to see who would head the military Arm of Amalgamated Worlds, with its huge budget, resources, and manpower. Barnstable, possessed of a strong conservative bent and vast support on Earth, had finally succeeded. His predecessor, Admiral Landreau, had been no friend to Doonarrala. Barnstable was known as a decision-maker, a good administrator and negotiator. Todd felt Barnstable, though not entirely perfect, was a significant improvement over Landreau. At least, Doonarrala had had no trouble from Spacedep since he had been in charge—until now. Barnstable wasn't so reactionary as to favor Human Separatism, but he was sure to support the inauguration of a base on the subcontinent; a base that would be as useful to the Hayuman Space Arm as to the Hrruban. Another point that Todd had tried to emphasize in his contentions was that Spacedep had no right on Doonarrala; had always meant trouble to the community. And now they wanted to invite Spacedep *in*?

Barnstable accorded his Hrruban opposite numbers a sharp, respectful half-bow, eyeing them as keenly as they did him. Then he gave an odd, convulsive shudder and frowned. "Confound it, I can't believe it's safe for a body to shift planets so fast. Ten minutes ago I stood on a grid on Earth, and then I was decanted on Doona."

"It saves time," Prrid said, lifting his upper lip in a toothy Hrruban grin.

Todd was relieved to see that Barnstable was familiar with the awesome sight of a Hrruban smile.

"I imagine you do not favor further grid installations on Doonarrala," Todd said to Prrid, seizing the opportunity for some subtle indirection.

Prrid's unexpectedly orange eyes regarded him, the pupil slits narrowed to a thin line.

"Zat will depend, Leader Rrrev. Zat will depend."

"Come now, Reeve," Admiral Barnstable said, turning jocular. "Surely you won't stand in the way of progress."

"If I were certain it was progress . . ." Todd let his comment trail off. So Spacedep was, as he anticipated, eager to obtain a legitimate position on Doonarrala.

"Now, Todd," Jilamey Landreau said, appearing at Todd's elbow, a-jingle with the tiny bells sewn in patterns on his stylish motley-colored attire. "It's not like you to resist any change which improves this planet. The more grids, the merrier, what? Think of how many more people would come to the Snake Hunts," he added, grinning mischievously. Then he turned to the Senior Commandant and his aide, his round face ingenuous. "Todd saved my life on my first Snake Hunt, you know. By the way, Admiral, Commandant, I represent the Grid . . ."

"Save it till later, Jilamey," Todd said, grabbing his friend by the elbow and pushing him away from the military group.

"Oh, I can take a hint . . ." Jilamey said with mock dismay, marching off into the conference room with an agitated jingling of his tiny bells.

Todd sighed to himself: it would seem that all his erstwhile friends were aligned against him. But Jilamey was "Grid" mad. If civilians of either planet could have had matter transmitters, Jilamey Landreau would have been first in the queue. Perhaps it was as well that the Hrrubans were so paranoid about sharing their technology.

To benefit from a trade and spaceport installation, the Hrrubans would have to put down grid facilities, probably the largest feasible one—similar in size to the one they had originally used to transport their "village" in the earliest days of the Doonan colonization.

Todd couldn't really blame the Hrrubans for wanting a free trade port. Their lack of large cargo vessels had weighed heavily against Hrruban traders expanding their territories. Of course, there were grids transporting goods among Hrruban home and colony worlds, but there still didn't seem to be much metal-bearing ore available on Hrruban worlds for more than small two- or three-man exploration vessels. Those were hardly large enough for cost-efficient intersystem trade. Spacedep had persisted in its restrictions on the sale of Hayuman spacecraft to Hrruban merchants. On the day that the Hrrubans released information and/or licensed grid matter transmitters to Hayumans, Spacedep would lift its embargo on vessel transfers.

"Yo there, Reeve," said Fred Horstmann, a stout man with fair hair and a flamboyant gold-trimmed tunic, an independent trader affiliated with Codep's leading administrator and negotiator, Captain Ali Kiachif. That wily old skipper was already holding court at the near edge of the great oval table. Ali had not changed in all the years Todd had known him, except for a little more gray in his hair and beard.

Some of the lesser lights chatted quietly at the other end of the table. Lorena Kaldon, with scarlet-dyed hair and a firm, pointed chin, was a banker from one of the major Amalgamated Worlds institutions. Her presence suggested that the project was favored by the money markets, and Todd's spirits sank even further. Damn it! Were they that certain this wretched facility would be approved? Her opposite number, Hrrouf, a financier from Hrruba, soon arrived with a pale-pelted female named Nrrena, whose limp air was belied by her scarred ears and forearms. Both were moderately broad Stripes, indicating that they were of good family.

Closely following them was Hrrin, a Rraladoonan from the Third Hrruban Village, who represented Hrruban independent traders and was an old friend of Todd's and Hrriss'. The stripe down his back and tail was narrower than Hrriss', and his leonine mane was much darker. Hrrin had kept his opinions to himself, so he might indeed side with Todd.

Barnstable and the two Hrruban Space Arm delegates moved straight for the conference table, to check their places.

Old Ali Kiachif caught Todd's eye and winked as he rose to take Barnstable's outstretched hand. It was too early in the day for a drink, but Todd could have sworn that the bulge in the old spacer's tunic pocket was a flask. It probably contained mlada, the Hrruban native liquor and Kiachif's favorite tipple in this lane of space. Though Kiachif had made port only a short hour before the conference was due to start, that was time enough for him to acquire "needful" supplies. Drunk or sober, the old man's mind was sharp, never missing the chance to turn an advantage his own way, occasionally even supporting the good of Doonarrala to his own detriment. But would Ali prove an ally or antagonist? He had every reason to want better shipping facilities on Doonarrala but he certainly wouldn't want to give up his edge on interstellar trade. Todd sighed.

Last to arrive, undoubtedly by design, was Hrrto, Second Speaker for External Affairs, currently the most senior administrator from Hrrestan's homeworld of Hrruba. This was the first time any of the Speakers had visited Doonarrala since the First Speaker, Hrruna, had "joined the Ancestral Stripes."

Todd knew that Hrrto, who had not always been a strong supporter of the Rrala Experiment, was under considerable pressure to make his mark at this conference. Rumor had it that he was on the short list of nominees for the post of First Speaker. He would be caught between his desire to win on his own merits and the necessity to compare favorably with his late superior in wisdom and probity. Comparisons were always odious, and even a Second Speaker from a well-regarded Stripe would not be exempt from them. The election was not far off, a fact that Todd knew would make Hrrto eager to conclude the conference as soon as possible so he could devote his time and energy to domestic matters.

Beside Hrrto, but one pace behind him, walked a female Hrruban in plain black robes: Hrrto's aide, Mllaba. Her hot yellow-green eyes showed Todd that her deference was deliberate, but not entirely out of respect for her employer. Todd found her a curious individual. Hrriss told him that Mllaba had abstained from cub-bearing and even companionship, in her drive to advance a political career. She came from a very broad Stripe, equal in rank on Hrruba to Hrrestan himself.

Hrrto turned first to Hrrestan and Hrriss, favoring his fellow Hrrubans with his first words, then came to face Todd.

"Speaker Hrrto," Todd said in High Formal Hrruban, bowing deeply. "You honor us with your presence."

"Zodd Rrev, I greet you," Hrrto said cordially, bowing slightly. Todd realized with a shock how much older Hrrto seemed. His tawny mane was almost all silver, and he moved with greater care, as if his formal red robes weighed heavily on his shoulders. "My assistant, Mllaba."

"Honored," Todd said.

"It is I who am honrrred." Mllaba replied in a low, throaty voice.

"Now that all the delegates are assembled," Todd said, "let us begin." He nodded at an attendant, who shut the heavy folding doors of the conference room.

Hrrestan politely led Second Speaker to his designated place and bowed him into it, before taking his own seat. Hrrin leaped up to move a chair from the row against the wall for Mllaba. She said nothing, but her tail twitched once before she draped it demurely to one side instead of sticking it through the gap in the chair back intended for the Hrruban caudal appendage.

As Todd took his seat he appreciated the irony that he now presided over proceedings in this chamber where he and Hrriss had once been on trial for their honor and more. The ultimate stake that day had been nothing less than the continued existence of their shared world, Doona/Rrala. In Todd's estimation, today's deliberations were no less critical. Doubly ironic was the fact that this was also his first chairmanship as Human colony leader, and he wanted it—against all odds—to fail!

He glanced around the table, meeting the eyes of friends and acquaintances, forcing a smile which he hoped would not appear inane or false.

"Friends," said Todd. "As co-host of this conclave, I welcome you all to this vital conference. I have to tell you that I am completely opposed to the formation of a spaceport and commercial facility on the Hrrunatan subcontinent." There was a murmur of surprise at his bald statement. "I feel strongly, as does my father and our former leader, Hu Shih, that such an installation is in direct conflict with the Decision made on Doonarrala thirty-three years ago.

"That Decision was ratified in a Treaty nine years ago, setting this planet aside as a peaceful, co-existent colony, specifically limited to an agrarian economy. To install an interstellar complex—even at the distance of the subcontinent—violates both Decision and Treaty. In light of this prejudice, I turn the meeting over to my co-leader, Hrrestan." He nodded to Hrrestan at the head of the table and sat down amidst a buzz of muted comments.

With great dignity, Hrrestan rose, nodding to Todd and holding up his hands, claws sheathed, to still the murmuring.

"There are many *good* reasons why the establishment of a *separate* and autonomous spaceport facility on the Hrrunatan subcontinent would benefit both our species. With the appropriate safeguards, ensuring the integrity of the work here"—he waved his hand to include the Treaty Island—"and what has been so successful on the main continent of Doonarrala, many of us feel that there would be no conflict, certainly no abrogation of either Decision or Treaty in having a free trade port. We must ensure"—he paused to accord Todd a respectful bow—"that all reservations and apprehensions are discussed and set to rest."

"With respect," Jilamey said, standing up and bowing to Hrrestan, motions which set off his minute bells. "I really do believe that this planet is ideally suited for three separate and diverse installations. Certainly it would be much easier to conduct trade in this sector of the galaxy, expediting"—he turned to the Hrrubans—"our allies' participation, at the moment seriously hampered by a lack of cargo transport." Sweeping the table with a glance, Jilamey managed to subtly criticize both Admiral Barnstable's Spacedep for its refusal to sell Hrrubans larger vessels that could handle the potential volume of trade, and the Hrrubans for refusing to reciprocate by releasing more of their matter transporters. "I will not, of course, at this point, mention the crucial need for more grids."

"Thank you for not mentioning that, Jilamey," Todd said, glaring at him to keep off a topic that made Barnstable, Prrid, and the Second Speaker all bristle with irritation.

Hrrestan let the claws on his right hand unsheathe so he could drum them warningly. Shrugging, Jilamey subsided, but there was the faintest smile on his lips.

"Speaker Hrrto," Hrrestan said, "are you willing to comment on the proposed trade center?"

The Second Speaker, absently smoothing the lapels of his ceremonial robe, rose to his feet. Mllaba, beside him, sat stiffly erect, ears slightly aslant to catch every word her superior uttered.

"Hrruban trade and commerce would significantly benefit from such a facility," Hrrto began, switching his thick hands to a firm and oratorial hold on the lapels. "Due to certain constraints"—he flicked his left ear and pointedly did not glance in the Admiral's direction—"only a bare trickle of Hrruban goods, some urgently sought on Hayuman worlds, manages to reach their destination. Ze cost is prohibitive, and subject to priorities which make deliveries uncertain. A universal marketplace would certainly improve industry on Hrruba and open up immense possibilities for further, mutually productive manufacturing. Having discussed this possibility with Hrruban officials in all areas of business management"—he held one hand out to Mllaba for a sheaf of notes which he then brandished as proof of his efforts—"ze majority would be quite amenable to such a project. With, of course"—he held up the notes—"safeguards to protect ze existing colony and ze Zreaty Island from any commercial contamination."

"How large a trade grid will Hrruba install?" Jilamey asked, all but physically pouncing on Hrrto, who recoiled.

"Zat subject has certainly not been discussed as yet, Mr. Landreau," Hrrto said repressively as Hrrestan simultaneously called for order, glaring at the unrepentant Jilamey.

"What I'd like to know," Tanarey Smith said, his voice overriding others wishing to be heard, "is whether or not the construction of such an installation will be joint?" His expression suggested that it had better be.

"That question is premature, Mr. Smith," Hrrestan said. "The matter to be discussed is the advisability of such an installation in the first instance, not who will build it."

"Ze Speakers must be assured zat regulations will follow zose already in force—" Hrrto began.

"Aw," Ali Kiachif interrupted, "let's not start that old keep-the-home-world-sacred stuff."

"Hell's bells," added Fred Horstmann, "there isn't a space captain worth his salt, Hayuman or Hrruban, who hasn't a fair idea where each homeworld has to be." He caught Hrrto's outraged expression. "Well, you only have to narrow the options available, Speaker."

"Don't we know each other well enough now, after thirty-something years," Tanarey Smith began, "to forget this nonsense about homeworld integrity?"

"No!" Second Speaker Hrrto leaped to his feet, the fur on his back bristling. "Homeworld integrity is not nonsense. It is ze most vital point of agreement between our two races and may not, must not, be abrogated. Never be abrogated."

"So is the Treaty!" Todd couldn't restrain himself from saying in a tone just short of a shout.

"The Treaty stipulates," Barnstable said, raising his own voice to top Todd's, "the conditions on which the Doonarrala colony is promulgated. It says absolutely nothing about that subcontinent nor the use to which it can be put. The Treaty specifies only the main continent, known as Doonarrala, and the Treaty Island, where observers are permitted and where any disputes are settled. This isn't an abrogation. It's an expansion."

"Well now, I shouldn't want to see anything violate the Treaty," Kiachif said, somehow inserting himself into the discussion. "I seen it start and don't intend to see it finish. How about a space station?" And he looked appealingly at Todd. Though Todd hadn't expected such a suggestion, he welcomed it.

The delegates, all speaking at once, responded excitedly. "Space station?" "Landside free port?" "Now, wait a minute!" "I thought the matter under discussion was the use of The Hrrunat!"

Appalled, Speaker Hrrto listened to the babble, his increasing outrage at such lack of courtesy demonstrated by the lashing of his tail.

"SILENCE!" Todd belted the word out in such a roar that there was silence, as much from surprise as to wait until ears stopped ringing. "You will all be heard in order. In order, I repeat. We may all know each other very well, but that is no reason to dispense with formality."

Even Mllaba regarded him with respect, and Second Speaker was mollified.

"Hrrestan . . ." Todd said, turning the meeting over once more to its chairman.

Having thrown out the suggestion of a space station, Ali Kiachif was acknowledged by Hrrestan to give particulars. He was listened to politely but when he had finished, five people vied to follow him.

Discreetly, Hrrestan acknowledged Hrrin, who spoke about the benefits to the burgeoning agrarian economy which could not profitably market its surplus beyond those few traders who regularly reprovisioned at the present small, and totally inadequate, space base. More people could be accommodated at a land base than a space station; therefore the agronomy of Doonarrala would certainly benefit more from a facility at The Hrrunat.

Lorena rose to support a space facility where the integrity of the colony would not be at risk. But, as she was speaking for bankers who would profit from either venture, she chose to fall on the side of the more expensive installation. Hrrouf, in terser language but with a thick accent, appeared to corroborate her statements on the Hrruban behalf.

Fred Horstmann wanted to be heard on the matter of the frail safety of a space station, whereas a land port wasn't half as vulnerable and furthermore could simultaneously accommodate far more vessels and cargo at a considerably lower cost.

"Costs could be reduced even further with the use of the bigger grids," Jilamey interjected, causing the Admiral and the Hrruban commandant to erupt in protest.

"Jilamey!" Todd said again, using his penetrating voice to cut through the rising level of peripheral conversations. "One more word about grid and you are O-U-T. Out!"

Jilamey's unrepentant shrug was on the order of it-never-hurts-to-try.

"I don't like gridding around," Barnstable snapped out, his crisp voice ringing in the big chamber, "and a big one wouldn't be any easier to endure than a small one. Brr! At least with a ship, you know where you are and how you got there." One of his ice-white brows lowered slightly as he turned in Second Speaker's direction. "But I would like to take this occasion, face to face, to ask the Honorable Senior Commandant Prrid and the Honored Second Speaker why the Hrrubans won't trust us with grid technology."

Hrrto's eyes gleamed, and the fur at the back of his neck bristled. Todd prepared to stand up and dive in.

"All I am prepared to say is zat it is not a question of trust, Admiral," Prrid replied. Second Speaker merely bowed to second that comment and turned his head resolutely from Barnstable.

"But will you say whether or not—if this project goes through—there would be a large grid at a free trade port?" Jilamey asked.

"No more will be discussed about ze grrrids," Second Speaker said with such finality that Jilamey subsided. "We discuss ze advisability of a free trade spaceport on Ze Hrrunat."

"Then let us get down to the nitty-gritty," Ali Kiachif said. "The size of the place, its organization. Will it be jointly administered?"

"Of course!" Mrrunda said emphatically.

Ali grinned at him. "Of course!"

Hrrto grumbled out a growl, shifting himself to face the old captain. "Hrruban trade has been at a disadvantage zat would be remedied by such a facility. I am instructed to make suitable arrangements."

So, Todd thought to himself, no reprieve was forthcoming from the Hrruban side. How was he going to delay the matter? A glance at the massive old-fashioned, long case clock in the corner of the room gave him the excuse he needed.

"Let us adjourn for lunch before we deal with details," Todd suggested, glancing about the table. "There's a splendid sampling of the local dishes, both Hrruban and Hayuman, for your pleasure. If you will follow me?"

Not every one of the delegates was pleased at such an interruption, but Barnstable was clearly in favor of a meal. The alacrity with which Second Speaker rose from his chair did much to sway other Hrrubans to follow his example. Hrrouf immediately sought Lorena Kaldon for a few private words as they followed Todd.

The wide marble hallways of the Federation Center were peopled by tour groups and employees hurrying to and fro. But these stood aside to allow the distinguished delegates to move freely toward the dining area. As they neared the facility, delightful aromas wafted out into the hallway. Todd took a lungful and began to relax a little. Hrriss' jaw dropped open in a contented smile. The anticipation of food was having much the same effect on the others.

"Friends, welcome!" a warm voice greeted them from inside the doors. "I'm your hostess, Kelly Reeve. Please, come in and make yourselves at home." She repeated her greeting in excellent High Hrruban, bowing low toward Hrrto.

Her coifed red hair ablaze in the room's pendant lights, Kelly Solinari Reeve beckoned them inside. She was a tall woman, whose graceful athletic figure was enhanced by the wheat-colored dress and short jacket she wore. As if caught in the act of making last-minute preparations, she set down the earthenware pitcher she was holding on the edge of a long table laid for a feast and advanced to the doorway, beaming.

"Mrs. Reeve, this is a pleasant surprise," Tanarey Smith said, bowing over Kelly's hand.

Ali Kiachif sprang forward to greet her. "A fine day, a fair lassie, and food fit for a Pharaoh. How are you, lass?"

"Wonderful, Ali," Kelly said, returning the old spacer's embrace with a kiss on his grizzled cheek. "How good to see you! And Jilamey! We're so glad you got here. I was very surprised to see no one but Barrington on the landing pad two days ago. We didn't know what became of you." Barrington, Jilamey's "gentleman's gentleman," accompanied him on almost every trip the young businessman made. He was a combination of amanuensis, mother hen, and genie from the lamp, to judge by Jilamey's accounts of his silent miracles of organization.

"Well, surprise," Jilamey said sheepishly. "I got a ride on the grid with Admiral Barnstable, hands across the water—or the void, so to speak." He winked at the Admiral, who ignored the cheeky familiarity. "I sent Old Patience-is-a-Virtue on by himself to breathe ship air and mind my parcels. He's marvelous. So I was able to stay home and tweak a few more deals before I came up. Grids are wonderful. You only grow lovelier, Kelly." He seized one of her hands to kiss.

"Well, your house is ready. I was up there only yesterday to check on it."

"I am in your debt," Jilamey said expansively.

The nephew of the late Admiral Landreau had bought a large house high on a hilltop southwest of the original First Villages, and equipped it via Codep transport ship with all manner of modern doodads, including private vehicles not specifically mentioned nor barred by the Doona charter. As for horses, he owned a few, but except for the weeks he was on-planet, they boarded in stables owned by friends. Except for the ambassadorial residences on Treaty Island, his was the only permanent home on Doonarrala owned by a nonresident But then, Jilamey was an exception to many rules.

"Well, sit down and eat," Kelly said, waving him to a seat. The table was laid with individual place settings, but the platters and bowls of food were intended to be passed from guest to guest. "How have you been?"

"I'm surviving," young Landreau replied happily. "How are the Alley Cats? And Hrriss' cubs? I'm looking forward to seeing them."

"And they can't wait to see you," Kelly assured him. "They all send their love. Nrrna is minding all the children while I play hostess."

"I've got a baby present for—what's her name? Hrrunna?"

"You're so good with them," Kelly said, shaking her head. "You should have some of your own." She caught herself and threw him a little shrug of apology.

"Not me." Jilamey laughed, without a trace of discomfort. "I'm much more definitely uncle material. Besides, I couldn't spoil yours so well if I had my own tagging along behind me."

"How is my youngest grandchild?" Hrrestan asked fondly, his voice dropping into intimate mode, as he stopped to rub cheeks with Kelly.

"Growing," Kelly said with a grin. "She follows everything

with her eyes now, and that tail of hers is positively prehensile. When she doesn't want you to stop patting her back, she holds on."

"Hrrunna is named for our dear First Speaker," Hrrestan explained to Hrrto. "She was born a mere four days after he joined the Ancestral Stripes."

"A most touching sentiment," Hrrto said, with a mere suggestion of a drop-jawed smile. "It is good to know those so far away from the homeworld would recall him and pay such a tribute. We of the High Council all regret the loss of our senior statesman."

To Todd and Hrriss, Hrrto's regret didn't ring entirely true. Hrriss shook his head, recalling that Second was enmeshed at present in a difficult contest to win the vacant speakership for himself, which likely overshadowed any real feelings he might have.

Kelly burst in to dispel the uncomfortable silence. "Well, come along, everyone. I hope you enjoy everything. Don't stand on ceremony. I'm sure you're famished." She came up to Todd and lifted her face for a kiss.

"How's it been going?" she asked in a hasty whisper as the others moved about the table to find the place cards with their names.

"From whose viewpoint?" Todd asked ironically. Kelly gave him a quick, worried look as he tucked her arm in his and escorted her up the length of the room. "Ali tried to help by suggesting a space station. Jilamcy's doing his best to irritate Hrrto and Barnstable with his constant nudging about grids. But—" She sighed as he conceded, "the majority see it as a way to improve their credit position one way or another! Even Hrrin sees the spaceport as profitable to the agricultural community."

"Oh? A new outlet for surplus. Hmm. Well, it would be. Ooops, sorry, love."

Smoothly, Kelly ducked away from him toward the Second Speaker.

"Ah, gracious sir," she said in her impeccable High Hrruban, "we have the urfa pie you so much enjoyed the last time you favored us with your presence," and she steered him toward his place and began serving him.

Then she turned her bright smile on Tanarey Smith, who beamed under her charm.

Soon everyone was seated, with filled plates and glasses, looking all too pleased with the morning's meeting. Despite the fact that the menu included two of Todd's personal favorites, he could find no appetite and pushed the food about on his plate.

He could hear snatches of conversations and shook his head because, without exception, everyone favored the instant establishment of a spaceport on The Hrrunat. The instanter, the better, and why wasn't this suggested years ago?

Because Hu Shih and Hrruna had squashed that snake any time it came out of its lair.

Why wasn't I able to? Todd thought in miserable isolation. *Dad and Hu Shih are as certain as I am that such an installation abrogates both Decision and Treaty.* Why *am I unable to convince the others?* He sighed deeply, noting Kelly's anxious gaze on him. He smiled at her, though it was a feeble attempt, and pushed a forkful into his mouth. The food was almost cold but he chewed it anyway. *I must not be the leader everyone thought I was, if I cannot protect the community from an evil* I *perceive as encroachment.*

The jingle of Jilamey's bells broke through his thoughts, and he saw the enthusiastic entrepreneur bumping up and down on his chair as he explained, with many gestures as well as body language, some point he was trying to make.

Maybe, thought Todd, *I was foolish to stop Jilamey yattering away about the grids. Maybe if I let him irritate Hrrto, Prrid, and that bunch sufficiently, they'll leave in a huff. Todd, my friend, think with your head, not your heart. There're more ways to deflect a snake than ramming a boulder up its maw.*

He brightened considerably as he turned over the possibilities for sowing discord. Certainly, if he insisted on discussing grids, he'd disorganize the meeting so that nothing could be accomplished but a venting of temper. He'd have to be subtle, which had never been his best suit, but so much was at stake.

Just then a stray phrase from Lorena Kaldon caught his attention.

"Once again, I want to know if this project will be open for tenders?" She looked agitated. "And who will make the final decision?"

"Why, obviously, that must be decided by the villages," Todd said, smiling affably as if he'd been following the discussion all along.

"In this instance," Barnstable began, joining in with a verbal pounce, "since the matter concerns more than the villages, the parent worlds must have a voice."

Todd lifted one eyebrow and gave Hrriss a long look, which Hrriss shrugged off. That annoyed Todd even more. Was Hrriss blind that he didn't see how eager Spacedep was to get a legal foothold on Doonarrala?

"Parochial attitudes must give way to interstellar requirements," Tanarey Smith said, and Lorena nodded hearty agreement.

"Yes, but with both Earth and Hrruba complaining about costs already, where is the money coming from?" Todd asked.

"This project will interest independent financial sources . . ." Lorena began.

"Don't you worry about the financing," Tanarey said.

"All right, I won't," Todd said, "but how does the facility manage itself once it's built?"

"Tariff, of course," Fred Horstmann said, regarding Todd with surprise, as if that source was too obvious.

"Which includes a yearly rental?" Hrrestan asked in a bland tone. Even Todd regarded his co-leader with surprise at that nicely landed bombshell. Hrrestan dropped his jaw in a smile. "You did not think that we Rraladoonans would let you have a whole subcontinent rent-free from us, did you? A percentage of the annual income . . ."

Todd covered his eyes and bent his head so no one would see his grin. Maybe Hrrestan wasn't totally lost to common sense in this matter. In Todd's mind, however, a hefty addition to the colony's coffers did not quite compensate for the violation of the Treaty. As it was, Hrrestan's remarks effectively silenced everyone—except for the jingling bells of Jilamey's suit as, first he sank back in his chair, then abruptly sat up to cause more chiming.

"Of course," the young entrepreneur said, beaming at his sudden inspiration, "Doonarrala must benefit from the project. But I think it's only a matter of working out an acceptable figure. Think of all that has already been worked out here on Treaty Island so harmoniously." He gave his arm a hearty shake, grinning at the effect on those seated around the table.

In the small reception room on board the cruiser which was describing a temporary orbit just outside the range of Doona's most distant moon, a smartly uniformed Spacedep rating awaited the passenger of an admiralty scout ship that had just arrived. The esteemed visitor, a stocky man in his early forties with a commander's insignia on his uniform, had a broad spread of shoulders, a strongly drawn jaw, and sharp, brown eyes that made the rating quail inwardly when they momentarily met hers. There was something almost cold about him. His square, handsome face was unlined except for the disapproving indentations framing his molded mouth. The rating waited at attention while the visitor cleared decontam and slipped out of his pressure suit. The glassteel doors slid open one at a time, allowing him to enter the atmosphere lock, and finally to admit him to the lounge.

"Welcome aboard, Commander," the rating said, firing off a perfect salute. "The captain awaits you in her office. I'm to take you to her." Frozen like a waxwork, she held the pose, waiting for the guest's reply.

"Thank you," Commander Jon Greene said, returning the salute promptly, but not too promptly.

The rating relaxed subtly, as if the precise timing was what she had expected, and Greene smiled inwardly. Without a single glance back at the scout ship now being swarmed over by a crowd of technicians for its courtesy checkup, he strode off behind his guide.

Greene surveyed the various work stations they passed, glancing first at the hands and then at the eyes of the crew working at them. Each person, as Greene met his or her eyes, straightened up involuntarily, and went back to the task at hand with renewed energy. As Admiral Barnstable's personal assistant, Greene represented Spacedep command in the flesh, and expected efficiency and the stiff-backed respect of subordinate officers.

Greene himself had come up through the ranks. By virtue of sheer efficiency and drive, he became indispensable to his various superiors, working his way up to a position of trust where he was empowered to carry out tasks that required strategy and thought. By making his commanders look their best, he acquired a vicarious importance.

In time, he had managed to ingratiate himself with the new head of Spacedep, Admiral Barnstable. Greene was an ambitious man, and hoped to go higher still in time. Who knew what might await him in the future? The chairmanship of Spacedep? A seat on the Amalgamated Worlds Admin Council?

The Admiral was presently on Doona for the purpose of attending a conference to carve a Spacedep niche in the proposed spaceport and negotiate other details of interaction between the two races. The Admiral was an adequate administrator, and spoke only passable Middle Hrruban, but he was a better negotiator than anyone in the Spacedep hierarchy. Greene knew his own talents would be employed there, as an adjunct delegate, speaking for the rights of those governed by the Amalgamated Worlds Council, to facilitate Barnstable's agenda. Greene himself was not anti-Hrruban except where the goals of the Hrrubans interfered with what was properly due to Humanity.

Barnstable recognized Greene's talents, and made use of them on missions like this one. It was ostensibly a courtesy call, allowing Greene to visit the captain of the Spacedep cruiser, which was passing through Doonan space, for the purpose of asking her to join him at the negotiations. His visit had a sub rosa purpose: the Admiral suspected that Hrruban warships would also be in the area, maintaining a discreet distance from the planet, and Greene's primary mission was to find out what they were doing. If they were behaving in a suspicious manner, the Admiral wanted to be informed as soon as possible so that he could take appropriate measures. Barnstable wasn't an isolationist, but he firmly believed that good fences made good neighbors.

Greene and his escort passed into the rear of the bridge area and skirted the main dais, heading toward an alcove facing it on the left. The officers of the current watch on the bridge glanced up only briefly at the visitor and his escort. No inefficiency here. Greene nodded approval. Overt curiosity in a fleet officer was a fault.

The metal door slid away into a recess as he approached it. The rating stopped at the threshold to announce him. Beyond the door was a utilitarian metal desk behind which sat a short, muscular woman with ice blond hair and direct brown eyes that arrested Greene on the threshold. She looked up from her desk monitor as the young rating performed the introductions. Greene felt a tingle at the back of his spine as she summed him up with a glance. A most attractive woman and, by her expression, not unpleased by what she saw. By her record, she was also a successful, intelligent officer, on track for flag rank. A good person to get to know. He smiled.

"Captain Grace Castleton, I bring you greetings from Admiral Barnstable," Greene began very formally, approaching her. "I am Jon Greene."

Castleton stuck a hand out over the desk, clasped Greene's, then released it and indicated that he should sit down. Her deep eyes were frank and full of concern.

"Good to see you, Commander. That's quick work! We only just heard the Alert."

"Alert?" Greene gawked blankly, and the captain frowned at him.

"Yes, Alert! You've come about that orbiting monstrosity out there, haven't you?" Castleton swivelled her miniature viewscreen toward him. On it was the image of a hovering hulk. Shock hit Greene in the pit of the stomach. The odd-shaped vessel was huge. "The system perimeter alarms went wild! Can you make anything of it?"

The outline, a long, irregular cylinder like a tree trunk, was somewhat familiar to him, but he couldn't place it. Greene made a point of familiarizing himself with all makes of spaceships—naval, civil, and private. And he had seen one like this recently, too. He concentrated on plucking the circumstances out of his memory.

"Not the usual design of Hrruban warships, is it?" he murmured, struggling to grasp the elusive recall. With a deft tapping, he brought up the computer telemetry statistics and studied the image, trying to identify it.

"Can't be Hrruban," Castleton snapped immediately. "Furthermore, the ship doesn't answer any communication signal we've thrown at it, and I know all the Hrruban codes. It's heading for a high orbit around Doona. We've our weapons trained on it, though it hasn't offered any overt threat. But then, how could it?" And her grin was ironic. "It's not carrying any heavy armament."

"None at all?" Greene demanded. "Ridiculous."

"Look there." She pointed at another shape on the screen, so far in the background that it could have been painted on the starry backdrop. Statistics, expressed in hot yellow numbers, inscribed themselves on the screen around it. "See? There's the biggest registered Hrruban ship, armed to the nines, right where the Admiral thought it'd be. That one set off my weapons sensors all right. High-grade radiation, well-shielded but still detectable. Bastard's not supposed to be there, but I guess they don't trust us completely either, with one of their High Council members down there. The way they're hanging off the stranger, they don't know where it came from, either."

As if in corroboration of Castleton's assertion, the intercom rang through. "The commander of the Hrruban ship," a voice said.

"Put him through."

The images faded, to be replaced by the face of a middle-aged Hrruban. "Zis is Captain Hrrrv. Your other ship refuses to answer our hails."

"Captain Castleton here. It's not one of ours. Can't you identify it for us?" she asked pointedly.

"One cannot identify what one has never seen beforrre!" the Hrruban said, snapping his jaw shut.

"Then, something new? A Doonan dreadnought built in secret? It would be within their philosophy to build a ship without guns," Greene murmured softly, knowing he was not in the intercom's audio range. The instant he realized that Captain Castleton had heard it and was glaring at him, he gave her a facile smile as if he'd meant to be facetious. Castleton was not stupid and, while she couldn't express political opinions, from her expression it looked as though she might entertain pro-Doona leanings.

"I doubt that very much," she said drily. "Doona has no heavy-metals resource to produce a ship that big, much less a space dock that could construct one."

"Then where is it from?" Greene asked. His inner agitation increased.

Of all the possibilities he could have anticipated in coming to Doona for this conference, the incursion of another alien race was not one of them. Another race of aliens becoming involved in the already complicated political dance between the Humans and Hrrubans would not please Admiral Barnstable. A new variable in the equation would be the last thing he wanted. And the faint familiarity Greene felt for the ship on the screen plagued him.

"I'd sure like to know," the captain replied, staring at the screen, "but I'm rather short on answers, and I've initiated all the approved procedures for contact. Captain Hrrrv, shall we pool our readings?"

"You have obtained some, Captain?"

"I'm seeing the same thing you are, Captain." Castleton shook her head slowly from side to side. "Science Officer, have you anything to report?"

"Proceeding with routine scans, sir." Even over the intercom, his voice held little expectation of success.

The outline of the massive ship, Greene decided, attracted the eye. It was such a peculiar shape. A central tube pierced through an almost globular center section. From the upper and lower parts of the tube, smaller clusters sprouted, almost like tumors in a tree.

It looked harmless, but then so did a land mine, he mused.

"We have life-form readings, sir," the science officer reported. "But, sir," he added, "I think there must be something wrong with our instrumentation or the stranger is somehow scrambling them."

"How so, mister?" Castleton asked.

"Too big. Neither Humans nor Hrrubans grow 'em that size, sir."

"Captain Hrrrv, do your life-form readings concur with ours?" Castleton asked. "Patch readings through to Captain Hrrrv."

The next moment, Hrrrv nodded solemnly.

"Let us report the presence of zis vehicle and its anomalies to our superiors immediately. Over and out." As soon as the Hrruban's image had faded, Castleton called for her communications officer. "Get Admiral Barnstable on the horn." She frowned as Greene raised a hand for her attention. "Belay that. Yes, Commander?"

"He's in the middle of a conference with a number of civilian officials, Captain."

"Noted, Greene," she said crisply, but she smiled to take the sting out of her brusque reply. "Use Command Code, Barnet."

"Admiral Barnstable," the Treaty Island aide said in a low voice, bending down to the Admiral. "Message from Captain Castleton, Command Code."

The old man looked around for the audio pickup. "Can you pipe it in here, son? Don't care to leave present company even for a Command Code!" He gave a snort. "Whatever is up Castleton's nose now?"

"Admiral?" A woman's voice, sounding agitated, echoed from the satellite feed. The pickup was audible only to those nearest the Admiral.

"Yes, Captain. Nice to hear from you. Something go wrong between you and my envoy?"

"There's a matter of extreme importance . . ."

"Well, Grace, spit it out," the Admiral ordered.

Her words pinged crisply from the speaker. "There's an intruder, a huge ship beginning entry into distant orbit around Doonarrala. I've never seen anything like it in space before. It's seven times the size of Spacedep's largest flagship! Captain Hrrrv can't identify her, either. I'd appreciate it if you'd come upstairs and take a look, sir."

With this information, those who heard erupted into surprised protest and consternation. In a few seconds, everyone knew the substance of the message. Second Speaker glared nervously around him, as if expecting the intruder to appear in the room. A young Hrruban wearing the single bandolier belt of a Treaty Island employee ran into the room and slid to a kneeling position on the polished wooden floor beside Hrrestan. The aide began to whisper urgently in the leader's ear. Hrrestan's eyes narrowed, and he rose to address the gathering.

"That was confirmation, my frrriends, if we needed it. An unknown ship of great size entered our system over three hours ago, and it has made full orbit. Ze space centers are on rrrred alert. Until we know more, I think we may consider zat we are being invaded."

"Why do we have to assume," Todd asked in a low, angry voice as he and Hrriss ran for the nearest comlink terminal in the corner of the room, "that we're being invaded just because it's a strange ship."

"Because it's big," Hrriss murmured, inserting his sleek body into the chair before Todd could, "and no one recognizes it." His long fingers flew over the keys, his partly bared claws clacking. Using an entry code, Hrriss hooked directly into the computer net used by the three Doonan space centers. Panting, Ali Kiachif peered over his shoulder.

"That," Todd exclaimed with awed respect as the scan started, "is truly one big mother!"

Castleton hadn't exaggerated: the stranger was approximately 7.4 times the size of a Spacedep flagship, and of no configuration Todd had ever seen before.

"Do we classify zis scan?" Hrriss asked, his talons flexing slightly in and out over the keys.

"Let's just hope that we're not too late," Todd said, "and that someone isn't linking into the net right now. We don't need a panic. Classify it, need-to-know clearance only."

"Just what I was about to suggest," Admiral Barnstable said, dropping a hand on Todd's shoulder.

"Hrrestan?" Todd looked up from the screen to his co-leader. Barnstable might suggest but he was outside his jurisdiction right now. Hrrestan nodded agreement, and pulled Barnstable back a little way.

"Ze knowledge will become common soon enough," Hrrestan said with a little sigh of regret. "It is for ze leaders to preparrre others to receive it. In ze meantime, we will be gearrring ourrselves frrr whatever may follow."

"And if the intruder is hostile! Who will protect us?" other delegates demanded. Kelly stood, watching, her arms wrapped around herself but showing no sign of fear.

"Zere is no need to assume ze worrst," Hrriss said resolutely, echoing Todd's feelings, "before all facts are known, is zere?"

"We don't have to assume," Todd added, supporting Hrriss, "that a stranger, any stranger, comes only with hostile intent."

"That big?" Tanarey exclaimed. "What else could it have?"

"I've got a fully armed ship on alert upstairs," Barnstable was saying at the same time. "It's ready in case of any emergency."

"We don't know if we have an emergency yet, Admiral," Todd said. "We have a visitor, not a proven enemy. Hell, it isn't shooting at us, is it?"

"Enough of this," Barnstable said firmly. "I want to see this mystery visitor"—he shot Todd a sardonic look—"with my own eyes. I'm going up to the *Hamilton* immediately. As head of Spacedep, I need to be where I can make informed decisions as soon as sensor data are received and analyzed."

"As planetary administrator," Todd said instantly, "I need to be on hand for any decisions that affect Doonarrala."

Barnstable gave him a long, measuring look, then nodded his head sharply once.

"Zis surprise arrival affects more zan just Rraladoona," Hrrto said promptly. "I must be present, as well."

"I go, too," said Hrriss, glancing at Todd, who nodded agreement. Their estrangement over the spaceport was momentarily forgotten in this new crisis.

"I must accompany the Speaker," Mllaba said, glaring at Hrriss as if he had usurped some perogative of hers.

"Hrrubans on a Spacedep military ship?" Barnstable said with sudden pompous suspicion.

"Zese are exzraordinary circumstances," Second Speaker said urgently, his tense stance suggesting he would brook no refusal. "I wish to see what you see when you see it. We will coordinaze wiz ze Hrruban ship from zere."

"Dammit, very well! Come along! But let's get a move on!" the Admiral barked.

"We don't know that anything's wrong, love," Todd whispered to Kelly as he gave her a quick farewell hug. "Don't panic when there's no need."

Kelly let her head rest briefly on his shoulder, as if memorizing his touch and scent, then pushed herself firmly away. "I'll wait with Nrrna and the kids."

"Thata girl," Todd said almost flippantly. "Don't I always come back to you?"

Nearly giving way to the very panic he had mentioned, she caught herself in time and said, "Just don't take any unnecessary chances."

"Me? Never!" He gave her his most charismatic grin and then turned back to the emergency before him. "Ali, I believe that the Admiral's shuttle is already on the *Hamilton*. Can you get us another one?"

"No tussle, trouble, or toil there," the Codep captain said, cheerfully, "providing we don't get shot out of space on the way. Follow me, all."

CHAPTER 2

KIACHIF TOOK THE SKIFF OFF IN A FAST-CLIMBING orbit, cleaving the atmosphere. Crowded into its forward cabin behind Kiachif and Hrriss in the pilot's couches were Barnstable, Todd, Second Speaker and his assistant Mllaba, Hrrestan, Barnstable's personal aide-de-camp, and Jilamey Landreau, who squeezed on board through the closing airlock before he could be stopped. Rather than waste any more time, he was allowed to remain.

Below them, the vivid blue of the Doonan sky glowed, illuminating the nearside of vessels hovering in local space above. Communication satellites, merchant ships, and beacons went by unheeded. As soon as the skiff attained its first looping orbit, the unknown ship came into view, watched cautiously at a prudent distance by the Spacedep and Hrruban Space Arm vessels. The invader had made no overt movements, either hostile or friendly. It just hung there in space, circling the planet at a distance. Everyone stared in turn at the screens and the forward port, as if to make certain what they saw on the screen existed in real space.

"Where did that large leviathanic liner come from?" Ali Kiachif demanded. His eyes gleamed. "I'd powerful like to take her for a test spin, make no mistake about that. Wonder what fuel she runs on?"

"Brr! It looks dangerous," Jilamey exclaimed. "All those bits and pieces sticking out. Surely that's not good design." The visitor plunged into the nightside of Doonarrala, making itself a sinister shadow against the stars.

"Isn't that a breakaway orbit?" Kiachif asked, checking his sensors. "Is she doing a spit, split and flit if anyone so much as says 'boo' to her?"

Todd scrutinized the outlines of the ship as it reached dayside again. The vessel was slowing down.

"Seems to be settling into a stationary orbit, Ali," he said. Details were hard to pick out on the black hull. He could see nothing at all that he could identify as weaponry, nor did the skiff's monitors register any telltale radiation glow. "They look like they mean to stay awhile," he added very softly.

Hrriss, beside him, was the only one to hear that comment. "I know what I wish zey are doing here," the cat man said wistfully.

"Me, too," Todd agreed, smiling slightly. Once again, he and Hrriss were in the minority. He was positive that most of the others were reacting with various degrees of xenophobia. Had neither race learned anything from the Doona Experiment? Or were they two the only ones who understood the true significance of this unique colony? Bearing in mind the result of his father's initial encounter with two small Hrrubans over thirty years ago, Todd believed a show of friendship might once again prove more useful than overt hostility. The very fact that this skiff contained persons from two races, observing a possible confrontation with a third, surely meant some good had been achieved by the Decision at Doona. His grin for Hrriss broadened. "Well, if wishes were hrrrses . . ." he murmured in a very good imitation of Hrriss.

"It is a trrrifying giant," Mllaba said, exhaling with a hiss as she shivered.

The skiff caught up with the leviathan, passed underneath, and shot out in front. Kiachif turned the craft out of an ascension trajectory and headed for the Spacedep cruiser.

Captain Castleton was waiting for them at the docking bay. Todd had met her once before, two years back, at a Treaty Day observance. He didn't know much about her, except that she was a good dancer. Her crew considered her a tartar because she expected honesty and tireless dedication from everyone who served under her. She appeared unruffled and calm, saluting the Admiral smartly before holding out a firm hand to each of the others.

"Welcome on board the *Hamilton*, gentlemen, madam," she said. Mllaba shook her hand gravely.

"Grace, I'm glad to see you," Barnstable said at his heartiest. "We've just had a good look at your mystery guest. Damned if I know what it is. Any new info?" The Admiral turned to acknowledge another uniformed figure in the bay with a lift of his thick white eyebrows. "Ah, Jon, there you are. My aide, Jon Greene," he said to the others. "I'll want your reading on this ASAP, Greene."

"Of course, sir," Greene said, stepping forward. "My report is waiting for you."

Todd decided the aide was about his own age but a hand-span shorter, compact and trim in his dark blue uniform. Greene glanced at the civilians behind his CO, meeting Todd's eyes, then focusing, as if identifying him. Greene's look of concentration faded abruptly, dismissing the civilians as unimportant, and he returned his gaze to his superior. Todd felt a swift flush of irritation at being so negligently dismissed.

Castleton went on. "Sir, I've invited Captain Hrrrv of the Hrruban vessel to take part in this conference."

Barnstable nodded. "Good. In the ready room?"

"This way, Admiral," Castleton said, indicating the portside corridor.

It was then that Todd saw the two Humans in dark blue uniforms with security flashes on their shoulders. They peeled away from the group waiting behind the sliding doors and fell in behind the Hrrubans as they went down the blue-gray corridor. As everyone filed out of the bay, more of the ratings took positions behind the other Hrrubans. It was not very subtly done and Todd could see that Second's spine was stiff under his red robe. Mllaba's tail switched angrily back and forth. After so many years since the Decision at Doonarrala, it was infuriating to see that there was still such blatant evidence of distrust.

"Blast it out of space," the Hrruban captain suggested, his fangs clicking together with a sound of finality. He waved an imperious hand at the image hanging on the large screen. Hrrrv bore a broad, dark stripe down the middle of his gold-furred back, sure indication of his clan's high position on Hrruba. Both cruisers were now matching the stranger's orbit, but with one fourth the curve of the great blue planet between them for safety. The Hrruban's ship was just barely visible in the corner of the viewscreen. "I do not like its appearance," Hrrrv said, "I think it means us no good." He walked up and down one side of the ready room, switching his tail irritably.

"Captain Castleton, when the ship did not answer any standard hailing messages, did you try any other methods of communication?" Todd asked, exasperated by the military mind.

Grace Castleton regarded him with surprise. "I tried all known codes . . . on all frequencies available to my equipment." Her tone and look implied that she had the very best, state-of-the-art equipment. "Oh, I see what you're driving at," she said after a moment, her face lightening.

"Thank goodness someone does," Todd said, throwing up his hands in gratitude.

"And just what is that?" Admiral Barnstable demanded, annoyed.

"Sir, how can they communicate with us if there isn't a common language? Or symbols or even a medium of communication. My father had the advantage of being face to face with two members of another species."

"And how do you propose to emulate your father, then?" Barnstable asked.

"By going to meet them."

Barnstable's eyes protruded and his face flushed with either surprise or anger, but Todd kept his ingenuous smile in place. "Worked before," he said.

"That's why we ended up learning Hrruban," Jilamey broke in. When he saw Barnstable, Castleton, and Greene giving him a concerted cold glance, he demanded, "What was wrong with that? We learned it. I think Todd's got the right approach. Go meet 'em and find out what they want. It doesn't do us any good to sit here in space with that big thing looming over us, neither side making a move. Their ship may be bigger, but"—he waggled his finger around the room—"we got more. They could be the ones scared stiff to do anything, you know. Make the wrong move and get blasted out of space."

Todd rubbed at his mouth, trying to make his lips behave. Jilamey was making exactly the point that Todd wanted to.

"Landreau's talking sense," Ali Kiachif said. "Don't know why I didn't see it that way myself, since I've traded with some mighty odd folk, using signs and trying to savvy their grunts, groans, and gargles."

"D'you mean to say," Castleton asked Todd, leaning forward across the table, "that you're willing to approach them?"

"If you'll let us have a tender, Captain," Todd said equably.

"But . . . but that could be a vanguard!" Barnstable protested.

"A vanguard? That big?" Kiachif asked incredulously. "If that's Baby, I don't want to meet Papa, if you get my drift."

"An unarmed baby," Todd said, seizing the initiative again. "Unarmed. I'm more than willing to go . . ."

"I'll go with you," Hrriss said.

"I wouldn't mind the trip myself. Be sort of fun," Jilamey said, grinning in his eagerness.

"Now see here," Barnstable began, trying to regain control. "That is not standard procedure."

"I didn't realize there was a standard procedure for encountering large unknown spacecraft, Admiral," Todd said. He stood up. "If you'll be good enough to assign us a shuttle to make first contact, Captain Castleton . . ."

"Dammit, young man," and Barnstable thumped the table with both fists, "nothing's been decided."

"I know," Todd said, gesturing to Hrriss and Jilamey. "That's why I decided to do something on my own initiative as co-leader of the planet, which I do not honestly believe is in any danger from this visitor. But the sooner we establish communications, the sooner we learn exactly why they are in our space and what they want."

"They'll want to blast you to motes if you're foolhardy enough to approach them," Barnstable said.

"With what, Admiral?" Todd asked, feeling the tide of aggravation rising in his blood. "You've established—at least you say you have"—he glanced for confirmation at Castleton and Hrrrv—"that the ship is unarmed . . ."

Barnstable waved that consideration away. "You can't know what kind of weapons they might have. The whole ship, in that peculiar configuration, might act as an amplifier for some kind of huge energy beam! Who knows what those bulges on the surface are for?"

"I'm willing to take that risk, Admiral," Todd said, adding grimly, "I've also considered that they might have biological armament which doesn't require high-powered delivery systems. But I prefer to believe that they're friendly; only waiting for an invitation from us. Enemies barge in; friends wait for invitations."

"Good point, Todd," Kiachif said, grinning broadly. " 'Enemies barge in; friends wait for invitations.' Great notion."

A notion which did not appear to amuse many of those present. Hrrto's expression was unreadable, though his tail tip twitched. Mllaba's was extremely active.

"Admiral, remember that thirty-four years ago," Todd went on earnestly, "Humans discovered that we were not alone in the galaxy, that there was another sentient race with whom we could be friends," and he nodded solemnly at Hrrto, who looked pleased, and grinned at Hrriss and Hrrestan, dropping his glance lastly on Mllaba, who sniffed back at him. "The presence of a sophisticated spaceship that big means that whoever is aboard is not only sentient but of an intelligent and advanced civilization. The fact that they haven't opened fire or made any threatening moves against us, I take to mean that they are not aggressive. I'm willing to test that belief."

"So am I," Hrriss said.

"Me, too," Jilamey piped up, grinning in an inane fashion.

"So, do we have a shuttle, Admiral?" Todd was becoming more and more irked at the specious delays. He wouldn't call them cowardly, but certainly close to it.

Grace Castleton flicked a glance at Admiral Barnstable.

"You can use my skiff, Reeve," Ali Kiachif said then, with a glance of veiled contempt at the naval officers. "Glad to oblige . . ."

Barnstable was on his feet, so was Hrrrv.

"Now see here, Reeve, that's encroaching on military prerogatives . . ."

"It's our planet down there, Barnstable. C'mon, Ali, you can pilot while this lot dithers."

Grace Castleton slid in front of Todd before he had taken a full step. "Stow that, Reeve. I take your point, and I'm sure the Admiral does, too, even if your method is high-handed . . . especially while you're on board my ship." She gave him a wry grin. "You've volunteered to test the intentions of our . . ."

"Visitor?" Todd suggested in an edged tone.

She nodded. "Visitor. But Spacedep is responsible for the safety of all its citizens, and Captain Hrrrv for his nationals."

Todd gave her full marks for remembering the Hrruban presence, naval and diplomatic. "That is true, but as these are aliens, whatever form they take, the approach falls in the province of Alreldep, of which I'm a representative."

"Out of the question," Barnstable said firmly. "Alien Relations or no. Until these beings, whatever they are, are proven harmless, it is still a Spacedep matter. I concur that logic suggests that, Reeve lead a first-contact team . . ."

"And the elder Reeve," Todd said. "He has, after all, had more experience than anyone else in successful first contacts."

"Your father?"

"The very one."

"Humph. Well—" Barnstable cleared his throat. "Makes sense."

"I'll lead the armed guard." Greene said, taking a step forward.

"There'll be no armed guard," Todd and Hrriss said in unison.

Barnstable bristled but Hrrestan's eyes flashed. "A show of arms is unnecessary. And might even be considered an insult. A friend advances with open hands."

"It worked before," Todd said, exchanging glances with Hrriss. Out of the corner of his eye then, Todd caught a look of intense disgust on Greene's face. Here was one man who didn't hold with the pacific approach. And probably one who might be a borderline xenophobe. "I think we've discussed this matter long enough. Too long a delay might jeopardize good relations. They'll have seen the skiff arriving. Captain, may I get in touch with my father on Doonarrala?"

As Grace Castleton bent to the terminal to instruct the commofficer, Todd saw the resolute glint in Greene's eyes. That man's middle name might be "trouble," he thought: he had a skeptical and suspicious air about him. Then the line to the surface of Doonarrala was open.

Ken Reeve was delighted to be asked. "I wondered what the lines were humming so hot and heavy for," he said, his image beaming an ear-to-ear smile at them from the screen. "I knew the perimeter alarms went off because I was jawing with Martinson at the Space Center up here between the First Villages. It was too late for the shush order when it followed. The gossips hanging around in port spread it all over town in jig time. Everyone's speculating on who's come calling."

Barnstable looked grim. "I was afraid of that. What's the response?"

"Not exactly what you'd think by your reaction, Admiral," Ken said with a grin. "Doonans are more inclined to think that outsiders who don't come in shooting are minded to be friendly. We know we're not the only ones out there, and I for one am happy for a chance to be one of the first to meet these new friends."

"They aren't friends yet," Greene reminded him sharply. Ken glanced over Barnstable's shoulder at the commander, his black eyebrows mounting into his hairline.

"Nor yet enemies," Ken replied quickly. "How can I get up to you?"

"I'll send a shuttle for you," Barnstable said, cutting Ken off and putting an end to the argument. "In the meantime, this is still a security matter. Please consider this as top secret. You may not inform anyone where you are going or what you'll be doing."

"Right you are. I'll be ready," said Ken cheerfully, and signed off.

"I'll go get him," Kiachif said, rising from his seat. "My skiff's faster'n any naval shuttle and I want another look, leer, and laying of a lens on that big ship. See if I can't get any more on her, if you get my meaning. Back in a ten-count." The Codep captain nodded to Castleton and the Admiral, and left the room.

"Until Dad arrives and we can proceed with a first contact," Todd said, once the door shut behind Kiachif, "we must not make any moves which the . . . visitors could consider antagonistic or hostile. No more scans, no probes, no drones. They could think that latter two were weapons."

"Let's not be overcautious, Mr. Reeve," Captain Castleton said, studying the image of the ship in the holoscreen. "Their range of power fluctuations alone invites closer investigation. Surely if they're the advanced beings you speculate they are, they'd expect us to try and uncover any information about them that we could, short of intrusive hardware."

"Who knows what they'd consider intrusive?" Todd asked. "Beings more sensitive than our two races might find probe scan painful. Do I have to remind anyone here of the Siwannah Tragedy? No. Well, then. You've already done enough remote scans." He didn't add "for all the good it did."

"I would feel better if I had more on them than the long-range data my passive telemetry picked up," Castleton said. "To quote an ancient Earth philosopher, 'It is a mistake to theorize in advance of facts.' "

Jon Greene was beginning to find the endless beating of the air dull and purposeless. The Doonarralans—wasn't that a word?—babbled against logical research that would help guarantee safety for their own people, not to mention the ships orbiting around their planet. Any part of that huge ship out there could conceal weapons. It didn't make sense to remain uninformed when useful data could be picked up as easily as vacuuming space dust. He wished he could recall under what circumstances he had seen that sort of vessel before. Castleton looked annoyed, and rightly so, with civilians usurping the appropriate naval roles in this sort of contact.

Barnstable gave him a glance and pushed his clipboard across the table to him. Greene picked it up and read the note the Admiral had discreetly added amidst the leviathan's readings. "Send probe." Greene erased the words and entered a random jotting of his own. He stood up.

"Permission to be excused, sir?" Greene asked, coming to attention.

Barnstable glanced up briefly from the discussion, and waved a hand. "Go ahead, son. I'll call you if I need you."

"Aye, sir. Captain, may I see you outside?"

Castleton looked surprised, but followed him out of the room. Greene escorted her a few meters from the door and automatically checked the corridor before he spoke.

"Sir, the Admiral asks if you will authorize launching a telemetry probe at the intruder."

Castleton looked down at her feet a moment before her shoulders relaxed a degree from their tight set. When she tipped her head up again, she wore an expression of relieved approval.

"Reeve's overcautious, Greene. Personally, I'd feel better with more data about that leviathan on hand. The distance scanners aren't giving us much to go on. This way." He followed her to a waiting 'vator car. "Level four," she said.

On an impulse, Greene stood closer to her than necessary in the small chamber and was surprised and pleased that Castleton didn't seem to mind. He was even more encouraged when she returned his smile.

A Gringg in the cargo-bay operations room of the gigantic spaceship watched on a viewscreen as a tiny metallic cylinder floated casually in the direction of the bow of their ship. He leaned lazily over and touched the key of the intercom with a long claw.

"Captain?" He knew he would find her in the bathing room. "The others have begun to acknowledge us. They are sending something toward our ship. I estimate it will be here within the hour. It is very small and does not seem to be armed. Shall I take it aboard?"

Splashing echoed in the background, and the sounds of other Gringg conversing provided a pleasant hum; then the smooth, rich voice of the captain came out of the speaker. "Do, please, and inform me when you have it. I'll come down to examine it."

"Captain? Ken Reeve is here," the bosun informed Grace Castleton, "with Captain Kiachif."

"Show them in."

Conversation around the ready room table halted as the bosun stood to one side to allow the two men to enter.

Grace Castleton would have known Reeve anywhere as Todd's father. Both men were rangy and taller than average, with big shoulders and long arms, and both had a cap of smooth black hair cut straight across the forehead over decidedly stubborn features. Ken's hair was somewhat thinner, and there was more gray in it than in Todd's. Lines had been graven by time in his fair-skinned face, but he exuded the same boyish enthusiasm that his son did. With a new adventure arising, years fell away. He might have been the same youthful jack-of-all-trades who had landed on Doona with a handful of tyro colonists more than thirty years ago.

"Hello, friends! Speaker Hrrto, Admiral Barnstable," Ken said, coming over to clasp hands and bow respectfully to the Hrrubans. He pounded companionably on his son's shoulder.

Ken slid into the empty seat beside Hrrestan.

"Well, anything happen while Kiachif and I were on our way up?" He looked around the table, which bore the remains of a recent light meal. "He's filled me in on the discussion. We're still going to make the contact?"

"We'll have to, Dad; they're not making any move," Todd said. "Captain, could we have a rerun of the tapes for my father?"

"I was about to suggest that," she replied and toggled the board for the replay.

Watching the tape with keen eyes, Ken whistled softly as he read the telemetry codes around the image of the ship.

"So we know very little about our friends over there." Ken heard a soft snort but couldn't tell who had it come from. "Not friends?"

"That has yet to be established," Barnstable said in a neutral voice.

"By me," Ken said with a grin.

"By us, Dad," and Todd indicated the other volunteers of the first-contact group.

"Can it be established if they're oxygen-breathers?" Ken asked.

"We'll need to know how to dress for our meeting."

"Can't even establish that, Dad," Todd replied.

"Just like you to volunteer for a blind mission," Ken said in a mock-disgusted tone.

"Begging the captain's pardon," Commander Greene said, watching the codes change on the main viewscreen. "There's data coming through right now."

"Put it up, Commander Greene," said Captain Castleton.

"More data?" Todd asked, startled even as he scanned the new readings. "Where did you get it?"

"From a robot probe," Greene said.

"What?" Todd demanded, sitting angrily upright. "Who authorized the launch?" He stared accusingly at Greene.

"I did," Barnstable replied, his face reddening at Todd's imperious tone. "For the safety of all of us, including our Hrruban allies, I felt it was vital we obtain more information."

"Admiral," Todd said in a restrained tone, "I specifically requested that there be no more probes, drones, or even scans until we were ready to proceed with the first contact."

Barnstable narrowed his eyes to glare at Todd. "Until proven otherwise, this is a Spacedep matter, young man. I am acting in the interest of safety for all the sentient beings on this ship. I don't need your permission to proceed."

"This is Doonan space," Todd said. It made him furious that this bureaucrat would take a unilateral action that might endanger the whole mission. Hrrestan, who hated the high-handedness of Spacedep, would back him up.

"We must not show distrust," Hrriss agreed.

"We do not know if those aboard that vessel arrre worthy of trust," Hrrto reminded him sharply.

"Nor do we know they are not, Speaker," Hrrestan said with equal asperity.

"In any case," Castleton said, raising her voice to put an end to the argument, "the probe only transmitted readings for a short time. They stopped the moment the ship took the probe aboard."

Todd struggled to control his vexation. "It probably stopped sending readings because they disabled it, thinking it might be a bomb."

"If they have not by now discovered its . . . benign"—Greene drawled the adjective, staring at Todd—"purpose, then they're by no means as sophisticated a species as you like to think them." Greene was rather pleased with that shot at the officious Doonarralan. He felt malicious glee at Todd's surprise.

Todd knew he'd been outmaneuvered there, but a soft touch on the back of his arm came as a quiet warning from Ken not to pursue the point. His father, better than anyone else in the galaxy, knew how hard it was to control the infamous Reeve temper, and how much damage it could do when let loose. Normally Todd was in control, but the combination of Spacedep's xenophobia and the unknown potential orbiting his beloved home planet was enough to put him at his worst. He reminded himself that he was one step away from a great adventure, equal to that when his father spotted the first Hrrubans near the earliest settlement over thirty years ago. These narrow-minded people did not, could not, understand the sheer joy of reaching out to another race, joining the far, cold reaches of the galaxy together in friendship. He had to be on that ship first, no matter what. It was a longing as strong as love. He glanced back and nodded at Ken to show he was under control.

"Let's see what the probe did transmit," Castleton said, settling down once more behind the table.

Greene pulled open the hatch over one of the inset consoles. He punched in a code. The view changed to a much closer image of the great ship, which steadily filled more and more of the screen. An overlay of white characters sprang up, constantly changing as the readings altered.

"We deployed a Mark 24-M probe with advanced sensors," Greene calmly announced. "As you can see from the metallurgical report, the alien defense shields are very strong. Most of the inner core of the ship resonates as a power plant. It's well insulated, with main conduits running down the pith of that central pillar. There are power fluctuations that build up from half a megawatt to over five gigawatts. My estimate is that the strangers are prepared to attack with some sort of electrical weapon."

"So far, your assumption about their intentions is speculation," Ken said. "The ship masses heavy. What's in it?"

Greene pointed to the relevant data. "Mostly water."

"Water? You mean H_2O? What kind of beings are there inside?"

"Big. Look at the readings. There's one weighing two hundred thirty kilos."

"Individuals?" Ken asked, amazed. Greene nodded.

Jilamey whistled. "They're as big as Momma Snakes."

"That'd explain the power requirements, if you follow me," Kiachif said. "Maintaining mass gravity for massive beasties."

"Or for quick power-ups on the weapons systems," Greene added.

Todd shook his head in vehement denial.

On the screen, a circular opening appeared in the side of the ship, gleaming silver against the blackness. The little probe's eye moved into it, giving an impression of a vast entry area and a quick view of some kind of computer console, and then the screen went blank.

"That's all there is. As you can see, once it entered the ship, it stopped sending," Greene said. "There is no visual of the inhabitants."

Barnstable rewound the report and started it from the beginning. Stroking his chin, he studied the screen closely. "Wonder what they're using all that water for? Ballast? Weapon storage?"

"Nonssenssse!" said Hrrestan, hissing his sibilants. "This is all speculation. In any case, it isn't a destroyer of any kind. There's no armament to speak of aboard. No rrradiation patterns which to me would indicate dangerrrous or powerrrful orrrdnance."

Castleton scratched her cheek thoughtfully. "I'm just as glad they haven't returned our compliment. The *Hamilton*'s considered a peaceful ship, but we do have small lasers and missiles. I wonder if they've scanned us telemetrically."

"We prrrove we arre peaceful by ze composition of our landing prrrty," Hrriss said.

"All I hope is they don't think the probe was some kind of threat," Todd said grimly.

"Wish I knew what sort of survival equipment we need," Ken mused aloud.

"May I suggest," Ali Kiachif spoke up helpfully, "the fullest rig and gear the *Hamilton* has to offer?"

Capturing the small unit proved to be no trouble at all, for which the technician was grateful. Like all Gringg, he hated to expend unnecessary effort on any task. The captain, a magnificent female of their species, entered the cargo bay accompanied by her small son, a curious lad of eight Revolutions, and the chief engineer, a female of many Revolutions and much experience. The three of them sat down in a semicircle on the floor near the console. The technician retrieved the little device, hoisting it lightly by one arm. He set it down on the floor and settled opposite the captain.

"I have decontaminated it, but you will be pleased to know that I found no dangerous organic substances on it or within. It makes a noise," the technician pointed out, indicating the subspace receiver on his console. "I believe it to be a message of some sort."

"How kind!" the Gringg captain declared. "Ghollarrgh, I am so relieved to find that these people did not attack us upon sight. Homeworld will be pleased. We must try to answer it, an unprovoking message. They must see us as being completely peaceful. Match the frequency, and we will attempt to translate. Grrala"—she turned to the engineer—"you should try to construct a similar device so that we may send them our compliments in return."

"In time, Captain." The engineer yawned. "In good time. Now, may we see how this little toy works?"

Eager to please, the technician began to display the workings of the ship-sent device.

Aboard the *Hamilton*, the shuttle was being made ready for departure. Todd and Ken were fitted out with tough transparent pressure suits. An attempt was made to find one which would accommodate Hrriss' tail, but nothing could be adapted in the short time allowed. In the end, Hrriss decided to simply stuff the caudal appendage down one pant leg and be done with the problem.

"I'm satisfied," Todd said, fastening the last seal on his suit. "The three of us should be able to handle any situation that comes up—or get out fast if it looks chancy."

"I want some personnel from Spacedep to accompany you," Admiral Barnstable insisted. "This is still a matter under my jurisdiction, whether or not I go along with your interpretation. I've got a couple of volunteers out of Castleton's crew, one from xeno and one from medical. And I'm sending my assistant to be my eyes and ears: Commander Greene."

Todd suppressed his reaction to that unwelcome news. The last thing he needed was the inclusion of a xenophobic Spacedep regular, but he conceded with as good a grace as he could manage. "All right. Have them suit up and meet us in the launch bay."

"Hrruba must also send an observer," said Second Speaker, after a quick conference with Mllaba.

"We've already got a Hrruban in the party," Barnstable said, glowering at Second. "Hrriss."

"I am willing to go," Mllaba announced. "I intend to go," she added.

Todd caught Hrriss' gesture of ears-back, and shook his head.

"Six is more than enough for a first-contact team," he said carefully. "More could be considered hostile. In fact, six might be considered too many."

"Will you not trust me, Speaker?" Hrriss asked softly in High Hrruban, seeking to smooth things over before the argument put an end to the mission. "I will uphold Hrruban honor."

Hrrto studied the younger male, who gazed at him earnestly. He grunted. "It is not a matter of trust, Hrriss. I did but think to give you the support of another among all these Hayumans."

"One of them is my brother," Hrriss said, "as well you know."

Hrrto, forgetting his argument with the Hayuman admiral, dropped his jaw in a smile. "I have known this for many years, young Hrriss. Very well, a Hrruban and a half-Hrruban. I simply did not wish Hrruba to be disadvantaged."

"None shall see it that way. They shall believe that only one Hrruban—and a half—is needed to balance out any number of Hayumans," Hrriss said innocently. Behind Second Speaker, he could see Todd and Ken grinning at his quip. They were the only ones who understood the brief conversation.

"I believe it may be so," Second Speaker replied at last. He retired, with Mllaba and Hrrestan, to the reception room beyond the blast doors. Ken gave them a thumbs-up.

"I'd like to go," Jilamey spoke up unexpectedly. "As an independent observer. On behalf of Earth."

Just how much High Hrruban did Jilamey Landreau understand? Todd wondered.

Barnstable glared at Jilamey. Although the young man's uncle was no longer head of Spacedep, the name Landreau was a prestigious one on the human homeworld. Barnstable looked for a moment as if he were about to say no, until he took a closer look at the obstinate expression on the younger man's face. Jilamey himself was not without influence on the Amalgamated Worlds Council. If the Admiral refused him permission, there could be endless small roadblocks for funding in the future, and unfavorable reports in the press about his administration. If he agreed, it might conceivably work out to Spacedep's advantage. In spite of his flamboyant wardrobe and occasionally foolish mien, Jilamey was known for his shrewd and observant mind.

"You're on your own, Mr. Landreau," Barnstable said at last. "Bear in mind that you're vulnerable while on alien ground, and we cannot adequately protect you. But . . . I'll allow it."

"Great! I'm ever so pleased you see it my way." Jilamey patted the Admiral companionably on the back. It was cheek and Jilamey knew it, but Barnstable suffered it expressionlessly. "Now, where can I get a suit?"

"You guys act like you have nothing to lose," the xeno technician said as he suited up in the landing bay, listening to Todd, Ken, Hrriss, and Jilamey all eagerly speculating on what they might find aboard the alien ship.

Like all men raised on Earth, Commander Frill had a soft voice that was currently afflicted with a quaver of fear. His quiet manner of speaking prompted the creation of his nickname, Frail, which he was not. Frill was tall, a bare centimeter shorter than Todd Reeve, with thick, solid arms and a burly chest. He was an All-Spacedep champion wrestler. Neither he nor the medic assigned to the mission seemed to share the sense of exhilaration the Doonarralans felt.

"Wrong, friend," Ken said. "I have everything to gain!" He grinned with unaffected delight at the challenge he was about to face. "My batting average's pretty good in first contact, you know. Lighten up. You're making history. And it could be fun!"

"Fun, he says," the medic observed, checking his gear. Ensign Lauder had been volunteered by his section chief, an honor he clearly would have foregone if he could have thought up a valid pretext. A slender, brown-skinned man with narrow shoulders, Lauder was to run scans, with permission, on who or whatever they met. The rebreather unit on his back was cycling at twice normal speed. He was very young.

"Hey, easy does it," Ken said, laying a kindly hand on the medic's shoulder. "If you want to back out now, no blame'll be attached."

"No, sir!" the medic said, gulping. "I'm no coward." With an effort, he brought himself under control. His respiration slowed, and his face went from flushed ocher to a more normal tawny shade.

"No one said you were, son." Ken smiled.

"If there are no more delays?" Greene asked with a touch of rhetorical sarcasm.

Todd nodded as if the question had been serious and put his clear plastic helmet on his head. Grommets around the neck bolted to the bubble with a final-sounding snap.

"We arrre waiting for you," Hrriss said. His pupils had narrowed to thin slits, and his ears lay slightly back to avoid contact with the headgear.

"Let's go," Todd said.

The shuttle left the lock and dipped slightly below the edge of the bay before the engines engaged fully. Todd felt insignificant as they left the big ship behind them. Frill, who was flying the craft, nudged the controls to pilot a wide-angle route toward the stranger, approaching with the sun at their back to get the best view.

The leviathan lay before them, huge and black. Todd admired the shape, wondering what sort of naval architects had designed it and why this shape was chosen. Hrriss' eyes glittered in the lights from the console. He must be wondering the same things, Todd decided. What purpose was served by the irregular bulges along the length of the central core? Ali Kiachif had speculated that the ship had substantial artificial gravity, undoubtedly to help maintain the muscle tone of the massive inhabitants that Commander Greene's probe had revealed. As they drew nearer, Todd was flatly amazed at the incredible size of the vessel. Beside it, they were a pinpoint, a dust mote. Behind him, Commander Frill let out a low moan, and was quickly reprimanded by a shake of the head from Greene.

Todd recognized a thrill of terror underneath his enthusiasm and anticipation. Was this how his father had felt thirty-four years before, when he got his first glimpse of a nonhuman, sentient life form? What if, after all his proud and confident words, the creatures inside this gigantic ship were unfriendly? And what if the "visitors" mistook the purpose of the shuttle and shot at it now that it was getting so close? What if they refused to allow the Doonarralan ship aboard? Well, that only meant his assumptions had been wrong. But he hated to think that Admiral Barnstable and Captain Hrrrv could be right.

As they got closer, more detail became apparent to their unaugmented vision. The surface of the alien ship was not actually black, but a matte-charcoal color that probably repelled certain wavelengths of radiation or light. Spotlights dotted the hull here and there, mostly marking out the place where antenna arrays or access hatches lay. These features were only now visible, Todd noticed. The matte coating provided unusually good camouflage of such details.

The shuttle circled a third of the way around the big ship's central "trunk" until they found what seemed to be an airlock lens, the same one that the probe had approached and entered. Triangular panels pivoted slightly to the left, forming an irislike opening. As Frill resolutely piloted the craft toward the aperture, Todd had the eerie sensation of being swallowed, ingested in one insignificant bite. Smoothly, the tiny shuttle sailed through the enormous circular hatch.

From each of the shuttle ports the passengers stared at the size of the chamber into which they were moving. The landing bay was a virtual cathedral, with shining, metallic walls, at least one hundred meters long—and high. Several craft rested in dry dock inside. Each was at least equal in size to a Spacedep passenger ship. The largest was as big as the administration building that contained Todd's office in the Human First Village. At the far end of the bay was a set of double doors both tall and broad, made of a translucent gray material. Behind a clear window set high in the left wall the party could see a vast console with rounded viewscreens glowing blue. The maintenance equipment and freight-loaders were made for bodies a good deal bigger than any Human or Hrruban. Beside a low console not far from the landing deck Todd noticed a man-sized device with the Spacedep insignia: the missing probe. It was still signalling feebly, its colored lights drowned by the brilliant illumination in the bay. The strangest thing about the control console was that there was no sign of a chair. What were these 230-kilo creatures, giant snails? Frill set the craft down on a lighted circle in the shadow of a ship twice the size of an Alreldep scout. The shuttle touched down with a hollow boom.

"Amazing," Hrriss said, voicing the thought in everyone's mind. "Ourrr hosts must be immenssse."

"Seems like," Jilamey murmured, his mouth hanging open. Ken Reeve just looked around him and grinned in pure joy.

While the party surveyed their surroundings, the airlock wheeled shut behind them, and hissing sounds arose. Greene felt a surge of panic. He was beginning to remember where he'd seen this ship before. It had been on a tape sent to Spacedep by an exploration team. He couldn't recall any details yet, but he associated the memory with violent death. For once, he hoped he didn't remember too many details.

Formless shadows passed back and forth behind the gray glass doors. As soon as the hissing stopped, the medical man checked his sensors. All the passengers checked their suit telemetry.

"G-force is zero point five over Earth normal. What's the atmosphere? Can we breathe in here, Lauder?" Greene asked, his voice hollow in the bubble helmet.

"It's a nitrox mix, plenty of oxygen," Lauder said, carefully reading the sensors in the control panel. "Reads like a class-M combination. I mean, I'd call it safe if we came across it on a planet."

"No trace elements?" Ken asked.

"Some," the medical man admitted, checking his instruments. "Nothing noxious in any concentration. No bacteria known to be harmful to Humans or Hrrubans, at least in this section. I won't give the atmosphere a hundred percent clearance, though, simply because I haven't run a lab analysis on it yet. Keep using the rebreathers."

"So ordered," Greene said with a sharp nod.

"Let's go," Todd said.

Frill released the hatch and he climbed out. The ambient temperature in the bay seemed slightly cool. Ken put part of the chill down to the room's having just been open to vacuum, and his trembling to excitement. The bay was already warming up.

Lauder stepped cautiously onto the deck and avoided the lighted circle. He bent over his scanner. "I wonder if this is what our hosts breathe or if they just made it up for us?"

Hrriss followed the tech. "I wonder where they are," he said, craning his neck to look up at the high ceiling.

A roar sounded over an unseen intercom, startling them all with unintelligible syllables. The shadows behind the door grew denser, darker, larger, giving an impression of vast size.

"That sounds like the overture," Todd said facetiously. "Here come the players."

CHAPTER 3

AT THE END OF THE HALL, THE GRAY GLASS DOORS parted and slid soundlessly into the walls. Todd and the others waited, mouths agape, as their hosts entered the landing bay. For all their height and girth, they made little sound when they moved.

"Stars!" whispered Frail, his voice sounding hollow through the sides of his plastic helmet. "Mother always said I'd meet someone bigger'n me."

The first of the aliens to enter, a bulky creature covered except for its face and the pads of its forepaws with thick, long fur of light honey-brown, stood just over two meters in height. Its face had a square muzzle with a black, leathery nose, black-fleshed lips, and two deep-set, eyes the color of red wine protected by thick, smooth-skinned eyelids fringed at the edges with more honey hair. Todd was amazed to see that its facial features were arranged in the same way as a Human's or a Hrruban's.

Its shoulders sloped from a thick neck toward a huge rib cage, and downward over a powerful lower body supported by very short but thick legs. It wore a pouch-laden belt and ornately decorated collar cut from a scaly hide of some kind. Todd thought it resembled snakeskin—but what a snake! If the size of the scales was any clue, it had been equivalent to a Great Big Momma Snake. The alien blinked at the visitors curiously before standing aside to make way for the two other aliens. The being behind it, identical in appearance but black-brown in color, was nearly two and a half meters tall. It too wore a collar, this one more elaborate than the first alien's, consisting of woven strips punched and stamped with complex designs. From one side of the collar depended a loop of decorated hide that circled the upper part of the big alien's arm. Todd wondered if the attachment might serve some specific purpose, concealing miniaturized devices, or was it a mark of rank, or both?

The third alien, of the same dark brown as the tallest being, but with a white patch on the throat that covered part of its chest like a bib, was just over one meter high and wore only a simple belt and collar of scaly leather.

With plenty of hairy fur to protect them from weather, the aliens had as little need for clothing as the smoother-coated Hrrubans. The three moved forward with commendable grace, until they were within ten meters of the party. Then they stopped in a line facing the landing party, regarding their visitors with calm, wine-colored eyes.

At first, Todd was taken aback by their sheer size. These creatures were terrifying, as if animal giants out of a children's story book had come to life. With that thought, their appearance struck Todd as hilariously funny. He felt a childish urge to break into giggles.

"It's the Three Bears!" he whispered under his breath to Hrriss. "I sure hope they don't want me to tell them a story."

"I do not undrrrstand," Hrriss whispered. Inside his helmet, his ears were laid back tight against his round skull.

"Earth fairy tale. They look just like bears, creatures that were found on Earth up to the last century—ugh! Tell you later." He stopped talking as Ken elbowed him in the ribs.

"Shush! You notice? They don't want to appear aggressive," Ken said. He smiled widely at the beings, and let the set of his shoulders hang loosely. "They're waiting for us to close the distance."

"Wait a minute," Greene protested, grabbing Ken's arm. "Consider the size of them!"

"They're friendly," Ken said, calmly taking the man's hand away. "They've brought one of their young along to show us they mean us no harm—in fact, that they trust us. You'd never bring a baby where you intend to be the aggressor, nor where you expect threats."

"That's a baby?" the medic asked, agog.

"It must be," Ken assured them. "Look at the way it's acting."

Todd understood completely what his father meant. The small alien was more awkward than the large ones, and kept looking up at the tallest one for reassurance. "That's his—or her—cub."

"Well, I don't know . . ." Frill murmured, unsure. He swallowed nervously. The medical man stood with his mouth hanging open while his telemetry gear went wild making recordings.

"Keep your mind on the job," Greene said peevishly. "Come along!"

"Yes, Commander," the two navy men replied. The group moved closer to the aliens, and stopped three meters away as the medic faltered once more. The three creatures watched them calmly, waiting.

Ken steeled himself. "I feel inferior, inhibited, and intimidated, as Kiachif would say if he was here. The sheer size of them! One of us has got to take action." He swallowed, and put a hand on Todd's arm. "Well, as the first and most successful xenolinguist in Earth history, we'll see what sense I can make out of whatever noise they make. Wish me luck, boys."

"You can do it, Dad," Todd said firmly. He clasped his father's arm, imparting confidence.

"Find out everything you can about them," Greene added. "Tell them as little as possible about us."

Todd shook his head pityingly at Greene. The man had absolutely no idea how long it took to establish the most superficial linguistic exchange.

Ken opened his arms wide in a gesture he hoped projected friendly intent, and walked right up to the furred trio.

"Greetings, and welcome to the skies of Doonarrala," he said, speaking as cheerfully and enthusiastically as he could, though his heart was pounding in his throat. "We come in peace. We hope you do, too."

Echoing his gesture, the three aliens opened their upper limbs and stretched their flexible muzzles up and back so that their teeth were showing: sharp, white stalactites almost as long as a human hand.

"Fardles! Now, those are fangs!" Jilamey whispered. His face was pale but his eyes glittered in fascination.

"We must be very careful, Captain," the Gringg linguist said, glancing upward at her. He was nervous about the possibility of disease, though he had been assured by the ship's physician that an alien species was unlikely to carry germs that could infect them. Still, he, like all the others aboard, were volunteers. If it cost their lives to discover the truth about this species, so be it. The linguist swept the hold with one more nervous glance, to reassure himself that there was nothing there to discourage these small interesting beings. "One of them approaches. Remember there is certain knowledge we must not reveal yet."

"I know what to do. Is it a female or a male, Eonneh?" Captain Grzzeearoghh asked, looking Ken up and down curiously. "These creatures are all so skeletal! And so small and weak!"

"It is difficult to know. But since some of them wear garments under those protective shells and some do not, that is clearly the demarcation. The unclad one's body configuration slightly resembles our males, so that must make the tall ones female."

"So they have a female linguist or first speaker," Grzzeearoghh noted. "How interesting. We shall have to converse much on the divisions of labor among gender once we have established communication. But she moves like a Gringg, slowly and carefully. I am glad. I find hurry so disconcerting." The captain raised her head and called out a command that made the aliens at the other end of the hall jump. "Rrawrum? Have you sent the message notifying Homeworld that we have been contacted and are carefully following procedure?"

"I am getting it done now, Captain." Rrawrum's voice echoed overhead in the cargo bay, a little loudly to Grzzeearoghh's thinking. She would have to ask the technician to correct the sound level when she had a moment. It was making their visitors nervous. Every care must be taken to put them at their ease. The strangers should have no cause to view them as a threat. *My cub should help to reassure these small aliens*, the captain thought.

"Tell them also that we are beginning contact."

"As you wish, Captain."

"Mama," Weddeerogh interrupted, as Ken stopped a meter away. "What is she doing?"

"She is identifying herself, I think," the Captain said, patting her cub on the head. "A pity their voices are so soft. I was not paying attention!"

Ken activated the recording unit at his side and put his hands to his chest. "My name is Ken Reeve. Ken Reeve." He extended one hand slowly toward the largest "bear," and pointed. "And you?" He gave the words the strongest interrogative tone he could.

The massive head swung toward him, and the rubbery lips receded behind the teeth again in a passable reflection of the Human's smile. Ken was impressed by the flexibility of the aliens' faces, and their ability to imitate expressions. Todd was right: they did possess a superficial resemblance to Earth bears. Their coloring, shape, and musculature were very much like that of the ancient species Ursa. They seemed to be made for defense, armed with heavy claws and a thick, loose skin. And they were so unconsciously powerful. If they proved to be unfriendly, they could tear him apart without trouble. The likeness to bears was not exact, of course. These beings had tails about the length and thickness of his forearm, covered with shaggy hair. What purpose did the appendages serve? Balance? Defense?

He studied the faces closely. They had been growling among themselves. He had clearly heard distinguishable syllables, some of them repeated. The creatures had long, agile tongues, suitable for pronouncing the complexities of a well-developed language. It was disconcerting to stand next to beings who made him feel so insignificantly small, like a child among giants.

The aliens must have sensed his discomfiture, for all three rolled back off their feet and onto their tailbones. It was a graceful gesture, ending with the body being braced solidly with hunched-up rear legs and outspread tail. Their lower limbs were short in comparison to the length of the body, but they were heavy and solid, made for balance, not speed.

"I am Ken Reeve," he said again, pointing to himself as he hunkered down in his best approximation of their new posture. He wondered if he should ask Hrriss to display his tail. "And you?" He extended his hand toward them.

The largest of the aliens roared again, and waved a thick claw at him, turning it palm down and drawing it from the floor up to its head. Seeing that he didn't understand, it levelled out the claw at its eye, and drew an invisible line out toward Ken.

"What are they doing, Dad?" Todd demanded.

He smiled, delighted. "Oh, I get you. You're trying to equalize things. They want me to remain standing up, so that we're all at eye level," he said over his shoulder. "Ken Reeve," he indicated once more to the aliens.

"Grzzeearoghh," the largest replied slowly and carefully in its basso profundo voice. It sounded like the revving of an engine.

"Errizz-eer-oh?" Ken repeated uncertainly, trying to duplicate the growl.

"Grzzeearoghh," the large one said complacently, wrapping its forepaws over its belly.

The gesture made it look even more like the holos of Earth bears, and Todd suppressed a chuckle. Hrriss shuddered, his ears halfway back.

"Their voices make me uncomfortable," he said in said in Low Hrruban. "Do they always speak at such volume? Spoken so loudly, the deep notes reverberate harshly on my ear bones." He shook his head as if to relieve the pressure. "Hrrubans do not raise their voices unless they wish to attract attention or if they are angry. Could we have made them angry?"

"How could we? I don't think they're upset, or they wouldn't be looking so comfortable," Todd said. "And with the size of those rib cages, I'd be surprised if they spoke in soprano voices."

Ken tried the alien's multisyllabic name over and over again, until the large one smiled at him. "I think I've got it, chaps," he called. "Meet Grzzeearoghh. Looks like he's in charge here."

Todd and Hrriss cheered. The aliens looked surprised but not displeased at the noise, regarding their visitors with polite curiosity. Beside Todd, the Spacedep men seemed to be making themselves as insignificant as possible, except Greene, who stood boldly pointing his recorder at the aliens. Jilamey was taking in the whole situation with awed joy.

"We're communicating already! It's too fascinating!"

Grinning at Landreau's genuine enthusiasm, Ken pointed at the medium bear. "Who?"

While he was learning the complexities of pronouncing "Eonneh," the cub rolled off its haunches and waddled toward him.

"Look out!" shrieked Lauder, backing away. The young medic's face was pale.

"What for?" Ken asked, breaking off his language lesson. "Hi, there, fella," he said as the cub bent to sniff his shoes. While he waited patiently, the cub ran its shiny black nose up his suit leg, sneezing briefly as the acrid stench of the transparent plastic tickled its nasal passages. But it continued its olfactory examination, shoving its nose into Ken's armpit and down his arm to his gloved hand. It sneezed again. Ken threw a shrug back toward his party. The cub meant him no harm. It was only curious, like any youngster. When they all unsuited, the bears were likely to get a few aromatic surprises.

The cub threw both of its heavy upper paws up onto Ken's shoulders and dragged his face down so that it could look at him. It seemed puzzled by the helmet. Ken rapped on the plastic bell with a fist, then waggled his head back and forth inside, trying to show that it was an artificial covering. The cub let out a series of pleased grunts that sounded like stentorian giggles, and let go of him. Ken hunkered down and extended his hand. The youngster sniffed it and squealed. He noticed that the black nostrils of the other two were twitching, but more discreetly. Scent must be important to them; a fact worth noting. The trouble was that humans did not smell like plastic suiting.

"You're a real sweet little critter. What's your name?" Ken asked the delighted cub. "Ken Reeve," he said, carefully enunciating the two syllables as he pointed to himself. "You?" he asked, pointing to the cub.

"Weddeerogh," said the youngster in an unexpected baritone, then scooted shyly back behind the largest alien.

"Aw," Jilamey said. "Acts just like a kid, too."

"I guess," Frill said, finding his voice at last. "If you like kids that big."

"Gringg," the biggest one said suddenly, indicating itself and the two others. "Gringg."

"Gringg?" Ken asked. "Grr-ing?"

"Reh." The big alien tilted its head to one side and let out a short grunt. Ken fancied it gave him a look of approval.

"Hayuman," he said, pointing to himself. "Hayuman."

"Ayoomnnn."

"Good." He walked over to stand beside Hrriss. "Hrruban."

The red eyes followed him carefully. "Rrrrooobvvnnn," Grzzeearoghh said, growling the *r*'s rather than rolling them as a Hrruban would.

"Close," Ken said approvingly. "Good for you, little fellah. And we're all Doonarralans." He gave the leader a big nod and a smile, which it copied, as he indicated Todd, Hrriss, and himself. "Well, now we know what we all are. Let's start on things." He knelt down, and patted the floor. "What do you call this?" Ken asked the big bear. "We call it *rllama*. Rllama."

"What are you doing, teaching it Hrruban?" Frill demanded, indignant. "You should teach it Terran."

"One language at a time," Ken warned him. "We need a lingua franca, and both of *our* peoples speak Middle Hrruban. The Gringg can learn the niceties of Terran and High Hrruban once they've mastered this one. Now pipe down, unless you want to do this for me?"

"No, I sure don't," Frill said quickly, backing off.

"Urrrlllah. Ma," the alien intoned.

"We're making progress. Rllama," Ken said, rolling the *r*, and keeping his mouth wide open so it could see the way he rolled his tongue. The little one watched him from the shelter of its parent's body, trying to match his facial expressions and rolling its long tongue. Ken laughed.

"Do you know, I think I'm the first sentient alien they've ever encountered."

"How can you make an assumption like that, Reeve?" Greene demanded. He looked slightly sick.

"This all seems to be new to them," Ken replied. "They're not acting as if they're anticipating what I'm going to do. And I think they're enjoying it."

"Weddeerogh, you have no need to be shy," Grzzeearoghh said, turning her head over her shoulder to beam at her offspring. "This is becoming most interesting. Will you go and get writing materials for us? Now we are starting to work with vocabulary. I don't want to miss anything. This is a very important moment in Gringg history."

"Yes, Mama," the cub said, with one more peek at Ken. "What funny hands she has, with no claws. I do not like the smell of that stuff she wears. I would like to smell her. I hope her own skin smells better."

"She wears a protective covering, showing concern for our health and hers. I admire that," Grzzeearoghh said. "I did not know what to expect from another race, certainly not such scrupulous consideration. And we know we must act with caution. Now, please go."

"Yes, Mama." On all fours, the cub scurried toward the doors, which opened and closed behind him.

"Rllama," the strange female said.

"Rrrllahma," Grzzeearoghh intoned. Her pronunciation seemed to delight the visitor. "I do believe we are getting somewhere. Good! I wish the female's friends were more calm. One of the females and the male seem quite at home, but I think those others may faint. And that female with its limb stuck out holding the little device seems most uncomfortable."

"I must confess to a certain amount of nervousness, too, Captain," Eonneh admitted. "They are a feeble-looking race, are they not? No fur to speak of. I am almost afraid to move for fear of hurting them. We have all been shown how important it is to give the appearance of being no threat to any new race we encounter. And such amazing dimorphism between sexes. You'd think they were almost separate species. When the male speaks, his voice is so shrill it hurts my ears."

"Here it is, Mama," Weddeerogh said, galloping in through the blast doors with a tablet and stylus in his paw.

"Good, dear. Give it to Eonneh. Write this down, Eonneh. Their word for floor is 'rrrllama.' "

The Gringg male put the pad of thin but solid tiles down between his feet and hooked the two loops of the stylus over the first and second claws of his right upper paw. He sounded out the word to himself carefully before beginning to inscribe it. In Gringg culture, writing anything down with a living hand made it official. Gringg males made the best record-keepers, poets, librarians, even artists; they also mastered the theoretical sciences to forward development. Eonneh was unusually skilled in all the arts, and was considered a credit to his gender, though he was too modest to allow such compliments to his face. The females, larger by ten to thirty percent, organized, and exercised the practical arts, such as all forms of engineering, and tended to take the lead in exploration. In Eonneh's opinion, Grzzeearoghh was an excellent captain, and was handling the situation perfectly. The World Congress which chose her as their envoy to any possible sentients had made the best possible choice.

As the alien female looked on with interest, Eonneh made the characters for a short growl, followed by a lingual extension, then a nasal hum. The accents that went above and below the characters indicated the subordinate vowel sounds.

"I'm enjoying this," Ken said, coming close to the scribe for a good look at what Eonneh was doing. "Their written language is beautiful: a minor work of art if this is any sample. Nothing from even ancient Terran civilizations comes close to it." Showing his camera first to the two adult Gringg, he walked around and pointed it down at the pad to record the scribe's work. "I think he's trying to get it down in a phonetic fashion. That's what I'd do. Well—" He snapped another shot. "This is their attempt at 'floor.' "

"Can you tell how they phoneticize, Dad?" Todd asked.

"Hardly," Ken said with a laugh. "Not after just one word.

It's going to take a while to get anywhere useful."

"Don't worry," Hrriss assured him. "Our hosts have settled in for the linguistic siege."

Eonneh scribed busily at the big pad, with Jilamey behind him to watch how the handscript was made. The pen contained free-flowing ink that the scribe carefully controlled to make thick and thin strokes on the smooth surface of the tile. Landreau was clearly impressed by the skill required, for each pictograph was complex and beautiful.

"What's that?" he asked, pointing down at the character that Eonneh was patiently drawing. "Er, how do you say it? *Aaah? Bbbb?*"

"Vv."

"And that little one?" Jilamey moved his finger to a mark like an accent that went over the top right corner of the squarish character.

"Ooo," Eonneh said carefully, glancing up over his shoulder at the Ayoomnnn.

"Really? This must be the way you spell 'Hrruban,' " Jilamey replied. "And that?" He indicated another mark, this time set below and to the side of one of the elaborate pictographs.

"Hhhh."

"That's not a vowel," he protested.

"That's an aspirate," Ken said, coming over to look. "So the different notations are divided into hard consonant sounds and vowels? Good job, Landreau."

"Huh?" Jilamey frowned in query.

"Is it all like this?" Ken said to Grzzeearoghh, pantomiming the handwritten panel onto the nearest round screen.

"Be careful, Reeve," Greene called. He felt down his hip for his side arm, and remembered with regret that it had been left behind on the *Hamilton*. If these gigantic aliens got out of control, he had nothing but his skills at unarmed combat with which to protect the Human of the party.

The captain rose to her full height and padded over to the console. "The skinny Ayoomnnn female is both intelligent and curious," she told Eonneh. "See this, Genhh Rhev," she said, pulling up a textfile on the screen.

Ken, recognizing the slightly mangled pronunciation of his name, followed her to the console. As he watched, fascinated, the computer laid down lines of the complicated characters first, followed by the small marks above and below the lines. As

Grzzeearoghh sounded it out slowly to him, he realized his guess was right.

"They're going to be a little confused by written Terran," Ken noted. "If they're used to aspirates and vowels as separate notation, it's going to take them a while to get used to seeing the characters all the same size and on the same line. It'll be interesting to see how quickly they cope with such a difference."

"It's primitive," Greene said dismissively. "Inscribing information by hand is slow and inefficient. Technology like this must be a fluke."

"Oh, I don't think so, Commander," Jilamey said from his post behind Eonneh. "Even on Earth, the ancient art of calligraphy is still practiced and held in esteem. It seems perfectly normal to me. I spend a lot of time in the Artists' Corridor, where there's a good deal of reverence for the old forms."

Greene snorted. "You can't attribute Human characteristics to aliens who may turn out to be dangerously barbaric."

"I wish this could go faster," Ken said, sighing, as he studied the round screen. "It could take us an age to put together a working vocabulary." He went over a number of items in the bay, asking for the aliens' words, and giving them the Middle Hrruban equivalents.

"And what's this?" he asked, pointing at the Spacedep shuttle.

"Va'arrel," said Grzzeearoghh.

"Va'arrel?"

"Reh."

"Good," Ken said. "Well, what do you call the big ship?" He gestured in a wide circle, indicating the vessel around them. The big alien followed his hand with its eyes.

"Va'arrel," the Gringg repeated.

"This is the same? Va'arrel?" Ken pointed at the shuttle. "Va'arrel?" He circled his arm.

Grzzeearoghh seemed to be listening carefully for something, and was mildly disappointed not to hear it. The alien shook its large head from side to side. "Va'arrel."

"But that's what I said," Ken insisted. "What am I missing? Va'arrel," he said again, pointing to the shuttle. The alien sat back with paws folded. "Va'arrel."

"Morra," the Gringg corrected him. "Va'arrel."

"There is no difference," Frill complained.

"Wait a second," Ken said. "I thought I got a sense of something there. It's possible I'm not capable of hearing the difference between two similar sounding words, and yet there is one, isn't there, old fellow?"

The dark-red eyes were sympathetic but encouraging. Ken grinned. "Your voices go so far down I wonder if you're dropping past the registers that we Hayumans can hear. Or perhaps it's a somatic element I'm missing. Of course, I could just plain be pronouncing it wrong. Only practice will help with that. Let's collect some more examples of Gringg speech to take home with us."

To speed things up, Todd and Hrriss volunteered to work with the other Gringg to teach one another vocabulary, leaving them with plenty of data when the Doona party finally left.

Ken, with the loudest voice, found himself talking to Grizz, as he nicknamed the Gringg captain. The big alien approved the shorter form with a dropped jaw and a discernible twinkle in its eye. In its slightly nasal voice, the elder Reeve's name came out as *Genhh*.

Eonneh, Hrriss, and Dodh, as the Gringg pronounced Todd's name, were already working out the pronunciation of more words, and writing them down on the pad. Frill, who was beginning to become interested in spite of his initial apprehensions, hung over their shoulders, kibitzing. The navy medic, still nervous but growing bolder, circled around. Greene maintained his distance, making the occasional comment into his recorder, still prepared to defend himself if necessary. Jilamey hunkered down on the floor in front of the cub, with his knees akimbo.

"Hi there, little guy. I'm Jilamey."

"Chilmeh!" the cub echoed happily, and reached out to push the Human's knee companionably. Jilamey pushed back, and found himself rolling over the floor in the crowing Gringg's powerful embrace. His helmet hit the ground with a clonk.

Greene ran after them and interposed himself, on guard, between the alien and the Human. The largest of the Gringg tensed, watching carefully.

"Be careful, Landreau," Greene cautioned the younger man, who lay gasping and breathless with laughter on the deck. With one arm, he pulled Landreau to his feet. "You have no idea what your actions may mean to these aliens."

"Aw, he's playing, Commander," Landreau said. The cub's tail swished from side to side like that of a large dog, and Jilamey ruffled the fur between its ears.

"It'll think you're a child, too."

Jilamey pouted. “Oh, don’t ascribe Hayuman assumptions to him, Commander. We’re learning a lot about each other, aren’t we?” he said to Weddeerogh, who blinked shyly at Greene.

“I’d like to bring some of these fellows home with us,” Ken said to the navy medic, “but I’m afraid they might not survive on Doona. We don’t know anything about their physiognomy, nor they ours. What are your impressions?”

“I wish I could get some samples of skin, blood, and hair,” Lauder replied. “I could tell you a lot more if I could do microscopic analyses.”

“When we can speak a little more of their language, we’ll ask,” Ken said. “It’s presumptuous to try before they can understand just exactly what we want. And why.” He turned to Frill, whose attention seemed to be wandering. “How about you? Any ideas?”

“Sorry, sir,” Frill said, reddening slightly. “My stomach’s rumbling. I, uh, couldn’t eat before we left. Hope they don’t misconstrue the sound.”

Ken smacked him on the back. “Good idea. Food! We’ll offer them some of our rations, let them analyze them, see if our food’s safe for their insides. There’s got to be emergency packs in the shuttle.”

“There should be, Dad,” Todd said, “if it was stocked according to regulations.”

“Naturally the shuttle was prepared according to regulations,” Frill said, regarding father and son with horror. “You’re not proposing to give them our food, are you?”

“Why not?” Ken asked reasonably. “It will give them an idea if our biosphere is compatible with theirs. They appear to be carnivorous, with those teeth—maybe even omnivorous. Be interesting to see if their comestibles are at all similar to ours.”

During this discussion the Gringg withdrew to have a conference of their own.

“Our visitors seem willing both to teach and learn,” Grizz said thoughtfully. “I feel it is safe to risk the second step. Move slowly and give them no cause for suspicion.”

“As you wish, Captain,” Eonneh replied, watching Genhh Rheu expostulating with the rest of her party. “I’ll go get what is required.” Grizz shouldered him companionably as he left the room.

“Go quickly, my mate. If this works out as we hope, you’ll have plenty of material for an epic poem, with yourself as the hero!”

Todd, Hrriss, and Commander Frill went back to the shuttle. According to Spacedep regs, emergency gear, including "rations ready to eat," or RRE's, were always kept in a locker beneath the co-pilot's couch. The ring latches securing the cubby door were frequently stiff, but a quick twist and tug by the powerful Frill opened the door without trouble.

"Don't give it all to them," Frill asked, eyeing the RRE's as Todd stacked them into a heap. "Leave me one, won't you?"

"You won't faint dead away on us, will you, Frail?" Todd grinned, and got an answering smile from the Spacedep officer.

"Not now," Frill answered, a little sheepishly. "Not as long as I get something to eat."

"Don't worry," Todd said with complete understanding. "I'm a big feeder myself. You can be the one to taste it in front of them so they can see that we warrant this food as safe." Willingly, Frill picked out his favorite from the sealed packs, and split up the rest to carry between himself and Hrriss.

"Todd," Ken called as they emerged from the shuttle. "Our friends here had the same idea."

Todd grinned. Piled high between Ken and Grizz was a quantity of wrapped and unwrapped goods. Eonneh and another medium-sized bear, whose coat was colored a dark, dusty cocoa, had Ensign Lauder by the console, showing him a program that displayed changing views of complex designs that Todd couldn't distinguish from where he stood. As he closed the distance, he imagined that he recognized the designs.

"You know, if those were on our computers," he suggested, "I'd think they were molecular diagrams. But of what?"

"The proteins, or whatever's in these goods?" Ken asked. He pantomimed to Grizz, pointing to the items on the floor and back again at the screen. "Is that the substance of this?" The big ursine roared softly, a triumphant sound. "I guess that's what he said."

"Reh!" Grizz acknowledged, crossing huge paws across his chest once more.

"How about it?" Todd asked Lauder. "Would a molecule like that be safe for Hayumans and Hrrubans to eat?"

"No doubt about it," Lauder replied, showing him his pad screen. "It's a common protein chain. The others are complex carbohydrates, pretty similar to stuff we eat. It's strange, because their digestive systems are very different from either of our two races."

Greene frowned. "In what way?"

"More efficient, I'd say. My scans, though I can't absolutely warrant the accuracy on alien biosystems, pick up a kind of 'afterburner' below the stomach, just after the pyloric valve. Well, that's what it'd be on one of us. For their size, I bet one of them doesn't eat much more than one of us does."

"Speak for yourself," muttered Frill, disconcerted.

Todd slapped him on the back and escorted him to the Gringg leader. "Now, Commander, you want to demonstrate the purity and deliciousness of one of our RRE's for our hosts here?" he asked. Collecting a nod from Frill, he and Hrriss placed their armloads of packages in front of Grizz, next to the heaps of Gringg offerings. "These are examples of our food. We're giving them to you for your examination. First, we'll eat a sample." He accompanied his speech with pantomime, which he hoped was comprehensible to the aliens.

As the Gringg watched with interest, Frill eagerly tore open the pressed-plastic packet, then looked dismayed as the difficulty became obvious.

"The helmet," he said, glancing at Todd for help. "How'm I going to eat wearing a helmet?"

Todd and Hrriss looked at each other and then at Ken.

"Well, one of us is going to unseal sooner or later," Todd said. He attacked the grommets around the base of his helmet, twisting the fastenings loose.

Greene sprang forward and grabbed his wrist. "What do you think you're doing, Reeve? Attempting suicide? If you choose to take foolish risks, I can recommend to Lauder here that we have you brought back to the cruiser in restraints to wait until a psychiatrist sees you."

"I never take foolish risks," Todd said. He shook off the man's hand. "The ensign here has already told us that if he encountered an atmosphere like this one planetside, he'd consider it safe. Isn't that right, Ensign?"

Lauder, not eager to get into the middle of a battle between a renowned planetary leader and a formidable ranking officer, quickly nodded his head. Encouraged by Todd's friendly smile, he added very timidly, "I'd think we were lucky, too, if the air on the *Hamilton* was this fresh, Commander." The medic swallowed hard as Greene turned his stare upon him, but he didn't recant.

"Therefore I consider the odds very much in my favor." Todd unfastened the plastic bubble and took it off. In the same instant, Hrriss removed his own headgear, and both took a deep breath.

There was a murmur of approval from the Gringg. Todd almost choked with nervousness as the warm air hit his lungs. The two of them waited, watching each other for signs of anoxia, wondering if they had made a mistake, each ready to slap the helmets back on.

One minute, two minutes, passed. There was no sound in the landing bay except for a mechanized hum deep in the heart of the giant ship. Todd could almost hear the sweat trickling down his back. It was hard to believe that only a couple of hours ago he had been sitting at the head of a tableful of voracious and self-seeking delegates who intended to ruin a special part of his planet to satisfy trade requirements. If he guessed wrong, if the data that the young medic had been carefully monitoring was incorrect, he could be about to die. Todd felt with every nerve-ending the touch of moving air on his skin. It was pleasantly warm. His lungs dragged it in and pushed it out. It took more of an effort than breathing usually did, but he was in a slightly heavier gravity than what he was used to. He was consciously tasting each breath for poisons, but there was only the cloying smell of recycled air and a musky, not unpleasant aroma, probably exuded by the Gringg.

He felt lightheaded. What was it they said? That after five minutes without oxygen one became irreversibly brain dead? Everyone was looking at them, expecting a reaction of some kind. Hrriss's nostrils twitched, and his ears swivelled forward expectantly. Todd suddenly realized that he was holding his breath. If there'd been enough oxygen to sustain him for the last five minutes, the next breath should be fine, too. With a halfhearted laugh, he let go and sucked in a deep lungful of air. Nothing adverse had happened. He was alive. Hrriss was alive. They and the Gringg breathed the same sort of air.

"It's all right." Todd nodded at his friend, and they fell into one another's arms. "Go ahead, Frill," Todd said, as he and Hrriss pounded each other on the back in relief. Ken Reeve was smiling. "Lauder is right. Our atmospheres are at least compatible."

"So they could live on our worlds, if they disposed of us," Greene said, his eyes cold.

"Enough of that, Greene!" Todd said firmly. "There are no indications whatsoever that these creatures are aggressive. On the contrary, in fact! May Commander Frill assist me now with a food demonstration?"

Grudgingly, Greene gave the order. Frill saluted and began to undo the helmet fastenings.

Watching Todd and Hrriss all the while, the big Spacedep officer lifted off his helmet and put it on the floor beside him. He, too, took a few tentative breaths before relaxing.

"It's real air!" he said simply, a grin spreading over his big face.

"This'll cause speculation among the scientists," Ken said. "Are all spacefaring races oxygen-breathers? Or do oxy-breathers tend to be pacific? There's a theory in there someplace." He took off his helmet, then peeled off his gloves. The baby Gringg toddled toward him again, this time chortling joyfully to itself that Genhh now exuded a totally different, and much more preferable scent—one compounded of many subtle smells. Ken was sniffed over from toe to crotch to pate.

With no hesitation, Jilamey removed his helmet. Timidly, with a glance at Greene for permission, Lauder opened his a crack, testing the air against what was in his rebreathers. Only Greene remained sealed in his protective gear, like a disapproving robot glaring at the others.

The Gringg, too, seemed to be happy with the removals, grunting low, pleased sounds to themselves, though only the littlest one made tactile, and nasal, contact.

As the Gringg watched with considerable interest, Frill consumed an RRE. He tore mouthfuls away from the bar of compressed protein, chewed, and swallowed them. The carbohydrate wafer crunched loudly in the metal-walled room, and the packet of fruit conserve went down with a slurp or two.

"Uh, see?" the officer said, twisting the packets into a little ball and tucking them into the empty box, a little uncomfortable to have his greed witnessed by such a crowd. "That's good food. Not as good as fresh, but okay."

"O-kaayy." Grizz echoed the word.

Todd thought that the big alien understood. It signalled to Eonneh, who undid one of the sausage-shaped packets and ate the contents, patting his chest to indicate satisfaction when he had finished. Todd caught a whiff of his scent. Not too bad, he thought. It smelled a little like smoked snake.

"Here, try this one," Todd said, pushing aside containers of tuna fish, Doona snake, bean curd, turkey, and cheese, to open one of his favorites. It was popcorn, in a self-heating hemispherical container. Cautioning the Gringg not to touch, he pulled the seal. The disk-shaped base started to glow. In a few seconds, the whole unit began to shake. Weddeerogh jumped, letting out a squeal of surprise, then hunkering down, getting as close as it dared to the twitching and bulging package. Todd grinned. Popcorn was not only food, but entertainment. Grizz watched more calmly while the silver dome unit expanded one pop at a time, until it had reached four times its original size. A small red spot appeared on the top of the dome, signalling that it was through cooking. Todd burst open the thin covering and took a handful of popcorn.

"See? This is really good." He ate it piece by piece, crunching each between his teeth with obvious satisfaction.

"Goo-ood." Using its long claws, the Gringg picked up a single puffed kernel and looked at it, a giant examining a grain of sand. Then it indicated to Ken that he should take the other Gringg rations, and sat, continuing to study the fluffy morsel of corn.

"Great," Ken exclaimed, collecting the bundles and putting some of them in his equipment pouch. Lauder, his hands shaking slightly, picked up an armload of the supplies and stowed them in his equipment carryall. "Thank you, Grizz. We'll be happy to take these. Soon as we have a good close look, we'll know if it's safe for you to come back with us." He bowed to Grizz and nodded to the others. "Thank you for letting us visit. We'd better get back, boys. The Admiral and the others will be going spare wondering what happened to keep us so long."

"One more thing," Greene said quickly, planting a hand on Ken's shoulder. "Tell them they've got to keep their ship in this orbit. If they move, we'll consider that an act of hostility, and we will attack."

"Now, how do you expect me to explain that to them?" Ken demanded, fed up with the Spacedep commander acting the eternal wet blanket. "I don't even know how to say 'how are you?' much less 'stay put.' "

"Oh, draw them a picture," Jilamey said impatiently. He knelt down beside Eonneh and held out a hand toward the Gringg's two-finger stylus. "Can I borrow that?"

Surprised, the honey-colored alien put the drawing implement in his hand and pushed the tablet toward him. Jilamey whistled at the weight of the instrument, then fitted his fingers into the twinned loops. He drew a little circle on his hand with the point, and smiled up at Greene.

"Now, what kind of orbit do you want them to stay in?"

Glancing at the Admiral's aide for permission, Commander Frill slumped down beside Jilamey, and looked up at the Gringg captain. "Draw Doona there," he said to Jilamey, indicating the center of a blank tablet page. "Now, draw a big circle around it, far out, beyond the moons—better draw in the moons—and put their ship on the big circle. Boy, this is undignified," he complained, looking up at Ken.

"Go on," Ken encouraged him. "You're doing fine."

"Well," Frill said, showing the tablet to Grizz. "This," he said, following the circle around the planet, "is good. Uh—This"—he took the stylus from Jilamey and drew a tangential line leading away from the circle with an arrow—"er, is bad." He crossed out the line. "This is bad, too." Red to the ears, he drew in another tangent, this one leading inward toward Doonarrala, and crossed it out. "Do you understand? Stay on this orbit." His finger traced the circle around and around.

"Reh!" Grizz said, following his gesture. "Orrrbitttt. Nggh yaahrr mmmmonnya." The Gringg showed a mouthful of long white teeth and black gums to indicate comprehension.

"Well done, Frill. Satisfied?" Ken asked Greene. "Again, Captain Grizz, our compliments. Until we meet again?" He bowed and turned away. Together, the party walked back toward the Spacedep shuttle.

For big creatures, the Gringg could move surprisingly fast. Eonneh and the strange bear who had brought in the Gringg rations waddled swiftly past them, and stood by the shuttle. The party stared at them, their initial fears returning.

"Now what is this?" Greene demanded, stopping at a distance from the ship. He felt again for his side arm and cursed Todd Reeve's insistence on coming unarmed. "Are they preventing us from leaving? Are we prisoners?"

"Eonneh gerrvah," the light-brown Gringg said, and indicated its companion. "Ghotyakh gerrvah aui'd." The other, its rubbery mouth drawn back in the imitation of a human smile, waved at them and set a gentle paw down on the top of the shuttle.

"Quite the opposite," Ken suggested, eyeing this gesture with amusement. Ghotyakh must be an engineer, if he pats spaceships like ponies. "I think they want to come with us as emissaries."

"Impossible!" Greene was alarmed at the thought of Gringg loose on a Spacedep ship, or amuck in the colony itself.

"Not at all." Ken glanced back at Grizz, who raised a giant snout in their direction. The intelligent, red-brown eyes were calm. "They're showing that they trust us."

"They could die from exposure to toxins or bacteria on Doona."

Ken shook his head. "Obviously, Commander, they're willing to take that chance. That's something they need to learn from us, too: if both species can exist in the same biosphere. And I get the impression that if we don't take them, we don't leave."

Jilamey blinked. "Who do we leave behind as volunteers? As our ambassadors?"

Ken grinned pointedly at his son. "Any volunteers?"

"Hrriss and I will stay," Todd said quickly, barely beating out Hrriss' call to remain.

"We are the logical choices," the Hrruban agreed. "We already serve the diplomatic arm for both Hrruba and Earrth, as well as Doonarrala."

"Wish I had your background in languages, Dad," Todd said, "but I think we'll get along."

"I have all the faith in the galaxy in you two," Ken said, and his eyes twinkled. "Good luck."

Hrriss and Todd shook hands in turn with Ken, Jilamey, and the two Spacedep officers. Greene continued to look disapproving.

"You should return to the cruiser with us."

"Not a good idea," Todd said promptly. "The Gringg have trusted us with two of their people. They might take it amiss if we don't reciprocate. Remember, it's their initiative."

"We shouldn't take them aboard, not until the Admiral has cleared such an important decision."

"Spacedep isn't involved in this aspect of the encounter, Commander. Alreldep is!" Todd told him. "Hrriss and I are Alien Relations. Report that to the Admiral."

"Two of our new friends are staying with us," Grizz said contentedly, watching Dodh and Rrss stand by as the other Ayoomnnns entered their fragile little vessel. "We have much to ask them. Go in peace," she called.

"Errrrungh!" The cub called out his farewell to his new friends before the shuttle door closed.

"Goodbye!" Ken called back, waving.

The cub let out squeals of glee. "Errrrungh! Gggbyyy!"

Just then the comunit in Todd's helmet began to crackle. Todd picked it up and held it close enough to hear any message.

"Frill here, Reeve. If you can hear me, nod." Todd obediently nodded. "We'll keep sending on our way back to the *Hamilton*. Give some answer as long as you hear us. Okay?" Todd nodded.

"If we can't stay in touch, we'll come back for you in twenty-four hours!"

Todd nodded vigorously, relieved.

The last sight Ken had of his son and the Hrruban who was nearly his second son was the two of them disappearing behind the gray glass doors with the dark-furred aliens. For a moment Ken was afraid, wondering if he had made a mistake leaving them behind.

It was a tight fit in the cabin with the two huge Gringg each spreading across two couches intended for one Human-size body. They were muttering excitedly to one another, their intelligent eyes scrutinizing all elements of the interior of the shuttle. Ken smiled to himself. The Gringg captain was probably having the same misgivings about sending two of his people with them.

"Good luck, son," he said quietly as Frill lifted off the little shuttle from the launch circle.

CHAPTER 4

COMMANDER FRILL GOT A CERTAIN AMOUNT OF PERverse pleasure opening a communications channel to the hovering Spacedep flagship and giving his message.

"Exploration shuttle returning at 1815 hours shiptime with two aliens aboard. Please inform the Admiral we will be with you by 1847. Frill out." That'll bring 'em running, he thought.

Out of the corner of his eye, Frill could see the colonist in the co-pilot's chair grinning like a fool. Frill had to admit he felt the same elation. They'd gone out on a dangerous mission and had returned not only intact, but in the company of two members of a new species. Although at first the assignment had made him nervous, Frill was grateful that Castleton had selected him. The aliens'd be well worth getting to know. For all his xeno training, he'd never had contact with any other species—apart from the Hrrubans, of course—that was sentient, let alone so eager to cooperate. Humanity deliberately avoided contact with intelligent extraterrestrials, lest such encounters result in a disaster like the Siwannese Tragedy. Despite his excitement, Frill was grateful that two of the smaller specimens had been sent. The giant ones were going to take a lot of getting used to.

The two Gringg were silent until the shuttle was inside the *Hamilton's* landing-bay doors, then began quietly muttering between themselves. Commenting on the differences? Frill wondered. The Spacedep bay walls were enamelled a spanking-clean white and stencilled with the Spacedep logo, and everything was smaller. A lot smaller. When he considered the size of the Gringg themselves, the volume of their ship wasn't so extraordinary. They needed a lot of head and elbow room.

Personnel in the Spacedep shuttle bay were fully clad in protective suits, and the board was showing full Red Alert. Frill thought that was rather overdoing security measures. If he had reported that they were under duress, or had given the covert danger code, it would have been appropriate. He had to remind himself that he had just spent a few hours on an alien vessel, and that those who remained aboard ship had no idea what the visiting party had experienced. He grinned again.

Setting down the shuttle smoothly, Frill began to switch off systems and run over the cross-check list, ably assisted by Ken Reeve.

Outside the small ship, a security force had been deployed. Marines, armed with powerful slug-throwing and laser weapons, hurried into a line surrounding the craft and knelt, waiting for the aliens to emerge. Behind the glass doors separating the bay from the waiting lounge stood Admiral Barnstable, Captain Castleton, and other interested parties.

Ken Reeve emerged first, grinning, followed by the Gringg. Frill had a good look at the reactions: the marines, to a man, recoiled and tightened their hands on their weapons as the huge bearlike beings hunched to get through the portal and then stood up and stretched to relieve the cramp they had endured on the small shuttle.

"They're friendly and they are not armed," Ken Reeve said, raising his arms, elbows out and away from his body as he maneuvered himself between Eonneh and the nearest marines. The Gringg followed suit.

"They're very friendly," Frill added in a bellow, grinning as broadly as he could to reinforce his words.

Castleton's voice echoed over the P.A. system. "Security, assemble at a safe distance. Await further orders."

"Yes, sir," replied the lieutenant in charge.

He signalled to his men, who re-formed in a close group beyond the shuttle. Frill felt his face redden.

"Captain," Ken Reeve said, frowning with annoyance at such overt hostility, "aren't you being a bit paranoid? They've shown no signs of aggression at any time."

"This is a security vessel, Mr. Reeve," the captain said in sharp tones.

"So it is," Ken retorted sarcastically. "I'd forgotten."

"There are definite procedures for this sort of thing, you know," Frill added, with a glance of apology at Reeve.

"Don't apologize for doing your duty," Greene snapped. He marched toward the decontamination booth.

Following Commander Greene, the party went through one by one. Ken and Frill stayed behind with the Gringg to reassure them as best they could, by smiling and trying to appear totally relaxed, that this was customary procedure. Neither of the two emissaries seemed dismayed, ignoring the actinic lights and the fans that fluffed up their fur. Ken admired their phlegmatic behavior in a totally foreign environment. Certainly there had been no similar procedures on the Gringg ship.

Barnstable was waiting as Greene, then Jilamey, followed by Lauder, emerged from the launch bay. The Spacedep chairman was containing himself with difficulty. Behind him, Castleton couldn't keep her eyes off the massive figures now passing through decontamination. Greene saluted and made directly for a computer terminal and began to enter codes.

"Whew, aren't they big mamas?" Ali Kiachif breathed.

"My son?" Hrrestan asked of Jilamey, the fur at the nape of his neck erect with fear. "He did not rrturn with you?"

"He's fine, Hrrestan. Stayed on board the visitors' vessel with Todd," Jilamey said soothingly. "They've volunteered"—he wrinkled his nose and grinned—"to be our ambassadors to the Gringg. These are our new friends. The gold one's Eonneh, and the other's Ghotyakh."

"Amazing crrreatures," Hrrestan said, gazing up at the two Gringg with wide eyes.

Snapping off the computer terminal, Greene marched up to his superior officers and saluted. His face was pale.

"Sirs, I must see you immediately," he said.

"Commander, how could you so mislead me as to the size of these . . . these . . . things?" Barnstable demanded.

"They aren't things," Jilamey retorted indignantly. "They're Gringg . . . and intelligent folk."

Barnstable brushed that observation aside. "This is a Spacedep vessel . . ."

"Currently assisting Alreldep," Ken said, bracing the Admiral, "in establishing friendly communication with a new species."

Barnstable glared fiercely at Greene. "When I sent you along as a Spacedep representative, Commander, this was exactly the kind of lamebrained, irresponsible behavior I expected you to counter."

"In point of fact, Admiral, encouraging this . . . delegation is not irresponsible." Greene aimed a very significant look at Barnstable. "They are, as you see, larger than any of us."

Barnstable cleared his throat. "Yes, there's that." He began to reconsider his position as Eonneh approached, passing close to him as he entered the lounge. "Did you . . . ah . . . manage to establish communications?"

"No, sir. We've exchanged a few words, nothing more. The rest was accomplished through a primitive sign language, and demonstrations." Greene shot a jaundiced glance at Ken Reeve. "Then they wouldn't allow us to reboard the shuttle unless we brought them"—he cocked his thumb at the Gringg—"with us." He glared again at Reeve.

"Well, what do we do with them?"

Greene flapped one hand indecisively. "Whatever one does with a new species . . . sir. They came voluntarily. Just as young Reeve and Hrriss remained. Sir, permission to speak to you privately concerning the Gringg. It is urgent."

"Watch it there, Greene," Jilamey said in a firm and angry voice. "The Gringg may not understand our spoken language, but your body language is sending hostility signals. Lighten up."

That made the two Spacedep men pause and glance suspiciously at the aliens.

"We have to know what we're dealing with," Barnstable said.

"I don't know about you, Admiral," Castleton said, "but the size of them makes me nervous."

Ghotyakh waddled in and began to exchange quiet murmurs with Eonneh.

"We'll keep them here long enough to run tests," the Admiral said.

Emerging just then from decontam, Ken heard the last sentence.

"Hold everything, Admiral," he began, noticing Jilamey's agitation. "If there's going to be any testing done, physicians affiliated with Treaty Island or Alreldep and Hrruban Alien Relations should administer the tests. Spacedep isn't involved."

"I agrrrree," Second Speaker put in, taking a step forward. He seemed much put out by the huge aliens' appearance and was maintaining a discreet distance. The one with the light-colored pelt leaned his way, sniffing. Affronted, Second clutched his robe tighter around himself. Undaunted, the alien turned its huge head toward Mllaba and snuffed at her. "You cannot sequester such data."

"You may perform your own examinations when we have finished," Barnstable said stiffly.

"You're not getting the message, are you, Admiral?" Ken said, stiff with indignation. "These aren't lab animals. They're sentient beings from a highly sophisticated culture and they're here as envoys, not creatures to be dissected. Get that straight now, once and for all. They are to be treated with honor and respect!" He let out a breath—"Because that's how we hope they're treating our emissaries."

"Surely," Kiachif put in silkily, "you don't want unwelcome, untested, and unauthorized aliens aboard your flagship any longer than you have to? I'll take 'em off your hands right smart."

"Since Spacedep may have to clean up after you Alreldeps mess up this first contact . . ." Greene began.

"I didn't mess up first contact before, did I?" Ken said in a voice that was cold with threat. "Ali, we accept your offer of transport here and now."

"Just a living minute, Kiachif," the Admiral began, clearly determined to keep the aliens aboard where he would have control of their disposition. "Castleton, escort these . . . these creatures to suitable quarters."

The captain stared at the aliens, and turned to her commanding officer.

"With all respect, Admiral," she said, "we haven't any quarters big enough for them outside of this lounge"—she gestured about her—"or the wardroom, which cannot be secured. . . ."

"Dammit!" Ken Reeve said in an exasperated roar. "The Gringg are not subject to Spacedep authority. They are Alreldep's. They're coming down to Doonarrala with us. And that's that!" His bellow made everyone look at him in surprise. The Gringg rumbled and shifted their big feet.

"Now look what you've done," Jilamey said, glaring accusingly at Barnstable and Castleton. Making reassuring sounds and waving his hands in placatory gestures, he went up to Eonneh and Ghotyakh, who blinked rapidly but made no move.

"Relax, lassie, they don't have any weapons," Kiachif said to Castleton, who had instinctively reached for her side arm.

"Just claws and teeth," she replied, but she dropped her hand to her side. Greene seemed poised to move between her and the Gringg if she so much as gestured.

"They look so dangerrrous," Mllaba murmured, still standing closer to Second Speaker than protocol allowed.

"Then we mustn't upset them, must we?" Kiachif said, rather enjoying the navy's alarm.

"Especially at the outset of what should develop into mutual respect and harmony," Ken said in a disgusted tone. "Now, let's get these good . . . creatures," and he made the term far more a title than Barnstable had, "down to an environment that is not bristling with hostility and weapons."

With ill grace, Barnstable finally agreed.

"The Kiachif vessel has leave to depart," Captain Castleton said into her comunit to the bridge.

"Captain, will you also make contact with Admiral Sumitral at Alreldep?" Hrrestan asked, then turned politely to Second Speaker. "Sir, you will wish to inform the Hrruban Council of this development."

"The Terran Council will hear of this," Barnstable said.

"Along with the rest of civilized space," Ken said, shedding all trace of his previous aggressiveness now that the navy had acquiesced.

"Sometimes, Hrrestan, you exceed your authority," Second Speaker remarked in a taut voice.

Even as Hrrestan bowed low in apology, he wished that the old First Speaker were still alive, with his wisdom and forbearance available to help them through this tense situation.

"I thought you would not wish to be seen in the same light as that Hayuman admiral," Hrrestan said meekly.

Hrrto regarded him through slitted eyes, and his tail switched just once. He pulled his nails through his muzzle whiskers and then dropped his jaw ever so slightly.

"A point, Hrrestan. A point."

"Shall I also give permission for Sumitral to use the grid for conveyance to Doonarrala? Alreldep has always been the most intelligent branch of the Hayuman authorities."

Hrrto considered the question for a moment, then with a flick of half-bared claws signalled his assent. It would do him no harm in his campaign for the First Speakership to be seen to side with the Alreldep, always the nemesis of the conservative element of Hrruba in vying for influence on Rrala and in the lanes of space.

Hrrestan turned to Castleton and swept her a graceful bow. "Please let it be known in the Federazhon Building that we request the most immediate prrresence of Admiral Sumitral in the First Village complex. I am most grrrateful for your assistance."

"This way, folks," Kiachif said, gesturing broadly toward the bay in which his shuttle was docked.

"I'm to be kept posted, do you hear me?" Barnstable shouted as Ken and the others swept toward the connecting link.

The security force drew back, hands convulsively closing on their weapons as they swung through.

"This way, gentlebears," Jilamey said, skipping in front to lead the way. "Next stop, a fine little planet that I'm sure you'll adore."

After a quick huddle with Captain Castleton and Admiral Barnstable, Greene followed the Second Speaker and the still apprehensive Mllaba as they started to leave the bay.

"A moment, Honored sir," he said in good Middle Hrruban, laying a hand on Hrrto's robed arm, "of your most valuable time."

"For what reason?" Second Speaker asked stiffly, glancing down at the offensive hand. Beside him, Mllaba let out a hissing breath.

"I beg your pardon." Greene snatched his hand back, bowing apologetically. "Honored Speaker," he went on in a humble tone, though Hrrto recognized in the Hayuman a warrior's bearing that showed he bent the knee to no one, "please let the shuttle depart without you. Admiral Barnstable and Captain Castleton wish a few words with you. About this new species. It will delay your return to Doonarrala only a few moments."

"Very well," Second said, without inflection or expression. Greene nodded to the captain, who lifted her communication unit.

"The shuttle may depart now," she said. The blast doors closed before anyone on board the small ship could question the absence of the Hrrubans.

The Hayuman glanced toward the brilliant light of the shuttle's exhaust port, fast disappearing over the curve of the planet. Second Speaker followed Greene's gaze, then directed a curious stare at him.

"The Admiral thought that perhaps you are not so sanguine about the nature of these new beasts." The brown eyes searched the slitted green feline ones. "Perhaps you, too, believe that more caution should be exercised in regard to these Gringg."

"Perhaps," Second said, very cautiously. "But why should you share these thoughts with me?"

Greene moved closer to him, into uncomfortable proximity. Though he was shorter than the Hrruban, he seemed to loom.

"Because, Honored sir, you have power and influence here and on your own homeworld, and you are known for your sagacity in their use," the Hayuman said in a low voice. "The arrival of these beasts complicates the equation that already exists between Hrruban and Hayuman and interrupts proceedings that have long been on the agenda. Should this be allowed to occur? And at this critical point? There is more to this than meets the eye. Admiral Barnstable and the captain beg a few moments to discuss their views with you. Nothing official, or binding, certainly. Merely a friendly chat."

"You interest me, Commandrrr," Second said, his pupils narrowing. He stepped away from the Hayuman, restoring his breathing space. He found the commander almost more threatening than the Gringg. "Very well, so long as it is understood that this is only a small chat."

Kelly Reeve fidgeted. When Todd and his party had departed to investigate the strange spaceship, Hrrestan's assistant had addressed the remainder of the delegates left in the dining room.

"Honorred frriends, we must postpone frrthrr deliberations until the others have retrrrned. We have zaken measurres to ensurre yrrr comfort while you are here, and we will keep you inforrrmed about the ship orbiting above us. Please do not dizcuss what you have hearrrd with anyone who does not have ze proprrr classificazhon. Securizy is vital."

The financier from Hrruba was the only one to voice a protest. "Our time is valuable. Zis interruption must not interferre with ourr negotiations," he said.

"We have not a choice," his assistant replied. "We may not continue in ze absence of ze honorred Second Speaker and half our membrrrs."

Putting aside her nervousness, Kelly smiled at the Hrruban executive. "Perhaps you would care to return with me to my village? I would be delighted to make welcome one who is so invaluable to the High Council."

"Zank you, no. I will remain on ze Zreaty Island until ze Speaker returns. I have calls to make zo ze homewrrrld," the banker said in cold, if polite, refusal. The delegates dispersed, muttering, to their guest quarters. Seeing she could nothing else to help, Kelly transported back to the Hrruban First Village, to Nrrna and the children.

It was still early morning on this side of Doonarrala. Children, not yet summoned by the school bell, raced around the green of the sunlit common. Worried about Todd, Kelly forced herself to smile at the serene picture they made.

"Mizzis Rrev," a Hrruban youngster shouted. "Where are Alison and Alec? Zey will be late zo school! It iz almoz time!" A crowd of children carrying books and tapes ran past them, heading toward the Friendship Bridge.

"They're not coming today, Zhrrel," Kelly said, fighting to keep from letting concern show on her face. "They're at Mrrva's, with me and Nrrna. Will you tell Hrromede I'll call him to explain?"

"Yes, Mizzis Rrev," Zhrrel said, turning almost on his tail and racing for the bridge as the bell began to toll. "Aiee! I'm laze!"

Mrrva, lithe and graceful in spite of her sixty years, hurried to put Kelly at ease, and would not let her speak until they were all seated comfortably in the garden with hot morning drinks. Perhaps in spite of her importance as the head of Doonarrala medical services she prized her reputation as a genial hostess, and she was as fond of Kelly as she was of her son's mate.

Nrrna appeared in the doorway, with her two younger children in tow. She was a soft-furred female with pretty green eyes and pointed cheekbones that made her look very young.

"Gelli, whateverrr is wrrrong?" she said in her soft voice.

She held the children close while Kelly told as much as she could and still be discreet. Ourrh, only a year older than his newborn sister, silently watched the faces of the adults with no comprehension of what had upset those who loved and protected him. Solemnly, he nestled close to his mother's chest and put one arm around the baby. Knowing that all the villages would have learned of the strange ship's presence, Kelly could, and did, describe its awesome size and appearance.

"Then they just piled into Ali Kiachif's shuttle to go take a look at it. Sometimes, Todd Reeve is enough to drive a woman to mlada!" Kelly finished, letting righteous ire dissipate some of her inner fears. "But, best of all, the pair of them went off together, Nrrna. Just like always."

The estrangement between the two best friends over the matter of the spaceport had been of great concern to their wives, and other discerning friends. It had seemed incredible that any matter could have strained the deep bond shared by Todd and Hrriss.

There had been tension even on the Double Bar Gemini Ranch, which Todd and Hrriss owned in partnership. Even the children had become aware of some stress between the two adult males, though for the most part they continued their games and running in and out of the two ranch houses as always.

"If these aliens have brought about a reunion," Mrrva said in Low Hrruban, "then they are thrice welcome in *this* house. So don't fear, Gelli," she added, patting Kelly's knee, "Hrriss and Zodd are resourceful. And never more so than when they face a mutual challenge. I have earnestly wished to help, you know." She tilted her head to gaze into Kelly's eyes.

"I know you have, Mrrva." Kelly smiled and grasped the slender furred arm. "It's just so utterly . . . weird that those two could ever find something to quarrel about." She closed her lips then, for she had to be loyal to Todd's principles even if, in her innermost thoughts, she didn't *see* why he so disapproved of the spaceport. Trade would expand, and the Doonarrala economy would improve enormously. A spaceport would make it so much easier for everyone. "I just hope we don't have to wait too long to hear what that infamous pair are up to now." She brushed away a vagrant tear because they *were* once more up to something!

"The most difficult part will be for you, waiting until they return! You are both welcome to stay here, since they must come through the village grid from the Zreaty Island."

"Thank you, Mrrva," Kelly said. As long as Todd and Hrriss were together, perhaps they'd also find a way past this spaceport difficulty, too. "It'll be like old times," she added, making her smile as genuine as possible.

Outside the house, she could hear the yells and hoots of her twins and Nrrna's two oldest children. They were accustomed to their fathers jetting off on special trips or being involved in colony business at Treaty Island. As Kelly had also been busy with the Treaty Island business, she had left her pair with Nrrna and Mrrva in First Village. So, totally unconcerned and giving their all to this extra day of leisure, they raced around Mrrva's front garden, playing out their notions of what was going on. Kelly sat on the stoop watching them, reassured by their carefree presence.

Her twin children were tall for their eight Standard years, and skinny as a pair of saplings. Early muscular development and plenty of exercise gave Alec and Alison such innate grace of movement that they resembled a pair of young Hrrubans, hence their nickname, the Alley Cats. Alec had his mother's red hair, but had inherited intense blue eyes from Todd. Alison was a more exotic combination, with shining black hair and eyes with golden, black-rimmed hazel irises. Except that they were obviously male and female, the twins' faces were extraordinarily similar in feature and form, though Alison's was slightly rounder than her brother's. Often friends would remark on how glad they were that they had different color hair, for in a losing battle to keep their locks from being eternally tangled messes, Kelly had clipped both heads short.

Also eight years old, Hrrana was slight and very shy like her mother, Nrrna. Hrrunival was a chunky six-year-old with wise eyes. He was the youngest of the four on the lawn, but tended to be the ringleader in games and feats of daring. The children had, of course, heard of the appearance of the strange spaceship in orbit.

"Zoddandhrriss will burrrst into ze alien vesssel," Hrrunival said, punctuating his phrases with zooming motions of his hands, "and drrrag out ze aliens and say 'What are you? Where do you come from?' " He was wild with excitement, dancing around on light toes. His elder sister, Hrrana, grabbed him by both ears to hold him still. He spat and batted at her.

"Then they will find out everything there is to know about the aliens," Alison said, calmly releasing Hrrunival from his sister's grasp and fluffing up the fur between the offended aural appendages. The Hrruban boy's eyes slitted pleasurably at Alison's fussing, and he wrinkled his nose at Hrrana. Unconcerned, the female pirouetted and did a boneless somersault, to land lightly on her feet again.

"And what happens then?" Kelly asked, distracted from her dark mood by the children's fancies.

"They'll make friends with them," Alec said, triumphantly spinning toward his mother, clapping his hands like cymbals, "like in the story where they brought all the Rralans together. Don't you think that would be nice, Mommy?"

"Yeah!" exclaimed Hrrunival.

Kelly sighed. The story of how Doonarrala was founded had become almost a legend, with "Toddandhrriss" the boy heroes whose names were always spoken together until they became an indistinguishable mass of syllables. She hadn't been born when that happened, but if Todd as a youngster was anything like eight-year-old Alec today, it was no mystery how he had insinuated, or rather, cannoned himself into the midst of a delicate situation that could have had disastrous repercussions for both races. The unexpectedly deep bonding between the young Todd, so out of phase with Earth social protocol, and Hrriss, had surprised and touched both Hayumans and Hrrubans. It was this friendship, and Todd's determination to enjoy it without adult-conceived hindrances, that had been the cornerstone for amicable co-existence between the two species. Which had resulted in the Decision at Doona.

The true adventure gave the children of Doonarrala heroes of their own age to admire and emulate. It also prompted the occasional outbreak of rope tails attached to the trousers of Human youngsters. If being the sons and daughters of legends made things a little tougher for the Alley Cats and Nrrna's brood, they never acknowledged the problem. Possibly their peers never connected the Todd and Hrriss of the stories with the two very accessible adult males, fathers of their friends, who played with them daily and who led the annual Snake Hunts. Those occupations, Kelly reminded herself, were adventurous enough for eight- and six-year-olds.

In the meanwhile, two hours had stretched into five, and five into nine. Worrying about Todd, Kelly ate a lunch and dinner she didn't taste. She tried to tell herself that the long delay was because things were going well, not because there'd been problems. Problems one usually heard as soon as they occurred. But she couldn't completely discount her nagging premonition of trouble, however nebulous it was.

After the early evening meal, Mrrva retired into the back garden to leave the two younger women alone. Nrrna dandled baby Hrrunna on her lap, playing with the small cub's perfect little hands and feet. The baby's fur was light gold with a mahogany-brown stripe down her back, a contrast to her mother's tawnier pelt. The cub fussed a little, and opened a little pink mouth to emit a weak, mewling sound. Nrrna, reclining on her side to expose the four gentle swellings nearly hidden in her fur, put Hrrunna to a nipple. The child began to suck, settling its little rounded ears back at an absurd oblique angle: a peaceful tableau, if not for the presentiment of danger plaguing Kelly.

Unable to sit still, she thought of calling the Federation Center again to see if they'd had any word from Todd and the others. Arms crossed over her chest to keep her fingers from twitching, she paced over to the console, wondering if it was too soon after her last call.

"What time is it, Nrrna?" she asked, tightening her fingers on her arms.

Nrrna shifted to her other side and nestled Hrrunna in the crook of her other arm so she could look at her wrist chronometer. "Only half past six."

"Hmm," Kelly mused. "That means it's nine-thirty on Treaty Island. Do you think there's anyone in the Space Center office?"

"There was not half an hourrr ago, Gelli. Why do you not try to relax?" Nrrna settled the nursing cub, peering at the concentrated little face with its tight-shut, shell-like eyelids.

"I don't see how you can stay so calm!" Kelly said. "Hrriss and Todd could be in great danger."

Nrrna let out the low, musical growl that was a Hrruban laugh. "I must stay calm or this tiny one gets gas through my milk," she said. "It is an exercise in self-control. I myself do not think of danger to Zodd or Hrriss! You could go to the Treaty Island?"

"What good would that do?" Kelly grumbled, pacing to the window at the opposite side of the room. "No. I'm not going."

"I am glad you do not," Nrrna said, jaw dropped in a gentle smile. "I prefer that we are together and not alone."

Kelly glanced down affectionately at the Hrruban woman. "Me, too. I guess that's why I didn't stay this morning. I'd get that 'useless female' reaction and be acidly asked what I thought I could do about anything. That lot at Treaty don't worry about people; they worry about treaties and agendas and . . . things! Besides, it'd be unfair to leave my two monsters here! Look at them out there!"

The Alley Cats were in the midst of a rough and tumble with Hrrana, Hrrunival, Ourrh, and a group of the neighborhood youngsters, freed for evening games until darkness. As Kelly watched, Alison was pulled to the ground by a couple of Hrruban cubs, and shrieked happily, coming up dusty to drag her friends over with her.

"Where do they get the energy?" Mrrva asked with a sigh as she walked up and gazed at their spirited racings.

"It's not fair, is it?" Kelly said, shaking her head. "Ooops, there goes Alison's shirt. Well, it was an old one," she added. "Once they knew they weren't going to school today, I had to fight the two of them into clothes, and now they're half-naked anyhow. 'If Hrrana and Hrrunival don't have to wear anything but belts, then why can't we?' " Kelly piped, in a flawless imitation of Alec at his most difficult. Nrrna chuckled again. The baby squirmed and let go of the nipple, licking her tiny chops. Her mother repositioned her, and with eyes still closed, she placed her head on her front paws and went to sleep.

"Take joy in the differences, that is what I think they should do," Nrrna said in Low Hrruban.

"Try telling them that," Kelly said wryly, then shouted out the window at the children. "You're playing too rough! Look out for Heeranh's nose! Augh!" she exclaimed, and started pacing again. "I don't know where they get the idea that they're indestructible."

"From their fathers, no doubt," Nrrna said. Hrrunna twitched in her sleep, and gave a squeaky little moan, which brought a loving smile from her dam. Nrrna glanced up at Kelly, who was biting her own thumb. "They will be all right, you know that, Gelli. They always are when they are working together."

"I guess so." Kelly paced back to the window, glanced out, and recoiled in shock.

"Mrrva!" she shrieked. "Get the snake rifle!"

The Gringg stepped off the grid in the midst of the Hrruban First Village and looked around them with great interest. First they had been landed on this new world in full dark; now they had entered twilight. They were glad to be able to see where they now were.

More Rroobvnnns had met them in the orbiting ship, including one very quick-moving male clad in black, and many more Ayoomnnns. From the ship, they had been transferred to a larger shuttle, flown by an engaging Ayoomnnn with black-and-gray hair who showed his teeth frequently and spoke in a poetic cadence. Once this vehicle had reached the surface of the planet, they had been ushered into a large white-stone cube of a building and down a corridor which echoed when one trod on the floor. The Gringg had obediently followed their guide to a small platform with pillars at each corner. When they stood upon it, the room became misty. Suddenly, they found themselves here. Eonneh was impressed. This form of transport was much more effortless than any he had previously encountered. The Gringg had much to learn from the Rroobvnnns.

A second group of four emerged from the mist. Genhh gestured to Eonneh and Ghotyakh to be patient and wait.

By some of the scents, the Gringg decided that the Rroobvnnn Rreshtanh lived here. The smell of the green groundcover and some of the flowers had been in his fur.

To one side, a high escarpment bounded the valley in which they stood, which was rich with trees and flora. Like the life forms they had seen so far, even the trees seemed less substantial here than on the Gringg world. But it was a beautiful place, and the air smelled good. In the distance, they could scent the musky odors of wildlife. One creature, which they guessed must be a service animal, unlike the Ayoomnnns or Rroobvnnns, stood tethered, calmly eating long strands of yellow herbage. It had not noticed them, but many more Hrrubans had. They were coming out of the little houses, staring and pointing at the Gringg. Most of them did not react with fear, but with interest. Eonneh found that to be heartening. Much more reassuring than the emotions he had perceived on the large orbiting ship.

The Rroobvnnn Rreshtanh was much honored here. Most of the Hrrubans spoke to him before circling around to look at the two aliens. Eonneh returned their gazes for a while; then, because there was little variation between one tawny-gold face and another, he became more interested in the scenery. There was much greater variation in color among the Ayoomnnns.

"Act as if there was nothing unusual in the way we were just transported," Eonneh said to Ghotyakh. "Though we have only seen a small part of this world, I am relieved that we seem to have been taken into the living places of these people. Even in the place where we first stopped we have seen nothing of the weapons carried by the guards on the ship. Accept anything they do with padded claws. Let us be sure not to frighten them."

"Observe the shapes of the domiciles, Eonneh," Ghotyakh said, turning a slow circle. "Square roofs, as had that building into which we were first taken. Everything is built using flat planes, and nearly all of them above ground. Curious."

"It is so. They do not build as we do, in echo of the natural shelters of the motherworld." Eonneh stared at one dwelling. "I would guess they have better ventilation than our homes. Perhaps their seasonal changes are not as drastic as ours. A very pleasant place." His tail wagged slowly. "I shall enjoy our time here."

The gesture seemed to interest his hosts. Genhh had no caudal appendage, as Eonneh had already observed. The angry male in black, who appeared to be subordinate to the male wearing an ornate red robe, both of whom had remained behind in the ship, had long, flexible tails that switched back and forth all the time.

"What interesting creatures these are," Ghotyakh said, glancing at the Rroobvnnns. "There is so much variation among the members of one sex. And do you notice that all the males seem to live on one side of this place and the females on the other? Look how many Ayoomnnns are coming from that direction. None live here."

"Reh. It is most curious. Is there water about? I'm thirsty, but a swim is even more necessary."

"I hear some running over there," Ghotyakh said, peering in the direction from which the Ayoomnnns were coming. "There is a bridge." Curious to see a Doonarralan river, the two ambled toward the sound.

A shout from behind reminded them that they were not alone.

"Oh, I apologize, Genhh," Eonneh said politely, turning to the Ayomnnn female. Her thin, nearly hairless skin was reddened from the effort of running. Eonneh noted again how small and weak the creatures of this world were. The tall being showed her teeth, and spoke. The Gringg listened, catching a word here and there, but comprehending more from the accompanying gestures.

"We will follow where you go," Eonneh said agreeably.

"They speak so quietly, Eonneh! I will be so glad when we work out what it is they are saying," Ghotyakh said. "They give every indication that they wish to learn our words, although it is also clear they want us to learn their language. I am glad we at least are no longer being watched by Ayomnnns carrying weapons, but this is in its own way a threat."

"I, too, still worry that they do not trust us. It is vital that they see us as harmless. Let us continue to shield our reactions and walk among them to reassure the small ones. If Grzzeearoghh commands that to speak their language is the best thing for Gringg to do, we shall do so, as we will deal with whatever else befalls us," Eonneh replied, following Ken into the heart of the Hrruban village. "For myself it is worth the risk. I am delighted to learn an alien language. It is easy to master other Gringg dialects, for they are all based upon the one mother language. This—this is genuinely different, and challenging. I have been waiting for a chance like this all my life."

The Gringg, gliding along in the midst of their escort, seemed fascinated by their surroundings. Ken pointed out objects, attaching names to each, but they paid scant attention to him. They did seem to be taking everything in with all their senses. Occasionally, Eonneh or Ghotyakh stopped to touch a tree or the wall of a house, feeling its substance with the sensitive pads of their handpaws.

A crowd of Hrrubans had gathered, and as word spread of the visitors' presence, Hayumans came over the Friendship Bridge to watch—at a respectful distance, having noted the aliens' size, teeth, and claws. The Gringg noted them placidly, and went on.

"What are these monsters? They look like giant mda!" demanded Anne Boncyk, riding up on a skittish horse. She was a dainty woman with a decided chin and large, fringed brown eyes.

"Our latest visitors," Ken said affably. At times, one didn't know which way Anne would jump. "They call themselves Gringg. Their ship is in orbit around Doonarrala."

The horse stretched out its neck to sniff at the Gringg. It sneezed once, but didn't shy away. Anne looked surprised.

"What about that? I'd've thought he'd be off across the compound," she said. "They don't scare him. Good lad!" And she gave her mount an affectionate slap on the neck.

"I find," Jilamey said mischievously, "that horses do not tend to judge by appearances."

"All ze children are still here," Hrrestan noted, sorting out the whirlwind of small bodies that whisked back and forth across his front garden. "Our sons' mates are waiting together." The older Hrruban paused. "You are certain that Zodd and Hrriss are safe?"

"Have you ever known a situation where they were at a loss?" Ken said lightly. "Except for that dratted spaceport issue. Seriously, old friend, I wouldn't have left them if I felt them to be endangered. I have a gut-strong reaction that these fellows are peaceful. Otherwise, they wouldn't send the captain's own archivist with us, and that's what I judge Eonneh here to be." Then he grinned, poking Hrrestan in the ribs. "Let's see what the grandkids think of our new friends! If I remember rightly, Todd trusted you on sight and he's never been righter."

"You'rrre not inzending to let zese strangers near childrrren, are you?" Hirro, Hrrestan's nearest neighbor, was shocked.

"The advantage is on the kids' side, Hirro," Ken said patiently. "This is open ground, and you must know how fast Hayuman children can move if they have to."

"Who are zey?" Hrrula, one of Ken's oldest friends, shouldered his way up to walk beside Ken. The Hrruban's big green eyes were shining.

"Gringg," Ken said, grinning.

" 'We arrre not alone,' " Hrrula quoted, dropping his jaw so far it nearly dislocated. "Mrrrvelous!"

The Gringg, largely ignoring their escort, caught sight of the cluster of children. Eonneh's ears seemed to perk up when Hrrana let out a shriek of mock fear, and ran away from her brother, who was stretching out a hand to tag her. Her tail, streaming out behind, whisked out of the way just as he was about to grab it. Fascinated, Eonneh and Ghotyakh moved closer to watch.

"Beep-beep!" shrieked Hrrunival, poking his sister in the belly when she twisted around to avoid running into a rosebush. "Now you have to say that!"

The other children dodged away from the Hrruban female, who finally caught Alec up against the pillar supporting Hrrestan's porch.

"Beep-beep!" she cried, and changed the symbol by tugging Alec's ear lobe. "Mrow!"

"Uh-oh!" Alec yelled, and ran around trying to catch someone else to be It.

"Uh-uh!" Alison cried, as Alec made a dive for Hrrunival. "No fair grabbing tails!" The pudgy Hrruban boy rolled away just in time and ran behind Alison.

The Gringg stood entranced by the children, ignoring the adults' efforts to move them along. Eonneh let out pleased little mutters at seeing younglings at play.

Suddenly Alec caught sight of the Gringg. "Look at them!" he shouted, standing stock-still and pointing. "Are they bears, Granddad?"

"What are bears?" Hrrana asked, swivelling and then standing as rigid as her friend.

"Earth animals, and these are not really bears," Ken explained, "but close."

All the children had paused in their noisy game of symbol tag and turned to look. They stared wide-eyed at the Gringg, who stared back. Shock held the children immobile for a moment. Hrrunival was the first to recover. Nose a-twitch and tail straight out in defiance of his own uncertainty, he squared his small shoulders.

"Who are you?" he demanded, walking up to Eonneh. The child wasn't quite as high as the Gringg's hip, but size wasn't going to deter him. The Alley Cats and Hrrana, holding Ourrh firmly by the hand, followed in close support. The baby's tail wrapped and unwrapped around one hind leg and his yellow-green eyes were huge, the pupils outspread across the irises.

"Totally unafraid," Frill muttered, watching this exchange. "What do you think of that?"

"Amazing," said Jilamey. "Unless you know Ken's family."

"Doonan children," Ken said, shaking his head. "They don't even know they're supposed to be afraid."

"Mrrva, hurry! Where's that rifle?" Kelly shouted again, as the children, aware of the beasts staring at them, stopped their play.

"Why?" Hrriss' mother came running, her tail lashing. "Where's the peril?"

The baby woke, crying. Nrrna snatched her up, holding her protectively to her chest.

"There are two absolutely gigantic mda out there looming over the children!" Kelly exclaimed. "They might attack at any minute. The kids are just standing there, frozen. Oh, my babies!" She followed Mrrva's pointing finger toward a closet, and was on her knees loading shells into the chambers of Hrrestan's powerful snake gun. "Call my brother at the animal hospital. Call the colony buildings. See if there's anyone in Animal Control!"

Nrrna ran for the commlink.

There was a rap on the door behind them. "Anyone home?" Ken called, then pushed the door open, aware of agitated movement within. "Oh no, Kelly! No, wait!"

She looked up at the sudden appearance of her father-in-law, her hands moving as if of their own volition. "Ken! Where's Todd? There are two huge mda out there! They never come so close to villages. These must be killers. I have to protect the children." She snapped the gun shut.

"They're not mda! They're our new friends. They're from the strange ship." He put one hand on the rifle barrel and deftly relieved her of it.

"From the ship? The one that came in out of nowhere?" Kelly swallowed hard, trying to grasp his statement as he unloaded the heavy-bore rifle. Behind him, Nrrna, green eyes huge, still clutched her baby.

"These fellows are peaceful. Their ship isn't even armed." Ken grinned reassuringly. Had all Kelly's training in Alreldep gone down the drain since her marriage? He smiled more broadly before he said, "Todd and Hrriss are staying aboard their ship. In exchange, we've got a couple of visitors. They really are friends, Kelly, Nrrna."

"Friends?" Kelly repeated, her voice sounding unsteady even to her. Her hands were shaking, and she didn't seem able to focus. "And you left Todd and Hrriss on board that immense ship?"

"They volunteered, but I wouldn't have agreed, dear, if I didn't truly believe it's the right way to deal with this unexpected situation. After all"—he winked at her as he helped her to her feet—"your father-in-law's had some practice in this sort of 'unexpected' encounter." Not quite certain, Kelly gave him a shallow grin. "So come on out and meet the Gringg. Even mda'd stay away from something that sizable!"

"Are you bears?" Alec wanted to know, confronting Eonneh, not too close, but close enough so that he could see the Gringg's furry features. "Why are you wearing belts? That's a very beautiful belt. I didn't think bears wore belts like Hrrubans. They have pockets in their belts, too. What have you got in your belt pockets?"

Eonneh was delighted that this red-topped Ayoomnnn seemed unafraid of him. It appeared to be asking about his belt, for the slender little finger was pointing at his chest. But courtesy came first. "Eonneh," he said, pointing at himself.

"Honey?" Alison asked, joining her brother in a semiprotective fashion. "Is that your name? Honey?"

"Reh. Ghotyakh," Eonneh said, indicating his companion.

"I can't say that!" Alec said. "It sounds like gargling."

"Don't be stupid, Alley, it sounds like Kodiak," Alison said. "That's a kind of bear. I guess they must be bears."

"But what are bears?" Hrrunival wanted to know.

"They're an Earth animal," Alec said, somewhat pompously. "Mommy read us about them in a storybook."

"I thought there were only Hayumans on Earrth," Hrrunival said. "Hrruba has no ozzer animals."

"Well, Earth did and does," Alec informed him condescendingly. "You've seen the pictures in the book."

"They're Gringg," Jilamey said, coming over to kneel beside the children. Following his example, Eonneh, renamed Honey, rolled back on his mighty haunches, bringing him closer to their level. "They've come to Doonarrala from their own world to meet us."

"You do not have any assurrrance of zese fine senziments," an older Hrruban male snapped. Ken recognized him as Trrengo, a relative newcomer to Rrala.

"I think we do," Alec said, suddenly turning an incredibly adult expression on Trrengo. "Uncle Jilamey says we shouldn't be afraid. He doesn't lie to us. You're friendly, aren't you?" He held out a hand to Ghotyakh, who engulfed it completely in his vast paw.

"Wait, don't let him touch you!" cried one of the Human colonists, Bob Lawrence.

"He's okay," Alec said, shaking hands solemnly. Alison followed suit, putting her hand into Ghotyakh's other paw.

"Just like their father," mumbled Macy McKee, patting his wife's hand where it rested on his arm. "I remember the first time Todd brought us a passel of Hrrubans to meet—" He broke off and looked about in surprise. "And hey, these fellows don't make me sneeze!"

"By analogy that should prove that these fellows are dangerous," Lawrence said sardonically.

"What a bizarre way to distinguish friend from foe," said Dr. Kate Moody in her caustic way as she pushed past her neighbors. "Allergies apart, they're sure not acting hostile. And the Alley Cats aren't the least bit skeered. Nor young Hrrunival. Look at them hunkering down to get level with your kids. Evening, Ken," she said cheerfully as he approached. "Back to your old habits, huh, finding aliens. Well, a man has to keep his skills honed or lose 'em. By any chance, are these the patients I was told to examine? I don't see any wounded lying about. Of course, the fellow on the Spacedep cruiser wasn't sure if they were a job for Ben Adjei, as head veterinarian, or for me, so we both came. And I'm glad we did! The size of 'em! Well-grown lads!"

Ken had brought Kelly, Mrrva, and Nrrna, still clutching her baby, all three women somewhat hesitant. "Come on, ladies, let me make you known to the Gringg. This is Eonneh. Go on! Introduce yourself. Tell him your name. I need more recordings of his responses to get more of their inflections."

Kelly glanced at Ken to make sure he was serious. With one hand he urged her forward, showing the recording device in the palm of the other.

"Kelly," she said, turning her thumb to her chest. "I'm Kelly." Then she turned her thumb to the smaller of the two Gringg and raised her eyebrows quizzically. "Your name?"

"Gelli," Eonneh repeated carefully, thumping his furry chest with an immense fist. "Eonneh. Eonneh."

"Honey!" the children chorused, delighted with such a name.

Ken made the rest of the introductions, laying his hand on each child's head and saying the name. Then he turned to see which of the neighbors were willing. Most of those who were, he noted with amusement, were members of the original Doonan colony or those who had arrived just after the Decision. Hrrula was delighted by the Gringg, especially the way they sniffed, very politely, at each person they met. The others, mostly recent arrivals, watched cautiously from a discreet distance.

The children had none of their parents' reserve. They were eager to meet Honey and Kodiak, as they'd been renamed. The Gringg tried to pronounce each new name, causing some of the kids to muffle their giggles in their hands. Made bold by their curiosity, more children came out of the surrounding houses and came forward timidly to see the visitors, then retreated, loud with relief, having experienced nothing more terrifying than a handshake.

"Come on, Nrrna," Ken said, urging the shy Hrruban forward. "They're really very friendly."

Still clasping Hrrunna, Nrrna slowly approached Honey and Kodiak. When she got close enough, she stood on tiptoe, her tail balancing out behind her, and looked deeply into their wine-red eyes. Both Gringg saw the sleeping cub and exchanged wide-eyed glances. Kodiak urged Honey forward, almost prodding him toward Nrrna. Very cautiously, as if afraid to frighten her or disturb the sleeper, Honey crept forward, eyes always on the curled-up infant. He hunched his shoulders and extended his neck, twisting his head from side to side, all attention focused on little Hrrunna. Then, ever so slowly, Honey held out his huge paws and gave a single, soft interrogative grunt. As one in a trance, Nrrna held the sleeping cub toward him and slipped her into his great furry paws, where the little Hrruban was cradled with tender care. Nrrna ignored the gasps around them.

Hirro even went so far as to leap forward, as if to snatch the cub from Honey, but, as if she hadn't even seen his movement, Nrrna stepped in his path.

"I trust you," she told the Gringg in the Middle Hrruban most of the onlookers would understand, her voice clear and strong in the sudden silence. "There is no harm in you that I can sense. You do come as friends."

The aliens were obviously entranced with Hrrunna, and ignored everything else. Ken could barely contain his delight in Nrrna's actions and words. In the hush that fell on the crowd, he could plainly hear the tiny whirr that meant someone was recording this on film, too, for which he was very grateful. He'd been so concerned with getting Gringg sounds down, he'd forgot to attend to a visual account.

Now Honey let out a tiny coo, the softest sound Ken had heard a Gringg make. The baby opened her eyes and briefly stared up at him, then stretched her pliant body across Honey's broad palms. The coo seemed to soothe her eyes shut. She let out a little sigh, and went back to sleep, curling her tiny tail about her. Honey's coo turned into soft melodic sounds, hovering just above audible level.

Ken turned up the gain on his recorder, hoping to get every note. Maybe it wasn't a Gringg lullaby, just Honey murmuring under his breath, but the tableau the Gringg presented was an effective one as far as a crowd-pleaser went, for soft looks were exchanged, and people definitely relaxed. Against their original intent, the settlers were being persuaded of the Gringg's pacifism by the gentleness shown a cub. Even the skeptics, with the exception of Hirro, regarded the large Gringg with less obvious apprehension.

"Music," Ken murmured to Kelly. "If that's what we're hearing now, is one more common language. I wonder what their reaction will be to Terran classics."

"Wagner? Mahler? Mtxainah? Hrnatn?" asked Kelly dubiously. "I can't help but be prejudiced *toward* a race that genuinely likes our young," she added, listening while Eonneh and Ghotyakh continued rumbly bass notes in soft harmony. She swept away a red wisp of hair from her sweaty forehead. "Whew! I thought they were mda! Just as furry, but much nicer."

Commander Frill seemed equally charmed by Hrrunna, too. He hung over Honey's arm, admiring the cub.

"This is the tiniest Hrruban I've ever seen. She's beautiful," he told Nrrna. "How old is she?"

"Born within the month," Nrrna said proudly.

"The youngest ambassador in the galaxy." said someone behind Ken. He turned to see Admiral Afroza Sumitral, his gray eyes alight, waiting beside Ben Adjei.

"You got here quickly," Ken said, shaking hands with his old friend.

"Not quickly enough, I see," Sumitral replied, half chidingly. "Once again the legitimate function of interplanetary diplomats has been usurped by the children of Doona. I wonder that we don't just induct the whole colony into Alreldep. Will you make me known to your friends here? Everyone else seems to have met them."

Laughing, Ken made a sweeping bow, from Sumitral toward the Gringg. "Introduce yourself. That's what we've done."

"And now," Kate Moody said when Sumitral had completed the formality, "if we've all finished becoming acquainted, I'd like to take a professional look at these two bruisers here. Ken, can we sort of maneuver them toward the Medical Center?"

"I am puzzled, Ghotyakh," Eonneh said, following the new Ayoomnnns through the village. "That Rroobvnnn with the small cub was at first very reserved with us. When we gave it back, it made suckling motions toward him as if looking for the source of milk. Could he, in fact, be a she?"

"A distinct possibility," Ghotyakh agreed. "We may be in error in our original assumptions. Previously I thought all the ones with tails were the males. Have we erred?"

"We must not be hasty in this. The appearance of the first Rroobvnnn we met closely matched our generative configuration. Perhaps they change after they have borne young?"

"Oh, I see!" Ghotyakh exclaimed, his roar of comprehension alarming some of the Ayoomnnns. "Our first visitor must have been a heifer. We must ask Genhh for the truth of this. I would not want to bring back specious data to Grzzeearoghh."

CHAPTER 5

CASTLETON ESCORTED ADMIRAL BARNSTABLE AND his party back to her ready room. The two Hrrubans were very nervous, and kept looking back at the escort of security guards that followed. She regretted the necessity of upsetting them, but regulations were regulations, and anyone on board who was not Spacedep had to be accompanied at all times. At least the rules allowed for the safe passage of visitors. Thank heavens Admiral Barnstable was more moderate than his predecessor.

The Admiral waited to speak until they were all seated and had been served refreshments.

"Good," he said when the door was quietly shut. "This room has been secured?" and when Castleton nodded, he continued. "We must address the matter of the Gringg. Now that we have some data to analyze, we can consider whether or not we are being rushed into intimacy with a potentially hostile race by overanxious individuals."

"I find zem most zrreatening," Mllaba said firmly. "Zey seemed so complezely unafrraid when zey boarded zis ship for ze first time. I felt as if zey had previous intimazhons of what zey would encounzer here."

"Too confident," Barnstable agreed, nodding. "That suggests a very sophisticated culture. Accustomed to dealing with alien species. You didn't sense any probes, did you, Grace?"

"None at all, Admiral," Castleton replied. "I would have said they made no attempt whatsoever to scan us. I find them interested and curious, but not overtly hostile."

"I am not so surrre," Hrrto said. He was torn. On the one hand, it was important to establish good relations with an obviously sophisticated new sentient race. On the other, he realized that it was foolhardy to rush into such relationships, without having a firm understanding of mutual intentions. So far, the Gringg had made the Hrrubans and Hayumans come to them, thereby giving them what the Hayumans called "home court advantage." It would not look well to the Hrruban High Council to appear in a subordinate position. Such loss of face could be fatal to Second's hopes in an election year.

There were many candidates standing to take over the now-vacant First Speakership which Hrrto felt he had to win. In his opinion, very few of the nominees had either the experience or acumen for the office. The prime Speakership should not be allowed to fall into the hands of some dilettante or partisan who might involve the Council in irrelevancies to please his supporters: someone with no standards or appreciation of true Hrrubanism. He felt himself to be the best possible choice. Having been Speaker for External Affairs for more than forty years, he understood what could happen to their carefully maintained civilization if Hrruba was badly led, and he was determined not to allow that to happen. If he was seen to be in the wrong in such a sensitive matter as dealing with the Gringg, his popularity, and his reputation, would plummet. Public opinion was fickle.

"In my opinion," he went on when he realized that a polite silence prevailed in expectation of his next words, "caution is indicated. I would like more data as soon as possible. Should we not be hearing from ze medical examiner on Rrala about now?"

"I doubt there could be any comprehensive results so soon," the captain said. "Laboratory work takes time."

"Yes, of course," Hrrto replied, fingering his robes.

Across the room from the Second Speaker, Jon Greene was busy over a hooded monitor, his fingers flicking swiftly over the controls. Grace Castleton eyed him, wondering what he was seeing that gave him such a worried expression. Mllaba flexed and stretched the claws of one hand along the tabletop.

"Well?" she said at last and with some impatience in her tone. "Do we go? Or stay? You must not waste more of the Speaker's most valuable time."

"Sirs, ma'am, Captain, the wait is worth it, I assure you," Greene said, straightening up, "for I have finally found what I've been searching for. Now, this is the tape made while we were aboard the Gringg ship." He manipulated the controls, and the holoscreen displayed a still frame of the Gringg landing bay. One by one, the landing party entered the frame. Castleton drew in a sharp breath as she realized the scale of the big chamber.

At its far end, the Gringg entered the room and began to interac with Ken Reeve.

Second Speaker's tail lashed in surprise as the largest Gringg spoke, its roar rattling the tympanum in the speaker unit. Greene allowed the tape to run for a short time, then sped it up so the action was telescoped into a few minutes. The Hrrubans watched in silence, then turned questioningly to Greene.

"Zo, we zee the firrst meeting of these creatures. Zey show intelligence and caution in zeir approach. No less did we," Hrrto said, as impatient as Mllaba. "What of it?"

"That it was only Ken Reeve's impression that they have never met sentient beings before. Just wait, sir," Greene said The commander froze the last frame of the three Gringg waving to the team as the shuttle lifted off, then blanked the screen.

"Now, this is a tape sent to Spacedep by an exploration team less than a month ago. It is coded classified, but Admiral Barnstable has given permission to allow you to see it. I feel it is vital to our understanding of the current situation."

Everyone drew shocked breaths when the new tape showed an uncompromising picture of a planetary landscape brutally torn and burned by conflict. Wrecked hulks of buildings of an unfamiliar architecture had been sliced in two with some potent destructive weapon. Battered shafts that did resemble known weaponry littered broad open spaces that must once have been graceful avenues. Castleton peered at the screen, looking desperately fo signs of living creatures. A series of scenes of stark, dead forests and the stumps of shattered cities flashed past without relief Nothing living interrupted the bleak landscape. Of the residents only a few skeletal remains could be found, and those were darkened and twisted: by radiation, the captain thought, somewhat familiar with the look of such deaths. Nothing moved except ashy debris swept around by the wind that howled eerily. The statistics overlaying the image showed readings of heavy radiation The changing symbols also showed that biological and chemical weapons, and an unknown energy weapon of great force had been deployed.

"This planet is in the Fingal system," Greene said, narrating "Spacedep interdicted it as soon as they received the exploration team's initial report. No life forms higher than deep-sea algae remain on a world that, to judge by the artifacts left behind had an advanced civilization. Estimates are that it would take over two thousand years for radiation levels to drop sufficiently to allow Humans to live there."

The image faded, to be replaced by that of an orbiting spaceship. Hrrto caught his breath as he realized it was identical to the one currently circling Rraladoona. It seemed subtly different, and as the exploration team's camera drew closer, he could see that this ship was derelict, its hull riddled with jagged rents caused by explosive charges and the neater, milled holes of laser bolts. The image, now recorded by a handheld unit, moved through darkened corridors, the white glare of its lights resting momentarily on the occasional floating corpse. Hrrto's tail twitched in surprise. There was no doubt about the identity of the dead. They were Gringg.

"It would seem that Ken Reeve's assumption was wrong. The Gringg have met other sentient species before," Greene said. His eyes met Castleton's. "And they destroyed them. The population of an entire planet, wiped out."

The captain felt a cold finger trace down her spine. She shuddered. Greene moved his gaze from Castleton to Barnstable.

"In the light of that"—he gestured toward the screen—"this hail-fellow-well-met attitude toward the Gringg has gotten a trifle out of control. Hasn't it, Admiral?"

The Admiral shifted in his seat. "Damned straight. It's turning into a regular circus animal act already."

"Perrhaps too much openessss was ssshown," Second agreed, edgily, "but zince it iss shown, what is to be done about ze steps Rrev hass already taken?" And he gestured toward Rraladoona.

Barnstable brought his big fist down emphatically on the tabletop. "Get in touch with him immediately and require him to show some restraint, that's what. Don't show so much damned much hayseed cordiality until we've got a tap on what they're really here for. This dumb show of theirs, so polite and open, could mask invasion procedures," and he waved his hand at the screen and the devastation it still portrayed. "They could be softening us up so that our defenses are down when their main fleet comes powering in."

"With all due respect, sir, the Gringg have done nothing—here—to arouse suspicions of their intent," Captain Castleton said with some restraint. Even a ship's captain practiced tact in dealing with an admiral. Greene's evidence was upsetting but incitement made her twice as cautious. "Their ship sent no probes. They waited until we made contact. To me that shows peaceful intent. Envoys have been exchanged—which I feel is a mark of amazing trust on their part, considering we're two species to their one. So far all those envoys have seen are the insides of a shuttle and the reception area of this ship. Right now, they're on an agriculturally based colony world, not one of our homeworlds which are not in the least bit endangered." She grinned to relieve the tension, for the Admiral was scowling even if he was listening to what she said. "Not that we know where the other's homeworld is," and she inclined her head in a courteous bow to Hrrto. "How can their mere presence on Doonarrala constitute a *serious* threat? Surely they are more vulnerable than we. Their vessel's not armed."

Greene cut in. "We don't know that they're completely without armament, sir. When you consider the devastation of the Fingal planet, they might have some new weapon we can't identify."

"Zat is true enough," Captain Hrrrv said thoughtfully. "All we know iss zat zey have no nuclear weapons or what we consider usssual orrrdnance."

Finding an ally, Greene continued forcefully. "Other weapons with less sophisticated delivery systems might be concealed aboard: powerful incendiaries composed of unknown substances and not easily detectable. I suspect whatever that ship used on Fingal Three could be easily hidden in that mass of water in the central globe of the ship. They are a new race. We don't know what they are capable of. All we do know is that they can destroy a planet. Since we have no direct verbal contact, I feel it is necessary to limit what they are allowed to see, and establish verbal communications as quickly as possible."

"They ought to be allowed the benefit of the doubt," Castleton said, appealing to Barnstable. "How long ago was the war in the Fingal system? Have the usual tests been done to discover how long that ship has been floating in space? How do we know that isn't a Gringg world and those were the defenders and not the aggressors?"

Greene shot her a dire look which she ignored. "The point is, Captain, that ship was armed, and Ordnance is still trying to puzzle out their weapons systems."

"Has Admiral Sumitral been briefed on the Fingal Three discovery?" Castleton asked.

"How could he be when the matter's been classified? He's Alreldep anyhow, not naval, for all his title," Barnstable said, then waved his hand to dismiss that consideration. "The fact remains that a ship of indisputable Gringg design was discovered in orbit around Fingal Three—call it circumstantial evidence, if you wish.

Grace—which has been absolutely wasted. That's enough to give me pause to consider very carefully how to proceed with the Gringg. I trust"—he looked around the table, nodding politely to Hrrto and Captain Hrrrv—"that you all realize that this meeting is not to be discussed at all? Good. You'll remain on Yellow Alert, Captain Castleton. Second Speaker, I'd appreciate your giving the same orders to your ships. Forewarned is forearmed!"

Castleton could not fault those orders as she sat staring at the frozen frame on the screen. Her initial impulse was to trust the Gringg, but intellectually she understood very well the need to remain on guard until both sides were satisfied of the other's peaceful intent. The Amalgamated Worlds had been at peace for centuries. The very thought of an interstellar war chilled her. She felt a warm touch at the back of her hand, and looked up to find Jon Greene watching her with his brows drawn upward, asking a silent question. His molded lips curved at the corner in a small smile of confidence. She nodded at him, returning the smile in spite of her worry. The expression in his eyes became warmer. Despite their obvious differences of opinion, she was inexplicably attracted to this man. But she was now on Alert status and there was no time for any private life.

"Of coursse, all waits upon being able to speak to each otherrr," Hrrto said.

"At least the most experienced man we've got is in charge of that," Grace Castleton said, finding relief in the fact.

"Sumitral?" Barnstable asked. "Has he arrived?"

"Not that we've been informed, Admiral," Grace said, "but I meant Reeve."

Barnstable gave a little grunt. "I heard that he learned Hrruban first." Then he remembered the presence of Hrrubans in the room, and smoothly went on. "Which was only logical at the time, of course."

"I hope he's the right man to do the initial work," Greene said, looking concerned. "Some people get so wound up in their own specialty that they fail to see the broader view."

"Rrev has proved his competence on several levels," Hrrto said, surprising himself as well as Mllaba. "He prrotects, as alwayss, Rraladoona." He dropped his jaw in a slight smile.

"Of course, Second Speaker," Greene said quickly, "but I found his manner of taking charge of the first contact a shade officious."

"He was asked to do so," Castleton reminded him. "After all, he expedited them to the planet, which protected the technology on the *Hamilton* from their scrutiny."

"Aye," Hrrrv agreed. "It waz wise to rrremove zem from zis vessel at once."

"Zo, Admirral," Second said, folding his arms across his chest. "We wait?"

"I'll instruct Sumitral," Barnstable said decisively, "to find out as soon as possible—using whatever methods, signs, sketches, are needed—what part of the galaxy they come from, and how they found their way here."

"Zat, surely, can wait, Admirrrral," Mllaba said smoothly. "Ze threat is here, now, not wherever ze Gringg home system iss."

"But the Gringg fleet?" Barnstable held on to his concern.

"No evidence zat zere is any. Nothing is detectable in ze near reaches of space," Captain Hrrrv said.

Castleton confirmed it. "I've checked with my telemetry officer. He agrees. They came in alone."

"Each one of them is an eight-hundred-pound warrior!" Barnstable barked. "They're a potential danger to Humanity!"

"And to Hrrubankind as well," Hrrto added.

"And from that tape," Greene added, "it doesn't look as if it takes more than a single ship to decimate a planet."

Mllaba was thoughtful. "Now what we really need is furzzer support for our position of caution. Ze Doonarralans will go on zeir merry way, never suspecting zat zey are set up frrr destruczhon until ze bomb falls on zeir heads. We require prrrsons of influence, who can prevail upon zem to move with greazzer care. What about zis Hayuman Landreau? Can we gain his support to suggest a more cautious approach to ze Rralan administration?"

Greene shook his head. "No, he's like a child with a new toy where the Gringg are concerned. In fact, he treats them rather like playmates. He's frivolous."

"Son, never call a Landreau frivolous," Barnstable warned him darkly. "His family has considerable influence on Earth and elsewhere. I'd prefer to have him with us than against us."

Second spoke up. "I shall endeavrrr to inform ze Hrruban High Council zat a wary approach is a wise one. Most of zem are conservative, and I do not zink zere will be protest. Perhaps more pressure can be brought to bear on ze Doonarralans from ze two home governments?"

"Direct intervention would be better," Barnstable said. "We need reinforcements, to have a physical presence. Trouble is we can't get them here quickly enough. It will take weeks for ships to arrive from Earth or any of the colonies where some of our potential allies reside. We must be ready for any eventuality!"

"In zis I can help," Second said, "at least with regard to transportation. I will auzorize use of ze grid for ze specific purrpose of supporrt in zis possible crisis. A wise Stripe moves cautiously zrough a strrange forest."

"Honored Speaker," Mllaba began, "it would be wiser still to be sure zat ze grid operazors on duty are ones known to us, and zrrussworzy. Zey must not disclose who auzorized zis movement wizout your specific prrrmission."

"Discretion widens a Stripe," Second replied, nodding acceptance.

"I'd feel a lot happier if we had some sort of military backup, just in case the Gringg slough off the charm and turn on the heat," Barnstable said.

"Sir," Castleton said, an odd expression on her face, "need I remind you that we have a full marine complement on board the *Hamilton*? Not to mention the fact that her crew have won every single martial arts competition the fleet has put on over the past five years?"

The Admiral grimaced and raised a conciliatory hand. "Now, Grace, medals for exhibition affairs are not quite the same thing as military experience. . . ."

"Who's had that in God knows how many years?" she asked, pursing her lips.

The Admiral's face reddened, a sharp contrast to his mane of white hair. "Grace, don't overstep yourself. I'm in charge of the safety of this sector, and dammit, I'll protect it any way I can. I allowed Reeve to take those aliens to the surface of a peaceful colony and I'll make damned certain peace is maintained there."

"Yes, sir," Grace Castleton said. "But may I still counsel moderation?"

"I've taken your counsel, and now hear mine. We're on yellow alert, and I mean alert! We're going to be ready for any thing—" Barnstable paused, closed his eyes briefly, suddenly remembering that there were Hrrubans right there with him, so he hastily altered what he'd been going to say. "What I mean is, those Gringgs are naturally armored, those fangs, their talons; their forearms have the reach of any among us. Why, that thick furry hide of theirs could probably turn away slugs."

Mllaba put in silkily, "Perhaps permeability of zeir skin and skin tension can be one of ze tests performed by your medical technician."

"Good suggestion. Maybe. In the meantime, Speaker Hrrto, I'll take advantage of your offer to use the Treaty Island grid. And, bear in mind, please, that if those Gringg make a move before we're ready for them, one of those grid operators must reach Earth alive to let them know what went on here."

Hrrto nodded. "I will remain on Rrala," he said, well aware that the Hayumans might have thought he'd chosen the easy way out by grid. The Gringg terrified him, but he was in acute terror of losing face by fleeing.

"As you wish," the Admiral said, rising. "I'll get in touch with a few people, transfer them up here for a little conference." He turned to Greene. "Put the connections through yourself, lad. I want a stop put to this chummy foolishness, stat!"

"Admiral," Castleton said, also rising, "shouldn't we inform the planetary administration of our discovery?"

"Indeed we should not, sir," Greene said suddenly. He was still smarting from Todd Reeve's off-hand treatment of him while on board the Gringg vessel, and his flamboyant disregard of safety in embracing the aliens. "I'd recommend against it. For security reasons alone. We certainly don't want the grids jammed with people insisting that their department has to have representatives here, too. The necessary departments have already been informed and are present. No more information should be broadcast." And when eventually the Amalgamated Worlds knew, Greene thought with satisfaction, Todd Reeve would be disgraced, even removed from planetary office as a danger to Humanity.

The passengers aboard the Spacedep shuttle were silent on the way down to the surface of Doonarrala. Admiral Barnstable sat making notes on his clipboard, pausing occasionally to call up data from its small memory bank. Second Speaker, unaccustomed to travelling in Hayuman spaceships, stared over the shoulder of the pilot, reading the control panel as if reluctant to trust the Hayuman female's expertise.

Mllaba glanced occasionally at the Hayuman who was her opposite number. Greene was attempting to meet her eyes. She wondered what he wanted. It was unusual for a Hayuman to remain silent; normally they chattered away, regardless of the gravity of a situation. Perhaps this male was different.

• • •

It was the middle of the night on the Treaty Island Center. The cleaning staff, busy with brooms and a floor polisher, paid no attention to the mixed group on its way to the grid. Mllaba took her place behind the controls.

"Ze Firrrst Village grid," Hrrto said to Mllaba, as he walked between the upright pillars and assumed a dignified pose. The female's claws clattered swiftly on the keyboard. Second Speaker vanished slowly in the rising mists. Barnstable looked uncomfortable and wary as he strode up onto the dais and squared his shoulders.

"Bring me back in four hours," the Admiral directed. Mllaba inclined her head.

"I, too, must return to my homeworld to report to the Council," Mllaba said to Greene, when thc Admiral had been dispatched. "May I assist you to travel somewhere first?"

The Hayuman seemed in no hurry. "No, thank you. I've waited because I wanted to talk to you alone," Greene said, his warm brown eyes meeting her yellow-green ones directly. She could feel the power of his personality being brought to bear upon her. "You have no reason to trust me, and I don't trust you," he continued disarmingly, "but we could help one another to our mutual benefit."

"How?" Mllaba asked politely.

Greene turned and gestured to a bench facing the grid station. Mllaba shook her head, so Greene sat down alone. He drew up one knee and wrapped both hands around it nonchalantly. The arrogance of the pose put Mllaba on guard. She slipped her hands protectively into her robe sleeves and stood stiffly before him, waiting.

"I know that election for the Speakership is imminent," Greene said, gazing up at her. "If Speaker Hrrto were to gain that honor, a new Speaker for External Affairs would be appointed."

If Mllaba was surprised to learn that a Spacedep officer was conversant with the intricacies of Hrruban government, she did not show it outwardly. Inside, she felt a prickle of excitement. Greene spoke to the carefully tended ember of ambition she bore within her. She concentrated on keeping her tail tip from flicking back and forth.

"And should I display more zan usual competence in zis most difficult and dangerous affair," Mllaba said, "I should be ze favored candidate. Is zat your idea?"

Greene nodded, grinning. "I, too, am trying to stay on what we call a 'fast track.' I'm a risk-taker. I was sent to these talks partly to get me away from Spacedep HQ, and out of the line of promotion. So far, the Admiral is getting all the glory here, but I'd like a little of it to drop on me. If we work together to save Doonarrala, as well as Earth and Hrruba, from the Gringg menace, both you and I would gain favor in the eyes of our superiors. Wouldn't you agree?"

"And you in the eyes of ze attractive Hayuman captain?" Mllaba asked, and complimented herself on making a telling stroke. The naked skin of the Hayuman's face flushed red. Had he thought the signals going back and forth between him and Castleton were invisible to the others in the room?

"I'll tell you why Admiral Barnstable has really gone back to Earth," Greene said, changing the subject. "He is ordering the Human defense fleet to Doonarrala. Only he has the authority to do so. From its current position, it'll take thirty days for the fleet to get here. Then, if the situation warrants, the Admiral could declare martial law."

Mllaba nodded. "Hrruba should prepare a similar defense fleet," she said. *Second Speaker is not acting as decisively in this matter as he should be*, she thought. Hrruba ought to have been the first to take such steps, not Earth. He should have issued such an order. She resolved to bring it up to the Council in his name. "And so you and I will cooperrrate and share knowledge?" she asked. "Only because zis is a crrrisis, and zat is what is best for our own species, you understand."

"Of course," Greene agreed gravely. He stood up and put out his right hand to her, thumb upward. Mllaba stared at it for a moment before offering her own in the same position. He clasped her hand strongly, then released it. Hayuman customs were so strange! She tucked her hands primly back into her sleeves, and Greene stepped away. He respected her; that was good. She intended to maintain the upper hand in this relationship. He needed her cooperation far more than she needed his.

Mllaba set the grid controls for a thirty-second delay, and stepped onto the dais between the pillars. "I will return in four hours," she said. As the mists rose around her, she watched the Hayuman turn and stride away toward the landing pad.

The procession into the Human First Village had taken on the aspect of a parade. Hordes of children, led by Kelly's and

Nrrna's youngsters, danced around and around the cluster of adults walking with the Gringg. When they reached the doors of the Doonarralan Medical Center, Dr. Kate herded the Gringg, Ken, Lauder, Frill, Sumitral, and Hrrestan inside. Almost as an afterthought, she pointed at Jilamey Landreau.

"You, mind the children! I need Nrrna and Kelly as lab assistants. Okay with you?"

"Anything to help," Jilamey agreed cheerfully, and was promptly dragged away by Alec and Alison, demanding to hear all about the Gringg ship.

To the adults outside, Kate said, "Go on with you. We'll give you the news when we have any." She smiled, scattering them with a wave of her hands as if they were chickens. When the door had closed, she turned around and let out a deep sigh. "Well! Welcome to you folks," she said, inclining her head to the Gringg. "And welcome to you," she said to the naval officers. "Who's my lab partner today?"

Lauder raised a timid hand. "I am, ma'am. Ensign Mauro Lauder."

"Just Kate, all right?" She smiled at the young officer. "I'll call you Mauro. Everyone this way, please?" She led them to her office and pointed toward the waiting room. "The rest of you stay here. I'm going to take this bruiser first." She laid a hand on Ghotyakh's furry arm. "Be good and you get a lollipop."

The door to the examining room shut behind them. Ken looked around at the wooden-walled waiting area, remembering how many times he'd sat here with a sick child or a farm-related injury his wife, Pat, hadn't been able to mend.

"Now, Reeve," Sumitral said, beaming, "tell me all about the confrontation."

Ken recounted their adventure without benefit of the tapes he and the others had made, but he didn't think he left out any important details or observations. Sumitral, who believed that the mark of a good diplomat was to be a good listener, nodded occasionally as Ken talked, only interrupting once in a while to clarify a point.

"Very interesting," Sumitral said. "Very, very interesting. I want to see those tapes as soon as we're through here. Thanks to Hrruban technology, I got here a lot faster this time."

"I think we need you more this time than we ever did with the Hrrubans," Ken said.

Sumitral's eyes twinkled. "I'm good for show and to wrap things up nicely."

"Much more than that, sir," Ken said, protesting such modesty.

"I don't have your fine honesty and instinct, Ken, which incidentally I respect immensely. Anyway, you've more experience in first contact than anyone else here. And, with creatures as large as the Gringg, I'd really feel easier when we establish a communication medium! I don't want misunderstandings of any kind with folks that big." He grinned.

But the Gringg were not without ways of making themselves understood.

"Genhh?" Eonneh asked, then paused, as if puzzled how to make his question clear.

Ken sat up straighter. "Go ahead, Honey. What?"

"Rrss. Rroobvnnn?"

"Sure is," Ken said. "Er, yes." Eonneh cupped his forepaws together, the way he had while holding the Hrruban cub, then drew them to his breast.

"Nrrna. Rroobvnnn?"

"Yep. I mean, reh," Ken replied.

"This is fascinating," Sumitral said, studying Eonneh closely. "What's he trying to ask?"

"I don't know yet," Ken said. "Vocabulary's very limited."

"Rroobvnnn, Rrss? Genhh, Ayoomnnn?"

"Reh," said Ken.

"Gelli, Rroobvnnn?"

"Ah . . . ah . . . morra. No. Ayoomnnn."

"Morra," said Eonneh, disbelievingly. He made the sign for baby again. "Gelli. Morra Ayoomnnn?"

"Reh, Ayoomnnn, Kelly," Ken said. "She's my daughter-in-law."

"Nrrna morra Rroobvnnn."

"Reh, Rroobvnnn." Ken nodded firmly.

"What's the problem?" demanded Sumitral, exasperated to be on the fringe of understanding.

"I'm not positive, but I'm beginning to get the drift," Ken said with a wry smile.

They went through the pantomime several times, with Hrrestan and Frill attempting to guess what explanation Eonneh was trying to elicit. Eonneh took hold of his own tail and held up the end.

"Rroobvnnn, shrra. Nrrna, shrra. Nrrna," and he made the baby sign again. "Morra?"

Ken fell back in his chair and burst into loud hoots of laughter. "Oh, I get you now! Oh, no!" He clutched his sides and beat his feet on the floor.

The noise brought Kate Moody running out into the waiting room. "What's the matter?" she demanded. Lauder, Nrrna, and Kelly were right behind her.

"It's hilarious," Ken gasped, coming up for air. "They think 'Hrruban' is the word for male, and 'Hayuman' is the word for female. Or maybe the other way around." When the others looked puzzled, he sprang the other half of the joke. "They think we're one species!"

"How could they think that?" Lauder asked, appalled as well as slightly indignant.

"Why shouldn't they? We arrive together on their ship, so we are together. They see us living together here on the surface. Why shouldn't they think we're the same species? They thought the Hrrubans were males and Hayumans females. The sight of Nrrna with a baby who's obviously hers knocked their assumption into a tailspin!"

Sumitral grinned at Ken's inadvertent witticism, his gray eyes alight. "So we are a species more than usually dimorphic?"

"They thought I was a girl?" Lauder demanded huffily. "I don't think that's funny."

"Well, I wouldn't take it to heart, lad. You'd be a good-looking girl—if you were one, which you're not," Kate suggested mildly. "But, under the circumstances, I think the Gringg copped on to the error of their assumption pretty quick."

Noticing how politely Eonneh and Ghotyakh waited for some explanation of his unusual behavior, Ken shook his head. "I haven't got the words to explain laughter yet. Much less how to explain that we're two species, male and female each, from two different worlds."

"Watch it, Reeve," Frill said. "That's strategic information."

"It might be if either of us knew exactly where the other's homeworld is," Ken said in mild disgust. "Lighten up, Frill. A basic explanation won't give away any more than our kids get in primary school."

"We can't base a solid future relationship on deceptions," Sumitral said more mildly. "Can you help us with the gender explanation, Dr. Moody?"

Kate grinned. "Sure can. Take the bull by the horns, so to speak. While Lauder and I are taking samples, we'll show them tapes on Hayuman and Hrruban reproduction and birth. They'll get the idea."

Kate ran the tapes used for sex education in the Middle School, all the while taking blood, skin, and hair samples from her unprotesting subjects. Honey and Kodiak watched the tapes with every indication of understanding what they were seeing. They muttered—"A little like embarrassed twelve year olds," Kate said later—and growled furiously between themselves.

"I'm running a CAT scan on each of them. They seemed very interested in everything, the equipment and procedures. They're both very intelligent. By the way," Kate said with a grin, "they're male. What we'd classify as male. Both of them."

"How do you know?"

"I got them to give me urine samples. There's no way that a baby could be born through that orifice, and there's nothing else appropriate. I did a very careful physical examination. No womb, but very substantial generative organs. We went through some pantomime to confirm it. But that big captain on the tape, the one you keep calling Grizz, and referring to as he? She's female! All of her, and that squat one's her second-born cub. Honey's the sire."

"So they are dimorphic with regard to size, but the other way round to our two species," Ken said, nodding.

"Right. There's precedent for this configuration, living on Earth at this minute. The males are tercels, an old word meaning a third smaller, Terran birds of prey. The large birds, falcons, are the females."

"Well, I'm glad we got that figured without making a serious gaffe. It doesn't matter what gender one is, so long as we don't mistake one for t'other," Ken said.

Eonneh, emerging from his turn in the ring-shaped scanner, sought out Genhh and Frrrill and the new Ayoomnnn. They were sitting in the wooden room, speaking softly to each other. He sat down beside them.

"I am terribly sorry for mistaking your gender," Eonneh said in his own language, pantomiming disgrace, which involved drawing an invisible line from his bowed forehead to the floor. "You are larger than others of your species, so we thought you were female. We didn't realize you were males of two different species of alien."

"What's he saying?" Frill asked, mystified.

"I think he's trying to apologize," Ken said. "It's okay, you know," he said, putting a hand on the Gringg's upper limb. The fur was smooth but thick, like horsehair. "It's no insult to be thought female, or male, for that matter. I know you're trying to learn all about us, but who said you had to get it all right first crack?"

"Nereh?" Eonneh understood his forgiveness, but missed the colloquialism.

Sumitral sighed. "We have got to make some sort of device so we can start understanding one another."

"We've got one problem," Kate said, leaning out the door. "I can't get this lad into the X-ray. He's too big! It's only made for Hayumans and Hrrubans. We're going to have to take him over to Ben Adjei's unit at the Animal Hospital for a peep at his insides."

While Kate Moody continued physical examinations, Lauder made use of an unused biochemistry lab to start work on the Gringg tissue samples and foodstuffs. Nrrna, who worked in the bio-lab, prepared samples for the centrifuge and electron microscope.

"I'm a duffer at chemistry," Kelly informed them. "My training is in diplomacy. I'll wash glass, or whatever you need me to do."

"One thing I'll need," Lauder said, very tentatively, "and I'm not sure I should ask you, is a volunteer to taste the foodstuffs if they test out as safe."

"Ouch," said Kelly, wrinkling her nose. Nrrna looked alarmed. "Well, if you promise me I won't die of it, I'll try anything."

"Oh, you won't be the only guinea pig at the table," Lauder said with a shrug. "We need to try at least one of the Gringg on Doonan food. Once we've got results on the tissue, I'll know what we can offer them and what we shouldn't."

"That's good," Kelly said cheerfully. "I do hate to eat alone."

"Them?" Kate replied, when asked about the Gringg's gastrointestinal system. "They can handle anything that isn't moving too fast. I did a whole-body sonogram on Ghotyakh as long as I had him over at the vet clinic. He watched everything I did, and I got the impression he doesn't like to go to doctors of his own species! That digestive pouch you detected below the stomach is one tough little organ. I wouldn't try them on concrete, but there's not much shy of that they can't eat. My husband, Ezra, went home to get some supplies. We may as well all dine together."

• • •

In the Federation Center, Jon Greene waited before the transport grid. Only moments before the four-hour time limit, the mists arose on the grid platform and the form of Mllaba took on shape and substance. Greene stepped forward to greet her.

"Did you meet with success?" he asked. The glare of her yellow-green eyes warned him not to get too close. He stopped short and gestured a fine bow as she left the dais.

"I have accomplished ze firrst of my goals," Mllaba said, settling her black robes back on her narrow shoulders. "Others from Hrruba will be following me very shortly to aid in slowing down ze Gringg agenda. As frrr ze second, it awaits ze Speaker's own presence to be set in motion. But I have laid ze groundwork well," she added with a degree of smugness. The two of them discussed plans for a few moments, then Greene glanced at his wrist chronometer.

"Now," he said.

The Hrruban put her clawed fingers on the controls. The air over the grid thickened, gradually revealing a crowd of Hayumans exclaiming to one another at the novelty of transporting by grid. Barnstable was at their head. Greene recognized two of the men and one of the women as members of the Humanity First! movement. Another was a prominent journalist with a talent for rabble-rousing. Three others were minor politicians and animal-rights activists. Greene grinned. The Admiral hadn't missed a trick.

As soon as he was aware of where he was, Barnstable looked around. "No unauthorized personnel present. Good. My thanks, Mllaba, for our safe transport. Greene, I'll want a report from you in an hour's time."

"Aye, sir," Greene said, saluting.

"Your allies from ze Hrruban homeworld await you at the meeting point, Admirrrral" Mllaba said. "Ze Speaker is with them."

"Good. To the First Villages, then," Barnstable said, nodding at the Hrruban female. Mllaba's claws clattered quickly over the controls. She had just enough time to join the party on the platform before it vanished.

Unnoticed by the others, three men in mufti slipped off the rear of the platform and waited until the mists cleared.

"Bouros, Gallup, Walters," Greene barked. The three men stiffened to attention. "Follow me." The commander led them out of the building into the night.

• • •

"Quit staring at me," Kelly complained, turning aggrieved hazel eyes on Ensign Lauder. "If I feel my insides curling up, I'll tell you."

"Sorry, ma'am. I'm just curious as to what's going on with you." The young medic blushed and went back to his plate.

Kelly grinned. "I'm just fine. In fact, some of this is pretty good." She turned to her dinner partner, Ghotyakh, and pointed at a sausage-shaped mass. "What do you call that?"

"Raghia," Kodiak said. "Neehar, ar . . ." He made his four fingers into the legs of some animal and walked them in a lumbering gait across the table.

"Meat of some ruminant?" Ken decided. "We'll have to get him to draw us a picture later. These fellows have fantastic skill."

Sumitral took another helping of stew. "It's clear that it is an important part of his job, even class station, to be able to write and draw well. I'd say that they're at the top of their grade, by the way, though I observe that Ghotyakh defers to Eonneh."

"I think if they're organized like us, Eonneh must be Grizz's special aide as well as mate," Ken agreed.

Eonneh nodded, showing his teeth, having caught the gist of Ken's statement. He and Ghotyakh were making significant inroads on the pot of stew. When Kate's daughter Rachel had arrived with dinner, the Gringg's agile noses went into full twitch. They waited, looking wistful, while Kate did a quick test to make sure there was nothing in the meal that would disagree with them, and howled with joy when she led them to the table to be served.

"By the way, Lauder," Kate said, "you were wrong about one of them eating as little as one of us. That was Kodiak's sixth bowlful."

Lauder grinned lopsidedly. "I could eat the same, myself. This is delicious. You don't get meals this good shipside."

"My very thought," Sumitral said placidly.

"Go on with you," Kate said. "It's all last year's dried snake meat."

"No, it's terrific," Lauder insisted.

"Do not let Dr. Kate ovrrwhelm you with hrrr modesty," Hrrestan said, his jaw dropped in a genial grin. "Hrrr cooking has been praised widely by all, including my mate, Mrrva."

"Well, that one's a winner," Kelly said, marking the packet of raghia with a plus sign. "Alison would like it: tasty with a flavor rather like urfa." With businesslike fingers, she pushed it to one side and opened another packet. She was taking only small portions from each of the Gringg rations, to leave room for as many samples as possible. The next was a chopped vegetable in a messy red sauce. She spooned a little of it onto her tasting plate and took a mouthful. Her face wrinkled up, and she choked.

"What's the mazzer?" Nrrna demanded.

Hrrestan rose to his feet in alarm. "Shall I get the szomach pump?"

Lauder was out of his chair and beside Kelly in a moment. She waved them away. Her face had turned red.

"Salty," she gasped, gesturing at the water pitcher. Kate handed her full glass over and then he filled Kelly's.

"So that's what they use to keep up their electrolyte balance," Kate said briskly. "You might like to know, Ensign, that unlike Earth animals, they have sweat glands here and there under that great pelt. Suggests to me that they evolved from an animal with less body hair. And they have a tremendous lung capacity, more than four times ours, plus a layer of fat beneath the skin that ranges from three to five centimeters. Now what does that suggest to you?"

"Nozzing," said Hrrestan, shaking his head.

"They're swimmers," Ken guessed, playing with a piece of bread.

"That'd be my summation," Kate said with satisfaction. "Seems to me as if they must have evolved from something more like otters than bears. It would certainly explain the tail."

"Hmm," said Kelly, taking another packet. This one contained dried brown kernels shaped rather like Brussels sprouts, and coated with a fine tan powder. She crunched one tentatively between her teeth, and smiled with pleasure. "Um, these are great. Gringg candy," she said, offering some to Ken, who reached out to take it.

"Ah-ah-ah!" Kate scolded, putting a hand between them. "No one else gets to try anything until you, my dear, have gone twenty-four hours without a reaction."

Kelly gulped. "I guess I didn't realize what a serious job this was going to be."

"I'm sorry," Kate said kindly. "I'm sure everything'll be all right, but if you're going to run a proper experiment, control is essential."

"Oh, well." Kelly sighed, and opened another packet. "And what do you call this?" she inquired of the Gringg.

Commander Frill entered, his nose twitching almost as much as one of the Gringg's.

"Something smells wonderful," he said. He was holding an armful of tapes and a couple of small pieces of equipment.

"Sit down and have some," Kate invited him. "There's stew, tenderfoot chili, creamed potatoes, mixed veg, and plenty left if you can beat the Gringg to it. Your friend Lauder here was just saying that this compares favorably to ship food."

"Thank you, ma'am," Frill said with alacrity, sitting down next to Ken. He helped himself generously from the stewpot and tore a huge section from the loaf beside it. "I don't know when I last had a home-cooked meal." Between bites and exclamations of pleasure, Frill explained what he had found.

"One of the engineers at the computer control in town let me use the equipment," he said, "to listen to these tapes. I think I've found the problem," he went on, setting down the equipment: a hand-recorder, a speaker, and a paired unit with glass-fronted screens. Across the upper screen was a flat green line. The lower showed stepped levels in green light. He started the recorder, and they heard Grizz repeating words after Ken. "Here, watch the screens carefully. Now, this is Gringg conversation." On the oscilloscope, the green line etched peaks above and below the center line as the sound level rose and fell. The frequency monitor below showed peaks and valleys, too, but more peaks than valleys when Ken's voice was heard, with just the opposite whenever the Gringg spoke.

"Interesting," Ken said, peering at the numbers beside the levels on the frequency monitor. "That would explain why I couldn't approximate some of their pronunciations. Their voices dip down into subsonics."

"How low do they go?"

Frill checked his printout. "Thirteen to fifteen cycles, sir."

"We Hrrubans would merely feel zose lowest tones," Hrrestan commented.

"Ah," Sumitral said. "So the words go below the range of Hayuman and even Hrruban hearing."

"It would also explain why we felt nervous, sir," Frill explained. "Some of these low tones provoke fear responses."

Sumitral nodded. "That guides us toward what we'll need to make coherent contact with the Gringg."

"If I can ask a favor, Admiral?" Kate Moody said, standing up to dish out more food.

"I'll grant it if I can," Sumitral replied, watching her heap potatoes onto his plate.

Kate strove to keep her voice light. "Don't forget the little people who helped make this meeting possible, will you? The citizens of Doonarrala are wildly interested in helping to learn whatever they can about the Gringg, and want a chance to help. They're not afraid of challenges or they wouldn't be here. Don't shut them out."

"Madam, I don't discount the input from those who have helped so far, especially the children, to whom the Gringg seem very attached," Sumitral acknowledged. "And I'd be a fool to push aside volunteer staff who are so eager to be included, so long as they acknowledge that I'm in charge of this mission."

"Oh, I don't think they'll mind that," Kate said. "It's being left out that they'd hate."

"This is Doonarrala," Kelly said, indicating herself and Nrrna. "We take pride in getting to know others on equal terms. That's what our husbands are doing right now on the Gringg ship, and on behalf of Alien Relations, over the twitching frame of Admiral Barnstable, I might add."

"Cooperation made Doonarrala what it is today. I'm all for extending the principle," Sumitral said, smiling up at her.

"Good, because cooperation is going to start with someone else cleaning up after this meal," Kate said with a broad grin. "Rachel, organize a few volunteers from those outside, will you? Then we can get on with the tests."

"I must go," Nrrna said. "It is nearly time for Hrrunna's meal. I must find Jilamey and ze children."

Sumitral rose and helped her out of her chair. "You take good care of that small ambassador," he told her.

"Zank you, I shall," she said, beaming shyly at the ambassador from Alreldep.

"Make sure the Cats get to bed on time," Kelly called. "Jilamey will let them stay up till all hours, and they are not to stay out of school on Uncle's say-so."

Hrrestan yawned, slurring his words out of pure exhaustion. "I frrr one am wearry. I am adjuzzed to Zreaty Island time, and we started earrly wiz ze confrrnce zis morning."

Unexpectedly, Nrrna was in the doorway again. She gestured behind her.

"Zese people wrrr waiting outside ze drrr." She did not have a chance to move aside, for she was pushed in by the crowd of Hayumans and Hrrubans who forced their way into the room. To Ken, their uniformly stony expressions gave them the aspect of a mob, not yet touched off, but potentially dangerous.

At their head were Barnstable and Second Speaker. Sumitral, standing beside the table, crossed his arms and waited calmly, while the mob organized itself around the perimeter of the big room, keeping wary eyes on the Gringg but patently determined to be in earshot. Hrrestan rose and stood beside the Alreldep ambassador.

"Well, Ev, how are you?" Sumitral asked.

Barnstable ignored the courtesy. "These people wanted to have a word with the colony leaders about this situation."

"And precisely which sizuazhon is zat?" Hrrestan asked, his tone relaxed but his eyes moving warily over the faces.

"The interruption of our spaceport conference by these . . . things," protested Lorena Kaldon, jerking her hand at the Gringg. "I came here to talk construction, mortgages, and interest rates, not alien invasions. My time is valuable, as is that of my colleagues here."

"We must do what we came to do!" added a Hrruban whom Hrrestan remembered as being a crony of the now-retired Third Speaker, a notorious reactionary. "Send zem back where zey came from. I oppose negotiations wiz zese aliens."

"They're called the Gringg," Sumitral said, a pleasant smile on his face. Eonneh and Ghotyakh, recognizing that word, rose to their feet and turned to face the newcomers. Both Kaldon and the Hrruban, suddenly obliged to crane their necks up, stepped as far back as they could.

Swallowing, Kaldon continued, but her voice was considerably less contentious. "We came so far, planned so long for this conference. It has to continue. You must understand our positions."

"No one planned to have zuch an interruption, Delegate Kaldon, but ze conference cannot resume at this time," Hrrestan said, "and, as co-leader of Doonarrala, I muss ask your indulgence in zis matter. Surely you should recognize zat zeir appearrrnce has altered everything. For ze time being, all discuzhons about ze spaceport must be deferrrred while we learn more about ze new arrivals."

"But we've been working for months to make our bids on the construction of a spaceport," she protested indignantly. "We can't just call a halt and continue as before simply because of . . . hairy monsters. They aren't interfering with the spaceport project. Why can't we go ahead with it?"

"Now, my dear Ms. Kaldon," Sumitral said, stepping forward, "that wouldn't be wise. And indeed, the hold may be for a very short time. But look at the arrival of the Gringg from a different angle: you are witnessing an incident of immense international significance. It isn't given to many to be the first to see, and meet, an entirely new species of star traveller. And I put this to you, as well: once we have established communications, why we may even have to construct a larger spaceport. For, frankly, I suspect that their main objective in seeking other civilized or inhabited planets is to initiate trade." He pointedly ignored a growl of protest from Barnstable's direction. "Were I you, I would believe myself lucky to be in on the ground floor for those you represent. I'm sure they'll be delighted to learn of the possibility of even more customers at the space facility."

Kaldon regarded Sumitral with no little amazement, and obviously considered his advice.

"Admirral," Second Speaker said, stepping forward, "are you not prezuming too much? How can you speak of trade when zeir objectives are not known. Nor can zey be until we can speak to zem! And even zen, such matters must be carefully prrsented to our respective goverrrments for sober, mature reflection . . . not decided out of hand herre on Rraladoona."

"I speak as Alreldep's representative, who is always ready and willing to speak to inhabitants of our galaxy no matter what form they appear in or from what quarter of the Milky Way," Sumitral replied with great dignity and a gentle smile for the Second Speaker's querulous attitude.

"Msss Kaldon, zere is also ze unassailable fact," Hrrestan added, "that my co-leader, Rrev, has had to absent himself from our prrroceedings, so zey could not, in any case, continue without him."

Barnstable now beckoned imperiously to Hrrestan, Sumitral, and Ken Reeve to move to one side, away from Kaldon's group.

"See here, now, my friends," he said, scowling deeply and glaring from one face to another, "I can't approve of all this good-folks-at-home routine. These Gringg are an unknown quantity . . . and don't give me that they-came-in-friendship-unarmed guff, Reeve. How can you be absolutely positive these creatures are so pacific?"

"Suffer little children, Barnstable," Ken replied, more amused han irritated by the Admiral's attitude. "But then you didn't see, s everyone here did, how the Gringg."

Barnstable cut him off abruptly. "It's just not good tactics to e open with an unknown quantity."

"Do I have to remind you that it worked before, Admiral? idn't it, Hrrestan!" And now Ken included his oldest Hrruban riend.

The Hrruban co-leader, whose tail had begun to lash in short ard twitches, relaxed and dropped his lower jaw slowly.

"We were not quite as formidable in appearance as these. Is at what alarmss you, Amirral?"

"What alarms me is a basic disregard for caution. I don't want hese good folk unnecessarily alarmed."

"They 'don't' look so alarmed," laughed Kate Moody, joining hem. "And how'd they all get in here? Place is crowded with trangers."

"She's right about that," Ken murmured to Hrrestan, who also egan looking at the curious faces of those backed against the all.

"Now, that is not the issue," said Barnstable darkly, not likng Kate's interruption at all. "You really are most unwise to llow such broad contact between the Gringg and the rest of the oonarralan population. As the official head of the organization harged with the protection of this sector, I want all data kept ecure and the Gringg out of public contact until we know more bout them. We have nothing but their physical presence to go n as yet, and that bothers me."

"Oh, but we got plenty of physical *data* on them," Kate said ovially. "I've got enough test results to satisfy anyone—" She ave Barnstable a jaundiced glare. "And even more reassuring mpirical stuff. Gringg like snake stew. And beans give them as."

There were a few chuckles from the back of the crowd. arnstable turned around to glare at the group. "And what bout the safety of these aliens? They could come to harm in his environment," he protested, trying another angle.

"They're pretty sturdy," Kate replied. "Not much could hurt hem. I haven't found a single allergen or toxin that their tissues eact to, not even rroamal. They've got functioning immune sysems, ticking away beautifully right now, and they don't react to nything we do. I also can't find anything in their systems that

bugs us, except for the odd irritant, and that can be inoculate
against. They're strong, the air is good for them, and our gravit
is at least twenty percent less than they're used to fighting. They'
be almost super strong here."

That appeared to upset Barnstable further. "In that case, you ar
exposing an entire population to danger from accidents incurre
during casual contact. I can't allow it. Remove them at once."

"You do not have jurisdiction here," Hrrestan said, his eye
flashing.

Sumitral was calm, almost apologetic. "This is an Alrelde
matter, Ev, and you know that."

Barnstable could not refute it, but he hated to relinquish com
mand to another authority.

"You will keep me in the loop, of course," he said, not withou
a measure of sarcasm.

"But, of course, Ev."

"Dad?" Robin Reeve poked his nose around the door an
peered into the room. "Ah, there you are, Dad!" Reeve's so
seemed to have an energy level befitting a man younger than hi
early twenties, and the poise of one much older. "Have I inter
rupted anything critical? Mom sent me to ask you when you'r
coming home and if you're bringing guests. Them?" he asked
Robin's eyes gleamed in keen anticipation of such a happening
"They're just as big as advertised. I was out on the range whe
they arrived."

"You zee?" Mllaba hissed. "It has alrready ze aspect of
vreakshow!"

"Not at all," Robin said cheerfully. "We always turn out fo
visitors. Whew! Wouldn't they be something on Snake Hunt? Ca
they hang around that long? Hunt's only six weeks away!"

Barnstable frowned. "They must certainly be off-planet whe
the Hunt takes place."

"Why?" Robin regarded Barnstable equably "Everyone els
wants to join in! At least these Gringg wouldn't need to b
protected! For that matter, maybe we ought to protect our snake
from them! Let's ask Todd and Hrriss to invite them officially.

"What I should like to know—" said a new voice, belongin
to a woman who stepped out of the crowd that had been politel
but avidly, listening to what they could hear of the discussion
She had a pinched mouth set in a plump pink face and wor
rather dowdy clothing, neither travel nor leisure wear. "—is ho
you dare continue to hunt those poor snakes? Much less sho

such brutality to . . . to individuals who could only misconstrue the barbarism you exhibit."

"Barbarism?" Robin exclaimed as other Doonarralans started to protest. "Hell, lady, you've never seen what those snakes do to *our* domestic animals. A blow from a Big Momma Snake's tail can break the back of a cow or horse . . . then the snake eats the poor critter whole and sits there digesting it for weeks. Who's being brutal?"

The woman had turned quite pale, but she wasn't one to give up easily. "Then it is imperative that you not expose outsiders to such dangers. Why, I believe that some of the larger snakes grow as long as twenty meters." She regarded the Gringg, who were not twenty meters in any dimension.

"Those big ones are usually too canny to cause trouble," Ken said, striving to remain polite. "Have we met, ma'am? I haven't seen you at any of the Village Socials, and I make it a point to get acquainted with all our visitors from Earth."

"I . . . I've just arrived," the woman said, clearly flustered.

Barnstable felt that it was a good time to retreat. "We intend to remain on hand throughout your investigation, of course."

"Of course," Sumitral agreed, and Hrrestan nodded.

As soon as Barnstable and his cronies withdrew, Ken made for the communications console at the side of the room. In a few moments, he returned to the group.

"I've just spoken to Martinson at the Space Center and to Hammer at Treaty Island. No one fitting her description has arrived on the last couple of ships from Earth."

"Then how'd she get here?" Kelly demanded.

"The grid?" Ken said, a light dawning. "I think I'm beginning to smell a conspiracy."

"I zink you arrre right, my old frrrnd," Hrrestan said. "Both Spacedep and Second Speaker. I do so dislike inzerference from outside."

"And you can put it down to Spacedep's distrust of the Gringg," Ken said, aggrieved. "Present company excepted," he said to Frill, who gave a sheepish shrug.

"Second Speaker has also shown discomfort wherrrre our new friends are concerned," Hrrestan said thoughtfully. "It would be well to be preparrred against such azzacks in days to come."

"The best defense is progress," Sumitral said. "We're having a fine time chatting with these fellows,"—he smiled at the Gringg, who had remained silent throughout the confrontation—

"but it's too slow. We require some kind of device to speed our understanding of one another. I'd also like to know how they found us."

"I can ask the communications center to help me get to work on a . . . a voder," Frill volunteered. He turned to Hrrestan. "That is, sir, if you'll give me the necessary authority?"

Hrrestan was openly pleased that a Spacedep officer deferred to the local authorities without argument. Ken was glad, because he was getting to like the burly commander.

"Grrranted, gladly," the Hrruban replied. "In ze meantime, it seems we must continue with drrawing of pictures to obtain informazhon."

"How will you describe light-years in pictographs?" Sumitral asked blandly as he settled down with an artist's block between Ghotyakh and Eonneh at Kate's laboratory table.

CHAPTER 6

TODD HAD FELT A PANG WATCHING HIS FATHER AND the others enter the shuttle. He hoped that Barnstable wouldn't try to hold the Gringg on board the navy vessel. He wanted them safely on the surface of Doonarrala, where folk were sympathetic to aliens. He particularly wanted the Gringg out of the vicinity of Greene and Barnstable. But his father would take charge. After all, the matter was clearly an Alreldep problem.

But would his father wait for Admiral Sumitral to back him up? Of course he would! Todd derided his lack of faith in his father's common good sense. He also wished he could be in two places at once—to see the reactions of Doonarralans to the Gringg.

Best of all, he and Hrriss were in this venture together and he wished they could just forget—forever—all that nonsense about the spaceport on the Hrrunatan. But he couldn't, could he? Well, he could for the duration of the task at hand.

Then Grizz touched his arm and indicated that Todd and Hrriss should follow him into the long, high-ceilinged, semi-oval corridor from the landing bay toward the central core of the ship. Immediately, Todd applied himself to the task at hand—perception and observation, absorbing what he saw and felt as if all his pores had eyes and ears and noses. So, the bay itself was situated in one of those "knots in the tree-bole" he had observed from space. The walls were smooth, a silver metal—steel?—equipped with rows of hand- and toe-holds at two points in the parabolic arc of the ceiling, no doubt to cope in zero-grav.

"For no grrrav?" Hrriss asked, pointing.

"They'd have to turn off the artificial gravity from time to time," Todd said. "If they turned gravity off, we'd be in a right difficult case trying to get our feet from one of those holds to another. Look at the size of 'em and the distance between!"

"I am glad zese are peaceable creazures," Hrriss said fervently.

They stopped in a corridor that was split around a central pillar in which were set more gray glass doors. Grizz hulked between them and the pillar, indicating that they should wait. The captain poked a claw into a hole in the door plate, and it slid open. Grizz took one Doonan by each hand and directed them to look carefully up and down inside.

Against the far wall, narrow white platforms with transparent back panels slid endlessly upward until the perspective shrank the shaft down to a pinpoint. The bottom of the lift shaft was much closer. Todd could see the platforms were an endless loop: up on one side, down on the other. He and Hrriss grinned at Grizz to show that they understood the principle involved.

"Reh," Todd said.

Grizz roared approvingly and stepped onto an ascending platform. Together, Todd and Hrriss stepped onto the next one, which could easily accommodate two Humans. But the baby bear, Weddeerogh, also leaped aboard, landing in a heap of fur at their feet. They laughed and helped him up.

"Do you feel a strong grrrvitic pull behind us?" Hrriss asked, swaying back and forth to test it.

"Yes," Todd replied, watching columns of gray glass doors sink into sight and out again past his feet. "I'd say there's a spiralling core inside this central pillar. It's compelling me to lean back against the wall. I guess that's how they keep from having accidents in this shaft. It must go up for three hundred meters." He let the pressure drag him backward, and he put a heel against the upper flat of the panel. "Look at this!" He inched upward until it appeared that he was standing several centimeters above the floor.

Weddeerogh snorted his baritone laugh and threw himself at the wall, back first. He adhered at eye level with Todd, then deliberately inched himself around until his toes were in the air. The Doonans joined in the merriment, experimenting with the increased gravity. Hrriss found that he could squat perpendicularly to the wall.

"But it causes trrrible pressure in my head and neck," he said.

A roar from above caused Weddeerogh to wiggle right side up once more and urge his two friends to do so as well. The next set of doors they were approaching were open, and Grizz was waiting for them. Weddeerogh made a flying leap and landed in a shoulder roll on the floor. Todd and Hrriss circumspectly hopped from platform to floor.

This corridor was not as lofty as the lower level, and had only one set of handholds, running up the exact center of the ceiling. The Doonans followed the captain along, taking in as much new input as they could with quick looks inside the various rooms that opened off the broad hallway.

The Gringg medic was black and white with a kind expression in her light red eyes. Todd still couldn't easily distinguish between the sexes, but for the sake of argument decided to call this one female. There were beautifully rendered anatomy charts on the wall, showing skeletal, muscular, and circulatory systems for two genders. The black and white bear seemed to fit the female mold, as, to the Doonarralans' surprise, did Grizz.

"Wait until the scientists at home get a look at these," Todd said.

While he was studying the charts and trying to remember significant details, the medic prompted him to sit up on a raised platform, produced a device with a small drum at the end, and put it to Todd's belly.

"My heart's up here," he said, tapping himself on the chest. The medic grunted, and moved the diaphragm upward. She let out a pleased noise when the heartbeat registered in her device. That seemed to be what she was looking for. Todd counted his own pulse as she listened. It was faster than normal, probably due to the increased gravity of the ship.

The medical examination went very much like the one that the Gringg were probably being put through by Kate Moody, with the medic, whom Todd and Hrriss decided to call Panda, signing when and where she was about to take yet another tissue sample.

Panda seemed a little puzzled when Todd automatically pulled off his shirt but left his trousers in place. She plucked at the heavy denim with a claw and crooned a question.

"I always say you Hayumans put too much emphassiss on clothes," Hrriss said with a grin, as he unself-consciously pulled aside the decorative loincloth he wore.

"I don't have a furry hide, cat man," Todd replied in an undertone. "Stark naked suits you, but I'm getting goose bumps and how'll I explain them?"

Actually, the room was warm enough for comfort, but Todd still felt chilly. He pretended total indifference when Grizz and Weddeerogh, as well as Panda, leaned in to have a good stare at all his parts. The Gringg stepped back to have a conference, during which they looked from one to the other of their visitors with increasing agitation.

The argument ended seemingly without resolution. Panda resumed her examination, and Grizz sat back on the floor to watch. The medic handled them both very gently as she went carefully over their entire bodies, then guided them to a host of strange, Gringg-sized machines.

"X-ray? CAT scans? EEG's?" Todd asked.

"You must ask zem when we can understand one anozzer," Hrriss said. "Zere is somezing very wrong zat happens to me when zey speak. Do you feel uncomfortable, too?"

"Without clothes, of course I do," Todd said.

Hrriss gave his head a little shake. "I don't mean physical; I mean in the nerves of the ear and the mind."

"That's a relief, Hrriss. I was putting the agitation down to nerves, but if you're getting the same sort of unsettling nudge, it must be more than that."

When Todd emerged from the last machine, Panda drew him back to the table and handed him a cup.

"Oh, no," he said. The Gringg looked at him expectantly. Panda indicated the cup, and made a gentle arc with one claw, pointing to the interior. "No. I don't think I could."

"Go ahead. I have done it. Why do you have so much zrouble producing waste wazzer?" asked Hrriss, amused.

"Doing it under these circumstances—with them watching the whole process, is slightly inhibiting," Todd said, annoyed with himself, Hrriss, and the whole affair. He turned his back and shortly was able to provide a sample. Panda and Grizz spoke in a crisp dialogue, their bass voices sounding excited. He hoped that they weren't amused by his behavior. When he passed the specimen to Panda, he noticed that Hrriss was now holding his ears.

"Are you all right?"

The Hrruban's forehead was drawn in long furrows of gold plush. "It is somezing about ze way zey talk. It is loud, but I am used to loud speech. We who live on Doonarrala have always used louder voices zan on Hrruba. Ze Gringg are not just loud but grating."

"Subsonics," Todd said, snapping his fingers. "That could very well mean that they're not hearing everything *we* say, either. I'd sure like to see an analysis of their hearing range."

He gestured toward his ears, and made faces so that the Gringg could understand that sound was causing him discomfort. Panda took a small scope from one of her pouches and looked in his ears. She grunted, puzzled.

"That didn't work, Hrriss. Aha!" he exclaimed, pointing at his friend. "Your voice is higher than mine."

"So?" Hrriss asked.

"Talk in the highest register you can. Go up through falsetto. If their range is too low for us, chances are ours is too high for them."

Obediently, Hrriss began to hum in his own tenor range, then climbed gradually, a breath at a time, into a piercing shriek. Long before he topped the highest note he could reach, the Gringg were holding their ears. At the top of the range, they were looking at him closely. Grizz folded her thumb and forefinger together in imitation of a mouth and opened it to show she didn't hear anything.

"That's it," Todd said. "Up at that end they're only seeing your mouth move."

Enlightened at last, Panda put the two Doonarralans onto a frequency generator and tested their ranges of hearing. Hrriss was capable of hearing a few cycles lower than Todd, but the lowest tones to which the machine was set were inaudible to both. They could only feel the cycles that Grizz indicated she was still hearing.

"Zat one could shake my bones apart," Hrriss cried, much agitated, waggling his hands for them to stop it.

Grizz called for another scribe. When Grrala arrived, slow of movement but bright of eye, they were gestured to a table.

"We'd better call this one Koala, so we don't mistake her with Grizz," Todd suggested in a low voice.

Panda motioned Todd and Hrriss to sit at the table as Koala set up some kind of aural transponder and demonstrated how it worked.

Using the settings on what Todd identified as a frequency generator, he demonstrated which tones he and Hrriss could hear, and which ones were painful. The Gringg did the same, and the scribe noted them down busily. The engineer, with a device like a round-screened pocket computer in her great paws, was clearly busy drafting a design.

"Now I think we're getting somewhere," Todd said happily. "This thing should translate the tones they speak in to the ones we can hear, and vice versa."

"Zat will help mightily," Hrriss agreed. "I do not zink we should miss any of zeir tonal qualities. We need to hear all to understand."

After a while, Koala signalled that she had enough to work on. She and the scribe excused themselves and went off.

"Now, the question is, how long will it take them to whip up a frequency voder?" Todd said, grinning at Hrriss. As he moved on the table, his bare skin slid and he gave an exclamation. "Great snakes! I don't need to stay in the buff any longer!"

The Gringg watched him dress no less closely than they'd watched him disrobe. He winked at Weddeerogh, who squealed. Then Grizz stood up and stretched, allowing the visitors a splendid look at her fine, strong frame. Refreshed, she addressed the two Doonarralans.

"Dodh, Rrss, kwaadchhs?"

"Quadicks?" Todd asked, struggling to match her pronunciation.

"Kwaadchhs," Grizz repeated and, obviously demonstrating, moved her great arms in broad arcs, starting at her breastbone and pushing outward.

"Could she mean swimming?" Hrriss asked, turning to Todd in surprise. Todd shrugged, grinning for Hrriss to answer. "Yes, we swim."

"Rehmeh," Grizz replied, and ushered them back to the elevator platforms.

"Swimming?" Todd muttered to Hrriss as they ascended another level.

When they followed her lead and stepped off in what must be the center of the ship, they could even smell the water. Even knowing that the probe had showed a mysteriously large quantity of water in the center of the Gringg ship, neither Todd nor Hrriss were prepared for what they saw.

"Swimming," muttered Hrriss in mild shock as they passed the transparent doors that led into the most astonishing room.

Instead of weaponry or generators of any kind, the water-filled center of the ship turned out to contain a swimming pool, vast and deep. The central pillar containing the elevator system pierced straight through the heart of it, but also supported several levels above the water, on which a few Gringg lounged while dozens of others swam and sported in the pool.

"This is absolutely spectacular!" Todd exclaimed, astounded, letting his face reflect his opinion. He bowed and grinned broadly at Grizz, who seemed pleased by his reaction. "That is some pool."

"More a lake," Hrriss said, staring about him at the sheer size, and shaking his head at the quantity of water put to such use.

"Greene'll never believe this is what the water was for. Though what sort of a weapon requires water . . ." Todd trailed off, shaking his head.

"I zink he would prefer anozzer explanation," Hrriss said. "He is not a man to appreciate gracious living. Ah, but I can!"

"And look at the range of colors in the Gringg," Todd added, nudging Hrriss. "Pied, patched, white, brown, black, tan, gold. See the black fellow there with a white shirt-front and chin and white boots? My sister Inessa had a cat who looked just like him, remember?" Then he craned his head about, able to take in more details now that the first shock of the space-lake had passed.

The room was, indeed, remarkable. A full, curved ceiling of a soft blue that arched benignly over the lakelet had been made to appear a natural sky. Hidden ventilators provided soothing breezes and the occasional surprise gust that made the water's surface skip and quiver. Except for the toroid shape and the fact there was an elevator shaft running through it, it was hard to believe that the immense pool was situated in the heart of a space-going craft. The elegant homes of the very rich on Earth had once had such amenities, or so his father had told Todd, before living space on the planet became so constricted that such luxuries had been prohibited. Man-made lakes on the few resort areas were out-of-doors, and few would have been as large as this one. Todd wondered how close this approximated the living style of Gringg on their homeworld. He knelt to dip his fingers in the water and taste it.

"It's fresh, with only a slightly chemical taste," he said to Hrriss. From his pouch, Hrriss took a little bottle and filled it for later analysis.

Having enjoyed their reaction, Grizz now took off her collar, shoulder piece and belt, placed them on a rack filled with other such accouterments, and slid into the water. Beckoning with a long, slow wave of her arm, she signalled them to join her. Todd started to strip and was distracted by the workmanship of Grizz's adornments. He picked up the collar and felt the material. It was smooth and supple like leather, though thin as vinyl.

"Is this snakeskin?" he asked, showing the way a snake moved.

"Morra," said Grizz, and molded her face around a gaping mouth. She submerged, and Todd leaned close to the edge to see her. She opened and closed her mouth, using exaggerated motions of her lower jaw, and flapped her hands alongside her jowls for gills.

"Oh," Todd cried, enlightened, as she surfaced. "Fish. They must be whoppers!" He sketched a fish of great size with his hands.

"Reh, reh," Grizz said, adding another length to Todd's. He whistled.

"Oh, the one that got away," he said.

Squealing, Weddeerogh bounced off the side and landed belly-first in the water, splashing everyone. One of the adults swam quickly toward him, only its head and the line of a dark-brown-furred spine and rudderlike tail showing above the water. The cub paddled noisily toward his dam, but his pursuer caught up with him. As he made cries of mock distress, the larger Gringg picked him up, lifted him bodily out of the water, and tossed him. Weddeerogh laughed aloud all the way down.

The resultant splash caught Todd and Hrriss full in the chest. "Agh!" Todd cried. "I'm soaked."

"Zen come in alrreddy," Hrriss said, teasing his friend. "You can get no wezzer zen you arrre." He undid his belt and threw it across Grizz's, and jumped in near Weddeerogh.

"Here I come," Todd said, hopping out of his shoes and hastily pulling off his clothes. "Damned nuisance. If I'd known I was going swimming . . ." Stripped again, he stood poised on the side of the pool. Then, as the Gringg audience watched with interest, he leaped up and cut a beautiful arc, entering the water with scarcely a ripple.

When he surfaced, halfway across the pool, the Gringg applauded him, batting the water noisily with their palms.

"Very prezzy," Hrriss said. "I didn't know zat was possible in zis grravity. I zink zey have not seen diving of zis sorrt."

"No," Todd said, surveying his companions. "They're not really built for swan dives and jackknifing are they?"

At Grizz's encouragement, Todd demonstrated more Hayuman-style dives, using the highest of the pillar islands to do a half-gainer. The Gringg were impressed, calling out their approval to him in loud, gruff voices.

When he was worn out, he pulled himself onto a nearby level and lay back listening to a youthful male with a stringed musical instrument gutturally rendering songs requested by the other Gringg. Todd asked to see the instrument, which was not unlike a guitar.

"But far heavier," he told Hrriss. He bent his fingers around the long stem as well as he could. They didn't reach the fretting, so he laid the instrument in his lap as if it were a dulcimer and tried to make chords. The resultant sounds were harmonious, but nearly inaudible. "These strings are heavier than baling wire. It's more like playing tent spikes."

The doors swung open. Koala, followed by the scribe, padded into the swimming room carrying a crescent-shaped solid in one hand and, in the other, a device not unlike Todd's recorder, with a slot intended to take the moon-shaped piece. The two Gringg settled down beside Todd and showed him diagrams on the reader's round screen.

"That was quick," Hrriss said.

"Let's hope it works," Todd replied. With a little stretch of imagination, Todd began to recognize the complex molecular structure of proteins.

Koala pointed to one. "Ayoomnnn."

"Yes, if you say so," Todd agreed with a grin. "And that's Hrruban, right?" He put his finger on the other pattern.

"Reh," Koala said, and put a claw to a control on the viewer. The two patterns moved toward and then overlay one another. Atoms stuck out to either side of the chain, and Koala seemed puzzled.

"Hayuman and Hrruban," Todd explained, pointing to himself and Hrriss.

The two Gringg conferred, and finally it fell to the scribe to draw pictures. With care, he sketched Todd and Hrriss, then began to draw in lines around them.

"The quality of artwork is magnificent for such quick drawings," Todd said. "Jilamey could make millions for this fellow in the Artists' Corridor on Earth."

"And on Hrruba," Hrriss added.

The scribe's sketch complete, he turned it toward them.

"It's a family tree," Todd realized. The scribe dashed small symbols between the images of the two of them, pointing at one, then another, and asking for clarification.

"He's not sure if we are siblings or . . . mated?" Hrriss turned with twinkling eyes to his friend, dropping his jaw in amusement.

"Uh, no," Todd said, shaking both hands and head vehemently at the misunderstanding. With the scribe's permission he took the tablet and stylus. While Koala watched closely, Todd drew two different family trees and peopled them with figures not much more detailed than stick figures, but clearly male and female of each species: one with tails, one without.

"You are not as good an artist as he is," Hrriss said.

"Agreed, but let's hope they get the message, and see the difference." He patted his work to show it was finished and pushed the drawing to the scribe. "We're two separate species! See—tails, no tails!"

The revised drawing prompted another spate of conversation. The scribe depicted a planet with figures of Todd and Hrriss standing on top of it.

"Ah. I presume he now wonders how we came to be on one planet," Todd said. "How do I explain?" So he drew Earth, marking out the Western Hemisphere continents, then its moon and sun, added a creditable spaceship and a line leading it to Doona, depicting its distinctive continental masses. Then Hrriss took over the double-looped pen from Todd, and sketched Hrruba and its satellites, and a dotted line for a Hrruban ship's journey to Doona. Todd jammed a forefinger onto Earth and held out his hand to Hrriss, who shook it, while with his free hand he pointed to his homeworld. Then they looked to see if the Gringg had understood the pantomime.

The Gringg passed the drawing back and forth, mumbling in rapid bass notes with such intensity that Todd felt his ears itching, and Hrriss could not keep his tail still. When the sketch had done a complete circuit, the Gringg smiled and nodded their acknowledgment to the two friends.

"Wish one of us could draw better," Todd said.

"Scrawl or not, zey seem to understand," Hrriss said, but his tail tip kept twitching.

"Two races sharing a world in peace," said Grzzeearoghh with a blissful sigh. "How wonderful! These are species I want to cultivate assiduously. We must learn from them how they contrived to co-exist so successfully. That harmony must explain why they are so willing to accept our peaceful intentions. Perhaps they cannot conceive that we might intend them harm. I hope this is so, for it will make our job much easier. This will be of great interest to all on the homeworld. Now, let us show our guests the entire ship so that they know there is nothing hidden on it to harm them or their mutual world."

They led the Doonarralans on an exhaustive tour of the ship, from the living quarters to the galley to the cargo holds, and finally to the bridge. Soon, the small beings began to tire.

"Mama, perhaps they want to take a nap," Weddeerogh suggested when Rrss yawned and attempted to conceal the gesture.

Just then, however, Grzzeearoghh received a signal from Grrala. "First we will return to the infirmary, for Grrala has something she wants them to see," she told her son.

"I'd say they deliberately trotted us up and down this ship to prove that they're not hiding anything. I feel as if we haven't missed a corridor or a single level," Todd said wearily. "Certainly nothing resembled a weapons system anywhere. They didn't even stop you when you opened that triangular hatch."

Hrriss wrinkled his nose. "No one is in danger from a compost heap. 'Rhaddencch,' Grizz called it. Zey seemed to let us go where we wanted to go. But it is so big a ship; to really explore would take weeks. Now, zat bridge was interesting, was it not? So vrrry casual."

Todd gave a soft snort. "Did you notice the configuration of the switches, toggles, and buttons? No way either of us could manage that sort of control board . . . not unless we could grow foot-long fingers and treble our hand-spans."

"Zat does not worrrry me as much as ze absence of couches," Hrriss said thoughtfully. "How do zey absorb ze g-force in takeoff and landing wizzout padded couches of some zort?"

"Maybe there's cushioning fat under their fur." Todd suggested and bent over to rub his thighs. "Their normal g-force is enough to make my muscles ache."

Hrriss gave a snort. "It wasn't ze diving you did?"

"Come to think of it, I haven't done much diving lately. But I know the difference between gravity-ache and muscle strain."

When Grizz guided them back to Panda's office, Koala and Ursa, another engineer, had several small devices to show them. Ursa strapped one about her massive throat and offered Todd another one.

"How do I operate it?" Todd asked. Out of the device resting against his larynx, his words came out in a basso profundo that made him jump. "Was that me?" he asked, and the device repeated it.

"Dodh?" Ursa began. Her voice, instead of being a deep, chocolate baritone, had been raised to a pleasant tenor range.

"Zat is much better," Hrriss said.

"Promising," Todd agreed. He turned to Ursa. "Say 'v va'arrel.' " He encouraged her comprehension of what he wanted by zooming his hand around like the shuttle. Ursa glanced at Grizz for permission.

"Vamarrel," the Gringg said, sounding faintly ridiculous in soprano.

"Aha!" Todd said. "See, we were missing something. Now say the word for the big ship." He gestured all around him. "Va'arrel?"

"Vasharrel," Ursa piped.

"Wonderful! We're on our way."

Ursa signed to Todd to take off the device collar and pass it to Hrriss. The Hrruban fastened the band, and tried a couple of words. "Spaceship, food, wazzer, rllama . . ."

The Gringg voder repeated much of what he was saying in a deep bass, but skipped parts of the higher tones. Wielding a tool that was a cross between a laser and a screwdriver, Ursa attempted unsuccessfully to adjust the tympanum to encompass all of Hrriss' vocal tones. She grunted and raised her paws palm up to show helplessness.

"Not perfect yet," Todd said sympathetically. "The waveband it uses is too narrow. We'll just have to wait until we get back down to Doonarrala. Better still, we could make use of Spacedep's engineers. The *Hamilton's* still floating along behind us. The Admiral was hinting none too subtly that they wanted to be involved. Let's get one of their technicians over here."

With a little tinkering and a lot of luck, Todd was able to adjust the Gringg communication system to the frequencies monitored by Spacedep. The communications officer, Rrawrum, maneuvered up and down the band until Todd heard static, and gestured for him to fine-tune onto that narrow wavelength.

"Hello? The *Hamilton*? This is Todd Reeve. Repeat, this is Todd Reeve."

"Where are you transmitting from?" demanded the voice of the communications tech. "You're interrupting a secured signal."

"Sorry," Todd apologized. "I wasn't intending to break in on anything. I don't know the field strength of this transmitter. I'm aboard the Gringg ship. I need to speak with Captain Castleton."

"The captain's not available at present, sir."

"Then, Admiral Barnstable? The matter I have to bring up with him is pretty important."

"Not available either, sir."

"Strange," Todd said, frowning at Hrriss. "I wonder where they went?"

"I'm not at liberty to divulge that, sir," the Spacedep comtech said.

"Uh-huh. How about Commander Greene?"

After a short pause, Greene came on the line. Todd described the situation and told him what they needed.

"Wouldn't construction of a translation device be their problem? Surely they've had to deal with the other species they've encountered," Greene said slyly.

Todd sighed. Greene had been his last option for help. "I doubt it, Commander."

"Really? A virgin species. Ripe for the plucking?" Greene asked acidly.

"Certainly ready to, and helpful in forming a meaningful relationship," Todd said, trying not to let the other man's sour tones annoy him. "A frame of mind I doubt you've ever experienced. At that, Greene, I'd expected that a man of your caliber and ambition would be able to catch the moment and run with it."

"What do you mean by that, Reeve?"

"Spacedep wants answers about the Gringg, don't they? They don't want them secondhand, do they?"

"No," and the reply was grudging.

Todd grinned. "So send us a communications technician who can help us refine a translator. They've whipped up a voder but it doesn't compensate for under- and overtones . . . and they're necessary to establish communications. Get a two-way exchange going and we'll find out what the Gringg are really saying."

"Will we?"

"As an Alreldep representative, I'm asking you, a Spacedep officer, to provide assistance. You know, the sort of addition that looks so good on a code sheet. Or are you unable to function without direct orders from Barnstable?"

"I can't order Castleton's officers to suit you, or Alreldep," Greene said in a sort of a snarl. Then he paused. "If someone volunteers . . ."

"Yes, a volunteer is the answer," Todd said, trying to keep the irony out of his voice.

"Not that I think anyone in their right mind—" Greene began and then briefly shut off the channel. He returned shortly. "You're in luck, Reeve. There's a sucker on every ship."

"I knew I could count on you, Greene," Todd said cheerfully. "Send him across. And don't worry. We'll vouch for your reluctance to send a man into danger. Reeve out!"

"This thing's pretty good," Lieutenant Cardiff, junior grade, said as he examined the Gringg prototype voder, running a sonic probe over the exposed interior of the device. He'd brought two heavy tool kits with him. And Commander Jon Greene.

Neither Todd nor Hrriss were surprised that Greene had accompanied the signals officer. The Gringg had courteously retired from the bay once the little ship was safely docked in their massive vessel.

"Sound reproducer of some sort, huh? First, what is it supposed to do when it's alive and well and working right?"

Todd explained the difference between Gringg voices and theirs. He had acknowledged Greene's presence but had to ignore the suspicious and cynical expression on his face, determined not to be provoked by Greene's open antagonism.

"Yeah, well, they were nearly there, I think. This resonator, here, is really brilliant. Should handle any decibel range. It looks like something they mass-produce, by the way. This plastic core looks prefabbed and the chips are probably standard for all their audio equipment. But I think these relays are too cumbersome; that's why you can't fine-tune. Think I can alter that to suit the purpose." He grimaced, and settled his probe on one of the baffles. "This one'll poop out on you after a few too many high notes."

"Can you remedy the problems?" Todd asked.

"Oh, I'm a master fixit," Cardiff said easily, and grinned at Todd and Hrriss. He had very white teeth in a face as dark as Grizz's fur, and a mat of silky, silver hair which he continually raked upward with the fingers of both hands. He seemed to be one of those enthusiastic people whose vocation was also his avocation, and was more interested in a challenging job than the wherefores of it. "Got some tricks of my own, I have. I'll just tinker with these relays—here and here—strengthen this baffle, and put in a more sophisticated tuner. Odd how there're only a few ways of doing some jobs? Sound's one of 'em. These guys have some mighty slick gadgetry."

Cardiff frowned slightly, turning the voder from side to side, re-examining its components. "But why leave it as just a frequency modulator? I can add a memory chip so it uses terms in the languages as soon as we have equivalents, build up the usable vocabulary. I've got some multiprogrammable blank chips here that'd do the job stellar! That way, all three races get used to hearing one another's tongues."

"Zat would be much more useful," Hrriss said approvingly.

"Sure thing," the tech said. "You know, they're trying to build something like this on the surface, too. Or so I heard from Commander Frill. He was looking for a decent resonator. I ought to turn him on to this one."

"Well, pool your knowledge, Lieutenant," Todd replied. "No use in redundancy."

"Nossir."

"Cardiff can't work here," Greene said irritably, looking about contemptuously. "There's no work space in this . . . barn."

"Since you've now seen what needs to be done," Todd said, ignoring Greene, "the Gringg have set up a place where you can be comfortable. They stayed out of the way on purpose"—he flicked a glance at the commander—"first to let you examine the voder without distraction, and two, so I can reassure you how hospitable they've been. Three, so I can warn you that they're big, Cardiff, really big."

"I figured they must be, from the size of their ship," Cardiff said affably. "Won't bother me."

"Well, you have nothing to fear from them."

"Nothing to fear?" Greene said, his lip curled derisively. "With claws that could gut a space shuttle."

"Which, I remind you, Greene, they haven't done. Keep your xenophobia to yourself," Todd replied in a harsh voice.

Greene raised a taunting eyebrow, his expression supercilious.

"I'm ready, sir, I think," the tech said, slinging one huge tool case to his bony shoulder and nodding for someone to pick up the big padded one that held his inventory of chips. Todd hefted it. "Lead me to 'em."

Through pictures and pantomime, Todd had managed to convey to Grizz the need of work space for the technician. She and

Panda had shown him one not too far from the shuttle bay, one level up on the belt elevator, and a short dogleg. It was yet another mark of Gringg tact that they met no Gringg on their way to the workroom. That Todd hadn't expected, but it pleased him very much. Hrriss, too, grinned as he followed behind the others while Greene kept glancing apprehensively up corridors and around corners. The belt elevator had surprised both Greene and Cardiff, though they were familiar with such mechanical lifts.

"What are they like, these Gringg?" Cardiff said, listening to his voice echoing back from the high, smooth ceilings. "I was hoping for a glance, you know."

Todd indicated the door to the workroom allocated to them and opened it. "See for yourself."

Cardiff lifted one foot, froze, and stared into the huge room. "Holy fardling afterburners!"

Grinning, Todd gave Cardiff a little shove in the back so that he moved on. Nevertheless, as he himself entered, he had to admit it was an impressive scene. Grizz and Weddeerogh sat beside Chief Engineer Koala, who was working over a low table, tweaking the components of the second voder. Her scribe, and Rrawrum, the communications officer, lounged around. At the appearance of the Human, all of them turned toward the door and smiled.

"Great gods! What a set of cutlery!" Cardiff declared, his eyes focused on the long claws the Gringg had extended in her work. His ebony-dark face had an ashy tint to it, and his already wild hair seemed to stand out further. "D'you suppose they file their nails like screwdrivers? Do I gotta work with all of them? They're big enough to cramp my style, I think."

"The silvery one over there's the engineer," Todd said with a chuckle, pointing out Koala. She waved a gigantic paw, and Todd could see the technician's eyes riveted to the length of claw displayed.

"You all right?" Todd asked, bracing the man's shoulders with a sturdy arm.

Gamely, Cardiff gulped. "Even with you warning me, I didn't quite appreciate . . . Hell, I've seen a stuffed bear in the museum and I just thought you meant they'd be a *little*—but whew!" He whistled softly.

"Get on with it," Greene muttered.

"Button up, Greene," Todd said in a fierce undertone.

Greene glared back with a hatred which he now made no effort to hide, but he said nothing. He could contain himself now, in anticipation of the total humiliation of Todd Reeve in the not-too-distant future. The Gringg had never met another species, had they? When Reeve found out the truth . . . When he could not retreat from his untenable position . . . When they had all the proof they needed . . .

Meanwhile he watched as the lanky technician was urged forward to be introduced to the Gringg. Greene momentarily sympathized with the reluctance evident in every line of the man's body, but then, Cardiff had volunteered. Greene contented himself with a smile and settled himself on a low counter, while Cardiff eased himself down on the floor with Koala and the scribe, and put the voder he'd examined on the table beside the other.

"Now, this is a good piece of work," Cardiff said, removing the resonator chip from the heart of the device and brandishing it at Koala.

"The word for good is *rehmeh*," Todd told him, squatting down alongside. Hrriss joined him, leaving Greene by himself, glaring at the roomful of absorbed Gringg.

"Right," Cardiff said, grinning. "Rehmeh, this. Not rehmeh, that. Downright cow patties, that. What you need is a couple of these transformers; a different microphone assembly, something with real range, but solid, too; and a new power supply." He rummaged in the big tool case. "I've got the very thing—somewhere in here."

The language of engineering had intrinsic universality. Circuitry symbols might be different, but the way to diagram a circuit was surprisingly similar. In no time, Cardiff and Koala were communicating easily through the sketches, augmented by nods, smiles, frowns, grunts, and much gesticulation, oblivious to all else. Cardiff's long, thin fingers assembled components, using hot-tipped tools and minute pliers as Koala made suggestions by pointing and making hand signals.

"Where's my soldering iron?" Cardiff cried, pawing through his case. "I'm sure I packed it. Oh, never mind. I can use the laser tool."

"Rehmeh," Koala said, at last, giving the Hayuman technician a rubbery-lipped smile of approval.

"Right," said Cardiff, straightening up. "Let's teach these things to talk." He had made use of the original casings, but shuffled components from both worlds. Out of the kit, he pulled a frequency monitor, and ran the dial up and down the cycles. "This will compress the greater range of Hrruban tones into the range the Gringg can hear, and match Human stuff as well. It'll also translate any one of the ranges into any one of the other, depending on who it's set to be worn by. This switch has three settings."

"Aha," said Todd. "Now we're getting somewhere."

Cardiff strapped one of the voders onto his neck. "You want them to learn Middle Hrruban first?" He ignored Greene's belated protest. "Sensible notion, since so many of us can get along in that. So that's what we're going to record into the memory."

Todd began to recite the words for which he already had the Gringg translations. Grizz recorded the translations in her booming voice when Cardiff pointed to her. Back and forth they went, putting more and more into memory, slowly expanding a Gringg/Middle Hrruban glossary. Todd suggested the words for body parts, things in the lab, male, female, baby, and any verb he could think of for which he could express the concept. Grizz responded.

"Right. We've got a good starting vocabulary," the technician said happily. "Go ahead, try it."

Todd cleared his throat. "I'm Todd, not Dodh." His voice came out as a deep bass, but with more inflection than he'd had through Koala's preliminary model. "Todd. Todd Reeve."

"Todd," the Gringg all repeated one by one. "Todd Reeve."

"See?" Todd said with satisfaction. "Supersonics—at least super to them—are dropping out, as subsonics are for us."

Hrriss took the other voder, and let Cardiff tune it to him.

"I am Hrriss, and my people are called Hrrubans." His voice was reproduced, but matching his *h*'s and *s*'s without dropping out any of the hissing.

"Hrrissss. Hrrrroobans," the Gringg intoned.

"Piece of cake," Todd said, spreading his hands happily.

"Peess of kkayyk," the Gringg echoed, showing their massive teeth in a grin.

"Don't encourage them to smile," Cardiff said with a twitch of his lean shoulders. "It reminds me of K.P."

"Well done," Hrriss praised him. "Well done by you, too," he told Koala, who grunted at the compliment.

"Well, let's take these things away and replicate 'em," Todd said. "Because of the tone differences, anyone who ever wants to talk with the Gringg will have to use one. That means dozens, if not hundreds, of copies. I'll see what inventory we've got and what we can manufacture in a hurry. Maybe even arrange a license to grid stuff in."

"Happy to help, if I can," Cardiff offered. "This was fun! Usually, I'm bent fixing electronics blown up by the visiting brass. No offense to you, Commander Greene." The three visitors looked around.

"Wherre did he go?" Hrriss asked, springing to his feet.

Todd glanced at the Gringg and raised his hands questioningly. Grizz cocked her head, and addressed a question to the others. No one had seen the other Hayuman leave.

"Wait," Todd said. "Where's Weddeerogh?"

Grizz moved faster then than Todd had yet seen. In a moment, she was on her feet beside a crescent-shaped device on the wall. She fitted a claw into a hole and spoke into a slotted grille on the side. "Ahrgha, geerh vnamshola Hayuman, parghhen va Weddeerogh. Ahrgha, meena lorrangh." Todd and Hrriss could hear her voice echoing in the hallway.

The announcement, if it was an order to bring back any Hayuman found to be wandering the halls with Grizz's cub, was redundant. Two strange Gringg, one male and one female, appeared in the doorway with a struggling Greene between them. Weddeerogh loped in behind the party, and rolled onto his haunches beside his mother. Grizz's eyes were hot with anger, but her voice sounded calm when she turned to Todd with a question.

"Geerh rhaddencch?"

"No, I mean, morra, that won't be necessary," Todd said, standing up to pinion Greene by the arm. The Gringg male moved away to make room for the tall Hayuman. "I'm taking him out of here now."

"What did she say?" Greene asked.

"She said, should she take you and throw you in the compost heap," Todd said, trying to master his fury. "What are you trying to do? Ruin the good work that's been done today, sneaking off for a private pry around this ship? You could have asked and Grizz would have seen you had the guided tour. This your idea? Or Barnstable's?"

Greene gave him a look of total contempt. Only the place and company kept Todd's anger in check. One day he was going to square off against Greene!

"Captain Grizz," Todd said formally, switching on the voder as he turned toward her. "We have truly enjoyed our visit aboard the vasharrel." Grizz murmured approvingly at his correctly enunciated words. "We'll be speaking again with you soon. May we be guided back to our vamarrel?"

"Reh," Grizz said, allowing a glint of humor into her eyes. Weddeerogh trotted up to nose Todd's hand, then over to Hrriss, and back to his mother.

"See you soon, little guy," Todd said warmly. "All packed up, Cardiff?"

"Lug this, will you?"

"I'll take it," Greene said unexpectedly, stepping forward to sweep the tool kit out of Todd's grasp.

"As you will," Cardiff said amiably, then turned. "See you again, Koala," and he tipped a salute to the Gringg engineer, who waved one large silver paw in response.

They both paused by Greene, and Todd gave a curt nod of his head for the commander to precede him.

"I'm sure you know the way to the shuttle bay, Commander," Todd said with barely concealed sarcasm. "Or didn't you get that far before they hauled you back for poking about?"

Greene said nothing as he expertly caught the next descending platform of the belt elevator. To Todd that meant he'd gone this far. Had he gone up or down?

"As you pointed out, Reeve, it's catching the moment and running with it."

"Even at the expense of violating good will?"

"Good will?" Greene snorted explosively. "Yes, good will! I'll show you some good will one of these days—" He broke off. Now was not the time to let anger overset good judgment. He took a deep breath and refused the bait.

Their guide hopped off the platform and Greene followed, knocking the tool kit against the wall as he slightly misjudged his momentum. Its flap bounced open, and a small, rodlike device fell out.

"Hey, there's my soldering iron," Cardiff said, diving for it before it dropped off the platform. He straightened up to tuck it back into the carryall, and stopped, looking curiously at the remaining contents of the bag. "Shooting stars, what's that? I never packed that."

"What?" Todd asked. A growl from the corridor suggested their guide was waiting.

Todd held up one hand to the Gringg before he grabbed for the tool-kit strap, to summarily lift it off Greene's shoulder. Greene twisted away but Hrriss barred his way.

"Hey, what's the matter?" Cardiff wanted to know.

"I want to see what's in there that you didn't pack, Cardiff," Todd said and jerked at the shoulder strap.

Greene struggled hard, but with a powerful yank, Hrriss stripped the bag from his shoulder while Todd deflected the commander's blows. The powerfully built aide had an excellent repertoire of hand-to-hand combat dirty tricks, but Todd had been wrestling snakes every year since he was ten. When Greene kicked, Todd hooked his feet out from under him and sat on him while Hrriss continued his inspection of the tool kit.

The Gringg guide came back to see what was holding his party up, and growled a question.

"Morra," Todd said grimly, keeping his weight on Greene's back. "What's in it, Hrriss?"

"It looks like a small bomb," Hrriss whispered angrily. "I do not know what zis sssmall device on top is."

Cardiff took a quick look. "Remote control receiver," he said, his face expressionless. "No fuse, just need a radio signal to set it off."

Todd closed his eyes against the arrogance of a man like Greene, too ready to destroy what he couldn't understand. Though he wanted to close his fingers tightly about Greene's neck, instead he hauled the commander upright by handful of his tunic.

"So that's what you intended, skiving off like that? To plant this bomb. When were you going to blow the ship? While Hrriss and I were still on it? Or when Barnstable gave the orders?" His fingers clenched and unclenched in the tough fabric of Greene's uniform. Though his eyes did not narrow in fear, the commander watched him warily, offering no resistance to the mauling. "No wonder you let Cardiff come. I should have been suspicious the moment I saw you in the shuttle with him. When, Greene? When was this to be set off?"

"A fail-safe, Reeve, just a fail-safe," Greene said, grating the words out, adding, when Todd relaxed his grip slightly, "Should the Gringg suddenly turn hostile."

Disgusted, Todd pushed him out at arm's length and let go. Greene staggered back against the corridor wall before recovering himself. He then straightened his tunic with careful gestures and smoothed back his hair with nerveless fingers.

"Do marines require their officers to be paranoid?" Todd demanded.

"Paranoid, hell, Reeve! Marines protect! Which is more than

you're doing," Greene replied in a low, angry voice and strode down the corridor toward the waiting Gringg.

The two Doonarralans hurried to bracket him, making certain he took no further detours across the huge bay to the shuttle. Silently, Cardiff paced ahead of them, eager to get into the shuttle and out of the way before the others boarded it. Hrriss managed the Gringg words for thanks and pulled the shuttle door closed. The small ship waited until the bay doors opened and slowly left the Gringg ship.

"If you'd planted that bomb and the Gringg found it, Greene, all the strides toward understanding that we've made today would have been neutralized."

"Why would they look for something, Reeve? Answer me that! They have such peaceful intent, and you are so honorable, why would they look for anything? But, why won't *you* look at matters from another perspective. What if all their compliance is a cover?" Greene demanded in a hard voice. "What if the Gringg are hiding something from us?"

"Hrriss and I were taken over the whole ship, and looked wherever we wished with no hindrance or supervision," Todd replied, still fuming at the appalling brush with near disaster. "They trust us. We must return that trust, and that means you keep your little gadgets off their premises."

"That little gadget might have saved more lives—" the commander began, and stopped before he blurted out why he had reason to be concerned.

"For the last time, Greene, this isn't your business. This is Alien Relations business, and in the interests of Amalgamated Worlds and this invaluable alien contact, I'll have you denied further access to the Gringg. This time, my father and I have the authority to keep the brass and bureaucracy right out of the loop so we can get on with unarmed diplomacy!"

It was with trepidation that Second Speaker returned to Hrruba to bring his news to the High Council. He had gotten no satisfaction from the confrontation engineered by the Hayuman Admiral. Between the medical examinations and the invention of a communication device, things had gotten totally out of hand. The stakes were far too high. In the presence of these immense aliens, Hrrto felt reduced to insignificance, although he was of large stature among his own kind. Beings should not be made in such massive forms, should not be allowed to grow to such abnormal proportions. They must not be permitted to come to Hrruba to dwarf even the largest of his people. He hoped that more of the Hayuman contingent felt that way than the Doonarralans did. After all, so many of them were shorter than the average Hrruban. Which reminded him that he had not felt any physical or aural intimidation when he had encountered the Hayumans for the first time, certainly not the unnerving sort he experienced in the company of the Gringg. He did not understand why others were not overwhelmed by the Gringg's presence. Even young Hrriss, whom he trusted as a true Hrruban, had taken to these furry giants as if they were veritable beings of honor, integrity, and value.

Mllaba seemed to feel that the coming of the Gringg could be a great advantage to him in the upcoming election. He was at a loss to know how he could possibly present such hulks as advantageous, though Mllaba was usually shrewd in seeing possibilities and potentials. Still, he had been there at the beginning and that did give him an advantage from which to speak. If he could build on that, with Mllaba's assistance, he might indeed enhance his bid for the Speakership. He need only be calm—and pretend to know more than he actually did. Mllaba was up to something, he knew, and she would inform him when her maneuvers were complete.

As Hrrto entered the impressive, dark-panelled Council Meeting Room, his tail gave a single twitch. The place had not felt the same since the death of Hrruna. It had turned into a cold, unfriendly place, with whispering shadows.

Hrrto took his place in the second seat, beside the head of the table, facing Third Speaker for Internal Affairs, a moderate Hrruban named Rrolm. The First Speaker's place was, of course, respectfully empty, draped with blue and red. In the center of the seat was the precious blue stone given as a gift of peace to Hrruna by the Hayuman settlers in the very first days of Rraladoona. On his deathbed, Hrruna had directed that the stone should be displayed in the Council Chamber until a successor was chosen. To him who assumed the office would pass ownership of the stone, to remind him that peace with one's neighbor was as valuable and vital as clean air or pure water. Yes, Hrrto thought, peace and trust were necessary, but in good time, when the Gringg had proved, beyond the shadow of a doubt, their pacificism.

"Be confident, sir," Mllaba whispered from her place, a seat rolled deferentially back from the table, suitable for one who was not part of the Council. "Contain this situation firmly. It will be the key to the election. Your rivals do not have such a good opportunity to display leadership as you do right now with your intimate connection in the Gringg incident. Fifth Speaker backs Third now, but the few outside candidates have little chance of assuming the post. Be firm. Be confident. You have the advantage."

"I know the tone and stand to take, Mllaba," Hrrto said, with some irritation, and flattened his tail against the chair leg, hidden by his robes. At times her attitude bordered on the officious, and she was not in contention for any Speakership.

Word had already spread over Hrruba that intervention by an alien presence had put a halt to the spaceport talks. The delegates, not held to temporary residence on Rraladoona as were their Hayuman counterparts, had come home full of tales about the giant Gringg. Mllaba's initial report had made a strong impression on the Council. The Speakers were eager to hear more from Hrrto.

So Second Speaker first explained the circumstances of the Gringg's advent, then signalled to Mllaba to run the tape of the huge aliens who had visited Rraladoona as emissaries.

As Eonneh and Ghotyakh appeared on the screen, gasps ranged around the table, then modulated into murmurs of discomfort when the Gringg spoke.

"What horrible sounds they make!" Fourth Speaker said. "Barbaric garble! Threatening in sound and appearance. So monstrous. Bare-skinned Hayumans were peculiar enough to behold, but these are at the other extreme!"

"Alreldep, which agency you already know includes several prominent Hrrubans of good Stripe," Hrrto said, rising to his feet as the tape ended, "maintains that these Gringg wish to establish peaceful relations with both Hrrubans and Hayumans. They are to learn Middle Hrruban," he said with a smug smile, intimating that this was a concession he himself had managed. "We must, of course, wait until sufficient understanding of language allows us to communicate to purpose."

"Peaceful relations?" Rrolm asked. "How can we be sure of that?"

"Of course their ship was thoroughly scanned and probed," Hrrto went on. "No weaponry of any sort was discovered, that is true. Alreldep sent envoys who were treated courteously, and no show of force or violence occurred . . ." He let his voice dwindle ominously. "We have little hard data, except the results of physical examinations done by the Hayuman medical team on Rraladoona. Alreldep does tend"—he paused solemnly—"toward optimism." He gave a diffident shrug. "On the other hand, Spacedep has given me reason to suspect that the Gringg assurances of good faith and their appearance of defenselessness—as far as their vessel goes—could very well be false. Until we are absolutely certain of their intentions toward us, Hrruba and Hrrubans, we should keep the Gringg contained in the Rraladoona sphere, but prepare ourselves for all eventualities."

"I do not think we wish a close association with these huge creatures," Sixth Speaker said, assuming the speech-making posture he had lately adopted, evidently believing that it gave his listeners more confidence in his ponderous opinions. "Once again the Hayumans have forced an untenable situation upon our peaceful citizens. I must tell you that there is great anxiety among those with whom I have spoken at length when word of this new incursion was brought to me."

"I second that, Sixth," Third Speaker said brusquely and turned to Second. "Have you any action to propose at this time, Second?"

Hrrto smiled, for matters were proceeding well if Third deferred to him to act. Although that could be a trap. Still . . .

"Surely, Third," he said with a smooth growl to his tone, "that is obvious. The fleet must be"—he let one talon extrude slightly from his right hand—"discreetly mobilized. Held on alert, undetectable behind the Rraladoonan moons. I have been assured that there will be those on the planet who will turn a blind eye to the occasional anomaly on the surveillance screens. And, should it become necessary"—he paused again significantly—"the Hrruban fleet will be able to move with surprise and great speed."

The others reacted with varying degrees of approval or censure, muttering among themselves.

"You are convinced of threat?" Third asked, over the hubbub.

"The prudent Stripe is prepared for any eventuality. In the case of large, unexpected visitors, mouthing peace, prudence is only . . . ah . . . politic. To be frank"—and now Second turned confidential, addressing his remarks directly to Third across the table from him—"I would feel less threat, actually, if their ship had shown some armament. With none . . ." He lifted his shoulders, leaving the anxiety for others to enlarge. "With the fleet in place, Hrrubans on the planet are supported. And our allies can turn to us for immediate assistance in case this situation turns ugly. And it very well could!"

"How? From what source? If the alien ship has been probed as weaponless?" Fifth asked doubtfully.

Second bowed his head, miming reluctant silence. "This is, of course, to be kept among us. Spacedep offered me incontrovertible truth of the possibility that the aliens are by no means as pacific and genuine as they would have us believe. But such information is classified. Suffice it for you to know that my eyes have seen, and my shoulders bear the heavy burden for you all. For the safety and sanity of Rrala, it must remain so."

"The Speaker did observe to me," Mllaba said, standing up, "that while Hayumans have weapons capable of destroying a planet, they have shown a moral code which prevents them from doing so. These Gringg, on the other hand, seem cultured and peaceful, but the evidence, which I, too, was shown, suggests they have two sides to their nature. The one we have not seen is vicious and ruthless."

The timbre of her voice only emphasized Second's less emotional narration.

"Yes, well, no one has answered me on the matter of the spaceport facility," said the Seventh Speaker for Management, slightly testy. "What's happened to it? There has been so much preparation, so many negotiations and hard work. Surely . . ."

Mllaba bowed to him. She enjoyed being able to speak freely before the entire Council. "It has been postponed indefinitely, Honored sir. The arrival of the Gringg is considered a priority of utmost urgency, and the conference co-leader is intimately involved in the negotiations. There is no surety right now that the facility will be discussed in the near future."

Sixth Speaker cleared his throat. "Do we yet know what part of the galaxy they came from? And, if they have come so peacefully, might they not have come for trade? That is why we—and the Hayumans—took to the stars: to find new sources of metals and foodstuffs and new planets on which to settle."

Mllaba realized with annoyance that Sixth was not convinced of the deadliness of the Gringg threat, nor was Fifth Speaker. Fifth saw the Gringg as potential allies and customers, and Sixth was more concerned with the inability to shift Hrrubans goods anywhere and the current recession due to that inability.

Hrrto rose and immediately Mllaba seated herself.

"The Gringg claim their discovery of Rraladoona was an accident," he said. "When they visited the First Village, they managed to convey to Ken Rrev that their instrumentation discovered an ion trail which they followed to the Rraladoonan system. They were encouraged to enter the system when they also found the marker buoys and realized that the third planet was not only inhabited but obviously using sophisticated technology. Their level of technical expertise is high. I cannot say whether it is similar to ours or to the Hayumans.

"To be fair," Second continued, planting his hands on the table, "the public face that the Gringg show is one of thoughtful, creative civilization. Their standard of artwork and music is high, and they have been quick to comprehend symbolic communication. They may have much to offer us—not only trade goods, but cultural gifts."

"This suggests an understanding of technology and tenacity of purpose," said Fifth Speaker, combing his chin mane with thoughtful claws. "These Gringg could be useful and worthwhile allies."

"If they are not planning to destroy us," Seventh said in alarm.

"I don't like it," snarled Sixth. "They could be a threat to Hrruban independence and individual development. There are already too many outsiders with influence on the Hrruban way of life."

"I feel it necessary that the Hrrubans take the lead in all discussions," Hrrto said primly.

"It may be more important than ever for you to *manage* such discussions," said Fifth Speaker, his green eyes wide with alarm. "I have heard something from our returning delegates which troubles me greatly. Is it true that the Hayumans are becoming more insistent in their demands to share our grid technology?"

"Yes," Mllaba said, rising gracefully to her feet. "But the Speaker stated without equivocation that such a thing was impossible. The Hayumans were not pleased by his adamant position."

"You did not admit to them why we could not share that technology, did you?"

Hrrto was genuinely insulted. He controlled his voice, but his tail lashed once under his flowing red robes. "Of course I did not. If the Honored Speaker will recall, I voted in favor of the proposition to make details of grid technology and construction available only to Hrrubans of the homeworld. I am only too aware that our supply of the element purralinium which makes the grids possible will only last for a hundred years at the present rate of use. Expanding the network of planets in our Explorations Arm and colony worlds will deplete it faster."

"We may find more," Seventh argued.

"How? Without better ships we are unlikely to find other asteroid belts where novas have collided and the minerals have formed into purralinium. The Hayumans are our only source of those ships, but they demand access to grid technology in exchange for spaceship technology. They will hold firm on that point," Second finished with genuine regret.

"How they dare! They go too far," Sixth said.

"They are curious," Second explained wearily. "Hayumans wish to know how everything operates. I must admit that many of the arguments put forth by the delegate Landreau make sense. As we know from many decades of use, grids save time and lives."

"Has no more purralinium been found?" Fifth asked Sixth Speaker.

Sixth stood up. "Plenty has been discovered, as the Honored Speaker may know from reading his texts. But never with the key trace elements which comprise the compound needed. I think we must curtail the establishment of any but the most urgent additions to our transport network. Research is, naturally, on-going to find alternatives, but we must face the fact that we have a finite quantity of material which is not renewable. We would do well to accelerate alternative power sources."

"We cannot!" said Third Speaker, looking panicky. "We've thrown all our support into grid research. We haven't the funds to advance new research into space technology. If the Hayumans remain on a hard line of negotiation, we are lost. In a short era, we will be circumscribed on every side by Hayumans and possibly by these, these Gringg. Something must be done!"

Fifth Speaker smiled grimly. "I heard through some sources who live on Rraladoona that the Gringg were not surprised by the grids when they first used them. Is it possible they might also have discovered matter transmission?"

Hrrto dropped his jaw and waved both hands dismissively. "The chances of their discovering matter transmission are exceedingly slim, Honored sirs, especially"—and now he drew himself up—"since the Hayumans have been unable to duplicate our process no matter how hard they have tried."

"Yet you imply that the Gringg have searched many worlds," Sixth said. "Might they not have found purralinium somewhere in their travels? We must discover what they have seen during their explorations. We must ignore no opportunity to replenish our supplies. Especially if we must use a third of our dwindling resources to erect an efficient grid in the spaceport facility. Never must the Hayumans discover how important purralinium is to us or how little we have left." Sixth Speaker was all but babbling in his urgency. "We cannot fall from our present prominence and become vulnerable to either the Hayumans or these Gringg creatures."

"Sixth, do not exercise yourself," Second said kindly, for the old Stripe was spitting in his agitation. "After all, the Hayumans have treated fairly with us. The delay on the spaceport is actually due to Zodd Rrev's contention that a spaceport is an infraction of both the Decision and Treaty." Second smiled benignly. "Despite their desire to share our technology, I do not see Hrruba made vulnerable to Hayumans."

"It is recorded that those who live on Rraladoona have always conducted themselves with honor toward Hrruba," Fifth agreed, "but there are too many on the Hayuman homeworld who are willing to take advantage of us. We must protect ourselves, or our culture will be swallowed up and lost, as our natural resources—nay, even as the surface of our planet was—by our own carelessness. The spaceport is essential if we are to maintain the precarious balance of trade. In the matter of the Gringg, you must ensure that any concession from them that the Hayumans receive, so also do we Hrrubans."

There was a murmur of agreement. Second realized he needed to walk carefully if he wished to be successful. Fifth was a determined and intelligent rival for Hrruna's place. And yet he judged that he had not done so ill in this meeting. Mllaba seemed to be very pleased.

"I concur," he said. "Steps shall be taken to establish Hrruba's preeminence. And its safety."

CHAPTER 7

OVER THE COURSE OF THE NEXT WEEKS, HRRESTAN took over as many duties from Todd in their joint management of the colony as he could.

"Todd can get his tongue round ze new worrds bezzer zan I," was Hrrestan's comment, "for all my dam said I was borrrn grrowling."

So, except for brief consultations now and then between the colonial co-leaders, Todd was free to spend long hours with Ken and Hrriss as they parsed and rehearsed Gringg sounds, memorized what vocabulary had been exchanged, and figured out the probable syntactical forms. As often as he could, however, Hrrestan dropped in, earnestly trying to refine those phrases he could enunciate properly.

Kelly and Nrrna kept pots of coffee available and the herbal teas that Hrrestan preferred, feeding them whenever the women could get their attention long enough, and reminding them that a good night's sleep would do wonders for concentration. Finally Kelly laid down a law.

"No Gringg at mealtimes," she said firmly on the evening when Alec had tried to emulate his father's tones and inadvertently regurgitated his last mouthful. "Give it a *rest!*"

Surprised by Alec's mishap, Todd offered sheepish apologies for his behavior and refrained from practicing the deep gutturals at mealtimes.

"Not that that improved his dinner conversation in the slightest," Kelly complained to Nrrna and Mrrva the next afternoon. She made grunts and woofs to demonstrate. "Now that he's got vocabulary and syntax, he complains because he only has present tense verbs!" She rolled her eyes in histrionic resignation.

"But zey are working togezzer," Nrrna murmured, and the two

women sighed once again with relief.

When the matter of planning for the upcoming Snake Hunt would have interfered with language lessons, Todd reluctantly acceded to Robin's pleas that he could handle the pre-Hunt arrangements. Kelly offered to give her young brother-in-law a hand. That work gave her a respite from Todd's current preoccupation. Robin proved not only completely conversant with the complexities of the big event but efficient in checking minor details to forestall accidents. Todd and Hrriss, as Hunt Masters, would spare a few moments to answer his questions and go over his work schedules and estimates, but that was one less worry for them.

Todd, Ken, Hrriss, and Hrrestan, separately or as teams, escorted Gringg visitors around Doonarrala or accompanied volunteer linguists up to the huge Gringg vessel to build vocabulary and language links for the translation voders. The Alreldep scout ship which had been assigned years before to Todd and Hrriss was back in service, shuttling people up without having to go through Barnstable, Greene, or Castleton. Only two of the smaller Gringg, like Eonneh and Koala, were small enough to fit in the scout. Hrrestan tried hard to get permission to put a temporary grid in the Gringg cargo bay, but Hrrto was totally opposed to the notion. Todd and Hrrestan did, over a great outcry from Barnstable and Prrid, give permission for the Gringg to use their own ship-to-surface transport, the smallest of the ones they'd seen on their initial visit. It was a cumbersome vehicle, like a great box, and looked totally out of place on the common of First Village where it had space to land.

Hearing about this, some of the more vocal dissidents made strenuous objections on grounds of noise, pollution, and possible damage to the expanse of grass which doubled as a playing field. But the vehicle was quiet, emitted no noxious fumes, and used an air cushion for landing and resting, leaving no marks despite its mass. The Gringg pilot, an oddly misshapen individual, smaller than any other adult Gringg, courteously asked for landing and departure permissions every time and remained in the vehicle, though Buddy, alias Buddeeroagh, was quite willing to show anyone through it.

Alec told his father that one day he had counted nineteen men and women, all of whom had the odd gait of spacefarers, requesting permission to board.

"None of 'em are from any of the villages, Dad. Me, I think

that old Admiral's busting his britches to find out something against the bear people. Isn't he?" Alec asked his father, cocking his head with a shrewd look in his eyes.

"You might think that," Todd answered cautiously, busy assembling the latest Gringg sounds on flash cards. Once again he reflected that children often saw more than their parents. "Why were you counting in the first place?"

"Aw, Allie, me, Hrr, and Hrruni were chatting with Buddy. He kept getting interrupted by these jokers when he was showing us this neat game. You know, if we could charge 'em for a visit, we'd make a pile!"

"You've been listening too much to your uncle Jilamey, I think," Todd replied, amused by his son's acumen but privately embarrassed at such gall, "but we can't charge for . . . ah . . . curiosity!" When his son's face contorted in dismay, he added, "And the navy is here to protect us."

Alec gave a snort. "Ha! Then they should spend their time doing that instead of nosing about our planet's guests!"

"Well said, Alec!" and he ruffled his son's tangled curls and then had to wipe his hand. "What have you been into?"

Alec finger-combed his hair, inspecting the results. "Some sort of oil er somethin'. Musta got it when Buddy showed me how their drive works!" Alec beamed suddenly, but his eyes were twinkling with slight malice. "He didn't show anyone but us kids!"

Todd decided he didn't need to worry about Spacedep's interest in the Gringg vessel when the pilot displayed such discretion. He also decided that letting the village children tag along with Gringg visitors would be a subtle way of disrupting the surveillance Barnstable and Greene had set up. What was the old tag? *Qui custodiat?* Who watches the watchers? The kids of Doonarrala!

So the almost daily unofficial visits by Eonneh and one or more of his fellow scribes to gather information and understanding of their new friends took on a new perspective. Of course, there were some diehards who wouldn't subject their children to "such influences," but these were fewer than Todd expected. When Alec casually mentioned the presence in the group of some youngsters Todd knew had been prohibited, he did have a qualm or two of conscience but decided their independence of mind should not be discouraged.

The positive reaction of the youngsters was also a grand buffer between the Gringg and the doomsayers who had managed to arrive from both Hrruba and Terra.

Somewhere underneath the busy exterior, Todd knew he was exhausted, but he'd hardly ever been so enthusiastic about a project in his life. Well, not since he'd been six.

The Gringg and the majority of Doonarralans were as delighted as he, cooperating like a dream. Frictions that had been caused by disagreement about the spaceport were mainly discarded by the generally held desire to establish relations with the aliens. The barriers of speech and unfamiliar custom were dropping farther and farther every day.

Sumitral, far from showing impatience with the laborious progress, made it a practice to interact every day with one of the male scribes, or with Grizz aboard the Gringg vessel. The Gringg captain herself had not yet set foot on Doonarrala, nor had any of her female department heads, preferring to save that portentous event, Todd was made to understand, for the day when she could make an official entrance, able to speak for herself.

Todd was grateful for her forbearance. His office received enough complaints from the very vocal Human and Hrruban minority who reacted negatively to the tercel males who had requested permission to wander about. The gigantic females would only cause a bigger stir and more friction. But he did identify most of the possible troublemakers and set up contingency plans to prevent outbursts from those quarters.

Todd also had reason to be very grateful to Jilamey Landreau, who set up entertainments and unofficial meetings at his hilltop home, well out of the way of Todd and those working on the language project. Superficially Jilamey seemed to be working both ends against the middle, soothing the disappointed members of the interrupted conference while making no bones about his Gringgophilia. He evidently made much of his being included in the first contact group.

The austere Barrington 'copted down daily to bring private and encouraging reports to Todd. Todd took these with a grain of salt, knowing Jilamey's enthusiasms, but Barrington's manner of reportage allowed him to hope that much of what Jilamey said was true. Especially when Barrington relayed Jilamey's firm opinion, one Barrington seemed to support, that the Gringg's only objective was to establish trade relations.

It was on this point that Jilamey urged patience until the translation problem could be solved, and how he managed to keep the frustrated delegates from leaving Doonarrala. Ironically, Tanarey Smith became one of Jilamey's converts, especially after Landreau persuaded Eonneh to escort the shipbuilder around the *Wander Den*, a rough translation of the Gringg vessel's name.

Todd could not ignore the undercurrents of dissatisfaction, even among Gringg supporters, that the talks about the space facility had been put hold. When he had time, he gave some thought to that. As a child, he had absorbed his father's views about planetary cohabitation; as an adult, he shared his father's opinion about any intrusive invasions of Hrruban lands on the planet. All right, it was Human greed that his father feared and it was the Hrrubans who had initiated the spaceport project. But did it matter which species encroached? If the rule applied on Doonarrala, it applied for both!

Had the arrival of the Gringg now altered the equation? No. Although he was optimistic about the outcome, the Gringg hadn't been officially allowed to open trade on Doonarrala. Todd, well-conditioned by Captain Ali Kiachif over the years, considered trading a different matter entirely from occupation or habitation. The crunch came in discussions of *where* the spaceport could be sited.

Todd knew how cramped and inadequate the old Hall at the Spaceport was for the volume of commerce that flowed in and out of it. Something had to be done to expand the facilities. No one wanted a larger complex at the original landing site, oozing toward the First Villages, ruining the peaceful valley. So a new location was imperative. Each time Todd mulled over the problem, he still found himself opposed to siting a larger port anywhere on the lovely subcontinent that was now called Hrrunatan. *That* should be left as the natural memorial park to the old First Speaker, which he, and all Doonarralans, had intended for it to be. He finally decided to leave the sore subject for another time, when he was thinking clearly and logically, not so emotionally nor—he admitted to himself—close-minded. His brain was already working overtime trying to cope with a difficult new language.

Gradually the daily sight of the large, shaggy strangers moving about with their Human or Hrruban escorts took the edge off the "fearsome hairy monsters" appellation. The Gringg became the "big bears," or Bruins, to most Doonarralans. But xenophobic pessimists somehow began arriving from Terra and Hrruba, and familiarity was not going to appease them. They visited every village, Hayuman and Hrruban, whispering against the "fiendish Gringg." They muttered about "murders most vile" and "devastated worlds," but would slip away before they could be closely questioned.

Todd worked all the harder to get the one tool that would throttle doubters and doomsayers both, and allow the Gringg to speak for themselves. Couldn't people wait for that, instead of stirring up unnecessary fears and forecasts?

The voder that Cardiff had designed with Koala was a brilliant piece of audio-engineering. It made use of the tiny Gringg resonator, memory chips, and other components from both Terra and Hrruba in common use on Doonarrala, all fitted into a compact case seven centimeters by two by five. Worn about the neck on a cord, it "heard" what the wearer said and repeated it in Gringg or human. Its creators nicknamed it growl box, or simply, the growler.

Cardiff, with the help of two of the university engineers, worked long hours to turn out six of the growlers so that Ken, Todd, and Hrriss could discuss Gringg objectives with Grizz, Honey, and Panda. The session was filmed, and although Barnstable had a fit at being excluded and decried the secrecy in which the interview was conducted, Sumitral pointed out that not even he, as Alreldep head, had been included, in an attempt to provide as relaxed an atmosphere as possible. Once again, Sumitral reinforced the perogative of Reeve and Hrrestan to conduct their own planetary affairs. There had been some heated reminders that the Gringg vessel was the concern of Spacedep.

"I could agree with you if it carried armament," Sumitral had replied suavely. "It carries only peaceful visitors!"

For Todd and Ken particularly, the session was a golden moment, for they established relations and exchanged meaningful data.

First: that for many spans of time (which Todd and Ken thought meant generations, since the Gringg travelled in family groups), the Gringg had been actively searching space for other sentient species as well as suitable resource planets. (It was a particular joy for the Doonarralans to learn that the Gringg had eschewed planets which probes reported showing habitations suggesting the basic intelligence of indigenous species.) The Gringg also required the availability of certain minerals and soils on a colonial world, for, despite being omnivorous and able to digest more substances than

Hayuman or Hrrubans could, they had to have a certain range of dietary supplements.

Two: they were quite open about the direction of their homeworld; galactically speaking, north by northeast, though the speed at which their ships moved was still not translating accurately. They provided "strips" which, fed through a device, enlarged the data into star maps. The difference in eye structure made these difficult for Hayumans or Hrrubans to decipher, and Koala was working on an apparatus that would compensate for the different optics.

Three: they would be happy to establish trade with both Hayumans and Hrrubans. Which put Todd right back on the horns of that unresolved dilemma of an adequate spaceport now that there would be three species using it.

Four: it was confirmed that they had found their way to this sector of space by following ion trails, detected by their own equipment. When they had come upon the Doonarralan warning devices, they realized they had finally discovered a sophisticated culture, which they approached cautiously, but openly. They were overwhelmingly relieved to discover they were not the only sentient species in the galaxy. And there was great jubilation when they realized that they had encountered two such species!

"We are joyous to not be alone," Grizz had said during the conference, bowing her head almost to her knees to signify deep emotion.

Hayuman and Hrruban were hard put not to burst out in cheers. Instead, they gripped hands with the Gringg, allowing their broad grins to demonstrate how happy they were.

"All a little too pat," Admiral Barnstable told Greene and Castleton when they viewed the tape. "Buddy-buddy, lovey-dovey, but all too pat!"

"Especially as we can't read their star maps," Greene added, as if that fact vindicated his distrust of the bearfolk.

"Considering they've come into this sector of space from a different quadrant, you couldn't read them even if they had the same optics as we do," Grace Castleton felt obliged to remark. She knew these two wouldn't have believed anything the Gringg said, even if they'd agreed to drop buoys all the way back to their homeworld, like crumbs that marked the way out of a cave in some old children's tale. Even loosely translating their distances, the Gringg homeworld was one helluva way back in on this arm of the Milky Way.

When the tape was shown in every village on Doonarrala, there was considerable rejoicing, and some doubts were allayed. Copies were dispatched by courier to both Amalgamated Worlds and Hrruban High Councils. Inevitably that brought back the issue of a larger spaceport.

"Zodd, we must resolve this between us," Hrriss said in Low Hrruban when he managed to find Todd alone in his office.

"Yeah," Todd agreed unenthusiastically, exhaling a long sigh as he tossed his pen across a desk covered by little piles of flash cards. He managed a half-smile for Hrriss, his dearest friend. "Can't bury my head in a snake nest any longer. Not if we want to keep the Gringg."

"First of all, Zodd, you have to agree," Hrriss said patiently, settling on the edge of Todd's desk as he had so many times in the past, "it is not Hrruban encroaching on unused space. It is Gringg needing space"—he dropped his jaw at this play on words—"for the very size of them. But more importantly, they provide a neutral factor, cancelling the sort of single-race intrusion you dreaded. In a triangle, all sides are equal."

"Only if it's an isosceles," Todd said, weary to his bones with disputations and arguments, and mostly fearful of a resumption of the estrangement from Hrriss which had cost him much mental anguish.

"Equal sides," Hrriss repeated, his eyes liquid and pleading. "Equilateral."

"Two of us don't quite equal a Gringg."

"What can equal a Gringg?" demanded Hrriss, throwing up his hands in comic dismay.

"They *are* to be friends, are they not?" Todd said, suddenly propelling himself out of his chair. He gripped Hrriss by the arms, needing to have all half-doubts dismissed. He *had* to proceed positively, thinking optimistically; by sheer will power bringing about what he so intensely desired. That method had worked before.

Hrriss' hands returned his grasp and then pulled him forward into an embrace, thumping Todd on the back as was the Hayuman custom.

"Yesss, friend of my heart, yesss! Even as thou and I," Hrriss added in High Hrruban. Then, in the less formal speech, he added, "As I have told you hundreds of times now, not all of the Hrrunatan is beautiful."

Todd frowned as he released his friend. "Where?"

Hrriss gave a sigh. "Where we have always wanted to put it, only you would never let me explain . . ."

"I knew, I knew." Todd flapped his hand dismissively, then suddenly stopped himself and smiled with chagrin at Hrriss' careful expression. "I'm doing it again, aren't I? But you do mean that rocky area on the east coast where that massive subsidence was?" When Hrriss nodded, relieved that his dear friend for once was willing to discuss the problem, Todd said, "But that wouldn't be large enough . . ."

"If one filled in the lagoon that was formed by the little subsidence islands and extended a firm base to those islands . . ." Hrriss explained with the weary patience of someone repeating a well-rehearsed argument, and waited for his friend's reaction.

Todd turned away, shaking his head sharply from side to side, but then slowing the motion as his sense of fair play forced him to examine that compromise. "It would take years . . ."

"To expand, yes, but not to set up the initial facility . . ." Again Hrriss watched his friend's face, seeing indecision increasing. "The beautiful part of the Hrrunatan would be intact, untouched . . . untouchable!"

"If that could only be enforced . . ." Todd began reluctantly.

"Why not?" Hrriss said, shrugging his tawny shoulders and dropping his jaw. "The terrain is perfect. The first precipice, where the subsidence began, is a natural barrier to the interior, and we will see that the traders abide by our laws."

"Traders are born to bend laws," Todd said, but he knew that was a weak argument. He shook his head one more time. "All right. Put the port there, but seal off the rest of the continent!" He shook a stern finger at Hrriss' grinning countenance. "I find so much as an ounce of ship's flotsam or the trace of fuel discharge on the mainland . . . I suppose you've got rough sketches all ready?"

Hrriss growled a laugh. "Jilamey used them as a device to keep the discontented occupied while we struggled with our growls."

Todd made a disgusted noise in his throat and rolled his eyes at such complicity. "Only, I'll have nothing to do with it. I hereby empower *you* to attend any meetings on my behalf! My heart simply isn't in it and I've *got* to increase the working vocabulary. I'm much more useful doing that. And, one more thing, I don't even want spaceships overflying the Hrrunatan. They come in from the east. That sort of racket would be disrespectful to Hrruna."

"Ah, but"—Hrriss raised a digit, claw half-extended—"Hrruna was a far-sighted progressive."

"So you say—" Todd caught himself as he was about to embark on the arguments he'd initially used to try to stop the project. With a laugh, he put his fingertip on the claw and gently pushed it back in its sheath. "A triangle *is* the most stable geometrical figure." Another thought caught him. "Great snakes! We'll have to enlarge Treaty Island facilities, too, to accommodate the Gringg."

"So we will. So we will," Hrriss replied equably.

Besides conscripting one of the local manufactories to turn out the voder parts, Todd managed to get the local high school and university, as a work-experience for their students, to assemble the translation devices in their electronics shop classes under the direction of Lieutenant Cardiff. Cardiff was a find. If Todd could have replaced his Spacedep pension, he would have been happy to give him a place on Doonarrala. But Cardiff liked travel and he was used to the military life.

"Maybe I'll retire here, friend," he told Todd. "Meantime, you've got a thousand of these growl boxes ready to go."

The crew complement of the orbiting Gringg leviathan numbered one hundred fifty-four, so the remaining devices were split evenly among Humans and Hrrubans. Over protests from the contentious of both homeworlds, Todd insisted that a number be set aside for children. Much debate had shrunk his proposed allotment from one hundred to thirty, but he was satisfied. The point had been made to Alreldep that, once again, the children of Doonarrala were going to play an important part in the missions of peace. In spite of a cry of nepotism, four growlers were assigned to the elder two of Hrriss' children and to Todd's twins.

Twenty-seven days after the project began, Todd asked Barrington to bring Jilamey down to the manufactory.

"But don't tell him why," Todd instructed, trying to maintain an expression of innocence. The tall, thin manservant regarded him with a calm demeanor, but Todd could perceive a twinkle.

"Of course not, sir," Barrington assured him, and departed in the small aircraft.

Jilamey was a child when it came to mysteries. In no time, the personal heli was back, scattering dust as it descended next to the factory door. Landreau barely allowed it time to touch down before he sprang out, calling for Todd and Hrriss. With broad grins, they met, one on each side as they guided him into the building. Barrington followed at a more sedate pace.

"What's the secret?" Jilamey demanded. "Old Silence-is-golden back there wouldn't give me a clue!"

Without speaking, Todd escorted him into the quality-control room. At his nod, Lieutenant Cardiff came forward, bearing a small device attached to the center of a soft, flexible strap.

"In rrrcognition of srrvice above and beyond ze call of duty," Hrriss said formally, "zo wit, keeping ze nuisances out of our furrr, we want you to have ze first wrrrking speech zranslator."

"Truly?" Jilamey gasped, looking from one friend to the other. Todd wore a face-splitting grin as he nodded. Enchanted, Jilamey held still while the voder was fastened on, then cleared his throat. "My dear friends, this is ever so super!" The sound echoed, expanded, and dropped several octaves through the speaker. Jilamey jumped. "This will need some time to get used to," he said, covering the voder input with his hand, but his eyes were glowing. "I sound like a bassoon."

Lieutenant Cardiff took a sonic probe to the side of the voice box. "Your voice is not as deep as some, sir. I tried to leave a little personality in each one."

"How's it work? I warn you"—Jilamey peered out of the corner of his eye at the technician—"I'm dreadful with machinery."

"Well, it transposes the pitch of your voice, compresses your range a little," Cardiff said. "Gringg don't hear as many of the upper tones as we do. It has a full language memory, with plenty of bytes left for expansion. You'll notice a bit of a pause—that'll take time to get used to—between the words out of your mouth and the Gringg equivalent from the growl box. It'll translate Terran into Gringg or Hrruban, whichever you set it for. At least the words that it currently recognizes. Otherwise it defaults to Middle Hrruban, since Hrriss said you're fluent in that."

"We'd like them to learn one language at a time," Todd said.

"One language I speak better than any other"—Jilamey laughed—"and that's trade. I've been contacted by a consortium on Terra. I say, Todd, there's a bit of unfair play going on. The Hrruban trading contingent grows with every grid operation and, if it weren't for the presence of Kiachif, Horstmann, and that crowd that got here originally, you and Hrrestan would be in for real trouble from Terra. However," he added, swiftly shifting mood again from the semi-critical to the self-satisfied, "I managed to salve injured feelings and, if I say so myself, managed quite a coup." He preened a bit, which set his shirt to shimmering with a cascade of subtle color shifts. "I've been appointed agent for the biggest and most diverse consortium of AW."

"Congratulations," Todd said, grinning. "The Gringg'll never know what hit them."

Jilamey pretended modesty, but was quick to make a demand. "When *can* we get down to the nitty-gritty? I've been arguing day and night on your behalf, but, since you've solved the voder problem, when are we going to get to *trade?* That financier Hrrouf is like a Momma Snake, and I hear old Hrrto just gridded back in."

Although Jilamey could be discreet, neither Todd nor Hrriss mentioned that Second Speaker was here because he had insisted on a private conference with Grizz. That was the only way they could pacify the Hrruban after he'd received his copy of the initial voder-assisted conference. The same concession would not be granted to Barnstable, on the grounds that he was only an admiral and not the temporary head of the Hrruban world.

"You will be happy to learn that the original spaceport conference can be reconvened," Todd told Jilamey.

"Wow!" Jilamey rounded his eyes and dropped his jaw in astonishment. "I thought you'd never relent."

"The Gringg constitute a new factor," Todd said obliquely. "Hrriss has been deputized to stand in for me."

"Ahha!" Jilamey waggled a finger in Todd's face. "I knew you'd figure out how to renege."

"I haven't reneged, Jilamey," Todd said with an edge of rancor. "But"—he waggled his finger in Jilamey's face—"if we want to trade with the Gringg—and we do—the old Hall and spaceport are totally inadequate. And letting the Gringg come in and out of Doonarrala obviates the necessity for their knowing the coordinates of our respective homeworlds. I still don't like to see the Hrrunatan—"

"Corrupted." Jilamey finished off one of Todd's well-known objections. "But old Hrruna would have approved of consorting with the Gringg. You know that! And by utilizing that rocky eastern coast, your preserve will be sacrosanct."

Todd sighed. "Hrriss made that point, too."

"Humph! At least the Gringg have made you two friends again, haven't they?" And Jilamey peered anxiously into Todd's face.

"We have never been *not* friends, Jilamey."

"Still and all, you can't get me to believe that things weren't pretty strained there, just before the *Wander Den* put in its serendipitous appearance."

"Leave off, Jil," Todd said, and pushed the carton of voders at him. "These are for your guests. We're giving everyone a day to get accustomed to the growlers. Show them how they work, and put them to use tomorrow. When I told Grizz that the voders were ready, she assured me that her delegates would be here directly after lunch. I'm taking hers up to the *Wander Den* this evening."

He did not say that he'd also be taking the Second Speaker in the scout for his meeting with Captain Grizz.

Waiting until the old port facility was relatively vacant, Hrriss and Hrrto gridded there from First Village and got on board the scout just before Todd made a more public appearance. He whistled as he loaded the cartons of growl boxes, and waved affably to those who noticed him. The tower gave him clearance, and he made no mention of passengers.

As usual, Grizz had been cooperative about meeting Second Speaker, styled to her as the "Oldest Elder" of the Hrrubans. Hrriss also managed to convey that the Elder was . . . nervous about spaceships, which was the nearest he could manage with a limited vocabulary, to offset any lack of Stripe that Hrrto might display when finally faced with the reality of the huge Gringg captain.

"Weddeerogh," Grizz had told him and, using two fingers, pantomimed her son meeting and escorting the visitor to a private place to talk. "Two," she signed, holding up two digits and sliding her hands sideways, one above the other, making it plain that she and Hrrto would be the only ones.

Todd could tell by the tense look on Hrriss' face that his friend was not entirely happy about that. This meeting would be quite a test of old Hrrto's Stripe! Hrriss had hoped to be an observer. Still, Hrrto *had* insisted! Todd hid a grin and indicated that Hrrto would have the growlers to help the conversation.

Grizz did the Gringg equivalent of relieved smiling and much snapping of her claws in and out of their sheaths. Todd just hoped she would refrain from doing that in Hrrto's presence.

However, when they arrived at the Gringg bay, Weddeerogh stood there by himself, looking comparatively small and harmless. He was also wearing a growler, and someone had tied a reef knot in the cord that had been designed to encircle adult

Gringg necks. The knot stuck out behind one ear and made him quite appealing. Hrrto reacted appropriately, by dropping his jaw in a half-smile, though he was clearly stunned by the size of the bay and the immense boxy shuttle-craft parked there.

On the short trip from the planet's surface, Hrrto had practiced with the voder, getting accustomed to the growling guttural reaction to his spoken words.

"Good evening," he now said, inclining his head to the cub. "You are my escort?"

Weddeerogh began to growl, and then his voder started off with "I am"—there was no equivalent for his name—"male child of captain. Come with me!"

With that, the cub did an about-face that Greene couldn't have faulted and strode toward the interior.

"You will wait for me," Hrrto said to the two friends with great dignity and turned to follow his guide.

They were about the same height, though the Hrruban was longer in the leg. As they disappeared through the iris of the lock, Todd wondered if he ought to have warned Hrrto once more about the size of adult female Gringg. He felt Hrriss touch his arm, and the laughter in the cat man's eyes suggested that he entertained similar thoughts.

"I wonder if he will howl," Hrriss said mischieviously.

"Well, he demanded a private audience," Todd said and then began to unload the cartons. As soon as Hrrto and his guide had reached their destination, Eonneh and Koala—and probably half the crew—would arrive to receive their growlers and practice before tomorrow's talks.

Hrrto had been much encouraged by the size and dignity of his escort. The creatures at least understood the basics of courtesy. The stumpy legs of the Gringg made its hind end waggle as they moved down the corridor—rather like a young cub, not quite leg-long. Still, the creature wore a harness that even Hrrto could see was beautifully crafted. So he had been accorded a senior official as his guide. That was as it should be.

With these thoughts, he tried not to notice the dimensions of the hall they traversed. Door panels slid aside at their approach and they went down another, larger hall. Then his guide paused, used partially extended claws to scratch at a door. This slid aside, and bowing from his waist, he made a sweeping gesture for Hrrto to enter.

He began to growl, which translated to "Captain . . ." and then some incomprehensible syllables of which all Hrrto understood was "grizz." Well, Captain would do well enough, so Hrrto swept his robes up deftly and stepped over the threshold. There he stopped and didn't even hear the panel slide shut behind him.

The room was twice the size of the Hrruban High Council Chamber and looked even larger because it was painted a light shade of yellow and was virtually empty except for a pile of cushions; a magnificently ornamented chair and footstool, which his stunned mind told him must be for him; and two small side tables, each crowded with exquisite dishes piled high with tidbits.

But the room was otherwise filled with the most immense living shape Hrrto had ever seen. Its coloring was a sinister dark brown, nearly black, against which the icy shards of its teeth gleamed dangerously. Its head seemed almost to brush the high ceiling, and the frightening roar that came from its mouth—before the voder took over—resounded in the chamber.

Blinking, and rocking back on his heels, Hrrto nevertheless heard Middle Hrruban words that made sense to him.

"Welcome, Honored Second Speaker Hrrto," it said, managing to speak his name with a proper roll of the *r*, a feat few Hayumans accomplished properly. "I am captain of the *Wander Den.* You may call me Grizz as your friends do."

No friends of mine, Hrrto thought, trying to find some mental balance. *Why hadn't Hrriss had the courtesy to warn me of its* size?

"Be seated. Be comfortable. We talk." The words rolled out of the voder, reverberating. As if puzzled by a lack of response, the creature held up the device, and with the tip of a very sharp claw, made a minute adjustment—which Hrrto doubted even as he saw such a delicate movement performed—to one of the dials. "Too loud. Roars are not good for friendly talk."

Hrrto appreciated the adjustment just as he realized that he could not hesitate any further or be a disgrace to his Stripe. He bowed as deeply as he felt he should and dropped his jaw, remembering that Hrriss said the Gringg understood that as a positive action. He thanked the ancient gods that he had not permitted any witness to accompany him—especially Mllaba, who had been quite incensed at being left behind.

Steeling himself for the next action in this ordeal, Hrrto managed a creditable and stately progress to the chair which a massive furred paw indicated. It was only then that he realized the creature had been standing. It now squatted down, with its own peculiar grace, to the pile of cushions, and gestured again for him to be seated.

Still in a state of shock, Hrrto realized he would have to step up on the footstool in order to seat himself. He was wondering about the dignity of this as he did so, but once he was seated and turned toward this Captain Grizz, he found himself at eye level with her. Yes, Hrriss and Zodd had said that the captain was a female. He'd forgotten that detail. Out of nowhere he was reminded of an absurd joke that Zodd Rrev had told in his presence, about citrus fruits that grew so large that eight of them would equal a Human dozen. One of these Gringg was certainly a full dozen.

With an effort of will, Hrrto slowed his heartbeat and his quickened breath and looked her straight in her odd red eyes, pupilless but glistening with intelligence. He couldn't deny that!

"You are . . . (*gracious? kind?*) very good to receive me, Captain," he said, wishing that the voder would not hesitate in its translation. Would that be considered a sign of weakness? No, her device did the same thing.

Now she gestured to the bowls on the side table.

Growling; then the voder explained, "All Hrruban foods. Enjoy!"

She reached for her own table and took a gobbet of something, conveying it neatly to her mouth. Grateful for the diversion and the courtesy thus shown, Hrrto selected a tiny crisp-fleshed fruit and became more relaxed, for clearly these Gringg had taken the time to discover his preferences. They both chewed companionably.

"You were long on your way here?" Hrrto asked, abruptly deciding to be social in manner. His previously rehearsed speech was totally inappropriate.

The Gringg nodded her great head, dropping her jaw as a Hrruban would, but he wished her black lips did not retreat over her very white fangs. He reached down for a handful of refried meat cubes, another favorite tidbit. "Grrrr . . . two cubs born to me and a long time between them. I am captain."

"I see," Hrrto said, nodding at such information. "Will you return to your homeworld or a colony?" He hoped the voder translated "colony."

"Grrruuph . . . We are on peaceful mission for long as possible," she replied. "We wish to trade. With Hrruban. With Hayuman."

Subtle, too, Hrrto thought, putting his species before the Hayuman. But that was as it should be.

"Grrrummmm . . . glad to find two for one trip," and she dropped her jaw again.

Hrrto paused a moment, decided she intended to be humorous and dropped his jaw. Then, deliberately over his next words, he scooped up more of the meat cubes, nibbling delicately. He had long ago learned how to eat without exposing his own dental equipment.

"You have seen many other worlds, planets, systems . . ." All three nouns came out in assorted groans and growls. "Have you?" he added, making that a question rather than a statement.

The captain nodded, running her tongue over her teeth, fortunately with her mouth closed. Evidently they had several courtesies in common.

"Many. Not enough water for Gringg. Too much land is not needed. But land has certain minerals, earths, no smart peoples. We are a water people. Hrrubans like water worlds?"

Clever as well, Hrrto thought, considering this a deft ploy to gain knowledge of his homeworld.

"We are land creatures," Hrrto said, finally settling back in the chair and finding it comfortable. His back muscles had started jumping from inner tensions. "We are hunters. Are you?"

Another nod. "Eating is necessary."

One answer led to another question, and Hrrto found himself able to ask, and receive answers, to many queries. What he so desperately wanted to ask—about the Gringg ship drifting derelict off a shattered world—did not come to his lips. Such a query would have been inappropriate, he told himself; certainly not consonant with the social nature of this meeting, and probably would be deftly parried by the captain. Far better for him to think of trade, and most particularly of the need for purralinium, though he had to be most adroit in his questions concerning that desperately needed commodity. The captain readily admitted how many planets they had surveyed, but not what the surveys had discovered. She discoursed on many matters, some of her conversation marred by the insertion of growls, snarls, and woofs where the voder could not accommodate a translation.

"On your way, did you discover dwarf systems? Or do you have enough ores and minerals on your own planet?" Hrrto finally inserted as casually as possible. Only systems shattered by novas contained the purralinium with the impurities that could be used for matter transmission.

"Reh! Yes," the captain said, nodding her great head. "Three," and she held up three huge digits. "We always look for new . . . ah grrrmmm—metals, earths, useful raw materials."

"I see!" Hrrto could hardly contain his excitement over such news. Surely in one of those systems, there would be the purralinium the Hrrubans had long sought.

"Do you?" asked the captain politely.

"One always *looks*," Hrrto said, waving one hand in an airy gesture, dismissing that topic. "We search space, too. You must come from very far away."

"Our scribes try to find time parallels so can be accurate. No wish to keep back any information. Only special words not available yet."

Throughout their hour-long meeting, she appeared at ease and did not evade discussion of any topic Hrrto touched upon.

Finally, after noticing she had finished the contents of the bowls on her table, he realized that it would be diplomatic of him to bring the meeting to a close. She was graciousness itself, and the young Weddeerogh, her male cub, waited outside the door to guide Hrrto back to the bay, and his transport back to Rraladoona.

All in all, as Hrrto took his seat in the scout ship, he felt the meeting had gone well. The possibility of locating one of those nova-blasted systems was the brightest part of the hour. More important, he had survived it!

The next morning, when Second Speaker arrived at the Treaty Center with his entourage and swept into the Chamber, he had second thoughts. He had spent a night tossing and turning on his pallet, and he was one who usually found sleep easily. He had rehearsed query and answer many times. He also tried to figure out how to acquire the coordinates of one of the nova systems. Yet that would require very adroit maneuvering on his part. But, as he tossed and turned, a solution came to him. The scientist Hurrhee, who was one of his own Stripe, would surely be invited to attend any technological sessions. Hurrhee was completely trustworthy, in that he held science as the premier dedication of his life. He could certainly introduce the topic of nova-blasted systems. Perhaps the Gringg might even have samples of ores, earths, and minerals they hoped to trade. A simple survey would reveal whether or not the purralinium fit Hrruban requirements. Yes, that was how to handle that problem. Accepting judicious amounts in return for trade items would not arouse any suspicions.

Satisfied with that solution, Hrrto once again composed himself to sleep, only to find himself distressed by a second anxiety. Despite the evidence on the tape shown him by the Hayuman admiral, he could not equate such brutality with the courtesies shown him by the captain. Of course, her manner and charm—yes, she had been charming in her own fashion—might be serving her own ends by allaying his doubts, but Hrrto could not quite believe such duplicity. Certainly not from someone who had assigned her own flesh and blood as his guide. Had she come to Hrruba, he would have assigned his second-generation offspring as her guide.

Mllaba, of course, had wanted a word-by-word account of the meeting. He had touched on the details, privately wondering what her reactions would be when she was face to face with the stupendous reality of Captain Grzzeearoghh. That would teach her humility. Casually, he asked her to arrange a discreet meeting with Hurrhee as early as possible the next morning, before the Trade Conference began, and for once, she did not ask why.

The next day, the wide hall of the Treaty Center—almost as wide as a corridor on the Gringg vessel—was well populated with little knots of Hayumans and Hrrubans chatting amiably. Hrrto, walking with great dignity, sensed the air of pleased anticipation. In front of the chamber assigned to the spaceport talks, he recognized the fair-haired female captain of the *Hamilton* and the Hayuman commander. If there was purralinium to be had by congress with the Gringg, he would have to rethink that uneasy alliance.

Greene turned a precise half-bow in his direction, to which Second responded. The Hayuman had kept Hrrto's aide fully informed as to the progress of the Spacedep fleet toward Rraladoona. Neither that squadron nor the three Hrruban defense ships were close enough yet. Now Hrrto wondered if that action had been as necessary as the Spacedep person had insisted. Would it ruin the good start he had made with the captain and, at the worst, deny the Hrrubans a possible source of purralinium? If he had only been able to ask her about Fingal and the dead, orbiting Gringg ship! Maybe having both navies there was *not* a bad idea.

If the Gringg *were* as peaceful as they seemed, he could always say that policy had required him to inform the Hrruban navy and they had acted without his orders. Yes, that was it. On the other hand, the naval presence might forestall any devious Gringg scheme. Either way, he would be considered wise. Overnight reflections had not entirely dispersed his anxieties, but his little chat with Hurrhee had been most productive.

After briefing the scientist, he had reviewed the morning dispatches, which included almost insolent demands from Hrruban manufacturers and traders of all commodities to open dialogue. They clamored that they *must* have first choices, with such an obscene single-mindedness that for once Hrrto found himself disgusted with Stripes, wide and narrow.

He was here now, officially and publicly, to initiate trade talks with Captain Grizz. Hurrhee was primed to include ores as part of any trade payment. Once matters were underway in that session, Hrrto could then gracefully retire to the spaceport conference. He couldn't quite leave such negotiations to Prrid, Mrrunda, Hrrouf, and the others who had gridded in for that purpose. Only after he was sure that both meetings were proceeding with dispatch, might he then be able to get back to Hrruba and promote his personal ambitions toward First Speakership.

Mllaba was almost treading on his heels as she escorted him to the Trade Conference room. To his relief, the immense and shaggy Gringg had not yet arrived, though huge square cushions on the floor gave notice where they were to sit.

"Your place should be at the head of the table," Mllaba whispered, guiding him toward one end of the great oval board.

To their surprise, Hrrin was already seated at the end of the oval. He regarded them with glittering eyes when they approached, showing no signs of vacating his seat.

"Greetings, Honorrred Speaker," he said in proper High Hrruban, rising and bowing gracefully. "I have been deputized as Rrraladoonan spokesperson, but I will, of course, defer . . ."

"I had expected Hrrestan—" Second began.

"Ah, but he is conducting the spaceport affairs," Hrrin said smoothly. "It was our understanding that you would not stay here long, but go on to the more important conference."

Mllaba hissed slightly in Hrrto's ear. Sometimes she could be annoying about what was due his rank.

"We have arranged ourselves according to our origins," Hrrin went on, gesturing to the Rraladoonans seated to his right and the Hrrubans, onward to the Terran delegation of captains and Jilamey Landreau further along the table.

The room was full enough of bodies right now, and Hrrto jerked his shoulders and switched his tail, trying hard not to remember how the Gringg captain had dominated a room not much larger than this.

"Most commendable," Second said with an absent frown. In ordinary circumstances, protocol would have required a Hrruban to allow him the dominant place for however long he chose to stay in the meeting. Hrrestan would have automatically deferred, but this Hrrin was more Rraladoonan. Hrrto decided to ignore Mllaba's hissing. To demand protocol in a mere trade meeting would appear petty. It was more important for him to be prominent in the spaceport considerations than to bicker about what to buy from whom and at what price.

Noting that Hurrhee was present, Hrrto spared a glance for Nrrena, seated to the scientist's right. She was an intimate of Fifth Speaker and bore watching. She must not think that these seating arrangements constituted a discourtesy. Determined to put the best face on the situation, he nodded with great dignity to Hrrin. "How wise to show, even here, that Hrruba is distinct from Terra."

"I am so glad that you approve, sir," Hrrin said, once again making a courteous gesture to the chair placed well along the outer curve of the great table.

Smiling graciously to Nrrena and two Hrrubans he did not know, Hrrto moved to that seat. It was, he was relieved to note, more ornate than any of the others at this segment of the table. He settled himself in the deep chair, flicking his tail out under the armrest. Mllaba was growling under her breath as she sat behind him on a small seat she pulled from those ranged along the wall.

Hrrto looked around with practiced casualness. Zodd Rrev occupied the other end of the table. Hrrto noticed that neither he nor Hrrin sat at the exact head, but angled off slightly from the table's axis. He wondered what precisely that indicated in the negotiations to come. The Rraladoonans had their own agenda, he had no doubt, and were clever enough to push it through in spite of the best efforts of homeworld diplomats. See how they had begun by forestalling him.

Then he realized that he was directly opposite an as yet unoccupied place which had no chair. He would be facing a Gringg. He steeled himself for that, wary after last evening's encounter. That inadvertently brought to mind the Spacedep tape as well as last night's insomnia. Again, he saw the devastated landscape, and the floating frozen corpses, and could not control a shudder down his spine. Firmly, he put that vision out of his mind. To cover his spasm, he fiddled with the voder straps. Everyone here was wearing the contraptions, of course, and he devoutly hoped that Hrrin—or would it be Zodd Rrev who moderated this meeting?—made certain that only one person spoke at a time. Otherwise the resultant cacophony would be nerve-racking.

The Hayuman admiral noisily entered the chamber now, and took his place obliquely across from Hrrto, with curt nods to everyone in the room. The bearded Codep trader and the stout independent trader followed with the Alreldep admiral and the small Hayuman male from Terra and a gaggle of others he'd never seen.

Jilamey Landreau interested Hrrto. His spies had informed him that Landreau was well connected in government, industry, and the arts, and had tremendous credit. His financial acumen was much respected despite his youth, for none of his ventures ever seemed to lose money. Landreau dressed much more colorfully than any negotiator or diplomat should, in Hrrto's opinion; almost Hrruban in style. At least the Hayuman understood the order of precedence, as he greeted Hrrto first on entering the room.

"Second Speaker, you honor us by your presence!" Landreau said, bowing with hand on heart. His warm brown eyes held a twinkle. "Why, good morning, Commander Greene! You're looking well."

The Hayuman commander offered a meaningless pleasantry and swung immediately back to the Spacedep admiral. Landreau slouched into the seat between the scarlet-haired banker and Todd Reeve, and began a cheerful conversation.

More, totally unknown Hrrubans arrived, bowing sharply to Hrrto from the doorway. Then Prrid emerged from the group and proceeded to his side of the table.

"I must be here to welcome the Gringg captain," Prrid murmured in High Hrruban in Hrrto's ear. "Then I will join you in the spaceport discussions. Mrrunda attends it now."

Hrrto approved with a nod, and Prrid seated himself. The Space Arm commandant, too, would be facing Gringg. Hrrto mulled over Prrid's probable reactions to Captain Grizz. Quite likely it would only reinforce Prrid's doubts about the Gringg's real purpose in approaching Rraladoona.

There was a stir and a hubbub of voices in the corridor outside. Todd Reeve observed it, too. Hrrto tilted his ears toward the door and rolled them back again as he felt an uncomfortable sensation at the back of his neck.

"I think our third party has arrived," said Reeve, rising.

Hastily, Hrrin, as co-host, sprang to his feet. Into the chamber swung Grizz, looking even larger than before. Hrrto had to restrain an impulse to lean back, away from her. She was truly overwhelming as she strode into the room. The floor seemed to bounce with the weight of her and her four companions.

Someone, thought Hrrto, ought to tell her to keep her lips over her fangs, despite the fact that an open mouth was for her species, like his, a sign of friendliness. Then Hrrto noticed that the stripe fur of every single Hrruban bristled with an instinctive reaction. Except for his, he was excessively pleased to note. He could also hear the faint whistle of lashing tails as Grizz's head brushed the top of the doorway. The resounding roar she used for a voice filled the room, overpowering the efforts of the small translator at her throat to compensate. Hrrto's heart pounded. So bizarre for the female of a species to be larger than the male. She quite dwarfed the males in her entourage.

"Hold it, hold it there, Grizz," a narrow, dark-skinned Hayuman said, running up to the giant beast with a small tool. "We're getting harmonics here, lady bear."

Lady bear? Hrrto was taken aback by such familiarity, such lack of basic decorum. Beside him, he could sense Mllaba's tension. He gave her a warning glance to settle the fur on her nape, but when he turned to Prrid, the naval commandant had already smoothed himself. Good Stripe, that Prrid.

With five Gringg, the room became suddenly as crowded as a package of fish, and he could see more in the corridor. They were so imposing that just a few of them looked like an invading army. Perhaps calling the Space Arm had not been such a bad idea. The Hayuman made adjustments to the captain's speech device and stepped away.

"That . . . good, gggrrr, better, best," said the Gringg, swinging a huge paw to touch the male gently on the shoulder. Her voder had modified her speech to a much more pleasing pitch.

Without the subsonics exacerbating his nerves, Hrrto relaxed. Strange that just sound could produce such effects. But others looked very much on their guard. Merely the presence of the immense Gringg held an aura of threat. Did they count on that?

"Wrrrfgruh . . . I grrreet you all," Grizz said, turning her head to include all the occupants of the table. "Hayumans and Hrrubans both."

"On behalf of Doonarrala," Todd Reeve said, "I greet you, Captain Grzzeearoghh, and welcome you to the first in a series of talks which, we deeply hope, will benefit us all."

The device at his throat translated his words from good Middle Hrruban into inarticulate growls and coughs. Hrrto laid back his ears. Some of the growling fell below his range of hearing, and sound shocks flew up and down his spine.

The great captain inclined her head. Todd swept his hand around the room to include the cushions on the unoccupied side of the table. "I hope these will be adequate."

The captain nodded absently in approval as she asked, "Two peoples are you Hayumans and Hrrubans?"

"That is corrrect, Madam Captain," Hrrin replied, courteously. "Here on Rraladoona we proudly sharrre a world, but we are of separate origins and species. If you and your prrrty will be seated, we shall begin."

"No. Two rooms are needed," the Gringg said, and folded her paws over her chest with a gesture of finality. "I have brought two pairs of Gringg, to speak to you separately."

"But why?" Todd asked, surprised.

"Here are two peoples. We honor your individuality. It is possible you each need different things from us, that you supply us with different items or units. It is only courteous to give individual attention to each of you. Therefore, two separate negotiations shall be held." The translator punctuated the Hrruban phrases with growls and hums, but Grizz's meaning was clear.

Hrrto felt his ears lean backward. This was not proceeding according to plan. And yet, without the Hayumans in the room, the subject of purralinium could be brought up without fear that the Hayumans would understand its importance to the Hrruban economy.

Be that as it may, Hrrto did not entirely trust this new development. These aliens were dangerous. Did they intend to divide and conquer, to promise vital goods and services to the Hayumans in private, cheating the Hrrubans of equal opportunities? Purralinium was not the only raw material Hrruba lacked. Depressed, Hrrto could see complications looming.

Admiral Barnstable seemed no happier with the Gringg captain's proposal, for he leaned across the table toward Reeve.

"Conference, Rrev," he ordered in High Hrruban. Quickly, Reeve turned to the towering Gringg and made a deep bow.

"A moment's pause, Captain," Reeve said through the translator and beckoned urgently to Hrrin. "We had not expected a division."

The Gringg lifted a paw in acceptance and sat down on the cushions, waiting with cheerful patience.

Second Speaker, Hrrin, and Mllaba joined the Admiral, Greene, Captain Hrrrv, Castleton, the two Reeves, and Hrrin and Kiachif in the furthest corner from the Gringg. Mllaba's nape hair stuck straight out in agitation. Greene looked grim; Castleton, curious.

"This will not do, Reeve," the Admiral muttered as they assembled. "I insist that we establish a single round table for any trade agreements. Each of our two races must have absolutely identical treatment and consideration. No covert clauses."

"Nonsense, nails, and nuts," Captain Kiachif said, scoffing at the red-faced Spacedep official. "That'd be the end of free enterprise—see if it isn't. Why not let it be their way? What's the harm of it? If we don't like what they have to offer, we insist on a joint parley tomorrow, if you follow me. Nothing's to stop us from convening, comparing, and combining."

"Nor am I comfortable with zis," Hrrto said, covering his voder with one hand. "I prefer open confrrrnce."

"But isn't zis preferable, Second Speaker?" Hrrin asked. "Hrruba's individuality maintained, and ze same for Amalgamated Wrrlds."

Hrrto glared, but he could detect no note of sarcasm in the Rraladoonan's voice. Those born on this colony planet really did lack many of the basic courtesies and tact which he felt his due.

"It is a dangrrrous ploy," agreed Captain Hrrrv, eyes gleaming.

Reeve dismissed that remark. "If we want the Gringg to feel comfortable among us, we should do our best to accommodate a reasonable request. I concur with Captain Kiachif. Let's go along with the Gringg's wishes today. We can use, uh—" he glanced around for a view of the hall—"the conference room in the research library as the other chamber. It's just down the hall and around the corner from the spaceport business."

"This is not as planned," Second said, reverting again to High Hrruban in his dismay. "Hrruba and Terra must take the lead here, not these strangers."

"It would seem, Honored sir," Ken Reeve said, replying in the same language, "that we must oblige our guests—today, at least."

Only because the privacy suited Hrrto's needs did he give consent. Graciously leaving the Hrrubans in possession of the Treaty Chamber, Todd led the Hayumans, the Gringg captain, and one of the pairs of males out of the door and away to the right.

Hrrto watched them leave. Could he trust any one of the Hayumans to give him an accurate account of what transpired in their session? Possibly his erstwhile allies in Spacedep would not dissemble too much. Still, if he could get the purralinium, he might just win the election on that score. He caught Nrrena staring at him. His direct and haughty glance made her look away again, her chin lowered in momentary embarrassment. How dare Fifth's representative look askance in his direction! He nodded just once at Hurrhee, who gave the barest of nods in understanding.

As soon as the Hayumans and the three Gringg had gone, Hrrin gestured for the others to be seated. With only two Gringg in the room, everyone seemed to breathe more freely.

"As long as we are now together," he said in Middle Hrruban, dropping his jaw in a pleasant smile, "perhaps we should begin by introducing ourselves."

To Todd's surprise, the engineer Koala was waiting a little way down from the Treaty Chamber with Commander Frill, Lieutenant Cardiff, and a few other Gringg males whom Todd hadn't met before.

"Afternoon, Mr. Reeve," the burly xenotech said, grinning. "Didn't think you'd be free."

"Frill and I are going to show Koala the sights," Cardiff explained. "These are a few of her assistants. We've got a powwow later with a consortium of scientists from your colony and both cruisers. Nothing sensitive, of course, just general stuff, like that resonator of theirs. Good luck!" He escorted the troop of Gringg down the corridor toward the landing field. "You can raise me by belt radio if you need to!" he called over his shoulder.

"Thanks, Lieutenant," Todd replied. Weddeerogh waddled shyly up to Todd and touched his hand with a wet, black nose, then turned to bestow the same greeting on Ken.

"Hello, little guy," Todd said, pausing to ruffle the cub's pate hairs. "Welcome to Doonarrala." Then he turned to Grizz, and turned his voder on again. "The other room is just down here, Captain."

"Morra," Grizz said, looking down on them fondly from her great height. "I do not discuss trading matters. I seek to visit your home village. Much has been told me that I wish to see with my own eyes," she said in slow Hrruban. The translator produced remarkably accurate pronunciation. "These two"—she pointed a claw at Eonneh and another Gringg, a male with silky gray fur—"I trust to make best trade speech for us types."

"Of course," Todd said, surprised on the one hand but pleased on the other. He'd wanted Grizz to see for herself what her emissaries had. "I'll see you're gridded up to First Village. My wife, Kelly, and Nrrna, Hrriss' mate, will be delighted to host you in our homes. Allow me to send a message for them to meet you."

"You are most very kind," Grizz said, pausing between words to remember what was appropriate to say.

"Are you sure that is wise, Reeve?" Greene demanded, hand over his voder input. "Sending a . . . a being of her stature to a civilian habitation unescorted?"

Todd understood exactly what the commander really meant, and refused to acknowledge it.

"I admit it might be considered rude to ship the highest-ranking official of a delegation somewhere without the correct entourage, but perhaps," he said, with a bow and a smile to Grizz, "under the circumstances she will forgive me. She will be met on arrival, of course, by my wife, who is, by the way, an Alreldep representative, and quite capable of handling our new friends."

Barnstable shot both of them a look of annoyance, and Todd understood that the criticism must actually have come from him. Spacedep's paranoia was beginning to wear upon Todd. Grizz, who had followed only part of the swift, low-pitched conversation, showed her fangs amiably. The gesture made most of the Human delegates shiver, and Todd grinned back at her.

"I forgive without reserve, Todd Reeve," Grizz said. "I and my son look forward to seeing the beauties of your home which these others have described to me. And this one"—she patted her son's shoulder—"is eager to swim in Doonarralan waters."

"Well, Admiral, Commander," Todd said, "don't let me keep you from your duties. The spaceport conference is just down the hall, you know." Then he turned to Sumitral, Ali, and Jilamey. "You all know the place we're to use. Why don't you show our

Gringg negotiators the way? I'll join you soon as I can."

After he had called Kelly to tell her to meet her guests, he conducted Grizz and her cub out of the Treaty Building and to the grid facility. As there seemed to be no limit to the weight a grid could shift, he did not worry about the mass of a female Gringg.

But the mass of the personage to be gridded quite shattered the composure of the bored grid operator. The slim female Hrruban on duty froze, her neck hair bristling, and gaped in shock at the pair to be transported to First Village.

"Zis grid is only for small shipments," she protested, anxiously glancing over Todd's shoulder at Grizz.

"Oh, come now, the captain masses no more than some of those 'visitors' you've been bringing in all week," Todd said, cocking an eyebrow at her. Then he pointed to the schedule hung above her control board. "You've got an opening of almost ten minutes before you receive the next pallets. Captain Grzzeearoghh is a person of importance. She shouldn't have to hang about here with you, now should she?"

"No, sirrrr, no!" the Hrruban gasped. "Step up onto ze platfrrm, most honrrrred guests, please!" She gestured the Gringg between the slim transmission pillars and fumbled to key in the coordinates.

"I know you'll enjoy your visit, Captain," Todd said, waving. "Kelly will be waiting for you!"

"G'bye!" Weddeerogh said, waving both his paws energetically. As the mist rose and began to swallow him up, he squealed on such a note that the grid operator laid back her ears.

The conference room which Todd entered on his return was providentially carpeted, floor and walls, in a warm, burnt orange that complemented the golden woods of the furniture frames. The padding on the walls would baffle some of the more annoying overtones of Gringg speech. The chairs, upholstered in the same handsome orange, were set around a well-polished table of golden hardwood. Several computer monitors on swivel boards occupied positions on the tabletop and could be turned to face any direction.

Someone had brought in the cushions which the Gringg preferred and placed them on one side of the large square table. Ken Reeve, the merchant captains, Sumitral and Jilamey, and some Humans Todd didn't know were occupying the chairs on the opposing side. Todd was annoyed to find Commander Greene also present. Barnstable was eating his cake in the spaceport discussions and having it, too, with Greene here to listen to trade talks. Todd did recognize several Doonarralan representatives of the craft- and farm-collectives. These men and women were trying not to appear awed by the company in which they found themselves.

"Are you comfortable now?" Sumitral was asking. "I would be happy to sit on the floor. We could move the table."

"Eye to eye, please, is Gringg way," Eonneh said politely. "Sofas are fine for Gringg, chairs for you, thank you." The translator had picked up the unfamiliar word "cushions," and given the Gringg the closest equivalent it had. "New friends, I am Eonneh, named Honey by a child of this world. I approve the name, as I consider it the first step to close links with your people. This is Krrpuh. You call him Coypu—easier to say."

Todd had to restrain a broad smile. He recalled, and cherished, the memory of the Gringg being assigned "bear" names by his twins and Hrriss' two eldest. The youngsters took the naming responsibility very seriously, having made a list of every synonym or cognate for "bear" that could be found in Terran philology. He remembered Hrrunival being peeved that his planet had no corollary creature. They matched names as closely as they could to the Gringg sounds, delighting the recipients.

"We welcome you, Honey and Coypu," Todd said formally and started introducing those present. He could hear rapid footsteps on the marble floors as latecomers hurried to the new venue.

As Todd recited the Humans' names, the Gringg sniffed subtly in the appropriate direction, obviously pairing scent with face. Sumitral raised the corner of his mouth in a wry smile as he realized what they were doing. Horstmann was the only one who seemed slightly uneasy. Jilamey, seated at the far corner beside Honey, winked as Todd named him. The tool-and-die maker from Rompiel was frowning abstractedly, trying not to stare at the two Gringg. Commander Greene spoke in low, urgent tones to Horstmann, who turned a shoulder on him; then the navy man stared piercingly at Todd. Todd tried to ignore Greene. The man's blatant Human chauvinism grated on him.

Todd had had a furious discussion about Greene with Barnstable after returning to the *Hamilton*, concerning Greene's near-disastrous antics on the Gringg ship. That the aide had been responsible for initiating the intruder probe was bad enough, but carrying an explosive device onto a vessel assumed to be peaceful defied all reason. Todd had made it clear to Barnstable that either act could have compromised matters beyond recall, and he insisted that Greene be left behind on the flagship whenever Barnstable came groundside. The Admiral refused, demanding his right to such escort as he required. He resented Todd's criticism of a member of his staff, and pointed out again that Doonarrala's priorities and Spacedep's were not identical. Todd hoped he wouldn't have to go all the way to the Amalgamated Worlds Council to keep Spacedep from causing more trouble.

During the weeks of research on the voder, Greene had been around and about on Doonarrala, always maintaining his distance from Todd, but always there, like an annoying itch Todd couldn't get rid of. Since none of the ursine guests had mentioned Greene, Todd decided that they hadn't noticed the burly commander, or were choosing to ignore his surveillance. The Spacedep officers hadn't been subtle when following the Gringg, as if they'd hoped for some kind of incident which would allow them to step in and take command.

Nothing had happened, and Todd hoped Greene and his spies had gotten bored stiff.

Honey seemed to be in good spirits. He had visited Doonarrala nearly every other day, touring schools, factories, and farms, and spending much time in the villages. He was easily the most recognizable of the Gringg. His companion, who moved with a ponderousness dilatory even for a Gringg, seemed to be older than Honey, with a majestic, slow bass voice that was so low it rumbled through Todd's very bones. Both of them had small computer devices with sculpted depressions, which were probably operated by the rhythmic manipulation of claws, something like the device used by an old-time court reporter. As usual Honey held his ubiquitous tile-like tablet. Jilamey, at Honey's elbow, was keeping a close eye on the Gringg, waiting for him to draw or write something with the double-looped pen that lay atop it on the table.

By then, the tardy delegates had arrived, slightly breathless, and more time was taken up by introductions.

Of the seven newcomers, five were clearly alarmed by the size of the Gringg, and although they were wearing voders, only one had practiced with his device. And Todd instantly marked Emil Markudian, a swarthy-faced man with a prominent, hooked nose and black eyes, as trouble. His companion, for the man seemed unwilling to move away from Markudian's side, was Brad Ashland, and he was not only plainly terrified by the aliens, but his eyes had the glitter of the xenophobe.

When he noticed them darting quick glances at Greene, he decided they bore close scrutiny. Well, he should have expected something like this after Barnstable's little confrontation of assorted blow-ins at Kate Moody's office. The others who had arrived in the wake of Markudian seemed to be legitimate, since they all carried portfolios with the logos of major, diversified Terran or colonial companies. Two found Jilamey's presence distinctly unsettling. Remembering how chuffed Jilamey had been about his coup, Todd grinned to himself and then turned the meeting over to Admiral Sumitral, seated directly opposite the Gringg envoys.

Once introductions of the new arrivals had been made, there was a perceptible pause. Todd sensed an electrical tension rising among them, veiled excitement. *I feel as if we're about to start a high-stakes poker game,* he thought. *Who's going to bluff whom?*

"We begin from ignorance," Admiral Sumitral said, rising to address the Gringg. "You have been among us for many days now and seen us going about our work and play. We know nothing about your world, and desire similar information."

"Ah," said Coypu, resting his paws on his large belly, "very kind of you to ask. Our world is much like this, gravity heavier and more water in many big pools. We are four ships to explore. Long, long, long"—and he nodded his head to emphasize the span—"looking. It is good, great news to find two at once!" He dropped his jaw and looked about him, his eyes twinkling.

"You say your objective is to trade, yet you admit that you are very far from your homeworld. How can you possibly trade profitably over long distances?" Commander Greene wanted to know.

"Big ship," replied Coypu succinctly. "We come prepared with offerings. Trading is good with peaceful people. You have much here which will be tradable."

"Such as?" Greene demanded sarcastically.

"You are out of order, Commander," Sumitral said, turning slightly so that his body shielded him from the Gringg. He had covered his translator and spoke in a low but carrying tone, somehow managing not to move his lips very much. "As Spacedep personnel, you are present only to observe!"

"We have seen much here on Doonarrala that will be very appreciated on our world," Honey added. "We are peaceful traders."

"It's very easy to say that you come in peace," Markudian spoke up, his deep voice smooth but holding an edge.

That statement elicited quiet gasps around the table. Todd had seen no signal from Greene, but that didn't keep him from suspecting the two might be acting in concert.

Sumitral regarded Markudian with an expression of mild surprise and astonishment, but it was Coypu who answered.

"It is easy to say what is true," Coypu said, either not offended or deliberately not understanding Markudian's implication. Now he lifted his paws. "We come far from our homeworld, seeking new worlds, hopefully new peoples."

"You are peaceful types, also," Honey said, looking around the table and nodding his appreciation of that fact. "It is very good for Gringg to see that two different species can live in peace without acchggt-sppppput . . ." He turned to Coypu as his voder could not give a suitable translation of the Gringg word.

" . . . without tearing the collar?" Coypu suggested.

"Tearing the collar?" Sumitral asked, pointedly asking for an explanation.

Coypu touched his ornate neckpiece with one delicate claw. "Yes, to tear off the collar of a Gringg is to start fight, but only if there is no other honor choice."

"Oh, similar to throwing down a gauntlet . . . a glove . . . a hand protector," Sumitral said, ignoring the mutters from some of those nervous about this discussion. "Of course, duels with lethal weapons have long been considered against the law as well as against common sense."

Coypu seemed oddly pleased to hear that. "With us, too, the custom has declined. There are nearly always other choices. We enjoy peace. Gringg do not like to exert themselves. Peace takes much less energy than combat, do you not agree?"

Todd laughed at the beautiful simplicity of the statement. "War is too much trouble?"

"War?" Coypu asked, for the word had been carefully omitted from the voder's lexicon.

"War," Greene said, jumping at the opportunity, "is when many tear the collar and join a fight; the winners take all. A great exertion," he added sarcastically.

"War is a thing of the past for both species. It was always a useless exertion," Sumitral said in such an icy voice and with such an icy stare directed at Greene that the commander subsided, mostly in surprise at the Alreldep admiral's intensity.

"Good! Good!" Coypu said seriously. "I tire if I think about it. Cooperation takes so much less work."

"Then Gringg have had wars?" Markudian asked, leaning forward.

"Long ago," Honey said negligently, "to protect the family pool and the landing place, and our young when there was not enough to eat."

That mildly delivered statement brought quite a reaction around the table. Todd and his father exchanged concerned glances.

"Then, during the Great Heat, we were forced to seek refuge in the deepest caves. It was then that we were forced to eat many things other than the beasts which had been our natural food," Honey went on, blithely unaware of the effect his first statement was having. "When we emerged from the caves, we turned to the sea and began to hunt the big fish. Little ones, too, which are often very tasty."

"But you *were* cannibals?" Markudian demanded, with such an air of superiority that Todd knew the man was there to cause whatever trouble he could. Unfortunately Honey had just handed him a perfect opening.

As Sumitral was trying to explain the word "cannibals" to Honey, Todd leaned toward Markudian.

"The emphasis was on a trade vocabulary, Mr. Markudian. We cannot, and will not, at this time, accept the discussion of side issues."

When Honey and Coypu finally understood, they both looked mournful.

"When we were very young beings, long, long, long ago, before we learned to think what we were doing, before we learned how much easier it was to work together instead of separately," Honey said, leaning forward, paws crossed over his chest in humility—"we Gringg did many stupid things we do not like to remember doing. Perhaps this happened to Hayumans, too, when your species was learning wisdom?"

"Not cannibalism," Markudian said firmly.

Sumitral gave a droll chuckle. "Mr. Markudian, you are obviously not much of a student of Terran history or you would realize how wrong you are on that point." Then Sumitral bent a stern look upon the man. "But you cannot be so young as to be ignorant of the Siwannah Tragedy, in which humans caused an entire race to suicide. I also feel that you speak out too hastily, Mr. Markudian, and I advise you to think very carefully the next time you feel obliged to criticize." Then he turned to Honey and Coypu. "We also had to learn to cope with famines. I trust there is no famine on your homeworld now that has sent you out on your long journey."

"No, not famine," Coypu said. "We wish to find new worlds. We wish to trade with same peaceful people."

"Let's get back to trade talk, shall we?" asked Jilamey a bit impatiently, giving Markudian a very jaundiced look for his interruptions. "Let's talk about what sort of payment we'll use for trade items."

"Excellent idea, my dear Landreau," Sumitral said. He turned to the Gringg. "In trading with our Hrruban friends, we use certain minerals and metals on which we have agreed to a value."

"Do you not use symbolic currencies?" Coypu asked. There was a murmur of surprise among the merchants.

"Yes, of course we do," Jilamey said, "but our credits would be worthless to you in your own system, so let us find other values for barter."

Ken Reeve said, "Eonneh and I have discussed molecular structures of certain metals and minerals that we would like to acquire in moderate quantities. What mediums have value for you?"

"We discuss a common trade currency?" Honey asked mildly, rattling his claws in the holes of his computerlike device. "Held perhaps on this planet in a central place for all three to use? With . . . ahccccgg . . . writings that can be strictly kept accurate?"

Ashland looked stunned. Jumping from cannibalism in a distant past to modern finance was too big a leap for him. Markudian's expression became darker than ever.

"A banking system is, of course, an excellent idea," Sumitral said, raising his eyebrows in silent query at the two, who blinked agreement.

"If you become permanent trading partners with us . . ." Jilamey began slowly, allowing the possibility to sink in, "a central place would simplify all transactions."

"Trading partners for a long time we want," Honey replied, and gave them a huge white grin.

Kiachif whistled. "For critters who've never seen other aliens before, you sure take the long view."

Honey bowed to Kiachif, inclining his long torso. "We are hopeful creatures, and in that hope much discussion occupied our long travels and what to do if we find others." He hiked one shoulder in a very human gesture. "It passed the time, and now we discover that it was wise to plan for such acchtgg . . . possibles. For now"—he spread his big paws—"we put theory into practice. It is not much different to the trading we do between our homeworld and its young."

"Young? You have colony worlds?" Sumitral said.

"Or subjugated worlds?" Greene asked, his eyes glittering.

Honey looked down at his voder, and Coypu looked puzzled.

"Acchgg?" Honey asked in query.

"That's quite enough from you, Greene," Sumitral said with the first flash of temper Todd had ever seen him display.

"You have set up colonies of Gringg on your young worlds? Yes, both Hayumans and Hrrubans have done the same. Have you found worlds with the different species?" Ken asked quickly, smiling.

"You are the two first we have ever met. The other worlds were empty of *intelligent* lifes," Coypu said, and even the translator echoed the regret in his manner. "Creatures with no thought of more than full stomachs, or things that were inedible, even for Gringg. Each has its place on that world. We do not interfere unless threatened."

"And if threatened, what do you use to protect yourself?" Greene asked, ignoring Sumitral's exclamation of aggravation.

"We are able to defend ourselves," Honey said blandly, and unsheathed his claws. Coypu retracted his lips, uncovering his white fangs. "We are larger than any edible creature we have met."

"And not as dumb," Jilamey said, giving Greene a look of pure disgust.

"How many colony worlds have you now?" Sumitral asked before Greene could continue.

Honey held up four fingers. "Four! One with very good water." His jaw dropped and he gave himself a wiggle that suggested total approval of it.

"Far from here," Coypu added. "A very long journey, but not impossible to make for Hayumans."

"We are translating our maps to yours," Honey said. "Slow because of vision differences and because we are far from the star patterns we know and guide our ships by."

"Let's stick with trade values," Todd said, and leaned across the table to Honey with the chart he had been making on his keypad. "What's of value to you might not be as valuable to us, so we'll need to establish the variables and work out percentages of increased value for temporary rarity of stock and other factors. This one time, I hope you will accept the values we use to pay for traded things between Hayumans and Hrrubans. We think the values are fair."

"It is just what I expect of the peoples who live together in peace," Honey replied. His simple frankness drew mutters from the other delegates.

Todd was relieved that the two Gringg had evidently not caught the blatant animosity in Greene's words and manner. "We can discuss the subject of values in more detail at the end of the meeting so you can key it in your own language."

Suddenly Horstmann, who had been growing more impatient, slapped both hands down on the table to divert attention to himself. "Let's also cut this confounded cackle. Let's find out what commodities you Gringg are interested in. And what you have to offer us. Those resonators Cardiff used in these voders would make a good start. Small, powerful, and I haven't ever seen anything like 'em from Terra nor Hrruba. Can we do a deal on them?"

"Any technological items will first have to be cleared by the Scientific Council of Amalgamated Worlds," Greene said.

Jilamey brushed that contingency aside. "Not according to the Doonarrala Treaty, they don't, Greene. Look, Honey, you've had time over the last weeks to see just what's available on Doonarrala, which I think is a fair sampling of goods drawn from both Hayuman and Hrruban. Technology? Medical or scientific processes? Tools?"

"We have many desirable commodities to trade, as well as the product of our skills," Eonneh began ponderously.

"Good," Kiachif said. "My ships don't like to make the trip back to ol' Terra empty. Give us a f'rinstance or two, friend."

"Also, our four young—colony—worlds have many valuable minerals in quantity. To trade here are listed molecular patterns with Gringg names. Some I do not see in use here or do not recognize. Maybe we bring you new stuff?" Honey dropped his jaw, suddenly a little like Kiachif, anticipating a major trade deal. Todd put his hand to his mouth to hide a smile. "Our friend Chilmeh has spoken to us also about gaining credit from the sale of drawings and works of art. We are pleased to see that you consider these things to be of value. Culture has value on your planets even as it has on ours. We feel that we may also learn technology stuff from you, sharing information. Already we have share technology"—he tapped the voder with the tip of one claw—"with Lootcardiff." Sumitral, Ken, and Todd openly grinned at the combination of rank and name. "We are happy to share information freely in exchange for also you share freely with us."

Greene and Markudian both began to protest, but Ashland was eager to know "information about what?"

"You can't want just cultural things and to share," Jilamey said. "That could be very one-sided and we insist on giving equal value to trading partners."

Honey inclined his head. "You give equal value sharing with us the delights of this planet of Doonarrala."

Todd could see Greene interpreting that to mean acquisition, and hastily intervened.

"Peaceful people deserve proper hospitality when their intent is good," Todd said, and Sumitral stared Greene back down into his seat.

"The matter has been discussed thoroughly among the captain's staff and by space-transmission with the motherworld," the golden Gringg said. "What we search most earnestly—besides peaceful people—is a source of protein, for"—he turned his deep red eyes on Markudian—"we are civilized peoples who do not eat meat of each other. Especially when here you have many delicious proteins."

Greene's mouth was open in amazement at Eonneh's dry humor.

Eonneh showed all his teeth. "Hayumans seem to have the most superior idea of what is a good thing to eat."

"Well, as it happens, Honey," Jilamey said, beaming from ear to ear, "we process a lot of protein in nutritious and delicious forms, and I happen to represent a large consortium which can provide you with a wide range of truly delicious and healthful comestibles . . ." His voder faltered on that word. "Stuff to eat—eatables, edibles," he hastily explained.

Coypu gave a startlingly deep grunt, signifying pleasure, for he had dropped his jaw. "Good. We wish to import to our world bulk or packaged largenesses of snake meat, fishes, beef, poultry, and of course, the stuff you name popcorn. It is not high in protein, but it is most entertaining to watch it cook and it can be seasoned in many flavors."

"Food?" Sumitral asked weakly. "You want food? Not technology?"

"Morra," Eonneh assured him. "If at all, some forms of Gringg electrics—"

"Electronics," Todd corrected.

"—electronics are more efficient than yours."

"You think that?" Markudian said indignantly.

"Our scientists know that after talking with yours," Honey replied. "Scientific fact is fact for all of us."

"A science conference just is not possible at this point in time," Greene said flatly. "Discuss food all you want. That's safe enough."

"Nonaggressive science is also safe," Sumitral said with equal firmness. He put his hand over his translator. "If they have no ordnance, Greene, then why not discuss science? Now that we know what their need is, I think you can step down from that Red Alert you're on."

"Just so long as *we're* not the food resource they have in mind," Greene said, but he also covered the voder as he added in a savage tone, "These peaceful people of yours are not as peaceful as they've all conned you into believing."

With that, he rose from his chair and stalked from the room.

After Greene's ominous remark, Todd was relieved to see the back of him. He was undoubtedly going off to report to Admiral Barnstable. Greene's crack about the Gringg eating Humans was asinine—especially when the snakes were larger, more numerous, and far tastier.

"You don't require metals?" Markudian asked, surprised.

"Yes, some metals are in short supply with us, and please to give us samples of all you use," Honey said. "But mostly we need foods," and he leaned forward, an earnest expression on his face. "Already, many on the homeworld are most eager to try Doonarralan snake meat. Having heard the praise it has from those who have taste it here, it will be a much sought-after delicacy. Perhaps you can show us how to breed the snakes on one of our worlds. One snake can feed several Gringg. As we learn to know each other better, I am sure there will be other goods we want, but for the present, we are eager to obtain largenesses of Hayuman-manufactured eating stuffs. That is all."

"Unbelievable," Markudian said, staring perplexed at the Gringg.

Jilamey threw back his head and let out a delighted laugh. "After all of our posturing and careful management, timid questions, and demand for sureties, food is what they need!" The Reeves and Kiachif chuckled with him.

As the Hayumans and the Gringg left the room, Hrrto was for a long moment too annoyed to gather his thoughts. The only advantage to the new arrangement would be the privacy to mention purralinium—if the Gringg had it. There wasn't a Hrruban here who didn't realize how vital it was to replenish the supply of that transuranic ore. Even Hrrin would appreciate that. But Hrrto saw that he would have to remain here longer than he had anticipated, to be sure the negotiations secured them at least the hope of the grid metal. Mllaba was also irritated. It wouldn't be her preference to be stuck discussing trade when she considered the spaceport conference a better place for Hrrto to show his merits. But her irritation also stemmed from the presence of the two Gringg across the table from her who were settling their big haunches into their cushions. Beside him, Hrrin sat with folded arms, watching as if he expected the Gringg to spring forward in an assault.

The subsonics in their voices were not entirely masked by the voders, from the keener Hrruban hearing, so the buzz and annoying vibration were still present, heavy in the air. At Hrriss' tactful reminder, the Gringg had been careful to modulate the volume of their speech, but they could do nothing to cushion the impact of their mere presence. Hrrto was rapidly developing a painful headache, one of the first in a long and healthy life. He tried to concentrate on what Hrrestan, who chaired the meeting, was saying.

Hrrestan was assisting the Gringg in their translations when the limits of the programmed vocabulary failed. Hrrto felt some respect for the colony leader's ability to retain what sounded to him like the roar and sputtering of malfunctioning motors. He was feeling yet another painful twinge, when Mllaba leaned toward him, her hand over the translator input grille.

"I dislike the uncouth way they sniff at us, Speaker," Mllaba hissed under her breath. She spoke in a very high-pitched whisper which the Gringg were unlikely to hear. "So primitive."

All the homeworld Hrrubans attending the trade meeting were initially disturbed by the Gringg behavior, but as the aliens proved to be affable and intelligent, they began to relax. Hrrto did not—torn between the need to introduce purralinium and memories of that tape. He wanted to be able to at least warn these Rraladoonans—since they were, in the final analysis, also Hrruban—that the Gringg were dangerous; warn them not to rush into discussions that would display their vulnerability to the Gringg; warn them to learn as much about Gringg customs and culture as the Gringg were learning about theirs. But he could not yet speak of that tape, not until the combined navies were in position. They were still some days away. Until then, Hrrto was forced to dissemble. He also had until then to discover the coordinates of systems that might produce purralinium. With difficulty, he turned his attention to the proceedings.

While Hrrestan was basically a sensible Hrruban, he appeared to be badly infected with young Rrev's enthusiasm. Perhaps, Hrrto thought, it might be wise to tell Hrrestan about that damning tape. Hrrestan was of an old Stripe and did not deserve the fate that might await other Rraladoonans when their seemingly cultured and civilized visitors showed the violent side of their natures. But Hrrestan was so honorable a Stripe that he might feel obliged to impart that information to Rrev. No, no warning to anyone until the fleet was in place.

Then the aliens produced a computer program showing molecular diagrams of the minerals they were ready to use as trade mediums. Hrrto shot a warning glance at Hurrhee, who was already trying to see what was on offer.

"These ores are available in quantity now from our mining worlds," said the one called Kodiak. "We have printed diagrams for you to compare with your molecular data. If you require any of these ores, we are pleased to offer them to you as goods for barter against our own requirements."

"I am sure we can come to agreeable terms for all parties," Hrrestan said.

"Indeed we should," Hurrhee murmured, flicking a confirming glance at Hrrto. "We have often found a use for this"—he extended a nail to delicately single out one item—"impure as it is."

Hrrto inwardly sighed with relief. They did have purralinium to offer.

"What is Hurrhee doing here?" Mllaba demanded in an annoyed undertone to Hrrto. "He's a scientist, not a trader."

"He is here at my command," Hrrto murmured back, protruding the claw of his fifth digit to indicate the need for discretion.

Suddenly Mllaba became extra alert and leaned as far across the table as possible to get a view of the slate. Under the table, Hrrto pulled her roughly back. She nearly hissed at him, so great was her indignation, but one look at her superior's eyes and she obeyed, though stiff with the insult just given her. Hrrto ignored her manner. Nothing must indicate to the Gringg how important the purralinium was to the Hrrubans.

Although Kodiak and his partner, a black-and-white Gringg whom the children called Big Paws after Zodd's sister's cat, were speaking very clear Middle Hrruban, modulated into audibility by the voders, the edge imparted by the subsonics of Gringg speech wore on Hrruban nerves.

Hrrto wondered how long he would have to remain in such an ambience.

"Yes, you do have goods that might form a trade currency," banker Hrrouf said with extreme affability, his tail tip switching. Ah, Hrrouf had noticed the purralinium, too. And, in his high position in the financial world, he would know about the lack of new supplies of the metal. "What is it you would require in exchange?"

Big Paws regarded the Hrruban amiably and folded his enormous hands on the table.

"You appear to be comfortable without the clothes used by Hayumans to cover their skin. We Gringg also do not need coverings. We admire the way that the Hrrubans adorn their natural fur with the most striking ornamentation. Most especially I like these harnesses of hide." The black and white Gringg put out a claw and plucked at the strap of the handsome harness Hrrouf was wearing. "The variety of these and of other pretty stuffs are most desirable to us. Such will be need to be made much larger to fit Gringg, but we wish to trade for quantities of harness. Plain and with many sparkle stones."

"What?" Hrrouf demanded, unable to believe his ears.

Other Hrruban representatives were equally astounded, and if Hrrestan and Hrrin managed to hide their amusement, few of the others—expecting to trade advanced technologies of all kinds with the Gringg—saw the humor of the announcement.

Second Speaker sputtered, his headache forgotten. "Garments? Jewelry? Ornaments? You must be joking!"

"What is joking?" Kodiak asked, looking up from his electronic keypad. He turned to Hrrestan for clarification.

"He asks if you tell him something that is not true to make him laugh," Hrrestan explained solemnly.

Kodiak returned his dark-red gaze to Second Speaker. "Morra, very, I do not joke."

"This is what you wish to receive in trade from us? Not technology?" asked Nrrena. "Hrruban technology is famous. You must have observed the transport grids—"

"Sst!" Hrrouf hissed at her in a high whistle. The merchant stopped, embarrassed.

"Ah, yes," Kodiak said casually, observing the byplay. "The transport system. But it does not interest us. We travel fast enough and are comfortable doing it. Items of wear and personal adornment are more important. And we insist to be told new styles and modes."

Hrrto wondered at Kodiak's dismissal of the "transport system." Could it be that they *knew* the special use for purralinium and had matter transporters on their own worlds? And if they did, would they trade any of that precious commodity to the Hrrubans? Many of the Gringg had used the grids, getting about Rraladoona, but no reports had been made by any of the operators that the Gringg had shown any interest at all in the workings of the grid, or had even looked closely at either the purralinium columns or the floor grid, though these were, in any case, thickly coated by the conducting material.

"This is outrageous," Nrrena said in a growl, rising from the table. Her tail swished angrily, lashing her sides, and her eyes all but shot sparks. "I was made to understand that this was a high-level trading conference, not a fashion show. I have the honor to wish you a good day." The Hrruban made a bow to Second Speaker and strode stiffly from the room. Second was glad to see her go. She would report back to Fifth that the conference had been a charade. When Hrrto arranged for substantial quantities of purralinium, she would look a fool, Fifth would lose face and Hrrto gain it in the contest for the Speakership.

"Perhaps all should go," Hrrin suggested sourly, "and put an end to this pretense."

"Have I offended?" Kodiak asked Hrrestan.

"No, friend," Hrrestan assured him. "That Hrruban represents manufacturers on our homeworld and elsewhere. There is nothing in these current talks which interests her." Hrrestan also suspected that Nrrena would be grateful to get out of the range of Gringg speech. Kodiak accepted his explanation.

"Ah," the Gringg said, returning a bland gaze to those left at the table. "May we then negotiate terms? It is now to work out equivalencies of value, against that which we offer for that which we want." He ended up facing Hrrestan, who gestured courteously toward Hrrto.

"I may not speak for Hrruba," Hrrestan said. "I have lived on Rraladoona for over thirty years. It is the Second Speaker for External Affairs whom you must address." He bowed deferentially. Hrrto was pleased and mollified.

"Very," Kodiak said, and turned to face Second. Mllaba sat up straight beside him. "So you are empowered to act on behalf of all Hrruba in these matters?"

"I do not understand what he said," Mllaba snapped, turning to Hrrin. "Please translate once more."

With a little less patience for her, Hrrin repeated the Gringg's question.

Kodiak's brow ridges lowered halfway over his eyes, concealing all but a crescent of angry red irises. "I believe that the delegate understood me," he said, his voice shifting very slowly to a menacing growl. "We have come in good faith to this meeting. It is not the Gringg way to give offense or take insult. Lootcardiff caused this device to translate perfectly. As a Gringg scribe, my honor required me to practice diction until perfection came. Does this female have hearing problems? That is the only acceptable reason."

The word "reason" came out in as close to a snarl as a Gringg had so far mouthed. Mllaba jumped in her seat. She glared at Kodiak, her yellow eyes ablaze.

"You wrong me," she said in a low, dangerous voice. "My hearing is extremely acute and the roars you make injure delicate tissue. You know that certain sounds you cause unpleasant reactions in us Hrrubans. Perhaps you deliberately use them to upset us."

"Enough!" Hrrestan said, raising his voice. Hand over his voder, he turned to Mllaba, but his attitude was clearly cautioning. "There is not a thing wrong with my hearing, Mllaba, and I think you are the one deliberately upsetting the smooth progress of this meeting."

"Why should I?" Mllaba demanded.

"That I do not know," Hrrestan replied sternly, "but as I am moderator of this meeting, I will have no further obstruction from you."

"I am assistant to—"

"In this meeting," Hrrestan said calmly but forcefully, "rank has been suspended to the greater benefit of all Hrruba. Or have you had trouble, Honored Assistant to Second Speaker, which you are embarrassed to admit?"

Mllaba drew a deep breath in through her nostrils at what was perilously close to a direct insult to the Second Speaker. Hrrestan waited, his eyes intent on Hrrto, as though Mllaba did not exist.

"I have had no trouble understanding the Gringg," Second said, his eyes slitted. "I do find their voices and their presence oppressive."

"Oppressive?" Hrrestan asked, with mischief in his eyes. "How can you find oppressive a species which is so very interested in fashion?"

Mllaba's tail tip lashed.

"If the price is right," Hrrin said, deliberately trying to lighten the tension in the room, "we Rraladoonans are delighted to supply as many harnesses as the Gringg wish. Since"—he turned to the disappointed representatives—"we supply our homeworld with many such items, we may need to import skilled workers to supply the demand."

"Then we have wasted our time?" asked the senior Stripe of the merchants.

Hrrestan bowed graciously. "Consider it but the first offering in a trade that may develop in unexpected directions, and have the imagination to come forward with other examples of our *culture*"—he gave the last word considerable emphasis—"which might appear attractive or interesting to our large friends."

Then Mllaba, using a coaxing and wheedling tone, spoke up, her manner so abruptly altered that Hrrto decided his clever assistant must finally have grasped the significance of Hurrhee's presence and remarks.

"Hrruban textiles are much admired by Hayumans, since you are interested in adornment. A swift message and we can have many beautiful things to show you," she said at her silkiest.

"We Gringg are content to see all you will offer," Kodiak said, showing all his teeth in an affable smile.

"So," Hrrouf broke in, "you will not object if we ask for metals, ores, and suchlike as payment for our cloth, leather, and jewels?"

Kodiak lifted one shoulder. "Metals we have much of and can cheerfully trade them for what we wish of yours. Shall we talk of relative values now for such bartering?" He turned his slate and held it up so that all could see it. Gringg symbols were on the left-hand side of the slate, Hrruban equivalents on the right.

Purralinium was mid-list. "These are in order of value to us."

Titanium was at the top, and Hrrto recognized the symbols for tin, zinc, germanium, platinum, and some transuranics before purralinium. How many leather belts and neckpieces would be traded for enough purralinium to manufacture another grid? The very concept was bizarre!

He found himself holding his breath as weights and measures were being discussed. To his dismay—for surely Hrrestan knew their plight—the colony co-leader was settling for too low a quantity of metal. Or was he merely being cautious? Then Kodiak mentioned bulk figures for finished leathers that nearly made Hrrto drop his jaw. There would be more than enough purralinium. Now he worried that Hrrestan might ask only for that metal and signal its value to Hrrubans. But Hrrto had underestimated the leader's acumen.

Suddenly he began to fret that Hrrestan would get the credit for such dealing, and that he, Second Speaker, who had laid the groundwork in his initial conference with the Gringg captain, would not gain the face he deserved. Restlessly he drilled claw tips on the table until he saw what he was doing and forced his fingers to be still. That precious metal in return for acres of cloth, no matter how beautifully woven, seemed almost indecent. Could the Gringg really be so naive? Or their holdings so rich that they could make such ludicrous exchanges? That was a possibility that hadn't occurred to him before. Those rich in goods thought nothing of exchanging what they didn't need for what they coveted.

"We do not deplete your stores with such large orders?" Big Paws asked courteously. "We can space shipments so that each is full of what is required. With Hrrubans we trade for what the Hayumans do not show or seem to need. Therefore no bad feelings may happen. We are peaceful folk. We wish for peace everywhere around us."

Hearing those oft-repeated words, Hrrto felt the pressing need for some air.

"If you will permit me to withdraw?" Hrrto asked, and received a courteous nod from Hrrestan and a vague wave from Kodiak. He shot Mllaba a glance to signify she was to be careful, and left the room.

In the hallway, where fresh air flowed lightly in from the doors and open windows, his head seemed to clear. *Peaceful folk, peaceful folk, wishing for peace around them.* The repetition made him nauseous. Perhaps calling the fleets was not a wise idea. The prospect of almost unlimited quantities of purralinium was worth a certain risk, was it not? Ah, but with the navies in place, perhaps such information would be easier to obtain. Yes, that was the way to move now. They could show the tape to the Gringg and force them to admit to these atrocities—they had already admitted to being cannibals, hadn't they? Show them that their hypocrisy was discovered, and make them reveal what weapons had caused such destruction. With the fleet pinpointing one unarmed ship, surely they would accede to all demands. Before another Gringg ship could reach the heliopause of Rraladoona, they would have built defenses against such ordnance . . . Why should Hrruba defend Rraladoona at all? The thought suddenly occurred to Hrrto. Why not evacuate all Hrrubans? If the Hayumans were foolish enough to wait for Gringg vengeance, so be it.

But what if the Gringg should discover the Hrruban homeworld? Hadn't that fat captain been a whisper away from admitting that he knew where the Hrruban home system was? Hrrto had never fully subscribed to either the Decision or the Treaty, though he had been forced to give verbal agreement. Under his Stripe, he had known eventually they would live to regret it.

And what were the Hayumans wresting from the Gringg while Hrrubans were selling *harnesses and collars?*

Unable to resist, he found himself walking toward the other negotiating room. He heard voices ahead, and slipped forward, close to the wall.

He peered out from around a column and saw the small Hayuman, Landreau, in animated conversation with the fat and fair-haired trader, Horstmann. Horstmann was patting his protruding midsection with satisfaction which, at this time of day, could have little to do with the pleasures of the table.

The trader's voice rang loudly in the empty hall. "Even calculating in the cost of fuel and modifications to the cargo space, we could clear a pretty bundle. If I can get impactors, freeze-dry whatever, that'd increase space available. If we pack in drones, they'd take ores, refined or half, even raw for some of the unusual stuff, and your principals will be damned pleased with the results, Landreau."

"We can always use a steady new supply," Jilamey said, his eyes narrowed as he calculated. "Spaceships don't build themselves, you know, besides requiring hills of metal. So, if they'll trade us . . ." and, in a low voice, he began to enumerate items which Hrrto had to strain to hear. In shock, he thought he heard

Jilamey name purralinium. "That newest colony of theirs hasn't begun to deliver the quantities that assays suggest are available. And they haven't even thought of the concept of in situ space refineries. We got a lot we can teach them."

Half-reeling with the shock of such infamy, Hrrto moved off toward the open door. The Hayumans were obviously being given the more important trade items while the Hrrubans were being palmed off with trifles. He could not return to the Hrruban conference until he had recovered his poise.

He was halfway there when he heard angry voices coming from the chamber where the spaceport talks were being held.

"It would be foolish *not* to consider Gringg facilities, Admiral," Lorena Kaldon was saying in an aggravated tone. "Much easier to start off with buildings suited to their needs . . ."

"I am not discussing the Gringg," Barnstable said angrily, and Hrrto could hear him striding away, his booted steps echoing in the marble hall.

Hrrto heard Kaldon give a totally exasperated sound, the quick noise of steps, and a door that was closed as firmly as a slam. He hurried back to the Hrruban trade conference, pausing to arrange his robes and wondering just how many lengths of such expensive cloth it would take to garb a Gringg. How many *trmbla* of weight made a new grid?

His return coincided with the end of the formal talk, Kodiak and Big Paws rising from their cushions with a grace that Hrrto envied. They were physically large but all too clearly athletic. Polite farewells were made, with Hrrestan and Hrrin doing most of the talking, arranging additional meetings so that tomorrow the Gringg could see, and perhaps order, varieties of ceremonial harnesses.

Hrrto managed to drop his jaw as the occasion demanded, and by wrapping his tail about one ankle under his robes, managed to keep that appendage from giving any hint of his agitation.

As the others started leaving the room, he gave a little sign to Mllaba to wait, and she made a show of gathering up her books, checking on items until they were alone.

"I think that the Gringg have given the Hayumans purralinium," he told her, speaking in the merest whisper.

"Just as if they knew what Hrruba needed the most," Mllaba replied in angry exasperation. "While they deal in harnesses with us," and she stamped a foot while her tail switched violently.

"Is it possible the Gringg have developed matter transmission?" Hrruba asked, having to voice his worst fear.

"Really, sir," and she spoke impatiently, "even our matter technology was a chance application. The circumstances are unlikely to be repeated by Gringg paws."

He gave her an odd look. "And the Hayumans keep trying! Let us hope the scientists of both do not get together on such a project."

"Highly unlikely, not with Spacedep controlling all technology."

"I must have a few words with Hurrhee," Hrrto said as he finished gathering up his own notes. "Catch him before he leaves." Hurrhee would tell him what the Hayumans did with purralinium and whether they used the metal in its pure or impure state. "We must remain the only species in the galaxy with transport grids."

"As you say, Speaker," Mllaba agreed.

Recalled from a more pleasant occupation to be an observer, Commander Frill found himself growing sleepy through the talk of electronics, and the endless displays on the small computer screens of circuit diagrams which to him looked all alike. It wasn't really his subject. He excused himself for a breath of air and wandered out of the computer lab.

The corridor was lined with windows along this side of the building. Opposite the doors of the computer lab was a view of a stand of picturesque forested hills overlooking the landing pad. Frill could see the great hulk of the Gringg shuttle on the tarmac, an ostrich among chickens. There was someone lurking around it with a furtive air. Frill went out to investigate.

From the door, Frill could see that the man snooping around the shuttle wore the uniform of a Spacedep officer.

"Lieutenant!" the commander bellowed in his best parade-ground voice. The man turned slowly. Frill didn't recognize him. He must have been one of Barnstable's suspiciously increasing entourage.

"Sir?" the lieutenant said, tapping his brow diffidently.

"I don't think you're supposed to be touching that, son," Frill said. "Come on inside."

"Yes, sir!" the marine said. He snapped off a more creditable salute and strolled, not too quickly, into the building. "Good day, sir!" he said, marching purposefully up the long corridor.

"Carry on," the commander said vaguely, and turned away. He glanced back over his shoulder at the retreating lieutenant, but the man was gone. Puzzled, Frill went back to the conference.

CHAPTER 8

BY MIDAFTERNOON, EXCHANGE RATES HAD BEEN decided and some groundwork laid for an exchange board. Honey was also deftly inquiring what sort of warehousing would be available until a sufficient amount of goods had been accumulated to make a voyage to the homeworld profitable. Ali was trying very hard to negotiate a contract, but Honey was sidestepping him neatly, suggesting that they would prefer to build their own facilities on Doonarrala if some unoccupied space could be found. By dinnertime, Todd had a deep respect for Honey's skills as a negotiator. The Gringg fought hard for concessions from the Amalgamated World-based traders, and won a few, even from Ali Kiachif, who Todd thought would never yield.

"Such a facility not being currently available, we meet you halfway and do ship-to-ship transfers at designated points in space," Honey said in conclusion. "It will save transit time. From here it is far to the Gringg worlds."

"The same goes on our side," Kiachif said. "No trip, no tax or tariff. That's fair. But there's still a need for full transits, or else how are we to meet your folk and find out all about you for ourselves?"

Honey grinned, showing his fangs. "Reh," he said, noting the terms on his tablet. "We seek only equity."

"None of this is final until we check with Earth," Markudian warned, not for the first time. "It's subject to approval by the trade authorities and the Amalgamated Worlds Council."

"As you say, as you say," Honey agreed, nodding his great head. He had been incredibly patient with the man's continual complaints and criticisms.

Todd wondered why Barnstable and Greene had picked so obvious an agitator. Even Honey had displayed brief annoyance at Markudian's constant interruptions and trivial complaints. But, Todd supposed, that's why the man was there, to try and disrupt the meeting as much as possible. That Markudian had failed was due as much to the Gringg's unshakable affability as Todd's own determination not to let such ploys develop.

A loud, insistent clicking sound arose from the vicinity of the Gringg's collar.

"Communication device?" Ken whispered to Todd.

"Sounds more like a timer," Todd said. "I'll bet Kodiak and Big Paws just heard one of those, too."

Todd's surmise was correct. Honey carefully finished the last of his hieroglyphs and glanced up to nod at the assembled Hayumans.

"That is all I may do today, friends," he said. "I thank you most very. I will be able to give you final numbers when I have presented these terms to Captain Grzzeearoghh. She is who decides what is best for Gringg."

Todd rose and bowed to the Gringg. "On behalf of the people of Terra and Doonarrala, I thank you for coming, Honey and Coypu."

"Doonarrala," Honey said. "Have I not heard the Hrrubans say Rraladoona? Which name for your world is right?"

"Both, really," Todd admitted. "Each of our species had their own name for the planet: Hayumans called it Doona, the Hrrubans, Rrala. Now we each use both names combined, but putting the one from the original language first."

Honey pursed his rubbery black lips. "You defer in all ways regarding a common language to the Hrrubans, it makes sense to settle on one name, everyone use it."

"You know, Honey, you're right," Todd said, nodding. "Possibly we've just hung on to both names to please our respective over-governments. We really should be concentrating on unity. It's an acknowledgment that we're all one world, after all. Calling people Doonarralans or Rraladoonans is just another way of identifying them as Hayumans or Hrrubans, and that shouldn't be a consideration anymore. It was a point that hasn't arisen before. From this moment, I'll only use Rraladoon. It puts my native tongue second, but that should demonstrate how much I value peace and unity."

"Like Gringg," Honey said approvingly.

Ashland looked astonished and Markudian glowered. "Really, Reeve, I think you take too much on yourself."

"No, he's right," Sumitral put in. "The name ought to have been standardized a long time ago. I agree we should be calling this colony by the Hrruban-derived name. I don't think Reeve's co-leader, Hrrestan, will object," he added with a grin.

"Then so will the Gringg," Honey agreed. He and Coypu arose with more grace than their lumbering bodies suggested they were capable of. "We will speak to you again soon." Without further ceremony, they withdrew.

The Hayumans remained in place. Markudian was still out of sorts, drumming his fingers on the tabletop. Looking worn out, Ashland stared out the door after the Gringg. Even Ali Kiachif was subdued. Jilamey glanced up at Ken and Todd with bemusement.

"Did I just negotiate a concession for half an ocean of canned fish?" he asked, "For a small fortune in rare minerals."

Ken pushed back his chair and stretched his long arms toward the ceiling, listening to his ribs crack. "One man's trash is another's treasure. I don't know about you, but I'm desperate for a cup of coffee."

"Seconded," Jilamey said at once. "We've been here hours. Let's see if there's anything left to eat in the dining hall."

"Dammit," Horstmann said fervently, "I hope there's something to *drink*."

"I could swim a sea of mlada and never sink, if you get me, friends," Kiachif agreed.

The urge for refreshment had brought the Hrrubans to the dining hall as well. A few of the delegates from the spaceport conference stood in a corner, eating from plates heaped with cold meat and salad. They gravely acknowledged the Hayumans as they entered. The rest, locked in a deep discussion with Second Speaker, paid no attention to the new arrivals. Someone tapped Hrrto on the shoulder. Surprised, the Speaker turned to face Admiral Sumitral.

There was an awkward pause of a few moments. Sumitral recovered first. "A most fruitful afternoon, wouldn't you say, Speaker?" he asked amiably.

"Most interrrsting," Hrrto said. "Ze Gringg are most skilled at ze arrrt of negotiation, zough zis is not zeir native language." His voice displayed signs of strain.

"I trust you won some concessions from them?" Sumitral asked delicately. "Your own skills are not to be decried."

"You are most kind," Hrrto replied, bowing.

"Somebody find me a drink," Barnstable said plaintively, sinking down at a table. "Jonny?"

Greene stood up, looking about him for a refreshment cabinet. Todd rose to get drinks for the party, listening closely.

"Did you find their terms favorable?" Sumitral asked Hrrto.

"I am surre as much as you yrrrself did," Second replied, equal to Sumitral's courtesy. Now that he had the chance to ask what the Gringg had offered the Hayumans, his nerve failed him. He could not stand the humiliation of admitting what the Gringg had asked of them. He kept his eyes fixed on Sumitral's mild gray eyes, hoping he would speak first.

Todd found the wet-bar cabinet and poured out a good shot of Doonan-distilled whiskey for the Admiral. The sight of open bottles attracted a number of the negotiators, and Todd found himself at the center of an eager and grateful group, dispensing liquid comfort. Hrriss gave him a drop-jaw grin from the edge of the throng, and held up a jug of plain juice. Todd nodded enthusiastically.

"A spot of mlada," Kiachif requested, with a pretended whine like an old man. "Not too small, and don't you dare dilute it, laddie."

In the center of the room, the careful maneuvers went on, the tension growing. Greene hovered at Sumitral's elbow as if to snatch back any incautious statements the head of Alreldep might make.

"Might one ask what commodities were discussed?" Sumitral suggested.

"I do not zink I am at liberty to reveal zat at zis time," Second said blandly. Mllaba stared open-eyed at the Hayumans.

"Perhaps I should not, then, either," Sumitral said, but Todd could tell his curiosity was aroused. Hrrto was being more than usually cagey.

Ken and Hrriss stood next to the drinks cabinet as Todd poured another draft for Ali Kiachif. The captain inhaled that libation and held out his glass for a refill. Jilamey broke away from the group in the center of the room.

"I can't stand it any longer," Jilamey said to Hrriss under his breath, watching the two senior administrators waltz around one another. "What did they ask for? You must have got some humdingers."

"In a way," Hrriss replied, but his big green eyes were brimming with mischief. "But change yrrr expectations down razzer zan up!"

"You, too?" Todd asked. "The Gringg asked us for food!"

"Not what anyone was expecting," Ken said, "but I was charmed by it and trust Landreau here to have food processors and big freezer units in that consortium of his. The Gringg don't want our technologies; they seem content with their own. But they do want rather basic, simple items we have in quantity, and cultural things. Is that why Hrrto can't get the words out of his mouth?"

"Yes," Hrrestan replied, with a fit of low, grunting laughter. "Hrruba has been requested to send this yearrr's fashions in hrrnss and jewelled szraps, and the heavy cloth of which Hrrto's robes are made. Custom-made size giganzic, please, in quantity."

Kiachif grinned, his narrow, bearded jaws opening in amusement. "They were ready to say no to bombs and bullets, but they didn't have a position prepared on beef or baubles!"

"I am sure zey would have classified it as potenzially dangrrrous and not fit frr exprrt if zey had considrrred it," Hrrestan said, his voice hoarse with merriment.

Jilamey exploded in a fit of the giggles. "And when you look at the two of them out there, neither one able to spit it out—" He waved a hand, unable to continue speaking. He watched them for a moment; then his voice changed. "On second thought, I don't think this *is* so funny."

"Neither do I," Todd said, breaking away. Hrrestan, with a nod of agreement, followed him.

"I'll have to put the matter to the Amalgamated Worlds Administration on Earth before we can discuss this further," Sumitral was saying. "In the meantime, I am glad to see we continue with the spirit of cooperation that has characterized this world of Rraladoon for over thirty years."

"Pardon me," Todd said, edging adroitly between the two diplomats, "I see little evidence of cooperation in your faces but a lot of wariness. Speaker Hrrto, would you like to know what the Gringg asked for in our talks?"

"Reeve, no!" Markudian cried, outraged.

"Markudian, yes!" Todd said, rounding on him. "I see this as a real test of Rraladoonan integrity, not Hayuman/Hrruban competition. Consider this," he went on urgently, looking around the circle. "One of the reasons the Gringg thought we were a single species was the way we worked together. I was delighted by that because it showed we'd learned to trust each other. But the first stir of the pot from outside, and we separate into distrustful—and greedy—strangers." Todd stared at each one in turn, his glance gliding over Greene's smug expression. "So let's reinstate the honesty we have always used in dealings on Rraladoon."

"Prrrhaps if we begin again," Hrrestan suggested, "knowing zat we arrre among friends, who will not judge against you no mazzer what occurred?"

Sumitral was silent for a long time, then bowed deeply to Second Speaker. "Hrrto, old friend, I don't know whether I've been gulled or not. The Gringg asked us to ship them tons of comestibles from Earth and its colonies. They want fish, and beef, and chicken. Oh," he added, with a wry grin at Todd, "and popcorn."

Hrrto cleared his throat and ground his back teeth a moment before he could bring himself to reply. "From us"—and the words seemed reluctant to leave his mouth—"zey wish fine cloth, leather, and jewels for zose collars zey prize so much."

"You worked the more equitable bargain." Jilamey said. "Jewels cost more than popcorn and fish."

"Only on Earth," Ken Reeve said, grinning. "Here we pick 'em up like popcorn."

The tension in the room melted away like fog. Todd relaxed and grinned at Hrrestan.

"You should not have admitted such," Mllaba said, glancing at Hrrto but careful not to let Todd or any of the others catch her eye.

"I agree with the little lady," Barnstable said to Sumitral.

Todd grinned. "The truth is, we all feel a little absurd. Right?"

"Ze Gringg do not wish Hrruban technology," Hrrto said, his tail giving an emphatic switch.

Sumitral grinned. "They didn't want any of ours either. Not even for purposes of comparison. I admit that I'm a little puzzled."

"Maybe they are satisfied with the technology they have," Grace Castleton suggested from the fringe of the group. Neither of her superiors seemed to agree. Todd thought it was a fair assessment.

"Don't be so naive, Grace," Greene put in acidly. "Any objective observer could see that by asking for such trivia they are determined to allay suspicion."

Todd glared at him. "Greene, you're not what I'd call an

objective observer," he said. "On the other hand, you've been extremely suspicious from the get-go. Have you any reason that you're not sharing with us?"

"Grrrene is not ze only one who does not believe zeir asserzhons of peace," Hrrrv said, breaking in. "To me"—he put his fist against his chest—"zey are so very *not* curious about our technology, zat alone makes me suspicious. Or have zey been given prrivate brrriefings?" He stared a challenge at Todd, who felt his hands balling involuntarily into fists. Hrrrv stared coldly, awaiting action.

Hrrestan immediately stepped between them, putting a hand, claws sheathed, on each.

"Captain, I find such an accusation as insulting as Zodd does," Hrrestan said in High Hrruban. "For this one Hayuman, the safety of this planet has always come first, nor would he ever, ever, jeopardize it. You will withdraw the remark. Now!"

Unobtrusively, Hrriss had moved to one side of his friend; Hrrin, the other. For one tense moment, Hrrrv looked as if he would disobey, but then, with minimum courtesy, he indicated his withdrawal by nodding briefly.

"We beg your pardon for the intrusion," a booming voice said from the door. Hrrestan's hand fell away, and Todd spun around. The Gringg had returned. Honey stepped forward, gesturing to two of the other males to enter the dining room. Between them dangled a Spacedep lieutenant, struggling and angry. His uniform was mussed and he had a bruise on his cheek. "We return this Hayuman male to you. He had unaccountably found his way onto our ship."

"He what?" Todd exploded.

"He was concealed behind a storage hatch," Kodiak said. "But we smelled him. I knew immediately which Hayuman he was. I had smelled him before. He walks behind that one." Kodiak pointed at Greene.

Putting up his hands to quiet the room, Hrrestan came toward the Gringg. He touched the arms of the two holding Greene, and they released him. With a tight grip on the Spacedep lieutenant's arm, he bowed to Honey and Kodiak.

"We thank you for rrrsstoring him to us. He surely became lost and disoriented. We will see zat he does not wandrrr again."

Fortunately, the Gringg chose to accept Hrrestan's explanation.

"Then we wish you good day," Honey said with a toothy smile

at the assembly. The Gringg left, and the room seemed suddenly larger.

As soon as the door closed, Lieutenant Bouros shook off Hrrestan's grip and stood at attention. Greene eyed him with annoyance.

"Detected by smell," Hrrrv said in disgust. "A fine job of concealment, Terran-male. No Hrruban would have been so stupid."

"What in hell did you think you were doing, concealing yourself on the Gringg shuttle in the first place?" Todd demanded, looming over him.

"I don't answer to you, sir," the officer said, staring straight at the wall ahead of him.

"Reeve, this is a Spacedep matter," Barnstable said, pulling Todd aside and lowering his voice. Greene and Ken closed in on them.

"If he answers to you," Todd turned to confront Barnstable, "did you order him to penetrate the Gringg ship? Spying on them is no way to establish trust between our two peoples."

"The more we know about them, the more secure we feel in forming closer relationships," Barnstable said, his brows drawing down over his eyes.

"Ev, that's Alreldep's job, not yours," Sumitral said, mastering his irritation. "And to allow him to go without neutralization of body odor?" Sumitral rolled his eyes. "Have you learned nothing about the Gringg? Even the kids here know the Gringg have a keen sense of smell. Or don't they issue deodorants in your navy?"

"Reconnaissance seems an obvious course with unknowns like the Gringg," Bouros said, still staring straight ahead. "The ship wasn't secured, sir. It was easy to do a recon."

"A recon might have been acceptable," Sumitral said, though his expression was dubious.

"But you had hidden, hadn't you," Todd said, "intending to remain on board. For what purpose? To fumigate them into submission by overpowering them with your body odor?"

"Now that was uncalled for," Barnstable said, indignant, though clearly he wasn't happy that one of his men had been apprehended.

"So was this marine's illegal entry," Todd said, then addressed the lieutenant. "You may be under the Admiral's orders, but by all that's holy, while you're on this planet you are also under mine as planetary leader." Todd went on, his fury unabated. "The next time you overstep yourself, mister, you'll be subject to my authority."

"And mine," Hrrestan said with equal threat.

The marine kept his face carefully expressionless.

"Have we made ourselves clear, Admiral?" Todd added, turning to Barnstable but looking at Greene, too. "We're trying to forge an alliance with these beings, and there are to be no more juvenile war games during the proceedings."

"Has it never occurrrred to you," Hrrestan added, "zat ze Gringg will likely *tell* you morrre zan you could ever discoverr by spying?"

"With all respect, Leader," Greene said, "I doubt that very much."

"I wish zo know morrre about ze Gringg zen zey have told us," Hrrrv muttered sulkily. "As yrrr prrrecious Hayumans say, 'Know yrr enemy.' "

"Better, *recognize* who is your enemy," Todd said to the Hrruban captain, and swung a fierce gaze toward the Spacedep officers, which gave him the satisfaction of momentarily startling Hrrrv. He did catch the odd glint in Hrrrv's eyes, but he couldn't interpret it. "If you'd realize there are no enemies here at all, we could progress on all fronts!" He eyed the Spacedep officers with the same fierce gaze, but clearly, he'd taken much of the wind out of their sails. He allowed his temper to cool. He'd said enough, and to thc point, for one day. He'd best withdraw.

"Now, if you'll excuse me, I have other matters to attend to." With a bow to the assembly, Todd left the dining hall.

"A little strong, was that not?" Hrriss asked mildly, following Todd toward the grid. His naturally quicker pace kept him abreast of the Hayuman, who was still dissipating his anger.

"Aargh!" Todd said, stopping and twining his hands into his hair. "I wish they'd all pack up and go home, and let us handle the diplomatic relations. We'd achieve fair terms and a treaty, and they'd never have to leave Terra!"

"Or Hrruba," Hrriss said thoughtfully. "I don't know how zings went with ze trade discussions, but ze spaceport talks were constantly interrupted by Barnstable's objections. I zought he was an advocate."

Todd grinned. "Only if Spacedep's allowed its little bureaucracies. And with the Gringg a new factor, he's likely to insist on a heavy Spacedep presence."

Hrriss shook his head. "No, it's somezing else. We know zey do not trrrust the Grringg, but zeir paranoia is worse zan just mistrrust."

"And probably all a part of why Greene had an agent infiltrating the Gringg shuttle." Todd flattened his lips into a grim line. "I shouldn't have been so glad to see Greene leave our trade talks—where, I might add—he and that Markudian lackey of his were doing their damnedest to mess things up."

"He objected to selling zem food?"

"As much as Hrrto objects to selling them ornaments from Hrruba."

The two old friends grinned at each other.

"Greene had a notion that perhaps they wanted *us* for food," Todd said, with a shadow of distaste at being reminded of that incident.

"Ho! So long as you promised zem Rraladoonan snake, you skinny creatures are safe," Hrriss said with a laugh.

"All fooling aside, Hrriss, I think the Spacedep personnel bear closer watching. But come on," he said, with a sudden lightening of mood. "We've got to get the lists of Teams drawn up for the Hunt, or you'll see a hell of a hullabaloo when the snakes swarm!" He grinned at his best friend. "I wonder if the Gringg would like to participate. Not that we've a horse up to such weight."

"Ze way zey move, zey don't need a hrrss," Hrriss replied.

Todd's eyes twinkled. "Speaking of moving, c'mon! Race you to the grid!"

Forgetting for the moment that they were adults, with children and responsibilities, the two abandoned themselves to the familiar contest of their childhood. Todd was laughing by the time he caught up with Hrriss at the pillars.

After Todd had stalked out, most of the other delegates found excuses to leave. Jilamey Landreau collared Admiral Sumitral and led him away, talking excitedly about the tons of fish and snake which the Gringg would need. Hrrestan was deep in discussions with the craftsfolk about the availability of large quantities of well-tanned leathers, and they all left together. Only Castleton, Barnstable, Greene, Second Speaker, Hrrrv, Mllaba, and Bouros remained.

Greene spoke to Bouros. "You're dismissed, man. Report back to Earth." He turned to Barnstable. "We can't use him again now that Reeve and the others have seen him."

"Stupid way to be caught," Castleton said with a half-smile. "Especially after we saw them use their olfactory senses to differentiate between us."

"Bouros is not a clumsy operative," Greene replied, annoyed at her comment. She shrugged.

"Well, Castleton, see what your specialists can do to overcome that problem," Barnstable said, giving her a sour glance. That startled her, but she nodded her head in acceptance of the commission. "Somehow or other, we have got to gain more evidence against the Gringg that will hold up in the World Court. Grace, have we gotten anything new from the exploration ship?"

"Nothing yet, Admiral," Castleton said. "I renewed the request with an urgent tag on it through secured transmission again this morning."

"Confound it, we need that data." Barnstable pulled a chair away from the dining table and sank into it.

"Trivia!" Second Speaker burst out suddenly. Grace stared at him, wondering if he was accusing them. The Hrruban began to pace, showing all the agitation he had concealed while Sumitral and the others were present. His tail lashed back and forth. "The Gringg ask us for trivia. What does it mean?"

"It means," Barnstable said, "that they intend to keep up this charade until the last minute. The pretense is wearing my nerves to a nubbin."

He sat back in his chair and wiped his face with a handkerchief. Castleton knew precisely how he felt. After weeks of maintaining the *Hamilton* in a continual state of Yellow Alert, she was tired. Shore leave to the surface of Doonarrala was limited, and the crew were taking it hard. Frail Frill, one of her most loyal officers, had asked to be released from his duties planetside because it was causing jealousy among the personnel who had been denied permission to downside. Grace had been grateful for the presence of Jon Greene, who had lent her his deep well of strength during the alert. His consideration was only part of his attractiveness. He was the most zealous patriot she had ever met. All his actions and decisions were considered in the light of what was best for Humanity. Grace admired him, but found herself unable to agree completely with him about the treachery of the Gringg. Her own observations belied what the archive tape had shown; her own instinct disagreed with that proof. Still, she watched the computer scopes every day, tracking the approach of the Spacedep squadron. It was still too far away to be picked up on sensors. Nor was anything else closing in, which took care of the notion that the Gringg were waiting for reinforcements. Perhaps they needed none, whether for peace or war.

"What are the Gringg waiting for?" Mllaba asked, her yellow-green eyes wide.

"A display of physical aggression?" Castleton suggested. "They don't act, they react. If we don't press them, they might never attack us."

Barnstable waved away the notion. "How far off is the fleet now?"

"Six to seven more days, sir."

"Right. From now on, tighter security. But I still want a look at what they're hiding on that ship!"

"I have an idea how to accomplish that, sir," Greene said. "If you'll allow me a free hand."

"What? All right, Greene. Carry on."

Castleton paused, wondering how to phrase her feelings. "Sir, after having listened to them today, I hesitate to admit it, but I . . . I like the Gringg. Hearing them talk, it's hard to believe that they caused the destruction of an entire planet. Their behavior differs so greatly from what appeared on that tape. If I hadn't seen it, I'd never be convinced that they are dangerous."

"Besides that tape they are so big!" Hrrto exclaimed. "And so loud!"

Barnstable planted a firm finger on the tabletop. "Cunning, too. All that openness and charm . . . right up to the moment they're ready to take over this planet!"

Such an emphatic pronouncement silenced the others.

"Only a week, maybe less," Hrrrv said in a tone of some desperation, "and we'll have a superior force in Rraladoonan skies. Zen we will ze authority"—he paused and drew his lip back from his teeth—"zat will wring ze zruth from these 'bears'!"

"Reeve and Hrrestan can be removed as planetary leaders," Barnstable said, rubbing his hands together in anticipation, "as unfit to govern . . . since they've extended hospitality to so clearly a menacing species, endangering the citizens of both species."

"Speaker Hrrto and Captain Hrrrv, you would of course support this move for any doubting Hrrubans," Greene put in. "With an intelligent and dedicated administration, we'll soon put things to rights. We might even consider removing the Reeve family from Doonarrala as subversives, detrimental to the well-being of the colony, since they seem to be forever leading it into dangerous situations."

Just giving voice to that possibility gave Greene a certain measure of satisfaction. Grace Castleton regarded him with shock. She had no idea his dislike of the young planetary administrator went that deep.

"And Hrrestan with him," Mllaba said, "since he also espouses zese same courses."

"I do most respectfully suggest that you act only on provocation," Grace Castleton said carefully. "This is an independent and autonomous planet. We still don't have proof that *these* Gringg pose a threat to the planet or either of our worlds."

"I don't like hearing such sentiments from you, Castleton," Barnstable said, eyeing her fiercely.

The captain inclined her head a moment. "I am of course" required to comply with any orders you may give me, Admiral," she said in a colorless voice, "but I would not be acting in *your* best interests if I did not play devil's advocate."

"Oh? Well, there's that," Barnstable said, mollified. "The Gringg protestations of their pacific nature are hypocritical," he went on, "and the basis for trade with them ludicrous. Only consolidates my distrust of 'em. I'll have conclusive proof all too soon that they're dangerous! Why, the size of them alone makes them physically superior . . . I mean . . . well, you *know* what I mean! We've got to make these fool Doonarralans see that these bear types are the most dangerous species Mankind has ever encountered. Why, they could dominate the known galaxy. That cannot be allowed!"

"It will not, sir," Greene assured him.

By the time Todd reached home that evening, he was tired and wanted nothing more than a quick dinner and enough time to review the day's tumultuous and astonishing incidents. He could smell the dinner, but as soon as he swung in the door, he felt the atmosphere crackling.

"Oh, Lord, what've I done wrong now?" he murmured. The house only felt like this when Kelly was ready to scalp him.

"Ah!" She leaped from the kitchen and stopped abruptly in the middle of the living room, fists dug into her hips. " 'Would you mind entertaining Captain Grizz and her son, dear?' " She did a good imitation of Todd, further warning of his being in deep trouble with her. " 'Oh, all I have to do is entertain them this afternoon, show them how we live?' " she said, mimicking her own wifely reply. "But"—and now she advanced on him, her head down, her glower intense—"does my beloved husband drop me one little word of the essential difference between the bears I've met and our noble Captain Grizz? No, nary a word does he say!" With a practiced flick of her hand, she caught his outstretched hand with the hard edge of a whipped tea-towel. It stung, and even as he began retreating, she flicked the towel again, catching him even harder on the leg.

"Now, sweetheart . . ."

"Don't 'now, sweetheart,' me!" She snapped the towel again, and this time he ducked because she was aiming at his neck and she'd had too much practice at that art. "Only one phrase . . . just one phrase was necessary. 'Sweetheart, the females are bigger than the males.' "

"But you *knew* that," Todd said, reaching for the door to put it between him and her attack. "You knew that! We told you she was immense . . . that the males are tercels. I know we said it."

"But you didn't say it *then!*"

With unexpected force she jerked the door free of his grasp and he stood there, feeling vulnerable.

"Sweetheart, you're good at remembering details . . ." he began. Then panic swept through him. "Nothing happened, did it? With Grizz and Weddeerogh?" Surely someone would have got word to him about that.

Kelly turned on her heel. "No, nothing happened except Nrrna, Mrrva, and I were paralyzed with shock for five minutes. Evcn the grid operator was affected . . ." And then Kelly couldn't maintain her angry pose any longer. She burst out laughing, doubling over and clutching her sides.

"I don't think Grrirl, who was on the grid controls then, will ever forgive us," she said, wiping her eyes on her former weapon, "because he really did lose it . . . even if Nrrna and Mrrva pretended he hadn't. Even if you'd said something in your message, we still wouldn't have been prepared for the size of Grizz and Teddy." Her giggles were slowly subsiding. "He's adorable! All I could think of was 'a Bear of Very Little Brain . . . ' "

"Huh?"

"You know, Winnie the Pooh." She stared at her husband. "My mother read me those stories when I was a kid and I read them to our children . . . don't you remember? Eeyore . . ."

"And the tail that's all he's got," and Todd now remembered the charming stories. "*What* name did the kids give Weddeerogh?"

"Teddy," Kelly said firmly. "Not my idea. Winnie ought to have been obvious, but those kids of yours latched onto Teddy Bear and there was no arguing them out of it. My word, but he can eat. 'Sing ho for a Bear, sing ho for a Pooh,' " she sang. " 'I'll have a little something in an hour or two.' He can move in here any time his mother's away . . . Swims like a dolphin. So does she . . ." Another burst of laughter, and tears were now streaming down Kelly's face. "Thank goodness you dredged the lake last year or it wouldn't have been up to her knees and she does so love to float, flat out. We'll got to go to the seashore next time she's free or perhaps demonstrate how we shoot the river rapids."

Kelly collapsed onto a couch, then patted it for Todd to sit beside her.

"Sorry, love, but I had to get it out of my system. I mean"—she shook her head in remembered amazement—"I didn't think the grid could take anything that big!"

"*That* particular grid, as you well know, can handle a whole village. So, what was the captain's reaction? She wasn't offended?"

"I believe she thought we weren't sure how to greet her appropriately and instructed us," Kelly said, snuggling up to him. "And Teddy was no problem at all—especially after he saw Hrrunna. After that, when he wasn't in the water, he was rocking her. Thank goodness they eat anything, and almost everything. I'll have to do a major resupply tomorrow. Another thing, Grizz wouldn't come in here . . . she figured our floors weren't up to her weight . . . but she looked in through every window. On tiptoe she could even see into the dormer rooms." Kelly stifled another bubble of laughter. "She seemed to approve—but mainly of the lake. Thank goodness you and Hrriss dredged that lake!" she giggled. "How did your day go?"

"Well, now that you mention it, I am glad we dredged the lake," he replied at his most casual. "Gringg love water sports. There's the ocean, too. I'm not sure they have tidal seas . . ."

"Yes, but what do they want to trade?"

Todd affected a very serious expression. "Not what we expected at all." He wondered how long he could play this one out before he told her the "awful truth."

Once the details of trade items became public knowledge, there was great competition to show the Gringg what Rraladoon craftsfolk and farmers had to offer. Since the old Hall would be more inadequate than ever with even a few Gringg inside, every village offered its green as marketplace. Nearly half the Gringg on board the *Wander Den* wished to participate active ly in trading, so no village had a chance to feel deprived or neglected.

The remaining Gringg were interested in other facets of life on the planet. Their wishes were accommodated despite continued vehement protests and ominous warnings from Spacedep. Gringg were "adopted" for a day by people in every line of work. With scrupulous impartiality, Kelly and Nrrna acted as secretaries for such engagements. So it was not surprising that when Shhrrgahnnn asked to have a closer look at some of the four-footed beasts which were in such continuous use by Hayuman and Hrruban, Kelly asked her brother to oblige him.

"Only if the smell of a Gringg doesn't freak my patients out," Mike Solinari, a veterinarian, replied.

"The Gringg smell pleasant," Kelly remarked, a trifle sharply, "and my house pets and our horses have exhibited no reaction to their presence." She didn't add that dogs pretended the mountain of flesh wasn't there and the cats remained well beyond the range of even Teddy, but they hadn't exhibited a "physical" reaction.

"Well, sick stock doesn't respond normally. That voder contraption unnerves *me*," Mike said, "and I understand its purpose."

However, Kelly did agree to wait and help if the Gringg freaked out Mike's patients. So, early on the scheduled morning, Kelly Reeve delivered the guest to the hospital for a trial meeting.

"Now, bro," Kelly said, introducing the Gringg, "your niece and nephew have renamed him Cinnamon."

"I can see why," Mike replied affably. "He's got hair the same color as we do." Mike's poll was fiery red, much brighter than Cinnamon's, though both could be termed red. Where Kelly was dainty and slenderly built, Mike's features were heavier and his frame carried extra bulk. He had a friendly, open face that wore a grin of anticipation as the Gringg climbed awkwardly out of the Reeve family hovercraft.

"Cinnamon, this is my brother Mike," Kelly said, holding onto the Gringg's arm. Then she gestured toward a tall, hollow-chested Hayuman with black hair and a broad, blunt nose, and a narrow-striped Hrruban. "Bert Gross, who's also a veterinarian, uh, animal doctor, and Errrne. He's an intern. Studying to be an animal doctor."

"Fardles, he's a monster!" Bert muttered, nevertheless extending a hand to the Gringg. "Greetings, or whatever." The Gringg touched his claws gently to the middle of the man's palm. Bert drew back, pretending to make sure all his fingers were intact.

"I am most pleased," Cinnamon said after the usual preliminary growlings came through the voder. He showed his long, white teeth, and all three doctors swallowed.

"Bet he brrrush zem a lot," Errrne quipped weakly.

"I've never seen anything with red eyes before that wasn't stark raving mad," Gross added.

"All right!" Kelly said, keeping an affable grin on her own face, just as glad that neither Bert nor Errrne had translators. "Let's see what effect Cinnamon has on the stock. Today I've got to touch a lot of bases!"

"I dunno," Bert Gross said, muttering under his breath. "I've been hearing rumors that these guys are pretty dangerous."

"Oh, horseapples," Mike said. He liked the Gringg on sight. Cinnamon seemed friendly and curious, not threatening as some of those in-flow visitors from Earth had suggested. The Gringg stood looking around him, sniffing the air, nostrils wrinkling ever so slightly.

"I guess the barn does smell kind of pungent," Mike said with a grin, and wondered if the voder translated the tone in which words were said, or meant. "It's a warm day, and we haven't mucked out our patients' stalls yet," he explained to the Gringg. "Come along. You don't have to do any of it, but we can talk to you while we work."

The isolation stables were in a big airy barn that had ventilators along the roof line, to circulate air through the building without chilling the patients below. Sensing the visitors, some of the sick horses and mules started whickering nervously, and one animal kicked the partition in its stall. Mike promptly marched Cinnamon out again, while Kelly exclaimed in some dismay until Mike and Cinnamon re-entered the barn through the downwind door.

"Can't be too careful," he explained to his slightly puzzled guests, keeping his tone low, hoping the voder translation would be equally quiet. It was. "Horses are delicate. There are a couple of high-risk mares in foal. I don't want them to abort. Say, here's a fellow who's only in for a sore leg. Have a look." Leaning over the stall door, he beckoned the Gringg close.

A low hiss of admiration escaped Cinnamon's lips as he gazed at the young bay horse standing on the straw. The animal looked up from the hay it was lipping, wisps hanging from its muzzle as it gave the unusual shape a long stare before it started to chew again, but it didn't panic. It twitched its dark satin coat here and there as if flies troubled it, and raised its white-bandaged leg, curling the hoof under the protection of its body.

"See? No reaction at all," Kelly said, "I'm off!" And she departed before anyone could delay her.

"The creature is very beautiful," Cinnamon said, speaking more softly through the translator than Mike would have thought possible. "What is such an animal used for?"

"We ride them," Mike explained, gritting his teeth as the voder squawked back. The gelding switched its ears and rolled its eyes apprehensively, but didn't do more, since it also heard Mike's familiar voice. "We use them as non-polluting—well, non*toxic*-polluting—transportation around here. They run on hay instead of batteries, and besides, they can be good friends to you. Some of this type"—he pulled Cinnamon across the aisle to a sick cow—"are reared as food animals and their hides are used for other things."

Cinnamon gave the cow only a cursory glance and went back to admire the horse. "They are like gentleness and night and wood," Cinnamon said, struggling for Hrruban words to express his admiration. "Hrrrsses must surely be the most lovely creatures on Rraladoon." He spoke the new word with a trill that enhanced the Hrruban pronunciation.

"Well, we kind of like them, too," Mike said, a little overwhelmed to be on the receiving end of poetry so early in the morning. "Stay and see how we care for them. I've got to spend some time in the surgery this morning. Bert, you have the comm." He passed his voder over so that any queries Cinnamon had could be understood. Then, with a nod at the others to begin their work, he left for his office.

Cinnamon watched intently as Errrne and Bert hauled out soiled straw and spread fresh, doled out medication, checked bandages, and generally cared for the ailing hoofed animals. When the round device on the wall had its two indicators pointing directly skyward, work ceased, and Mike returned to collect the Gringg.

"Do you have any questions about what you've been seeing today?" Mike asked.

Considering, Cinnamon rolled his fleshy lower lip. "I want to know what is the purpose of this place. I have watched you. Why have a vet-er-i-nar-y hospital when you eat animals? Why not just eat the ones who can no longer serve you?"

Errrne and Gross thought this was the funniest thing they'd ever heard. Mike shut them up with an eloquent glance.

"You don't farm animals, do you?" Mike asked rhetorically.

"Morra," Cinnamon replied. "Only plants such as grain, vegetables, and fruits. All of our meat is caught wild. There is plenty of game around us, and we are good at preserving that which is uneaten."

"Well, there are more reasons to have animals than for food," Mike said. "Not all animals make good eating."

"Can you show me some?"

"No, I can't. Every beast we raise has a double purpose. These, for instance," Mike said, drawing Cinnamon to the sheepfold, "we raise for the fleece on their backs which makes our clothes." Capturing one of the merinos, he showed Cinnamon the depth and fineness of the wool and then demonstrated the difference with a hardier mountain sheep. The Gringg gingerly felt each fleece, nodding as he appreciated the different textures.

"The captain will want to know about these," he said.

The Gringg was careful to input all new vocabulary into the memory of the voder at his throat. By the end of the morning, he could discuss what he had learned with intelligence and a measurable degree of clarity.

"These bruins are smart," Bert commented, impressed.

"Tape-learning," Errrne said, shrugging his plush-covered shoulders. "He is amassing a bluffrrr's guide, zat is all."

Errrne looked puzzled when Cinnamon shoved away the chair beside their table in the lunch room. Then he realized that the Gringg was quite capable of reaching the table even parked on the floor beside it. Not knowing how much a Gringg ate, Mike had made arrangements with the cafeteria cook for double quantities of everything. As he watched the Gringg eat, though daintily enough for all his size, Mike was a little sorry that he hadn't made that triple. Cinnamon exclaimed with pleasure over everything he tried, and ended up consuming as much as all three Rraladoonans put together. When his plate was empty, he was clearly though politely looking around for more.

"You eat more than my brother Sean," Mike said, with respect, leaning over to speak through the voder around Bert's neck. "I didn't think anything short of a Great Big Momma Snake could pack it in tighter."

"Everything had a most delicious flavor," Cinnamon said, rolling back on his tail and running the tip of a claw between his teeth for stray morsels. "I admire also the variety of textures and aromas."

Mike grinned. "The grub is good here. What's Gringg food like?"

"We eat protein, carbohydrates, starch coming from different sources. I will show you some of our eatables at another time. Now I must be curious about all aspects of our new friends, who are so very different from Gringg."

"You can say that again," Bert said, surveying the alien with a narrowed eye, forgetting that he was wearing the voder.

"Why must I repeat it?" Cinnamon asked, drawing his brows together over his snout.

"Uh," Bert said, and looked to his friends for help. Mike guffawed.

"It's a colloquialism," Mike explained, taking hold of the voder by the cord around Bert's neck and bringing it to his mouth. "He means he agrees with what you said."

"Would it not be simpler to say 'I agree'?" Cinnamon asked, and the men laughed again.

It was impossible for anyone passing through the lunch room to miss the shaggy hulk of the Gringg. A few eyed Cinnamon warily and hurried on. Mike recognized those as interns from Earth. Most of the usual Rraladoon staff, however, stopped to be introduced. Cinnamon's head kept turning back and forth, trying to follow multiple conversations. Mike decided he was happy to be in the midst of everything. One by one, the medics and visitors recalled appointments, and disappeared, leaving the four of them alone at their table.

"Okay," Bert asked. "So, Cinnamon, what do you want to do this afternoon?"

"I wish to learn more about the pretty hrrrsses," he said eagerly.

"You and everybody else," Mike said, pushing away from the table with a mock sigh of exasperation. "Come on. We've got Mrs. Lawrence's hunter gelding in for an abscess on his rump. He's pretty calm. I don't think he'll spook at the sight of our pal here."

In the treatment barn, Mike greeted Nita Taylor, one of their veterinary assistants, who was washing out a bucket under the pump at one end of the horse barn. "Got a visitor here to see Amber."

Nita glanced over her shoulder, then stood up to take a full-faced stare at the Gringg. She was a willowy girl of middle height with light-golden skin and dark brown eyes and hair. The things most people noticed about her were her perfect cupid's-bow lips, and the fact that she was as shy as an urfa. She nodded, tilting her head toward the stall.

"No problem," she said, collecting her wits. "Like you ordered, I changed the dressing before feeding this morning so it might need replacement."

The chestnut horse stood half asleep in the sun. Mike hopped over the fence and approached with soothing sounds, running one hand down its back and to the rump. Its eyelids fluttered as it shifted a leg, denoting it was aware of Mike.

"Hey, watch he don't cowkick you, Mike," Bert said, nervously, "if he catches sight of Cinnamon!"

"He's all right," Mike assured him, turning to catch the tie-rope and halter in one hand.

The horse came fully awake and nosed at Mike's chest. He pushed away the gelding's muzzle.

"You're almost better, fella," he said affectionately. "Another couple of days and you can go home."

Cinnamon walked halfway around the fence to get a better look at the animal's face. Mike noticed the visitor was being very careful to stay downwind.

"We call horses the wealth of Doona," Mike explained, patting the gelding's cheek. "No one in the galaxy raises better stock than we do: jumpers, hunters, or just riding hacks."

"How is it ridden?" Cinnamon asked.

"I will show you," Errrne volunteered, taking a headcollar and lead rope from those on the peg of the turn-out field. As the Gringg watched, the Hrruban quietly approached an animal grazing just beyond the sick gelding. Deftly he slipped on the halter, then tied the rope onto the far side to make an impromptu rein. Then, with the ease of long practice, Errrne leaped to the horse's back and coaxed it into a walk.

"You hold on with your knees," Mike explained. "You don't need a saddle unless you're riding a long distance. Then it's vital for your comfort and the mount's. They've got sharp spines."

"Ah," the Gringg said, his eyes glued to the graceful form of horse and rider. Errrne coaxed the beast to a fast trot, then into a canter, which increased to a gallop.

"That Hrruban rides like he was part of the critter," Bert said admiringly. "He breaks horses freelance."

"He does what to hrrrsses?" Cinnamon asked anxiously, tapping the voder. Bert laughed as he tried to explain.

" 'Break' is not the literal translation," Mike said, his eyes dancing.

"Hello?" someone called.

"Back here!" Mike shouted back.

Footsteps ticked and scratched on the concrete floor of the barn. Nita blushed suddenly. Mike noticed her reaction with a grin. If she knew those boots just by sound, the wearer had to be Robin Reeve. The younger Reeve was a smaller, slighter copy of Todd. He had the same intense blue eyes, dynamite with the engaging grin that got him out of trouble as often as it got him into it.

"Afternoon," he drawled, then noticed the visitor. "Well, hi!" he greeted the Gringg. "I'm Robin. Which one are you?"

"I am this one," Cinnamon replied. "I am called Cinnamon."

"Welcome, well-met, and well-named," Robin said cheerfully. "As our old friend, Kiachif, would say. Are you enjoying Rraladoona so far?"

"Reh! Very especially the hrrrsses," Cinnamon said enthusiastically.

"Glad to hear it," Robin replied. "We're all horse-crazy here."

"Robin is my brother-in-law," Mike said. "His brother is married to my sister."

"A most complicated explanation of a simple relationship," Cinnamon observed.

"Sometimes it's very complicated," Robin agreed. "Say, Mike, I've got a sow in the flitter out front. She's due to farrow any time now, but she's running a temperature. I'm afraid she'll lose the litter."

"How in hell did you get a sick, pregnant pig into a hover?" Mike demanded.

"It's only because she knows she's my favorite that she trusted me enough. I have this way with women. Oh, hi, Nita," he said, mischievously peering at her sidelong from under his sweeping black lashes. Nita bent the bow of her delicious-looking lips into a shy smile, then retreated to the isolation stall.

"I'd better take a look at your pig, then," Mike said, grinning. "I hope she hasn't decided to give birth right in your car."

Robin looked alarmed. "I hope not! It's my sister Nessie's car."

Cinnamon barely noticed the two Hayumans depart, so entranced was he with the ruddy-coated gelding. He was mentally composing a poem to the species, and to this specimen in particular, when the

Hayuman Bert Gross pulled at his forelimb fur.

"If you want to see some more horses, we've got a whole bunch of them in a corral over to the other side of the building," Gross said, studiously casual.

"Reh!" Cinnamon exclaimed, picturing a sea of the beautiful animals. "I would be most grateful."

The Hrruban pulled Gross to one side. "What are you up to?" Errrne said in a low voice.

"I'm gonna show our guest," Gross said with careful emphasis, "a whole *lot* of horses."

Errrne, understanding the joke at last, dropped his jaw in a big grin. "Let us go!"

The paddock contained some thirty animals, huddled together near the feed troughs. One tiger-spotted appaloosa stood near the gate, scratching the side of his nose on the post. It glanced at the Hayuman and Hrruban without interest, but started violently and snorted at the sight of the Gringg. As Cinnamon came closer, the horse retreated until it was well within the crowd on the other side. It wheezed a warning sound. All the others in the pen looked up and stared with wary brown eyes at the stranger.

"These are all two-year-old geldings," Gross said.

"They are not hrrrsses?" Cinnamon asked, puzzled. "When is a hrrrss not a hrrrss?"

"Is that a joke?" Bert asked, elbowing his Hrruban companion. "Uh, when a horse—ah, forget it. Yeah, they're horses. Nice, aren't they?"

"Reh," Cinnamon breathed. He felt a deep affection rising in him for the big liquid eyes, slender limbs, and smooth pelts of these animals. Oh, what very attractive creatures they were. "I understand why Rraladoon prizes them so."

"Why don't you just go in and get acquainted with them?" Bert asked, opening the gate and standing back to courteously gesture him through. "They're all well handled."

"Oh, I would like that," Cinnamon said, and stepped into the paddock. Bert shut the gate behind him.

"What if he hurrrrts zem?" Errrne whispered.

"Don't worry," Gross muttered back. "They won't let him get anywhere near 'em."

The veterinarian's prediction almost came true. Wearing a beatific expression, Cinnamon walked toward the herd. Instantly, it split into two groups and cantered past him toward the opposite side of the corral.

The Gringg was disappointed that the animals were so shy around him. His new friend had assured him that they were friendly. Perhaps he was just too unfamiliar. If he allowed them to smell him, they would become used to him and come close enough to touch.

Extending one paw forward very slowly, Cinnamon walked toward the horses again. For the first ten paces, they stayed where they were, watching him approach. He had not observed before that their huge brown eyes were edged with white under the lids. He took another step, and one of the bigger animals tossed its head. That seemed to set off the others, who cantered away in a bunch, skittering and neighing, leaving the Gringg facing nothing at all. Patiently, he turned about and tried his approach again.

Try as he might, Cinnamon could not get close enough so that any of the lovely animals could sniff at his paw. Intent on his task, he could hear the gasps and bursts of sound made by the Doonarralans behind him, but he did not see them slapping one another on the back. He tried another approach: when the herd was downwind of him, he stood still, allowing the slight breeze to carry his scent to them.

The musk of his fur made a few of the horses rear and toss their heads, but they didn't bolt or show other signs of alarm. In a few moments, they calmed down completely except for a twitch here and there. Slowly, very slowly, Cinnamon moved closer with his paw out. As before, as soon as he was within a Gringg-length or two, the herd melted to either side of him and fled. Patiently, Cinnamon tried again.

"We could let this go on all day!" Gross said, red-faced with laughter. Errrne grunted breathlessly beside him.

Over and over, the same actions were repeated: the bearlike Gringg walked toward the herd, which split up and ran away from him. The Rraladoonans were enjoying themselves immensely. It was funnier each time it happened, and the Gringg's disappointment increased their pleasure. Then one of the horses in the paddock began to rear and whinny. Its eyes showed wide arcs of white, and its nostrils were flared.

"What's with that one? It's spooking badly now," Gross said, pointing. "I don't want it jumping the fence."

At first there seemed to be no reason for the horse's growing anxiety. As the herd split one more time, the two men outside the pen saw why.

"A mare's in zat bunch!" Errrne cried.

"Oh, fardles, and her colt is there, too," Bert said, hurrying to jump the fence. The mare cut out of the herd and made straight for the Gringg, swinging her head back and forth, showing her teeth.

"Cinnamon, get out of there!" he yelled. "Back off!"

The Gringg stood waiting for it, his eyes wide with joy.

Even trained as he was for accurate recall, Cinnamon was not ever able to describe exactly how the collision came about. One of the hrrrsses came out of the herd, directly toward him. Welcoming, he put out a paw for it to sniff, but greeting him was not what it intended. He saw a flash of eye, then teeth, then hard, round hooves flailing at his face. It cut his muzzle, making him bleed. The hooves struck him on the shoulder, the chest. Cinnamon's paw came up to protect his face, and hit the mare's head instead. Her neck broke with an audible snap. As Cinnamon watched, stunned, she sank to her knees and, rolling to one side, lay still. A half-grown horse trotted out of the herd, and stopping uncertainly halfway there, it emitted a tentative whinny, which grew sharper when there was no reply. Cinnamon realized with horror that this was her young. He had killed a mother horse and left an orphan.

He threw back his head and wailed his grief. Then the horses began to stampede!

The instant the wild howling started, Mike and Robin exchanged a look and raced toward that side of the building. They'd never heard such a sound before—a cross between a siren and a foghorn, a very insistent and unhappy foghorn—but they knew it meant trouble.

In the stableyard, there was a penful of hysterical horses hammering themselves against the far fence, and Mike's two junior associates staring with horror at the Gringg.

"What happened?" Mike demanded, looking from one to the other. "Why's he yelling like that?"

"That beast killed a horse," Bert Gross said, pointing wildly at Cinnamon, who was sitting on his haunches in the corral beside the body of the dead mare. "They're dangerous! He broke her neck with one swipe!" He hoped that Mike would take his story at face value. Neither he nor Errrne wanted to confess their part in the tragedy.

"Better get Todd," Robin said grimly.

• • •

The Hayuman and Hrruban traders, chafing from their enforced idleness while awaiting the outcome of the postponed conference, had spent a lot of time in the pub of the Space Center. The Center wasn't a large building, though additions had been made as trade to Doonarrala increased. In fact, there was more pub than spaceport facility. Ali Kiachif made it a point to stop in at least once a day and swap lies with whoever was hanging about. Any of his captains who needed to drop a private word in his ear could find him there, and many potential problems were quietly defused in that milieu.

Fred Horstmann and a couple of the others involved in the conference were having an afternoon drink with Kiachif. The subject, as it had been for weeks, was the Gringg.

"I can't guess whether they're funning us or not," Morwood said. He was a middle-ranker, a Codep shipper who had been out a fair number of years. He wanted most of all to get a cargo and leave the planet. He'd been here far too long.

"Fun? For fish, flesh, or fowl?" Kiachif asked, ripping the seal off a fresh bottle of mlada and pouring himself a glassful. "I'd say they're telling the truth."

"But it sounds like a joke," Horstmann offered, taking a pull on his beer. "Hard to believe they'd settle on such simple stuff, if you understand me."

The other traders grinned. "You've been around Kiachif too long," Captain Darwin said, looking open and innocent when the Codep chief turned a surprised glare on him.

"Not so simple, but it's a foot in the door, to be sure, a foot in the door," Ali said. "Nothing will do but fresh and new, which will keep our ships in the spacelanes. I like that well enough, if you follow my reasoning, and you do."

The debate went on, with about two thirds of the spacers firmly in the Gringg's corner, and the others uncomfortable and unsure of the new aliens' motivations. It was shaping up to a fine brawl, when Kiachif spotted Jon Greene walking through the security gate toward the landing bays.

Thank the Stars I outrank him, Kiachif thought. *I dislike him more than I hate stale bread and water. And I hear he's sweeties with Grace Castleton, though you'd think a lass of her rank would have better taste*. Greene was sure set on roiling up ill-feeling, and Kiachif knew, from his sources, that the commander'd come an alm's ace to making an intergalactic incident *happen.* Which would have been bad for new trade possibilities and *that* was not on in Kiachif's lexicon.

It's time he had a piece of my mind handed him, Kiachif decided. He gulped what was left in his glass and excused himself.

"I'll be back," he called to the publican. "Another bottle of the same, to be waiting." The man snapped the towel he was plying on the inside of a glass pitcher, and nodded.

The mlada was burning a pleasant warmth in Kiachif's stomach as he made his way through the chilly concrete corridors. He told himself he preferred a quiet life, but a good mill always helped the blood run warmer. If Greene didn't tell Kiachif why he was trying so hard to queer things, it wouldn't be for want of persuasion—of one form or another. He might even persuade the commander to show good manners.

Around the corner, the corridor was empty. His prey had a good stride on him; Greene must be pretty far ahead. Kiachif passed the control room. He waved a hand in at the door, and kept walking. One of the female technicians, a young woman with chocolate-dark skin, nodded to him. She was having a quiet talk with someone who wasn't visible from the doorway. A lover's chat, perhaps? Kiachif slowed down as he recognized the man's voice: the importunate Commander Greene.

He doubled back and put his ear next to the doorpost.

Whatever was going on in there, it wasn't love talk. He heard Greene say something about sensors, followed by a low and indistinguishable question. Chancing a quick look inside, Kiachif saw the woman shake her head.

"No, sir. It's all been by the book, I swear," she said. She sounded panicky, and her skin had a moist look of stress Kiachif did not like to see.

"And the records of the scans have all been filed under coded seals?" Greene's voice was smooth and low, but there was an unmistakable threat in it.

"Yes, sir." The woman's throat constricted on the second word, sending it up an octave. Kiachif's eyes went wide.

"Blank that screen!" Greene commanded. Hastily, she reached for the control, and the sensor pattern she'd been monitoring vanished. Kiachif hadn't had time for a good look at it, but he fancied he could reconstruct it, given time. There'd been three ships on the screen—three ships with the yellow dataprints of heavy weaponry. Fleet ships? But where bound, and why?

"It's a crime to reveal secure data to anyone without the correct classification," the commander said, continuing his harangue.

"I know that, sir," the technician said. "I'd never do that, sir."

"Good," Greene said, standing up and moving into Kiachif's line of sight. He leaned over her in an ominous fashion. That he scared her was obvious from her distraught expression. "See that you don't. You are to keep me or Admiral Barnstable posted on any change, but no one else, do you understand? An infraction of the regulations could put you into a one-by-two cell in a military prison on Earth for ten years."

The woman's eyes widened until Kiachif thought they'd pop right out of her head.

"Well, if that gall don't grease a goose's gizzard," Kiachif muttered. Abandoning his listening post, he strode boldly into the office.

"Afternoon, pretty lady," Kiachif began cheerily, as if he hadn't a care in the world. "I've got a ship coming in from Tau Ceti way. Wondered if you could give me a vector and an ETA. If it's no trouble, that is. Oh, hello, Greene. Leaving, are you?"

The Spacedep commander fixed Kiachif with a hostile stare. He was clearly unhappy to have been interrupted before he had totally cowed the poor girl.

"I was just going," he said. "Remember what I said," he told the technician. "Security!"

"Yes, Commander," the technician replied unhappily. She watched Greene leave, then turned to Kiachif, beads of sweat visible on her forehead. "How may I help you, Captain?" she asked, readying her hands on the keyboard at her station. Her voice petered out, and she swallowed.

"Is that rattlesnake giving you trouble, my dear?" Kiachif asked kindly, sitting down on the edge of the chair Greene had just vacated.

"Oh no, sir," she said quickly.

"Now, now, you know, I don't believe you at all, if you follow me," Kiachif said, his voice soothing. "That one has no manners. I'm sure that asking nicely would have gotten him the selfsame smiling service from a nice lass like you." He glanced up at the digital clock. "Ah, you're nearly off shift, aren't you?"

With a grateful look of near-fainting relief, she glanced the same way. "Fifteen minutes," she said with a sigh and a sagging of her shoulders.

"Well now, you wouldn't think of joining an ol' space captain for a tot or so of mlada, would you? A sort of thank-you for checking up on my ship? You look like you could do with a jolt, if you know what I mean."

She shot him a tentative smile. "I don't know as I should . . ."

"Why not? Your shift will be over, duty done, and a little relaxation's in order. You've been under quite a strain, with all the shipping in and out, and many's the glass I've had that's taken the weariness out of me in such a situation. So I recommend it highly to you, if you know what I mean."

After Greene's manner, the kindly old captain whom she'd known for years soothed her rattled nerves. A drink or two in pleasant company *was* just what she needed right now. She swiped back her hair with a shaking hand. "Oh, Captain," she said in a low voice suffused with desperation. "I'd like that very, very much."

CHAPTER 9

SINCE EVERYONE ON BOARD THE *WANDER DEN* WAS so busy that there wasn't even company for swimming, Weddeerogh asked his mother if he could visit the young people at the Double Bar Gemini Ranch. Grzzeearoghh thought that an excellent idea and immediately inquired of the Hayuman Zodd if this could be arranged. Todd asked Kelly, adroitly in the presence of Alison and Alec, but fortunately his wife was amenable to the notion even without the pressure of their pleas.

"I told you Teddy could come any time," she said. "Pop over and tell Nrrna, will you, kids? Is Grizz coming, too?" she added, immediately cataloguing what she had on hand in the freezer.

"No, just Teddy." Todd said. "With all the adults out and about trading or kibitzing, the little feller's likely to be lonely."

"Little feller?" Kelly mocked with a sly smile, and raised her hand to ear level.

"Comparatively," Todd said, grinning. "Buddy'll drop Teddy off right here. Save you a trip into town."

"Fine by me, as I thought the air cushions on the flitter would burst the day we collected the little feller and his sweet mommy from the grid." Kelly favored her husband with a sardonic look for the surprise she'd had when *all* of Grizz and her not-so-small cub had emerged from the mist.

"I'll clear up as much as I can in my office today," Todd said, "so I can join in the fun."

"Ha! Where were you when I needed you!" Kelly exclaimed, rolling her eyes but smiling. "Teddy's no problem, but *what* should I fix for him to eat this time?"

"Ask the gang," Todd suggested as he left.

• • •

News of Teddy's imminent visit sifted through other items of interest so that when Buddy skillfully landed the big Gringg shuttle, there were unofficial observers, too, as the five eager youngsters bounded to greet Weddeerogh. He had put on his best fish-scale collar and, at his dam's urging, brushed his fur until it gleamed. He had also shortened the cord of his voder so that it no longer prodded his ear or the back of his head.

Not that the voder could handle the shrieks and shouts of delight from the two Hayumans and three Hrrubans. He didn't even try to say the phrases of gratitude his dam had had him prepare.

"C'mon," said the Alec one, grabbing his hand and starting to pull him away from the house. "The (garble) just hatched and you've never seen baby (garble) before, Teddy."

Alison, Hrrana, and Hrrunival, either pushing or pulling him, started him on the way to the barn while the smallest Hrruban followed, wide-eyed.

"I must give your parent . . ." Teddy began, the translator stuttering at first until the Hrruban came out.

"Mom said you'd want to see the (garble)!" Alec said, tugging harder.

Teddy could see Kelly on the porch, waving for him to go with the children, so he felt completely excused from the courtesies his dam had insisted he perform in acceptance of family hospitality.

He found the newly hatched "chickens" (and he dutifully added that noun and "bantie" as "mother of chicks" to the vocabulary), delightful creatures, although he couldn't hear them peeping, as the others could, no matter how he fiddled with the voder.

Then he was taken on a tour of the hrrrses in the barn, and he pleased everyone by remembering the names he had been given on his previous visit. He wondered how long it would be before he could mention swimming in the lake again, but no, there were other newborn creatures for him to meet . . . katzz and kitthhhens. He did know the word "katz" . . . small furry being. Well, he must uphold the honor of his father, who was one of the most renowned linguists on their homeworld, so Teddy girded himself to remember the personal names of these new species. It wasn't easy to pick up new words: the Hayuman children talked so fast and the Hrruban brothers and sister interrupted them constantly, making it difficult for the voder to keep up.

"Here they are, Teddy," Hrrana said, beating the others to the place where the katz had kitthhhens.

Four tiny four-legged animals swarmed over Teddy, their mouths opening and closing, though the voder didn't pick up the sounds. Hrrana lifted one up to him and instructed him on how to handle the soft, squirmy things. It sniffed at him, as was proper, so he sniffed, very carefully, at it.

"(Garble) behind the ears," Hrrana said, and demonstrated. He asked her to repeat the first word and then added it to the rapidly increasing line of new vocabulary.

He gently extruded one claw only, because his digits were much larger than Hrrana's, and applied the appropriate pleasure. He could feel a rumbling through the palm of his paw.

"She's prrrring," Hrrana told him proudly, and he took this to mean the small creature accepted him.

"What is this kitthhhen? How big does it grow?" Teddy asked just as a larger, black and white creature of the same species came bounding over the hay-strewn place to investigate him. It sniffed at his feet, and courteously he squatted, bringing his head down to its level to get its scent.

"That's how big it grows," Hrrunival said. "Cats are from Earzz and are not intelligent."

"They are so," Alec replied with some heat. "Kasha's very intelligent."

"For a cat," Hrrana agreed, shooting a quelling glance at her brother.

"At least as intelligent as you, Hrrunival," Alec went on tauntingly.

As he evidently expected, Hrrunival charged at Alec, who lithely twisted out of the way and streaked for the wide-open barn door, Hrrunival in close pursuit. Clucking (rather like the chicken had), Alison removed the kitten from Teddy's paw.

"We'd better make sure the fight's fair," she said, and with Hrrana and Ourrh, who hadn't yet addressed the Gringg cub, she followed the boys. The little Gringg had no choice but to follow as fast as he could waddle. At the door, Alison looked back.

"Wait, Hrrana! We're leaving Teddy behind!"

"Ooops! He can't run verry fast, can he?" Hrrana observed, slowing down.

"He's doing the best he can," Alison replied.

Alec suddenly remembered his manners and grabbed hold of Hrrunival, evading the punch that came his way. "C'mon, let's do something that's fun for all of us. Hey, Teddy, what do you want to do?" he called out.

"I would like to swim," the cub said. "Swimming here last time was much pleasure."

"Should we try the creek this time?" Alec asked his twin.

"No, he wouldn't get very wet in the creek," she replied, scanning the girth of their guest.

The ducks on the farm pond scattered with noisy protests when the children, stripped naked, waded into the water and started to splash one another. Teddy unfastened his collar and laid it and his voder on those of his hosts.

"Confirmed," Lieutenant Gallup whispered, crawling on his knees and elbows into the ditch where Lieutenant Walters crouched. His long, sallow face was filmed with sweat under the camouflage makeup, and his brush-cut black hair was dusty. "The Gringg cub *is* there, with the Reeve and Hrruban kids. They're swimming in the pond, mother-naked."

"And the pond is right out in the open," Walters said, squinting through the tall grass into the sunny yard. His light blue eyes were two pale spots in an irregular stripe of black greasepaint. Raising his scope, he scanned the grounds of the Reeve and Hrriss farms. "D'ja see anyplace we can grab him alone?"

Gallup shook his head. "Not so close to the houses. The kids'll set up a ruckus. We'll have to wait until they're farther away. Too bad the pond's visible, 'cause they've all stripped off comms and voders. Damn!"

"Let's ooze down there anyhow. That fancy collar of the cub might be interesting to examine. Can't know what sort of technology's hidden in it. All the bruins wear something of the sort all the time they're downside."

Under a sky bluer than any he had ever seen, Teddy dived and swam and played with his new friends in water that smelled of fragrant grasses and weeds. It tasted unusual but very nice.

The Hayumans and Hrrubans taught him games by demonstrating between themselves how they were played. One required each swimmer to keep away from one chosen to be "tagger." Alison lost that draw, and the game required lots of splashing and swimming and shrieking for those eluding the tagger. Another game made use of a colored ball which the players were required to catch with their hands. Teddy had to be careful of his claws, which inadvertently unsheathed to make the catch, indenting the surface of the ball. It made him realize how fragile Rraladoonan toys were, as were the persons of Rraladoona. It was also very difficult to throw the squishy ball any great distance, depriving him of the advantages that strength and speed gave him in the other contests, to the evident joy of the younger Hrruban. Hrrunival was so determinedly competitive that Teddy started losing on purpose to keep the young felinoid from feeling bad. The object of the game was to get the ball over cross poles at each end of the relatively oval pond. After a certain number of these objectives had been attained, Hrrunival gestured for Teddy and the others to join him at his end of the pond, pantomiming that they should now swim as fast as possible to the other end. Bored, Ourrh went back to the house. Teddy wished that the voder was waterproof. He was losing valuable words which he was certain no other Gringg would collect.

The children quickly discovered that though Teddy couldn't move as quickly as they could on land, none of them could touch him for speed in the water. His big paws scooped waves out of his way, and his powerful tail gave him extra thrust. No matter what kind of a head start he allowed the others, he was always at the other side of the pond before any of them were halfway across.

"No fairrrr!" Hrrunival cried, spitting out a mouthful of duckweed at the end of another unsuccessful race. "He's got a ruddrrrr behind!"

"You've got a tail, too," Alec told him. "Use it!"

"Mine does not wrrrk zat way. Also, all my furrr is so wet, it holds me back. Your bare skin is an advantage."

"Teddy's got fur, too," Alison said, shaking her black mop out of her eyes. "Lots more than you do, that holds liters more water."

"I'm tired of losing," Hrrunival said, pouting and splashing with his arms. "What if we have a test whrrr Teddy swims, and we run on ze bank? We'll see who's fastrrr all over."

This motion was carried as a good idea and the alteration explained to Teddy. He never objected to staying in water. The Rraladoonans climbed out of the pond and shook the water from their skins and fur. Taking his voder from the pile, Alec named himself as official starter.

"Okay, once around the pond to this point here," he said, drawing a line in the soft earth down to the waterline with his toe. "If anyone falls down or gets hurt, the race stops right there."

"Agreed," Teddy said. This Hayuman was most careful of the safety of others.

"Okay," Hrrunival said. The girls nodded.

Teddy braced his toes in the thick mud. The others bent down with one foot behind, their hands touching the ground on either side of their forward feet.

"On your mark, get set, GO!" Alec shoved off, running. His long legs gave him an immediate lead over the two Hrrubans and his sister. Teddy thrust off powerfully from the bank and plowed across the pond.

Alec was a swift runner. Hampered by having to avoid reeds and water plants, Teddy needed to concentrate closely on his stroke to keep up with him. He could hear the Hrruban boy yards behind them, grunting with frustration as he drove his short legs to their fastest pace.

A small fish, disturbed from its hiding place among the reeds, leaped into the air like a rocket, directly underneath Teddy's face. Thinking of the predatory fish on his motherworld, he jumped up to avoid it. It fled him. Sputtering, he rolled over in the water to clear his nose and mouth. Alec gained a few paces and Hrrunival was closing faster now. Teddy kicked to right himself onto his round belly, and paddled furiously to regain the lead. He was nicely buoyant, but the water plants all around him were dragging at his fur, slowing him down.

Only a few lengths to go. He spat weeds out of his face and sucked in a deep breath of air to sustain himself for one final burst. In three strokes, he crossed the shallow line etched in the bank. Alec was still right beside him. Alison and Hrrunival were nearly together, coming in second. Hrrana was dead last. Teddy heaved himself out of the water and stood dripping to congratulate Alec.

"It's a tie!" Alec said, slapping him on the back and splashing all of them. "You're fast."

Teddy reached for his voder and put it on. Alec repeated his last words.

"You are . . . fast, too," Teddy said. "I worked hard, but we both won." He turned to Hrrana. "I am sorry." He meant to console her for losing, but Hrruban words failed him.

The girl seemed to understand his intentions perfectly well. She shook her head with cheerful resignation. "It is all rrright. I nevrrr win," she said, "so it does not bozzer me."

Hrrunival was not such a good loser, but he tried to cover his disappointment. "Well, that . . . was a good . . . contest!" he panted, still short of breath. "Wanna . . . zry rrriding hrrses?"

"Yes! But I do not know how," Teddy said, looking around for his collar. Surely he had put it right with the voder. No, there it was on the bush. He shrugged, not too concerned that it was other than where he thought he had left it. The children finished dressing and strapped on their voders and belt-radios.

"I'll teach you," the young Hrruban said, condescendingly patting Teddy on the arm.

"Hrrrrrrunival," Hrrana said, fuming with embarrassment at her brother's tone. "You haven't ze patience to teach anyone to *hop*."

Not looking back, he twitched his tail at her and led Teddy away, water still dripping off their fur. (Alec and Alison followed, grinning.)

"Close, but no luck," Gallup muttered under his breath as they watched the children leave the pond. "Didn't have long enough to check anything on that collar. Good thing I got it to hang on the branch." He and Walters had been within meters of the pond when the children climbed out.

"Commander Greene wants that little bear stat," Walters said. "Figures questioning the kid's our best chance to find out what the Gringg are really doing here. He might even be our ticket aboard their ship, if his folks want him back safely."

"The Hrruban kid said they're going riding."

"Couldn't be better," Walters said, grinning. His teeth glinted. "We'll let 'em get clear of the yard, jam the kids' comms and be ready to snatch the bear. He's sure to fall off a time or two and we ought to be able to isolate him from the others. The flitter's waiting for us just this side of the woods."

Teddy had already been introduced to Tornado and Fairy, the twins' mounts. Looking over the other mares and geldings, Alec and Alison tried to choose one for their guest while the Hrrubans went back to the stables for their own ponies.

They came back, leading their mounts, before Alec and Alison had decided which horse suited Teddy best.

"We need something so bomb-proof you could drop a Big Momma Snake on its back and it wouldn't spook," Alec decided.

"That's Teabag, then," Alison said.

"What saddle, though?" Alec asked, critically examining their guest's body.

"We'll look for something," Alison said. "Hrrana, will you saddle my gray for me, please?"

"Ssure," the obliging Hrruban said and expertly threw a pad and then a saddle over Alison's gray pony mare. Hrrunival went so far as to help bridle her. Teddy stood to one side watching, feeling considerable respect for his new friends.

Teddy was unused to the idea of having pets larger than he was. Yet the hrrrsses, who stamped an occasional heavy and dangerous-looking foot down on the concrete floor of the building, seemed content to scrve. There were no longer large animals on Teddy's homeworld, though his dam had told him there had once been many different kinds. How lucky were Rraladoonans to have such a variety. Then Alec came out of the barn with his bay animal.

"Now, Teddy, watch me! This's how you mount," Alec cried, and sprang into the saddle, wiggling from side to side to show how secure his saddle was. "There! See how easy that is?"

"Alec, you nit," his sister admonished him. "Teddy couldn't vault that. He'll need to mount from something."

"Yeah, I guess he would," Alec said, dismounting and looking around for a suitable surface. "Sorry, Teddy, we were just about born in the saddle."

The mental picture this evoked for Teddy made him gasp. He could not picture his dam awkwardly poised over the back of an animal. Surely it could not be true! Alec caught his expression of open-mouthed horror and started to laugh. Teddy realized his statement had been a joke, and added sheepish staccato grunting to the merriment.

Alison looked him over with a measuring eye.

"And Teddy's a different shape from us, not much leg. There's no way he could rise at the trot," she said, turning to her twin. "But old Teabag's a pacer, isn't he?"

"Say, wouldn't a pack saddle give Teddy a lot of support?" Alec suggested. "I mean, remember when we used them for jousting-saddles when we played knights and ladies?"

"Ze very zing," Hrrana said. "We can pad it wiz extra blankets and a sheepskin."

"Worth a try," the redheaded boy said. He jumped off his horse, ran up to the end of the barn, and came back laden with a strange contraption and an assortment of blankets and numnahs.

Together, the twins prepared his mount, the golden-brown hrrrss named Teabag. The children explained that Teabag was a "single-foot," which confused Teddy, who could see that the animal had four legs, just like all the other hrrrsses. He was a bigger animal than the children's ponies. And his back, where Teddy was to sit, was higher off the ground.

"Daddy always gives Teabag to people who've never been on a horse before," Alison explained with gay reassurance. "He knows more about riding than we do," and she giggled.

Her preparations complete, she signalled Teddy to approach. Teabag turned his head to eye this unusual form, and he breathed noisily between his lips. Each time the small Gringg attempted to get close to the horse, the animal edged his backside away. Then Alec pulled sharply on the reins.

"Get up there," he ordered, and the horse sidled close to the bales of hay that had been piled in the form of a mounting block for Teddy's benefit. "Jump up on these, Teddy, and we'll get you in the pad. We've even got a neck strap for you to hang onto. No one's ever fallen off Teabag."

"Safe as houses," Hrrunival said, snickering a little as Teddy dutifully climbed up on the bales.

"Throw your right leg over," Alec said, pushing against Teabag's right side so the old horse couldn't dodge his would-be rider.

Teddy managed that, though he could feel himself stretching the skin between his legs. Maybe Gringg were not meant to ride horses, even if Hrrubans could. Still, it was not uncomfortable and there was support for his lower back and a slot for his tail to fit through, too.

"Yeah, the pack saddle even has a tail hole," Alec told the others. He grinned up at Teddy. "Now, these are called reins. Reins. They guide the horse. Pull left and he'll go left, pull right and he'll go right. Pull both reins back hard and he'll stop."

"Ol' Teabag'll stop more zan he starts," Hrrunival said with another snigger.

Teddy nodded, trying to assimilate the knowledge while the horse moved from side to side under him. Inadvertently he clutched both reins, leaned back, and convulsively tightened his legs against the sides of the animal.

"Whoa there, Teabag," Alec said, grabbing at the bridle by the bit. "Hey, you did just right then, Teddy, leaning back and tightening your legs. You'll be a rider in next to no time. Just sit deep in the, ahemm . . . pack saddle. Grab on to the crosspiece, here—" Alec showed him the leather-covered bar. "All you have to do on ol' Teabag is sit and let your body move with the horse!"

"I will try," Teddy promised.

"Oh, Alec, I'm not sure if he'll be able to stay on," Alison said, frowning at the shortness of the Gringg's leg despite stirrups shortened to the very last hole in the leather.

"He'll do fine," Alec said, nodding his head with assurance. To justify such confidence in his abilities, Teddy determined that he would.

"Here we go!" said Alec as he once again vaulted to Tornado's back. As soon as he saw the others were mounted, he dug his heels into the horse's flanks and Tornado moved forward. Teddy, right behind him, followed his example. To Teddy's absolute delight, Teabag immediately obeyed, forcing his rider forward. Startled, Teddy grabbed at the crosspiece and that gave him a feeling of more security. Then they were all out of the barn and walking briskly away from the yard. To his surprise, Teddy enjoyed the movement. It was exciting. The hrrss smelled good, too, always a propitious sign. He felt that it might not be a bad thing after all to be born in the saddle.

"Where do we go?" he asked.

Alec swivelled around to face him. "How about just down to the river and back?" he suggested. "We'll go near the marsh. Maybe see some drrr-frogs?"

"Toward the marsh," Gallup said, scrambling out of the hollow on hands and knees. "Ready to deploy the jammer."

Walters was right behind him. Keeping their distance, they trailed the string of horses. The five young riders kept their horses to a slow steady pace, moving farther and farther from the security of the ranch houses. When they were far enough ahead, the two Spacedep men dropped away to one side, pacing silently through the standing crops until they paralleled the little group.

"Be ready to grab him," Walters said.

The path was a worn ribbon of earth drawn through flower-strewn meadows, skirting golden crop-fields and going over green hills. Where the path was level with the surrounding terrain, the horses walked abreast. Alec and Alison sat so naturally in the leather cradles that they appeared to be part of the animals. Hrrunival would occasionally hurry his hrrrss forward ahead of the others, then turn back to rejoin the formation. Nobody minded the pudgy Hrruban's plunges and darts, least of all Teabag. It was a peaceful day. Avians winging in the sky sang sweet chirrups, and the breeze smelled delicious and intriguingly different. Teddy felt happier than he could ever remember. He wanted to stay on Rraladoon forever and ride hrrrsses every day until he rode as easily as Hrrunival did. The children chatted and laughed, asking Teddy about life on his world and matching his experiences with some of theirs.

"I am sad," said Teddy. "I am sad to know that in the future I will be too big to ride these beautiful creatures. This is more fun than anything I have ever done!"

The four other children regarded him with sympathy.

"Would plow horses be big enough?" Alison asked her brother, eyeing the young bruin.

"Uh . . ." Alec said, measuring Teddy with an eye. "Not for a really fully grown-up Gringg. Not Captain Grizz's size, for sure. But Teddy is a male and will never be that big."

"What was it like to come all this way in a starship?" Alison asked then.

Teddy's Hrruban vocabulary did not include many superlatives, so it was difficult to find the words to explain.

"I was not yet born when the voyage started," he said, no longer aware of the hesitation in the voder turning his Gringg into their Hrruban, "but I have been travelling all my life. Always stars around us, some very bright and big. Some dim. We came to one place where there was nothing but big rocks in orbit. My sire said that the sun had burst open in one great whoosh. We have orbited several planets, but I was told they were not right for Gringg. Then I had to learn what was right for Gringg, which is right for Hayuman and Hrrubans, too. Much more fun to see than to learn." And he made a broad gesture, dropping his jaw to show them how happy he was. "Were you born here on this planet?"

"Yup, all of us," Alec said. "Mom was, too, but Dad was born on Earth. And hated it."

"Earzz?" asked Teddy.

"Yeah, Hayumans originate on Earth and—"

"Hrrubans come from Hrruba," finished Hrrunival.

"But you are Rraladoons?"

"We all are," Alison said from where she rode slightly behind Teddy. "Let's see if Teddy can manage to trot a bit, okay?"

When they pushed their horses to faster movement, Teddy made a tentative grab for the crosspiece, but Teabag seemed to flow forward and soon Teddy released his hold, leaning back so his tail would keep him steady.

"Hey, Teddy, you're doing just great," Alison called, but somehow Teddy did not trust his balance enough to turn around and thank her.

Soon they pulled the horses back to a walk, for they had reached a forested area and could no longer ride spread out. Teddy's fur was beginning to dry in long rats and tangles. He combed at a few of the worst knots with his claws, fearing the thorough brushing at the hands of his sire if he arrived back at the ship so untidy. Eonneh was never unkind, but he was merciless with tangles in his cub's thick fur, and smoothing them out sometimes hurt Teddy. Eonneh threatened, not seriously, to plait all of Teddy's fur and leave it that way if he could not keep it neat. Working carefully with one hand, he undid a mass of stringy fur and extracted a strand of lakeweed. It smelled interesting, so he tasted it. Not bad.

Hrrunival was behind him now. He was careless and inclined to show off. Without a strong hand to control it, his hrrrss had its snout almost up Teabag's tail, probably continuing some private argument on-going between the two animals. Teabag kicked backwards with one hoof to discourage the untoward familiarity. Hrrunival's mount reared and whinnied a protest, moving in again. Teabag stopped short, making Teddy rock violently forward in the saddle, and turned to snort, as if to demand the other hrrrss leave him alone. Instead, he caught a sniff of hot, wet bear, and his eyes rolled white. The hrrrss's neck arched, its nostrils flared, and Teabag swung his head forward.

"What is he doing?" Teddy shouted, alarmed, clutching for the saddlehorn.

Alec turned to look, and his eyes went wide. "Hold him! Hrrunival, grab his lead. Teddy, pull back on the reins!"

"It does no good!" Teddy bellowed.

The sound of the Gringg roar was the last straw. The spooked gelding shot off along the trail with Teddy bouncing on his back. The little Gringg struggled to hold on, gripping as hard as he could with his knees to keep from tumbling off. He pulled at the reins, but the horse refused to respond to the pressure. It was running away as fast as it could from the funny smell.

"Come on!" Alec shouted, spurring Tornado after the wailing Teddy. "We have to stop them before they hit the marsh. There could be early snakes rising."

The other three wheeled to follow. They were responsible for Teddy. How could they ever go home again if their guest got hurt? The ground in the swamps was notoriously unsafe. The horse could slip on the unsteady path, both mount and Gringg ending up in deep, viscous mud. And what would they say to Grizz if Teddy got eaten by a snake?

"The horse bolted with him," Gallup radioed to Walters, now a dozen meters behind him. "We've got him alone. Deploying jammer."

"Following," Walters said. "Stay out of sight. Radio silence, now!"

Keeping their eyes open for the other children, the two men pelted down the hill, following the runaway horse and rider into a stand of young trees at the edge of the meadow.

Teabag charged off the path down into a deep gully, twisted down the sloped sides, then bounded across a narrow but fast-flowing stream. One of his hooves slipped on a stone in the middle of the brook, throwing Teddy forward. Anchored by only his frantic grasp of the crosspiece, the reins had somehow got wrapped about his arms, effectively tying him in the saddle with just enough slack to let him bounce with every jolt of the runaway horse.

"Help!" he cried and shifted one paw, his claws instinctively extending so that he dug into Teabag's neck. The horse, already frightened, now reached the stage of terror where all he wanted to do was rid himself of what was on his back. Teabag charged up a bank and headed directly into a thicket, hoping to brush the predator off. Teddy had to cover his face with both hands to protect it against the thin branches that whipped past. The reins wound tightly around his palm jerked again and again as Teabag tossed his head wildly from side to side. He brushed against tree trunks and shot through bushes, snorting and neighing furiously. The Gringg, afraid of being thrown off, shifted his grasp to the crosspiece again, digging his claws into the wood beneath the leather and shut his eyes tight.

• • •

"Hurry!" Alec shouted. Tornado crested the bluff overlooking the summer-creek and came to a halt. The other horses cantered up beside him.

"Where's he gone?" Alison demanded.

Hrrana scanned the woods on the other side of the stream and pointed to where the bracken was disturbed. "Zere!" she cried.

"We can't get zrough zere," Hrrunival said, gawking. "It is solid forrrrst. Ze hrrses won't obey if we zry to frrce zem in."

"You're right," Alec agreed. "Teabag must have been scared so much he just went through like a rocket. We'll have to go around on the path and hope we catch up with them."

He guided Tornado down the gully and up the other side so that they skirted the woods. They found the path, which was marked by yellow streamers tied around two small trees flanking its entrance to show it had been widened and cleared of dangerous plants. As hers was the steadiest horse of the four, Alison urged Fairy in first, leaving Alec to bring up the rear.

Once under the roof of leaves, the group scanned the area to their right, looking for clues of Teddy's passage. There was nothing moving in the woods except for an urfa that looked up, chewing, with tender leaves sticking out on either side of its narrow jaws. It fled when Hrrunival sat up high in his saddle and yelled.

"Teddy! Teddy! Can you heeaaaarrrr meeeee?"

There was a slight echo as the trees caught his cry, but no answer.

Alison led them as fast as she dared. The path was narrow, and wound to avoid big trees and fallen trunks. Several small brooks cut through the floor on this side of the Bore River. The riders forded the streams, only centimeters deep.

The four took turns calling out. "Teddy!" "Are you all right?" "Answer us!" "Teddy!" "Teddy!"

"If we don't find him soon, we'll have to call for help," Alec said, peering ahead as he felt along his belt for his handset.

"Oh, no," Hrrunival protested, as his friend pushed the signal button. "Do not. I will get in zrouble. It is all my fault. My hrrss made his nrrvous, and it rrran away. Please let us find him frrst."

"We'd better," Alison said, looking at Alec, stricken. She punched furiously at her handset. "My communicator's not working."

"Neither is mine," said Alec with an eloquent groan. "Mom

will feed us to the snakes!" He shouted out again, "Teddy! TEDDDDIEEEE!"

"Can't . . . keep . . . up," Walters called to Gallup. The horse with the young Gringg was well ahead of them, vanishing in the thick cover of shrubs and trees. "You go on. Going . . . for . . . car!" Walters slowed to a stop, and bent over to catch his breath.

"Aye!" Without looking back, the other Spacedep man shouldered his light pack and kept running.

The forest thinned eventually, fading away to whippy saplings and high grasses flattened where the deer and urfa slept at night. Alison led them around to the right, toward, as Alec put it, "Teabag's probable trajectory." Beyond the woods, the ground was soft and soggy. The riders skirted the edge of the bright green patches of bog, hoping that by staying close to trees, which their fathers had told them liked "to keep their toes dry," they would be able to stay out of the clutch of quickmud.

About a hundred meters from where the path left the woods, Hrrunival's sharp eyes spotted the first signs of Teddy's passage. A long streamer of dark fur hung on the point of a broken twig about two meters into the forest on their right. To the left, the mud was churned up. Green-tinged water already filled hoofprints that pointed arrow-straight into the heart of the marsh.

"There could be snakes! We've gotta find him," Alec moaned, voicing what all of them were already thinking. It was early, but even a Big Momma Snake might be wriggling out there. "If anyone's afraid, you'd better go home now. Get Mom, or Aunt Nrrna, or go call Uncle Robin or Uncle Dan."

"I'm not afraid," Hrrunival said at once, though his green eyes were saucer-sized and his tail lashed.

"Nor I," Hrrana cried. Alison just shook her head.

"Okay," Alec said, taking a deep breath. "Here we go."

The land changed around Teddy. First, branches stopped hitting him in the face and feet. Then, stinking, sticky mud got thrown up at him by the hrrrss's hooves. Suddenly, the mud changed to wet sand, then very dry sand. Teabag's feet foundered and slid. Teddy cried out as the hrrrss fell down and rolled on top of him. He wasn't hurt, because the sand was so soft, but he was scared by all that weight on him. Suddenly it lifted, yanking the reins one more time, and they ripped free of Teddy's hands.

Teabag scrambled to his feet and shook himself vigorously, splattering sand everywhere. Realizing that at last he was free of his rider who was floundering in the sand beyond him, the horse made straight for the safety of his home barn.

"Stop!" Teddy called to him. "Don't go! I am lost!"

The Gringg roar only served to speed the gelding on his way.

Teddy pulled himself up out of the sand and brushed at his coat. Now it was not only matted, but dust and grit were ground in all the way to the skin. He scratched at his belly, which emitted a deep, rumbling sound.

"They did not feed me yet," Teddy said wonderingly, "and I am hungry." Such a thing had never happened to him before. But what was there to eat in this hilly desert overlooking the smelly marsh, or in the big river he could see down the hill to his left? If his new friends were here, he could have asked them. This was their world. They would know what to eat here.

Wait, there was a smell! It was faint because the air was so dry, but he was sure he had caught it.

The breeze that carried the scent was coming from behind him. He turned and clambered on all four paws up the dune. At the top, he saw a dark-furred being with its head busy over its front paws. It was eating! Teddy was so excited that he scrambled toward it.

The crest of the dune gave, and tumbled him bawling with surprise into the bottom of a sandy cup. In the midst of a sandy nest of eggs, a mda looked up, startled. When Teddy appeared at the top of the next dune, it met his eyes.

"Are you Gringgish?" Teddy asked hopefully. It was unlikely that more true Gringg had come here, but he might be one of the sort of Gringg that lived here. It was not impossible, Teddy thought, remembering katz and Hrrubans. "I am Weddeerogh, of the *Wander Den*, cub of Grrzzeeraoghh and Eonneh. Can you help me? I am hungry and lost. What are you eating? It smells good. Can I have some?"

The mda, accustomed to living by itself and avoiding creatures that talked, was taken aback to hear unfamiliar sound emitted by another mda. It eyed Teddy with suspicion. The animal was fully his size, Teddy noted, and obviously meant to attack to defend its find. But surely courtesy would require this Gringgish creature to offer him some?

"Please. I am only a little Gringg. Will you not share?" Teddy waited politely. The strange Gringg did not reply, other than to start a low growling which reverberated in gibberish through the voder. Confused, but unwilling to leave a source of food, Teddy rolled back on his tail and settled in to wait.

That calculated act suddenly unnerved the mda. Attack it could understand, and knew how to defend itself. But the smell of this creature was different, subtly menacing. Suddenly the mda decided that it had had enough egg. Growling with annoyance, it picked its way gingerly across the hot sand and disappeared among the marsh plants.

That was a decision of sorts, Teddy realized, galumphing down and up the hill of sand toward the good smell. If the strange Gringg had none of his words, this was his way to tell him it was all right to share, and that he wouldn't measure how much food Teddy ate.

The stranger had already eaten many eggs, to judge by the number of shells strewn around, but the nest contained many more, half-uncovered in the sand. Teddy picked one up carefully and it sagged around his handpaw. He sniffed and the smell was good, not tainted by unpleasantness. His father had told him that most of the food the planet offered was good for Gringg to eat. Reassured by both smell and paternal remarks, he tore it open with his claws. He plunged his muzzle into the heart of the egg and drank the delicious yolk. Extending his long tongue, Teddy licked his lips and square muzzle with pleasure. There were enough eggs here to make several good meals for a small Gringg. He would not be greedy. He'd eat only enough to take the edge off his hunger. He picked up another egg, pierced one end of the shell, and sucked the contents out. That way he would keep his face fur clean.

He had emptied quite a few eggs in this fashion when he heard hoofbeats. Teddy stood up and, peering over the dunes, saw Alec approaching on Tornado. He pulled so hard on the reins that Tornado stood up on two hind legs, which delighted Teddy.

"He's here!" Alec cried, and the others quickly joined him. "But you're in the dunes, Teddy! We've got to get you out of here! It's dangerous."

"You've found him?" Alison cried in relief. "And Teabag, too? Is he all right? What's he doing?"

Alec squinted at the little round figure, who was waving something white at him. "Teabag's not here, but Teddy's eating snake eggs."

They climbed up to meet him, panting in the dry air. Teddy was ecstatic that his friends had found him.

"Have some!" he said. "These eggs are good to eat, and I am so hungry. The strange Gringg let me have some. Are you hungry?"

"Well, yes," Alison admitted, but looked queasily at the raw egg. "But we usually eat these cooked."

"Ooh, cooked!" Teddy opened wide red eyes. "That would be good, also!"

"I like zis little guy," Hrrunival said. "He's got class!"

"Wait," Alec said, squatting down beside Teddy. He, too, refused the egg, so Teddy felt obliged to eat what he had opened. Then Alec looked at him queerly. "What other Gringg?"

Teddy swallowed a mouthful of yolk and pointed the way the stranger had gone. "He never spoke to me, but that is not unheard of," he said.

Hrrunival scrambled to look at the tracks that led away from the snake nest. "It was a mda!" he gasped. "And it left you alone?" His voice cracked on the last word.

"Reh. It did not speak to me, but we have not been introduced."

Alison was laughing. "Mda can't talk. They're not intelligent."

"Like the katz?" Teddy asked.

"Not like cats at all," Alison said, her face screwed up in earnest. "Mda're dangerous carnivores, Teddy."

"What is carnivore?"

"It eats meat!"

"So do I eat meat!" the young Gringg protested.

Hrrana, ever cautious, was checking the perimeter for snake signs. "I see no tiddlers, but zere are ozzer nests already made. We should go away as quickly as possible."

"It's zoo earrrly for anyzing but tiddlers," Hrrunival said, holding his head up to sniff the breeze.

"Snake Hunt is only dayz away," his sister reminded him.

"But not yet."

Since no one moved away, Teddy went back to eating eggs. They were so delicious, he could not understand why his friends did not want to share them. Nor why they kept looking around them nervously at the dunes.

Gallup spotted the white-eyed horse with the torn pack saddle plunging toward him on the swamp trail. The young Gringg had been thrown off, then. He had only to find the cub now. The horse saw him and shied away, continuing its panicked gallop down the track. Gallup palmed sweat out of his face and kept moving. He surveyed the path for footprints, but there were none except those the horse had just left. It must be heading for home. All he had to do now was follow its tracks back to the cub. The stink of the marsh was dying away as the terrain sloped up and into less fertile soil. Ahead of him were the snake dunes. Wonderful Spacedep maps warned him against going into the desert unarmed. The big Rraladoon snakes were capable of eating an entire horse, let alone a winded lieutenant.

As he topped the next rise, he looked down onto the dunes. And there, on the top of one of the sandy hillocks was the little bruin. Alone, too! A perfect opportunity! Gallup reached for his side arm. If the kid agreed to come quietly, Gallup wouldn't have to use force, but after a chase like that one, his patience was gone. The kid was looking down, busy with something messy. Gallup crept around the edge of the dune, staying just out of sight.

Behind him, he heard rhythmic pounding on the sand. He jumped into cover just in time to avoid being seen by the four youngsters riding out of the woods. The little Gringg glanced up and waved. Gallup snorted in annoyance at the lost opportunity. By mere seconds. He hoped Walters would get to him quickly with the flitter. He checked his tracer stud to see that it was still working. This was their last chance to grab the Gringg. He and Walters would have to carry him off in full view of the other children. If they protested, he'd have to take care of them, too.

Kelly was busily preparing a big lunch for the kids, who would surely be hungry after swimming. It was only as she walked into the living room that she realized there were no sounds coming from the direction of the pond. She had also just realized that there was a horse tied up to the door-post and a hovercar on the drive, when the doorbell rang.

"Who—?"

"Kelly, my dear!" She opened the door to see Jilamey Landreau, finger poised over the bell for a second stab.

If she'd thought that Jilamey had toned down his wardrobe in the years since she had first met him, she was profoundly mistaken. He was dressed in bright, bull-angering red that stood out from the surrounding landscape like an out-of-season poppy. Still, when Kelly considered it, the color was perfectly becoming to him. She didn't know why she thought men shouldn't wear bright colors.

"Hello, dear Jilamey," she said, leaning over to collect a kiss. "Barrington, this is an occasion." The gentleman's gentleman was waiting down beside the hover. He was clad in sober brown, a color that blended into the scenery as thoroughly as his master's garb did not.

"Mrs. Reeve." Kelly thought for a horrible moment Barrington would bow to her, but he only nodded.

"Old Caution there insisted on following me here in the car," Jilamey said plaintively. "You see why I don't bring him to Rraladoon very often? He mothers me, Kelly. Make him stop."

Kelly shook her head. "You need it sometimes, sweetheart. Come in, both of you. Where are Todd and Hrriss?"

Jilamey laughed. "Oh, likely in their office in the government building," he said. "I thought I heard something about 'too much to do before Snake Hunt' as they left."

"Sometimes, I wish they were both twins," Kelly said, her hands on her hips. "I love having these visitors, but I wish that things would calm down a little so I could see my husband once in a while." She sighed. "I can't damn the man for having priorities, but it does get a little lonely."

Jilamey laughed and seized her hand. "Now I know you're telling a fib, beautiful lady. Where are the children?"

"I'd just realized that it was too quiet out there," Kelly said. "Teddy, Grizz's cub, came today. With all the mighty discussions at full spate, no one has time for the youngster. Well, they won't want to miss their favorite uncle."

"Good!" Jilamey said. "I have a special present. It finally arrived from Terra on the latest shuttle."

"Good heavens," Kelly exclaimed, going over to the comunit and punching in the twins' codes. "What is it?"

"A model airplane, made from blueprints from centuries ago. It really flies! I tried it from the roof of Alreldep block."

"Only you could get away with that!" Kelly said, all too aware of the repressive character of Terran society. "That's funny. There's no answer." She punched in the code again, thinking she had gotten the signal wrong. "Nothing."

Nrrna arrived with her sleeping cub, greeting Jilamey graciously before she saw the anxious expression on Kelly's face. "Somezing is wrong?"

"I told those children to take their radios!—No, they did take them," Kelly said, glancing at the rack which held only one, hers. "I remember the Cats picking them up as they went out the door."

"So why do zey not answerrr?" Nrrna asked anxiously.

"I don't know," Kelly said, biting her fingers. "Oh, wait, maybe they're out in the barn. No need to turn the units on there. Only, surely we'd hear them . . ." She looked anxiously at Jilamey.

"Barrington? Search the barn for the youngsters, would you?" Jilamey said, and his servant moved with great alacrity, covering the distance to the main barn in seconds. "He keeps fit," Jilamey remarked as he gently extracted the comunit from Kelly's hand and punched in a sequence. "Just a little trick I learned . . . to see if the units are broadcasting. Ah, that's odd. There's interference from somewhere."

"A jammer?" Kelly cried, really alarmed now.

"Could be natural . . ."

"Maybe David's seen them." Kelly ran to her computer and called the ranch manager on the land lines. "He hasn't seen them at all," she said, severing the connection. "I wonder . . ." She punched in another number. "Todd? Hi. Are the children with you?"

"No," Todd told her. "Are they on their way here? I'll keep a lookout for them."

Kelly winced, for suddenly she was sure that the kids were in trouble. But Todd had broken the connection before she could tell him that. Then Barrington mounted the steps to the porch.

"I'm sorry to report that there is no sign of the children in the barn or the pond. Further, five stalls are empty. Would that be significant?"

"It would! Oh God," Kelly said, "they should have *told* me they were going riding. And with a total novice in tow, too."

"The hovercar could be used to search," Barrington offered.

"And I can summon my personal heli from the house," Jilamey added. "We'll find the children in next to no time, Kelly. Don't you bother your head." He took the comunit back and called for his pilot to bring the heli immediately to the Double Bar Gemini. Then he strode to the wall where the big map was tacked. "Hmmm, let's see. Where do the children usually ride, Kelly?"

She shrugged. "They ride everywhere."

"But not everywhere with a complete novice like Teddy."

Kelly frowned, glancing at Nrrna for help. "No, they would probably go across the meadows and into the forest . . ."

"Well, that would require the heli. Barrington, you take the road toward the village in case they went that way. Your children are very resourceful, Kelly, Nrrna. I wouldn't worry—yet! No sooner do we leave than they'll come back, having done a tour of the meadow for Teddy's sake."

Not quite convinced, Kelly and Nrrna nodded uncertainly, each thinking of all the dangers that could befall five small children on Rraladoon so close to Snake Hunt time.

Just then, four things happened: a riderless horse clattered into the barnyard, Ourrh was found in the barn, asleep in the hay, Jilamey's heli arrived, and so did the big Gringg shuttle.

CHAPTER 10

ALTHOUGH KELLY AND NRRNA WAVED FRANTICALLY at the shuttle, it took off once it had deposited Grizz.

"Oh, Lord! And that's Teabag coming in all a-lather, too." Kelly groaned, hiding her face in her hands.

"With a pack saddle on?" Jilamey inquired, mystified.

"When I get hold of those twins, I'll larrup them to within an inch of their lives," she said so fiercely even Barrington regarded her in some surprise. "Jilamey—" She pushed the entrepreneur toward the porch. "You meet the captain, be gracious, offer her food and drink, while I see what I can find out from Teabag."

"He talks?" Jilamey said to Kelly's back as she strode off to intercept the gelding, wearily plodding toward the safety of his stable.

"No," Nrrna said, her eyes flashing, "but ze mud on him and ze grasses caught in ze girt will tell us where he has been. The young Gringg cub would be more comfortable riding a pack saddle zan a normal one. At least, zat Hrrunival cub of mine had some sense!" She was not one bit less annoyed than Kelly, though her aggravation was expressed by the lashing of her tail.

As he obediently went to greet Grizz, Jilamey mused on the maternal trait that caused each of the women to blame her own offspring for whatever had happened to Teddy. He devoutly hoped nothing had, for it might have a devastating effect on the delicate negotiations now in progress.

"How nice to see you, Captain," he said cheerfully. "Didn't realize you were expected. Kelly's had to go tend to that loose horse," he added, waving in that direction. "Are you hungry or thirsty? Kelly offers you hospitality. You've been here to the ranch before, I understand? Great place, isn't it."

Teabag, only too grateful to be home, allowed Kelly to approach him, especially as he had just stepped on the longer of the broken reins and answered the tug on his bit. But that was the least of the details she observed. The blanket under the pack saddle looked to have been sliced by a sharp object; Teabag's neck bore shallow scratches. His hide was sticky with half-dried sweat, so he hadn't come from all that far; the still slightly wild white eye he gave her as she caught up the shorter dangling rein proved that his fright hadn't been that long ago. She soothed him as she examined the claw marks on the crosspiece and noted the scratches on the thick leather of the reins, but apart from his scratches, there were no other bloody spots. Kelly tried to reassure herself that falling off a horse was part of learning how to ride. Probably even ol' bomb-proof Teabag had found a Gringg too much to bear. A real all-out howl from a fallen Teddy might well have made Teabag bolt. Nonetheless, spooking was most uncharacteristic of the docile Teabag. She felt his legs—warm but not hot, so no tendon damage. Her hand came away with swamp mud, the stink apparent even at arm's length.

"Well, clues of sorts," she said, still trying to reassure herself that Teddy had merely fallen off. In the swamp—which Teabag would have avoided on his own—Teddy would at least have had a soft landing. But *why* didn't the kids call in? Ask for reinforcements? Why were the comunits dead? That was disturbing. Quickly then, she stripped off the saddle, dropped some feed in his manger, and left Teabag in his stable to recover.

Jilamey and Grizz were booming at each other on the porch as she returned to the house. Kelly gritted her teeth. The truth was always preferable, even if it showed her up as a less than careful guardian.

"I am so sorry, Captain. The children have all gone off, on horseback, I believe, though the last time I looked they were all in the pond," she said, and managed a smile. "I didn't realize you'd be able to join us or I'd have kept them about the place."

"Grrgggl . . . the meeting ended sooner than expected," Grizz said amiably, glancing toward the pond.

"And you thought of a swim, no doubt," Kelly said, managing to act casually. "Well, while you're indulging yourself in some well-earned relaxation, we'll just go back along the trail and hurry the kids in. Here's Nrrna, too, Captain—" Turning her back briefly on the Gringg, Kelly beckoned furiously at the Hrruban to join them. "How fortunate you came by heli, Jilamey," and she firmly tucked her arm in his, elbowing him to fall in with her scenario.

"Easiest way to travel speedily," Jilamey said on cue. "This won't take long," he added as he guided Kelly toward the vehicle where Barrington waited.

"Any instructions?" Barrington, who had just rejoined, asked as they began to board.

"Oh, would you please man the communications channels, Barrington?" Kelly said, scrambling into a window seat. "And keep trying the kids' frequency." She gave him the code and he bowed politely.

The small craft lifted off and Kelly's heart did a flip as she saw Grizz, dwarfing Nrrna's slight figure, standing in the yard.

"Where do you think they went?" Jilamey called over his shoulder from the co-pilot's seat as they cleared the trees. The heli's engine was reasonably quiet, but no way to silence the *whup-whup-whup* of rotors tearing the air had ever been discovered.

"They must have taken a trail ride," Kelly shouted back and remembered then to turn off her voder before she damaged her eardrums.

"Then they might just have turned their handsets off?" he asked.

"No, a call alert would get through. Nothing did," Kelly said, disturbed by that. "Those units'll even continue broadcasting near high-power sources."

"Think they went mda-watching?" Jilamey asked.

"They wouldn't dare!" Kelly exclaimed, horrified. "Or maybe they would, the rascals. They were dying to show off the whole planet to Teddy."

"Would they have known to keep the pace slow for Teddy's sake?"

"Alison and Hrrana have more common sense than the three boys so they'd have kept to a reasonable pace. Turn toward the swamps, Jilamey. It was swamp-mud Teabag had on his legs."

"Swamp? This close to Snake Hunt?"

"Yes, I know." Kelly grimaced. "But Teabag wouldn't spook at any old tiddler."

"What about a Big Momma?"

Kelly shook her head impatiently. "I'll skin them, I will, when I find them. Let's backtrack Tea's probable route home. He came in on the swamp road."

"No sooner said than done, milady," said Jilamey.

"Look, where the terrain opens, can we skim to see if I can spot hoofprints?" Kelly asked, reaching for the case that held binoculars.

Jilamey, had taken the controls and was a deft pilot. In the soft ground of the track, Kelly could make out the darker color of disturbed ground in the even pattern made by a single-foot. Skimming along as far as they could until the bushes grew too close, she could also see where the tracks were those of a gallop stretch.

"Well, he was still running scared here," she said as Jilamey lifted the heli above the thick shore growth.

Now she scanned more widely as they passed over the marsh toward the dunes.

"This is getting all too close to snake-hatching grounds, isn't it?" he asked.

"It certainly is," Kelly said, leaning forward with the field glasses.

Jilamey had just angled the heli up and over another line of drifts, and a wide prospect spread before them. She caught her breath at the oh-so-welcome sight of a handful of small figures crouched on a blanket on a dune ridge. Slightly below them were five horses, apparently tied to a driftwood log. "And there they are, the scamps! Teddy's with them." Only then did Kelly admit to herself how terrified she had been that he'd be missing. "Set down!"

With one eye on the tracer screen and the other looking out for riders, Walters drove the small flitter around the edge of the dune where Gallup was waiting. He killed the quiet hum of the motor, and the small vehicle coasted silently to a halt. Gallup gestured for him to climb out, and pointed up the hill at the five youngsters. Walters nodded and swung the pack off his back.

"This place is full of snakes," he whispered. "Damn near stepped on one that was sleeping! They give me the creeps."

"Shh!" Gallup said, flattening himself on his belly on the hot sand. Together, they inched up toward the crest of the dune where the children were waiting.

The *whupping* of heli blades startled them. Hastily, Gallup and Walters burrowed into the sand and covered their heads with their arms. The copter set down on the sand hill between them and the children.

"Aw, hell!" Walters exclaimed, slamming his fist into the hot dry dust. "Commander Greene is going to be furious!"

Gallup plucked at Walters' collar. "Come on, we have to get out of here before they spot us." He reached into his pack and switched off the jammer.

Together, the two men crept backwards down the hill to the flitter.

"Snakes!" Kelly cried, pointing.

There were only a few, and relative tiddlers at that, but they were gathering just out of sight of the cluster of children. Kelly knew that the smaller reptiles wouldn't attack something big by themselves, but when they were hungry after laying their eggs, and there were a bunch of them, they'd been known to trap urfa or even small mda and rend the animals apart. Jilamey whirled the craft around so that the fine sand blew directly into the faces of the waiting snakes. Most of them fled over the dunes and into the marshweeds before he landed.

Kelly sprang out, ducking under the still-whirring blades. "There you are! Teddy, you're all right?" She fumbled to turn on her voder. "You've had us worried half to death," she scolded, running a hand down Teddy's sticky matted fur before she turned on her twins. "Why didn't you let us know you were in trouble?"

"We *tried*, Mama," Alison said, ducking her head in shame. "We tried."

"We did, Mom," Alec said stoutly, reinforcing his sister. "And we made sure the red 'charged' light was on before we took them off the rack. They just wouldn't work when we tried to call you."

"Well, you nearly caused an interplanetary incident, young lady," Kelly said sternly, but she hugged her daughter and ruffled Alec's hair before she plucked Alison's radio out of the belt clip. She thumbed the switch and then stared at the unit. "It's working now," she added expressionlessly.

"It wasn't before, Mama, honest!" both twins clamored, tugging at her arm.

"Alley tells ze exact truzz," Hrrunival said, twitching his tail for emphasis.

While it was just like these rascals to stick together, Kelly knew that they were always truthful. She compressed her lips tightly.

"Furthermore, you all know how dangerous the dunes can be at this time of year, so why under the sun did you bring Teddy here of all places?"

"We didn't *bring* him, Mom," Alec began in an exasperated voice, as if she had added insult to the injury of underestimating his common sense. "Teabag did, and Teddy didn't have much choice." Alec pressed his lips against a grin. "We followed."

"Well, then, young man, what spooked Teabag to run off?"

Alec shrugged his shoulders. "I was leading, Alison behind me, then Hrrunival with Hrrana now beside Teddy."

"Teabag just took off," Hrrana murmured, obviously upset and feeling responsible.

"Well, no one has been hurt and Teabag got home. Teddy, did Teabag actually run away with you?" Kelly turned back to the victim and only then saw the yolk streaking the fur around his muzzle. It gave him a ludicrous Pooh Bear look. "He'd had a little something this hour or two." The verse rattled unbidden through her mind.

Teddy shrugged, so reminiscent of Alec that Kelly had trouble keeping a straight face. "Grrbble . . . the hrrss did not like me on its back. It took time for it to fall me off as I clung tightly."

Well, Kelly thought, *since he's all right, there's no need to make an intergalactic incident out of this*. "So you've found snake eggs, have you, Teddy? Do you like them?" She grinned because his eyes sparkled and he dropped his jaw.

"Gracckle . . . Very tasty indeed. May I take some back? My dam would find them as tasty as I do."

Alec gave an exasperated snort. "We've been trying to get Teddy to move, but he's stuffing himself."

"Can we get started home now?" asked Hrrunival. "It's not much fun sitting around watching someone else eat when you're hungry, too."

"You'll be hungrier by the time you've ridden home," Kelly began, thinking that would be adequate discipline for this escapade.

Just then the horses neighed in alarm and began pulling at their reins which were tied to a driftwood log.

"Kelly, look out!" Jilamey cried, pointing violently even as he reached for whatever hand weapons the heli carried.

As swiftly and inexorably as a tsunami, a medium-sized tiddler boiled over the ridge of the south-facing dune, flowing its leaf-patterned sinuous body toward them with incredible speed.

Because they were beside her, Kelly gave her two children a shove toward the heli before she reached for Teddy, who hadn't even risen at Jilamey's warning cry. Hrrunival and Hrruna ran to safety. Teddy first had to rock himself to his feet, even with Kelly yanking at him. The snake, feeling the vibrations, moved in on them.

"Oh, fardles, Teddy, GET UP! That thing wants you for lunch!" Reflexively, she pulled out her belt knife, jumped in front of Teddy, and faced the oncoming snake. She just hoped Jilamey had a snake rifle in his heli. The worst she could do to the snake with her knife was deflect it briefly. But Teddy had to be protected.

Then the snake was close enough to stare directly into her eyes, pinioning her almost hypnotically. She didn't recall ever being this close to one when on foot before or armed with such an inadequate weapon. She stared with helpless fascination as its maw opened, the jaw unhinged as it widened, showing its extraordinary gullet. Gunfire, deafening in the usual silence of the dunes, startled both her and the snake. Sand kicked up almost in her face, and there was the smell of explosive propellant in the air. The snake was distracted.

"Move away, Kelly, so I can get a clear shot!" Jilamey shouted. He was sighting down a heavy-caliber hunting rifle. "You know I'm a lousy shot."

"I'll forgive you," she shouted back, "if you kill it!"

Kelly and Teddy dodged, getting out of the direct line of fire. The entrepreneur fired again, this time catching the snake in the tail, causing it to thrash back and forth in pain. Then it raised its head and stretched its jaws wide again, moving toward Jilamey. Teddy needed little urging from Kelly now, as she hauled him to the top of the nearby ridge and slid down the far side. They both lost their balance in the loose footing and ended up rolling down into the next valley.

"*Aaaaaaggghhh*!" Teddy cried, his vodered voice echoing in her ears. Above, below, beyond, and behind her, she heard the repeated boom of the rifle discharging.

She was still trying to spit sand out of her mouth and clear her eyes when Jilamey slithered down beside her, a wisp of smoke curling up from the bore of the rifle.

"It's okay. It's as dead as I could get it."

Kelly got her eyes clear of sand, but that didn't seem to help. She was at the bottom of a gully covered with sand, looking at what seemed to be a dozen people, their features foreshortened by height and darkened by the sun behind them. In a moment, they coalesced into four, then two, then one Jilamey. She released the fierce clutch she had on the Gringg cub and rose to her knees.

Teddy unrolled easily and waddled to his feet. "That was fun," he said. "I want to come back here and roll down hills again."

"Teddy, not here!" Kelly said firmly. "This is the breeding ground for those snakes. You could have been killed."

"Why didn't you tell me to defend myself from it? I was not afraid, and I am strong enough to have rendered it harmless," the cub said calmly.

Kelly started to protest that he was only a child, and then realized that the Gringg cub was probably a lot stronger than she, and might well have been a match for the tiddler. But snake-killing was not likely to be considered a desirable occupation for a species that said it did not like violence.

"Well, I knew Jilamey had a rifle and I certainly don't want to risk your hide on any snake-wrestling!"

"Oh, that is what one does with these snakes? Wrestles? I like wrestling. I'm good at it," Teddy said, looking disappointed that he had not been allowed to show his prowess.

"Fardles!" Kelly muttered under her breath and continued to de-sand herself. "Actually, Teddy, I think your dam expected you to play with our young, not wrestle the wildlife." She got to her feet and extended her hand to the cub. "But let's leave here *now*, because I really don't care to run into anything bigger than that one."

"How big do they come?" asked Teddy, intrigued.

"That one was small . . . a tiddler. Some of them are immense. The ones we call Great Big Momma Snakes are much, much bigger." She indicated girth with her hands.

"Oooh," Teddy said, impressed.

When they got to the top of the dune, he exclaimed in dismay, "It smashed all the eggs." There was yolk all over the place, and crumpled shells, for in its death throes the snake's body had convulsed, completely destroying the nest.

"We'll find more another time, Teddy. Come on. Your mother's waiting for you at the ranch. Let's go." Kelly gave him a gentle shove toward the heli.

"You didn't mention the mda," Alison muttered at Alec as they watched the dying snake.

"Do you want to be grounded for the rest of your life?" Alec replied.

"Well, no . . ."

"Then, shh!"

"Well?" Jilamey asked, steadying Kelly through the sand to the heli.

"Well, what?" she asked. There was sand down the back of her blouse, inside her trousers, and inside her boots. She was itchy and thirsty, and she didn't know whether to skin her children alive or just never let them out of her sight again.

"My second snake," Jilamey said plaintively, pointing to the twitching corpse. The children were admiring it and arguing amongst themselves over its length and probable weight. "After nine Hunts and not for want of trying, I have slain another snake. Might it count toward the Coming of Age Ritual?"

Kelly laughed, her voice echoing over the empty land. "Oh, I'm afraid not, Jilamey. I wish it did, you were so heroic. But it's got to be an official kill or capture during the Hunt itself, or we'd have poaching during the early season by obnoxious youths who want to make sure they qualify. Cheer up," she added, seeing his crestfallen expression. "It'll be good enough for a feast. We'll have a barbecue. Grizz'll enjoy fresh snake steak, and so will I. I only have to defrost the sauce."

Jilamey brightened. "I like barbecued snake!"

When the snake's corpse finally settled to an occasional twitch, they heaved it into the heli. It exuded a slightly musty odor, but the trip back to the ranch wouldn't take that long.

After settling Teddy inside the craft, Kelly turned to the other youngsters.

"You five go straight home, now," she said, shaking her finger at them. "No diversions, no detours. Got that?"

Two "Yes, Moms" from the twins and a meek "Yes, Aunt Gelli," from the three Hrrubans.

She let a grin break the scowl of disapproval on her face. "I'm just glad you're safe," she said, kissing each one in turn.

"I just wish they hadn't fibbed about those comms. This could have been very serious," Kelly said softly to Jilamey as he lifted the heli. Teddy had his nose pressed tight against the plasglas, watching the kids ride off.

"They don't lie as a rule, Kelly," Jilamey said. "Could someone actually have been using a jammer for some reason?"

"I'd prefer that explanation, but it isn't likely." She sighed. "Well, nothing really bad happened."

• • •

At the house, Grizz was on her feet, a living tower, waiting for the heli to land. Making a most peculiar-sounding ululation, Teddy climbed out of the aircraft almost before it had set down, and hurtled toward his dam. She embraced him fiercely, throwing him up in the air without effort and neatly catching him as he squealed with delight. Jilamey whistled at the careless exhibition of strength.

"And we've got a special treat for you," Kelly shouted over the slowing rotors as she walked toward the Gringg. "Fresh Doonarralan snake, courtesy of Jilamey's hunting skills. We'll have a real feast tonight."

The captain shook her head. "Morra. Please to take me immediately to the government offices. I have had an urgent communication from Eonneh. There is trouble. I must be there."

"Quiet!" Todd shouted, waving the crowd down. "One person, tell me what happened."

His office was full of angry people. The bad news had travelled all over the colony in the time it had taken Mike Solinari to inform him of the incident. Admiral Sumitral had come on the run from his office when he heard the commotion. Second Speaker arrived shortly afterward, with Captain Hrrrv and several of the visitors from Hrruba behind him. The rest were Rraladoonans of both species, all arguing at the top of their lungs. In the middle of it all was the Gringg male, Cinnamon, who said nothing and sat despondently waiting for whatever would happen to him.

"Mike!" Todd said. "The rest of you, quiet!"

"My two assistants and I were showing Cinnamon around the veterinary hospital," Mike began, shouting at first but lowering his voice as the others stopped talking to listen. Dr. Adjei, head of Veterinary Services, stood at Mike's shoulder behind Robin. "He was our special visitor today. I had morning surgery, so I left Cinnamon with my assistants, Dr. Gross and Intern Errrne. They took him around the place and ended up at the corral where we were holding about thirty animals, mostly geldings. I heard a howl and came running. The Gringg, Cinnamon, was in the corral"—Mike shot a furious glance at his erring employees—"with the dead mare at his feet."

"He killed it," Bert Gross burst out. "With one punch!"

"You're out of order, Gross," Todd told him sternly.

The plump woman from Humanity First! pounded on Todd's desk and thrust an accusing finger at Cinnamon. "This monster should never have been allowed to go unsupervised among decent beings! It could have been one of us!"

"It was an accident," Robin Reeve said firmly. "Cinnamon has repeatedly said so."

"I will recompense for its loss," Cinnamon said miserably. "I will adopt its youngster and nurture it."

"It'll need a foster mother of its own kind," Mike Solinari explained, but the spontaneity of Cinnamon's offer softened his harsh expression. "There's a couple of mares who have lost their foals. We can put the colt in with one of them. That part'll be all right."

"But he killed . . ."

"Ma'am, it's upsetting, but can we put the incident in perspective?" Todd asked politely.

"What perspective is that, Reeve?" Greene asked sardonically. He stood with fingertips poised on Todd's desk, not as loud or insistent as the angry woman, but somehow much more menacing. "That one of these gigantic aliens of yours killed a horse, or that he did it with one blow? They can break necks with as little effort as it takes for you or me to brush away dust. You've sown them among the population of a civilian planet like poisonous weeds. Where in this perspective do we find responsibility?"

"Oh, very picturesque, Commander," Robin Reeve said, applauding with sarcastic exaggeration.

Greene showed no signs of impatience or temper. "As Admiral Barnstable has repeatedly requested, these creatures should be sequestered."

"Locked up like wild beasts?" Hrrestan said, shaking his mane. "Unrrreasonable. You would not lock up a Hayuman for killing a hrrss. You would fine him and set him frrree. So would a Hrruban trrrbunal."

"Only in cases where malicious inzenz does not exist," Second Speaker Hrrto said. He was as far away from the Gringg as the dimensions of the room, and the crowd, would allow. Todd was relieved to observe that Barnstable was not present. "Ze question now remains if ze Gringg intended to kill."

"Why would he? And let me remind you that in our laws," Todd said, "as in yours, a suspect is presumed innocent until proven guilty. Prove that Cinnamon acted in malice."

"Our laws forbid violence," Eonneh protested, making his way forward to stand beside his colleague. The room seemed to shrink around them. The animal rights woman from Terra let out a squeak of surprise and retreated behind Mike and Robin, who exchanged a glance of disgust.

"I am sorry," Cinnamon repeated, staring at his big paws reproachfully. "I strove only to push away the hrrrss's attack. It hit me with its feet, here." He showed a torn patch on his coat where the mare's hooves had struck his chest, and the gash on his broad muzzle. "I did not realize I had struck it so hard until I heard—" And somehow he imitated the precise sound of a bone breaking. Everyone in the room shuddered. "I grieve to have killed a harmless animal, especially one prized so highly by our new friends. My hosts assured me that the hrrrsses were eager to have friendship. I sought only to make friends with the beautiful animals."

"Dr. Gross," Todd said, keeping his voice level and consequently forcing the crowd to hush to hear him. Inwardly, he was ready to roar with fury that a petty, though tragic, incident had given such fuel for trouble.

Bert Gross came forward and cleared his throat. His face was red, and he nervously rearranged his hands from pockets to belt to hip; his right hand twitched toward Cinnamon, and ended up scratching the nape of own his neck.

"Well, he, I mean the Gringg, went right into the corral, and he started chasing the herd around and around. Anyone with sense wouldn't have done that. Then the mare charged him, defending her foal. He struck her down like swatting a fly."

"It is so," Errrne said with a terse nod.

"Why didn't you stop him," Dr. Adjei asked, his eyes narrowing, "when you saw the herd reacting? You had the voder."

"Why would you leave ze Gringg alone in ze corrrrl in ze frrst place?" Hrriss asked. He had stood beside Todd, silent until now.

"Huh?" Gross looked at his Hrruban comrade. Errrne lifted both hands palm up, shrugging.

"I heard them." A very soft voice came from within the muttering crowd.

"You were a witness?" Hrrestan asked, glancing around the crowd. "Come forward."

A slender girl in a soiled coverall raised her hand. "I saw. Juanita Taylor. I work at the animal hospital."

Robin elbowed his way through the crowd to escort her toward the desk.

"Will you tell us what you heard?" Hrrestan asked her in a kind voice.

Nita blushed deeply, but Hrrestan kept his big green eyes fixed on her deep brown ones. "Dr. Gross invited the bear, I mean, the Gringg, to see a herd of horses on the other side of the barn. I . . . I didn't mean to be eavesdropping, but the barn's open all the way through, and there's an echo."

"No one's accusing you of anything, Nita," Todd said in a gentle voice. "You're helping us."

The girl nodded, and swallowed nervously. "They told him to get into the corral and get close to the horses. It was their idea. They were laughing about it. I didn't realize that anything was wrong until I heard the stampede, and then the mare screamed."

"So you say that the two Rralandoonans led him to believe the situation was controllable, and then failed to act responsibly and in time to prevent a tragic occurrence?" Admiral Sumitral asked.

"That's a leading question!" Bert Gross protested.

"You watch too many courtroom videos, Bert," Ken Reeve told him. "Will you answer, Nita? Just tell the truth."

"Well, my dear?" Sumitral prompted.

Nita nodded, not looking at the men. "I think they were trying to play some kind of joke on . . . Cinnamon, but it backfired. That mare was very protective of her foal. We had trouble getting close to her, and she knows us."

"So the mare reacted out of fear of a stranger," Todd said flatly. "I think that sums things up pretty well, don't you, Hrrestan?"

"I agrrree," Hrrestan said. "If it was not frrr zis witness who has come brrravely frrwrd, zeir dishonor would nevrrr be discovrrrd, since ze Gringg would continue to believe he was guilty of a crrrime."

"We," said Todd, including Hrriss at his side, "apologize, Cinnamon, that you were subjected to such infantile behavior."

"Hey!" Bert Gross protested. Errrne hissed. Todd met their glares with a cool stare. Both of them suddenly found something else to look at.

"I'll talk to the two of you later on," Todd said, his voice cold. "But I think Dr. Solinari might have something to say to you first."

"You're damned well right," Mike said grimly.

"I have a restoration to make," Cinnamon insisted, inclining his big head. "I did not mean to cause a loss of life. I wished to make friends."

"I am positive of that!" Todd replied earnestly.

"You are most courteous," Eonneh said, bowing.

"Is that all?" Greene asked. "You stand here and compliment one another ad nauseam, when this alien has shown the dismaying ability to destroy without effort?"

"Not at all," Todd said, as if he had noticed the Spacedep commander for the first time. "As Cinnamon has already offered to make restitution, what else could be demanded of him? A day in the stocks? A month of bread and water? Mike'll determine the value of the mare and how much fostering the colt will cost, and Cinnamon will pay what he owes. End of matter!"

"In whatever way becomes possible, I will make the value good," Cinnamon promised.

"You forget the loss of use of a valuable brood mare and any subsequent earnings," Greene said.

Cinnamon nodded his head obligingly. "That, too, is fair and can be decided. I await the decision."

"But we have formulated no schedule of payment or value," Second Speaker said, looking distressed.

"You can't just let these . . . *aliens*"—Greene larded the word with repugnance—"buy their way out of any incidents. This one involved only the death of an animal. You let the Gringg wander where they like. What happens—"

"We Gringg will cooperate in any way we can," Eonneh interjected, looking intently from Greene to Second Speaker to Todd. "The just reparations for accidents must be decided, clearly stated, and set down. This regrettable incident is unlikely to be repeated, but we Gringg are big and accidents can happen no matter how careful we try to be in our excursions."

Greene rolled his eyes, and was gathering himself to speak, when Hrrestan held up his hand.

"Agreement must be formulated with all dispatch," Hrrestan said, "so zat justice—unlike zis . . . inforrmal and crrowded hearring—can be calmly and sensibly rendered on any matters zat could be required. A tribunal of one each of our zree species should do very well, should it not, Zodd? Sumitral?"

"Now wait a minute—" Greene said.

"You are not, Commander Greene, a resident, norrr even a frequent visitor to Rraladoon," Hrrestan said, gently but firmly dismissing the man's protest.

"We Gringg agree," Eonneh said, looking from one to the other, "justice must be clearly stated and set down. It is the only fair way in which we can interact, now or in the future."

"A second Decision at Doona," Todd said, with a grin at his mentor. Today's accident—so nearly a tragedy—had provided a major forward step in the tripartite relationships. The Rralandoonans in the crowd cheered, but not all the visitors looked pleased by the outcome.

"Impossible situation," Greene protested, realizing he had lost control of the situation. "There are ramifications you cannot understand—" He broke off suddenly.

At Second Speaker's side, Mllaba stared at the commander, her huge eyes glinting, and a hot flush rose from Greene's collar to flood his face unbecomingly. In his presence, almost with his cooperation, the ridiculously naive Doonans had struck a bargain with their would-be destroyers. They proposed galactic policy with a dangerous species, and were grinning like idiots. Sumitral, beside them, who should have been wary, was behaving just as foolishly.

"This whole thing is an inappropriate response to the situation," he said through clenched teeth.

"Not at all." Todd raised his voice to be heard over the hubbub. "The malice was not on Cinnamon's side. If he had deliberately destroyed property, it would have been necessary for him, as it is for anyone on Rraladoon, to be disciplined in some fashion. However, we have established—haven't we?—that he was the victim of an ill-conceived trick."

"Hear! Hear!" Mike cried.

Robin, breaking off his quiet but intense conversation with a blushing Nita, echoed the vet's sentiment, glaring at the dissenting expressions of faces in the crowd.

"Since it seems that Rraladoon is fast becoming a popular spot for aliens to meet"—Todd went on, injecting some levity into the discussion, for which he was rewarded with a few grins—"it behooves us to consider contingency plans and guidelines until formal proceedings can be initiated. This is my world, and I am the Hayuman leader of it. Hrrestan, as my Hrruban colleague, do you concur?" Hrrestan nodded, his gleaming eyes never leaving Greene's face. "I could almost suspect"—Todd paused significantly, though he pointedly did not look in the commander's direction—"that the whole incident was manufactured by those intent on causing trouble between our people and our new friends. Our *guest*"—Todd emphasized the word—"has been most gracious, considering he was the butt of a bad joke. End of incident. Now, you all, clear out of here, and tend to your own business. Not mine!"

Greene stood staring at the desktop, then looked up to meet Todd's eyes.

"I . . . I agree with you, Reeve," the commander said, nodding his head slowly. "You should not have become involved with a tempest in a teapot. Delicate relationships between our three races should not be fractured. As Human colony leader, you are in a superior position to facilitate such guidelines. Spacedep wishes to offer any assistance you require."

Todd gawked at the Spacedep officer's sudden change of direction. He was unable to detect any sarcasm in Greene's earnest face.

"That's very wise of you, Commander Greene," Sumitral said. "And the sooner we can devise final terms the better. In the meantime, let us extend immunity to these stray visitors of ours until we have achieved a proper treaty with the Gringg." He sighed. "If only they came in a slightly smaller package, there'd be less objection!"

The officers were talking in a tight group as Robin and Mike were urging people to disperse, joking that the show was over for the day.

"Or were they less dangerous," Mllaba said, staring at the dejected Cinnamon. "It is not merely ze sheer size of the Gringg zat is off-putting."

"Not to menzion ze zurprize of zeir trade items," Hrrestan said.

Hrrto was shaking his head, and his tail tip twitched convulsively. He spoke Middle Hrruban in a low voice. "Perhaps if all business was conducted by comlink, there would be less need for protection."

"Why, Honored sir, when they offer no violence?" Hrrestan asked. "I think some responsibility devolves on us—to be sure they are not victimized, as they were today."

That aspect had clearly not occurred to Hrrto. "Yes, yes, I take the point, Hrrestan. But . . ." And he sighed heavily. His priorities were in constant turmoil. Only the prospect of the essential purralinium remained of constant importance. "It always depends *who* the victim is, doesn't it?" he added enigmatically.

"Hall's cleared now, so goodbye. I've got a hospital to run," Mike Solinari said over his shoulder as he firmly pushed the last of the curious out the door.

"Especially when the victim does not realize he has been made one," Hrrestan said, looking at the retreating figures of the veterinary contingent. "The laws of Hrruba are far more stringent than are needed here on Rraladoon, Second Speaker. Diplomatic immunity should be tendered. The terms of such immunity are already known to both Hayuman and Hrruban. Let us examine them first. Then we must learn the law forms of our visitors, so that there is no ambiguity or misinterpretation." As he spoke to Hrrto, Hrrestan leaned away from Greene, as if he hoped the commander would take the hint and depart. "We of Rraladoon will be honored to mediate such discussions if that would solve the current dilemma of jurisdiction."

Mllaba nudged Hrrto. "Such a project would greatly enhance your prospects for election, Speaker!"

"I . . . yes, of course it would, Mllaba," he told her testily. Then he turned to Hrrestan. "Justice for all is the primary purpose of the Council," he said. "And also of our allies on ze Amalgamated Worlds Council."

Greene, who had not taken the hint to leave, entered the discussion, also using Middle Hrruban. "Diplomatic immunity is certainly a good point at which to start, since we are all familiar with its workings. I was for a while attached to Spacedep Legal, so I would like to assist."

His offer surprised every one in the room, so that he was able to glance meaningfully at Mllaba without comment. She nodded, understanding that the two of them must have a private conference.

"Then it's settled," Sumitral said cheerfully. "Ah, Captain Grzzeearoghh, we've been expecting you. There's a matter of great importance I wish to broach to you."

Todd glanced up. The enormous Gringg filled the doorway, her red eyes nearly sparking. Behind her were her cub, Kelly, Jilamey Landreau, and Landreau's servant, Barrington.

"What matter is that?" Grizz asked carefully, her sweeping glance having taken in the forlorn Cinnamon. Eonneh went to her side and began to speak in a low voice. Grizz bent over him, and waved her claw now and again in assent.

"If I may," Admiral Sumitral began, nodding to Todd and Hrrestan for permission. Then he approached the Gringg captain. "As Honey undoubtedly informed you, there has been a slight mishap involving Cinnamon, which has been resolved under our laws. As guests of this planet, Rraladoon, you are now granted diplomatic immunity, the ramifications of which I will gladly explain to you. I can safely assure you that this will be immediately ratified by the governing body of Amalgamated Worlds."

Somewhat stunned by Sumitral's announcement, Hrrto forced his way over and said, "And by the High Council of Hrruba."

As he heard himself saying such words, he wondered that he had so spontaneously promised what he would have to argue at his most eloquent, in the Council, to obtain. And yet, all he had to do now was mention purralinium to them and they'd agree to any measures needed to procure the metal. Nevertheless, he had been forced to take an action which he ought to have discussed, at least with Mllaba, before committing himself. Could the Hayumans and Zodd Rrev have cunningly maneuvered him into agreeing? Or was it that Sumitral had once again made the Second Speaker of the High Council dance to his tune as if Hrrto were a mere apprentice in the halls of diplomacy? Perhaps both. Sumitral had always been a formidable mediator, and young Zodd had indeed grown up.

Then Hrrto wondered at the sudden shift in Greene. It had been the commander all along, declaring that the Gringg could not be trusted. What could be the reason behind such a switch? Then it occurred to him that under the guise of diplomatic immunity, "escorts" could be assigned to any Gringg on the planet—to ensure that the immunity was observed. *Ahh,* thought Hrrto, *that Greene is quick, clever, and shrewd. He had got the better of Sumitral, Hrrestan, and Rrev, and used the concession to forward his own aims.*

"Of course," he continued, hoping his pause had not been overlong, "all three interested parties, plus their homeworld representatives must be present to discuss a Trade Agreement—in the same chamber."

Grizz gave him a brilliant smile, her long fangs gleaming. "Of course, Second Speaker Hrrto," said the pleasant voice of the voder. "It would not be correct or courteous any other way."

Second Speaker bowed to the Gringg leader, suddenly feeling that twice in a short space of time he had been manipulated by a clever strategist. Zodd and the two Hrrubans were not laughing, but he thought they might be close to it.

"I would be most interested in a treaty between us all, especially if it will facilitate trade practices here on Rraladoon," Grizz said, addressing both diplomats. She put a maternal claw on her cub's head. He grinned up at her lovingly. "My son has been telling me how delicious are the eggs of the native species of snake of Rraladoon. How glad I would be to trade with Rraladoon for such a commodity."

"Now that you mention our friend the snake," Jilamey said, addressing everyone who remained in Todd's office, "I happen to have a delicious specimen which we can barbecue tonight. You are all invited to partake of the unique taste of Rraladoonan snake, a real delicacy. I feel a lot of policy can be discussed over a friendly sparerib or two, eh?" He winked at Kelly.

"You two are never, never, *never* to leave your handset off again," Todd said, towering over his offspring with uncharacteristic anger. Alec and Alison studied the ground and each other's shoes for a moment, then peeked up at Todd. "If there had been an accident, no one would have known where to find you until it was too late!"

"But everything came out all right in the end," Alison offered, fluttering the thick lashes of adoring golden eyes at her father. "We stayed with Teddy to make sure he'd be all right until Mama found us." She could sense him softening, and nudged Alec with her elbow. Her twin added the earnest plea in his blue eyes.

"Honest, Dad, the radios were working when we left! It's not our fault they failed," Alec said.

Kelly spotted the silent communication between her children and interjected her own comment. "It doesn't matter how it came out; it's how it began. Promise, or you'll never get to ride Hunt until you're old and gray. Promise!"

"She means it," Jilamey said, lounging in the porch seat while Barrington, elegant as ever, sliced snake up into manageable portions for the barbecue grills. "She nearly made me stay behind from my first Hunt because I didn't want to carry a handset."

The twins sighed and matched glances. They knew they hadn't been remiss but couldn't prove it. Being accused of a lie was almost worse than getting chased by snakes.

"I promise," Alec said at last. Alison nodded.

"We'll check and double-check from now on. We're very sorry to have caused trouble. And we washed Teabag and the other horses down and groomed them real good."

"And so you should have, kids. But it isn't what happened, it's what might have," Todd said, hunkering down to the children's eye level. "Teddy's a stranger here, and we trusted you to look after him. Your responsibilities make it imperative that you remember things like making sure that your equipment is functioning properly. You were unable to call for help, or notify anyone as to your location. Think of your mother and me. We'd have been devastated if anything happened to you."

The thought had passed through the twins' minds. They threw their arms around Todd, who hugged them tightly.

"We'll never let it happen again, Daddy," Alec said in a low, tight voice. Over their shoulders, Todd glanced up at Kelly.

When Teddy had emerged from the Gringg shuttle at the Double Bar Gemini, he was also visibly chastened. He stood, scuffing one foot in the dust, waiting for his friends to come out again to play. Hrrana and Hrrunival had been assigned extra chores by Nrrna as their punishment. Kelly watched Teddy mooch around the grass kicking a stone, bored and lonely. She relented.

"All right," she said, and the Alley Cats perked up. "Go and play, but when I call, you come right in, understand? I'm counting on you to help me with all the guests we're having tonight. You're my best assistants."

"Yes, Mama!" Like twin bolts of lightning, Alec and Alison raced down the steps calling to the small Gringg.

"And we wanted children, didn't we?" she said, taking Todd's hand and squeezing it as they watched the children play together on the grass.

"We did, and I wouldn't have it otherwise, even with double trouble," Todd said, gathering her under one arm and enfolding her tightly. "It's not an easy job, but I love it."

The smell of roasting meat made a tantalizing atmosphere for the negotiators who gathered over the course of the next hour or two. Robin and Jilamey acted as chief cooks, turning hunks of meat on the broad grills, and explaining to the Gringg what "barbecue" meant. Big Paws, the black and white Gringg, couldn't seem to stay away from the fragrant, spitting roasts. He stayed close, chatting with the chefs.

"I have had only preserved snake," Big Paws said, with a sidelong glance at a smallish steak, only centimeters from the edge of the grill, as if he'd swipe it if backs were turned. "I am looking forward to tasting fresh meat."

"This'll be the best," Robin said expansively. "Reeve family recipe. There's a secret to cooking snake to bring out the true flavor. First, you sear the sides of the meat, then season—"

"No. Season, then sear," Jilamey said, interrupting.

"Right," Robin said. "Then cook for four to eight minutes on a side."

"How is it a secret if he knows?" Big Paws asked, pointing to Jilamey.

"I'm practically family," the entrepreneur said, grinning. He sliced off a piece of rare steak and held it out on a roasting fork to the Gringg. "Taste."

The bite disappeared in a twinkling. "Delicious!" Big Paws exclaimed, licking his chops with his long brown tongue. "I would like to have much more of this. Is this barbecue the only way of preparing it?" He looked dubiously at the glowing coals.

"Whatever way rocks your jollies. Tell you what, come along on Snake Hunt," Robin suggested. "If you catch your own snake, you can cook it any way you want."

"Oh, I would love that," the Gringg said, his eyes lighting up. "I will make the suggestion." He raised his voice, already quite loud enough to be heard all across the yard. "Captain Grzzeearoghh, may I suggest a concept to you?" The black and white Gringg lumbered off toward his leader. Robin grinned at Jilamey and went back to turning steaks.

Hrriss passed among the guests with pitchers of lemonade and beer, filling glasses. He stopped to offer refreshment to Ali Kiachif, who looked at the contents of the two carafes, and shuddered.

"Unfermented fruit squeezings! Don't you have a decent tipple for a *man*?" the old spacer asked, reaching for the beer.

"I'm sure I will find something," Hrriss said, dropping his jaw, amused.

"So you're the chief meeter, greeter, and feeder for tonight?" Kiachif asked. "Where's your tail-twin? Scrubbing dishes?"

"Zalking," Hrriss replied, with a dropped-jaw grin for his long-suffering friend. "I am sure he would razzer be washing dishes. Zodd is engaged in deep talks with my father, Second Speaker, the Gringg, Spacedep, and Alreldep, so I offer hospitalizy on behalf of us both."

"Ah, one of you is as good as the other," Kiachif said airily. "And I saw your assorted offspring going about handing out baked taties, salad, and fruit like very pros. You're raising 'em right, young Hrriss, so you are."

"Thank you," Hrriss said, extremely gratified. "I will see if there's any mlada in the house."

"Ah, this picnic is doing wonders for calming overstretched nerves, so it is." Kiachif sat down on the porch seat to wait.

Mllaba and Greene left their seniors engaged in the informal Treaty talks, and made their way surreptitiously to a spot as far removed from the party as possible. Grace Castleton and Captain Hrrrv were at the end of the fence waiting for them. There was a small tray table before each of them. Hrrrv's platter was empty, and looked as if it might have been licked clean. Castleton's food was virtually untouched. She toyed with a beaker, picking it up and putting it down again without drinking from it. She felt she couldn't force anything past the tightness in her throat.

"I could not zink what you were doing, Greene, in agreeing to enter formal discussions with these creatures," Mllaba said, as soon as they were out of earshot of the party. "But it was cleverly done. We can szretch out zuch dialogues for many weeks."

"Glad you caught my drift," Greene said smugly, settling onto a chair beside Castleton. She glanced up at him with an abstracted smile. "And it had the effect of disarming Reeve's objections. The Admiral was very pleased when I reported back to him. The bruins have sworn to abide by a peace accord. Now they'll have one, and Admiral Barnstable is personally involved in drawing it up. It gives the fleets time. This diplomatic immunity also allows us to keep track of where the Gringg go. They'll have escorts everywhere. If once they show what they are capable of, we'll have witnesses!"

"How does the meeting go?" Hrrrv asked in a low voice.

"Second Speaker has become caught up in the dream laid out by Hrrestan and Rrev," Mllaba said, her eyes gleaming with faint disgust. "He will lose the election if he does not take care. All of them are so enamored of the concept of unity that no one listens to reason."

"They'd sign tonight if the Admiral wasn't there," Greene said, grinning with malice. "He insists on discussing each clause in the Diplomatic Immunity Handbook over and over again, then letting himself be talked into the original wording already set down."

"But very slowly," Mllaba said, laughing in short, breathy grunts. "A very cleverrr man, for a Hayuman. The Immunity Agreement will not be finished tonight. And yet they continue to look upon his involvement as helpful!"

The other two joined in the laughter, but it had a forced ring to it. Castleton took a sip from her drink, but did not taste it. The thought of deliberately sabotaging a safeguard for both Gringg and themselves worried her, almost more than the up-coming confrontation when the naval support ships arrived. Despite the tape, she found much to admire in the Gringg.

"Now Reeve has committed himself," Greene said. "the confrontation with the Gringg will make him look the idealistic fool he is. All we have to do now is stall. When the fleets arrive . . ."

"They're close," Grace said quietly. "The Terran fleet is within twenty-four hours of making orbit."

Greene looked at her, almost for the first time, and his expression changed from triumph to concern as he saw how worried she was.

"What's wrong?" he asked.

"Nothing," Grace replied carefully, glancing at the two Hrrubans. "All ship-shape, and observing radio silence."

"Ze Hrruban fleet will arrive just outside ze heliopause a few hours later," Hrrrv added.

"Very good," Greene said. "The Gringg are most likely to strike when we expect it least. Possibly while we conclude agreements and treaties they never had any intention of signing. We'll hold up the final agreement as long as possible until both fleets are in position."

"It cannot be held up long," Mllaba said. "Ze movement toward accord is inexorable. Ze Gringg, Sumizral, and Rraladoon are in agreement. Zere are reasons why Second Speaker will sign zat I cannot discuss, but no one will oppose him in ze Council."

"Then that trade agreement could be the last thing any Human or Hrruban does on Doona," Greene warned. "Admiral Barnstable has sent sealed orders to open fire on that *Wander Den* of theirs the moment their reinforcements arrive, or at the first hostile sign."

"Zousannds of lives are at risk," Mllaba added. "We have to stall until ze ships are in place to defend zem. Ze Gringg shipz must be blown apart before zey can attack."

"We shall be ready," Greene said, leaning over and speaking in a low voice so the others had to listen very closely. "Then we'll support Hrrto by telling the Council that he was on the right side—the side of caution—all along. The Admiral has the tape to justify our actions. That's our ace in the hole. Barnstable also wants to sabotage that scientific get-together planned for tomorrow."

"It is already being zaken care of," Mllaba said, her yellow-green eyes watchful in the twilight. "I attend ze conference again in ze mrrning."

"Good! This charade has gone on long enough," Greene said. "In the meantime, we pretend to cooperate and thus allay suspicion until our fleets are in position."

"Then we demand the truth of the massacre in the Fingal system," Hrrrv said, flourishing his claws. He stood up, bowed to Mllaba, and left.

"I, too, must go," Mllaba said. "Ze Council expects me to report on ze Zreaty's progress." Her black robes whispering over the long grass, Mllaba glided away. Like a shadow, she passed between the hulking figures of Gringg and Hayuman, and disappeared between the gateposts.

"Jon, what if we've been wrong?" Castleton asked Greene suddenly, in the thoughtful silence that followed the Hrrubans' departure. Her voice was too loud, and she forced herself to lower it. "What if they truly are peaceful creatures? What will the Gringg think when our forces surround them? They'll feel betrayed. They'll never trust us again."

Greene put a gentle hand on her wrist, and she shuddered slightly. "You've seen the tape, Grace. We can't ignore that proof. We have every right to demand an explanation, and to take reasonable precautions."

"I still don't agree with your conclusions," Grace said. "I'll fight, and even die, if I have to, to protect Humanity, but I still can't bring myself to believe in the Gringg threat. I'll just bc doing my job." She lowered her gaze, and sat staring at the ground between her feet.

"Yes," Greene said, moving closer to her. They were now knee to knee. She was aware of the warmth in his eyes and the scent of his skin mixing with the cooler aromas of the night air. "After tomorrow we might be very busy . . ."

"Or dead," Grace said, her eyes fixed on his.

"But not without having fought good battle," Greene said. He held out his hand to her. "Let's go back to the ship . . . and form our own plan of action."

With a sad smile, she nevertheless took his hand.

CHAPTER 11

COMMANDER FRILL COURTEOUSLY PUSHED BACK HIS chair and rose when Mllaba entered the conference room. He wasn't sure if protocol for a Speaker of the High Council applied to his personal assistant, but it was better to err on the side of courtesy. Mllaba spared him an annoyed expression, then made straight for his side of the table. He remained standing until she had taken a chair, and he assisted her in drawing it to the table. Cardiff, on his other side, glanced up at the Hrruban, but his conversation with a pair of Gringg engineers and the technician from the Hrruban warship did not falter. The Gringg were arguing a complex point about drive engines that the Hrruban couldn't believe, but wanted to. Vocabulary was not yet adequate for high technology, so most of the dispute was carried out in mime, with each side making subtle alterations in the technical diagrams showing on the computer screens set between them. Cardiff's talk was peppered with untranslatable military and Earth City Corridor slang that a couple of the Gringg were beginning to repeat back to him.

Hurrhee, the chief scientist from Hrruba, interrupted his talk to pay heed to Second's assistant. He was, as Frill understood it, a medium-wide Stripe, which put him among the upper class on Hrruba, but Mllaba was his superior. She muttered a long, low stream of grunts and growls at him, flipping off the control on his voder. Hurrhee submitted to that action, but Frill frowned and pricked his ears, though he only recognized a few of the glottal changes as belonging to High Hrruban rather than Middle. He wished he knew that dialect, because whatever it was she was saying, it sounded important.

"What is it, madam?" Hurrhee asked with just a touch of asperity. "I am in a most interesting conversation. I do not wish to get left behind in the details."

The assistant's gold-green eyes glinted with impatience. "What have you learned?"

"About their grasp of matter transport technology?" The military tech glanced up at the words. Mllaba stared around her in alarm, but no one else had comprehended.

"Yes," she said. "Speak in concepts, not terms."

Hurrhee lowered his voice. "Most interesting, madam. I spoke in a general way about crystalline focusing systems from deliberately impure mineral complexes. Those"—he nodded toward the hugest Gringg, a female, who sat beside the Hayuman scientist and a large, brown-patched male Gringg—"began to study the false diagrams I gave them. To my great delight, they have an idea how to prolong the life of the tuning crystals, madam. But I am now absolutely positive that the purralinium they are willing to trade us has the impurities we so urgently need. Though that metal did not come up in conversation, the dark-skinned Hayuman has made a suggestion that could very well result in still further protection for our supplies."

"What?" Mllaba replied, deeply troubled. "How could he? Hrruba has sought such advances for centuries."

"But a fresh eye," Hurrhee said in a grunting whisper, "may see things a jaded one cannot. I am most enthusiastic about pursuing this discussion. And Sixth Speaker for Production was eager that I should continue."

"If the Hayumans suspect what aim you serve, they will be in possession of valuable information regarding gr—that technology," Mllaba said sternly. "Discredit anything which comes too close."

Hurrhee shook his graying mane, disbelievingly. "But should these things be secrets, madam? Science is the only universal language which cannot lie. Sooner or later they might deduce it on their own. The Hayumans seek it now, and I believe the Gringg have a fair idea that purralinium is what powers the grid systems. The large female has asked several leading questions. I hate to keep putting her off, since who knows what advances she may lead us to?"

"But it could be advances the Hayumans might be able to share to the disadvantage of Hrruba, and that must not be. Our secrets must remain our own. Can you not equivocate?"

"No," Hurrhee said bluntly, but still in a whisper. "The facts would swiftly bear against me. There is more. A few of the naval

Hayumans are quite upset about it, and in fact tried to speak out against open discussion."

"Could you tell what the subject was?"

Hurrhee shook his head slightly. "I think it had to do with spaceship technology, maximizing poor resources for greatest effect. It may well be, madam, that both our technologies are short of essential metals to increase our respective transportation mediums. In my deepest heart, I feel cooperation, total cooperation, would benefit us more than the current secrecies."

Mllaba eyed him coldly. "Then it is as well that you are not in any position to make policy," she said in a voice devoid of expression. "Follow the instructions given you and do not deviate."

"Madam," Hurrhee replied with great dignity, "how can I, in my capacity as a leading scientist, ignore the chance to gain advantages which will result in massive leaps forward in many fields? I must know what these Gringg have to say, and to do so, I must be honest."

"Honesty!" Mllaba was astonished. "What is that when our security is at stake?"

"False security, I would say," Hurrhee replied haughtily.

Mllaba didn't trust herself to speak further. An outburst here would only serve to disgrace her office and that of the Speaker she served. Angrily, she pushed back her chair and stalked out. Hurrhee watched her depart, then returned to his discussion.

"Ah, Koala," he said, pleasantly. "Now, where were we?"

"Hrrestan, may I speak to you?"

At Second Speaker's voice, the Hrruban co-administrator glanced up from a stack of angry messages scattered across his desk, then rose hastily to his feet. The older male seemed agitated. "But of course, Honored Speaker. Please be seated. How may I serve you?"

The Hrruban settled himself into the padded chair opposite and attempted to compose his thoughts. "May I take you into my confidence, Hrrestan? You have always held the Hrruban cause dear."

"This sounds ominous, Speaker Hrrto," Hrrestan said, infusing a light tone into his voice. "It is true, I act for the best of all Hrrubans, but also to secure prosperity for my Hayuman neighbor."

"My request does not run counter to either of those purposes,"

Hrrto said. "You are aware of the scientific conference going on in the Treaty Center?"

Hrrestan inclined his head. "But of course. Your interest honors us. What is your request?"

"It is not a simple one to explain. I must tell you I disapprove of the openness which pervades there. Instead of discussing generalities, as I thought the conference was meant to do, the participants seem to have gone straight on to sensitive topics, discussing engineering and space sciences as if they were exchanging recipes."

"Scientists do tend to become enthusiastic about their pet topics," Hrrestan said. "If you wanted them to learn only names and formulae, that could have been done with simple teaching tapes, instead of allowing free-thinking beings to participate. The Gringg have their own sciences, some in advance of ours, from what I have been told. Evidently our own inventors and technicians have discovered they can proceed quickly to the satisfyingly and interestingly complex."

"No! That is not the way it should be operating," Second insisted, raising his voice almost to a shout. He stopped, surprised at his own lack of prudence. "There are reasons why we should be more discreet. I . . . I cannot be more candid at this time, but I am greatly worried that indiscretion reigns with creatures unknown to us a mere four weeks ago." Second Speaker allowed his alarm to color his tone, then controlled himself and went on firmly. "We take quantum leaps before we understand walking with them as partners. So much is at stake here."

"Indeed, but what exactly alarms you so?" Hrrestan asked earnestly.

"I beg your pardon?"

"From what I have heard, there has been accord and much exchange of information among our scientists, while others are busily discussing trade agreements. What specific problem agitates you so, Second Speaker?"

"Mllaba has been attending on my behalf while I dealt with the diplomatic immunity affair," Hrrto said in a testy tone; he had the right to use his assistant as an information gatherer. Hrrestan did not react adversely. Perhaps he, too, had spies. "Her sources suggest that the Gringg may have already deduced the workings of our grid transport system!" He paused to let Hrrestan absorb the significance of that before he continued. "We know they have impure purralinium on offer as barter. We must obtain all, *all* of the material. We cannot allow the

Hayumans to have any. Surely I do not need to remind you why."

"Pure purralinium is also on offer, and the Hayumans seem much more interested in that," Hrrestan said soothingly. "They like quality and insist on the purest assays."

"But the danger exists, and you should know by now how Hayumans can grasp a single word and end up with a statement! If they *ever* connected the impure purralinium with our grid technology—!" Second Speaker threw his hands up at the thought of such a catastrophe. "Mllaba has tried to slow the talks or divert them from discussions that would inevitably lead to its disclosure, but she has been unsuccessful. These scientists are so single-minded! Therefore, you must disband the science conference!"

"I must not do that. For shame, Speaker Hrrto," Hrrestan said, his large eyes flashing. "For shame that you will not allow the Gringg to prove themselves as strong and supportive allies. If they can deduce our poor technology by casual examination—as our Hayuman friends have never yet managed to do—and yet have offered their friendship and their assistance instead of taking advantage of us, you should be pleased and grateful instead of treating them with distaste and fear. I shall be proud to have them as friends, which is much more preferable than making them rivals or potential enemies. As you have said, I support Hrruba, and I say that Hrruba would benefit greatly by frank and honest interaction with such a race."

Hrrto regrouped his arguments. "But you do not fear them yourself? You do not find their size frightening?"

"Not at all," Hrrestan said, his jaw dropping in a slight smile. "Their voices are annoying, but they cannot help that. We become accustomed, and nape hair no longer rises when they speak too loudly. If they are large of stature, what of it? They are intelligent, caring beings. Yesterday, at the incitement of my grandchild, one of the Gringg picked me up and held me in the air like an infant. You were at the barbecue; you might have seen it yourself. It was a game the two of them were playing together, and yet the Gringg is the size of a large hrrss. My rambunctious grandson considered him a playmate. If my children and their offspring trust them, can I do less? Children are most intuitive. The Gringg value the same things we do, hold life as dearly. I find a great basis of mutual understanding already."

"I see," Hrrto said slowly, realizing that he could form no

alliance with this person. "Thank you, Hrrestan. It has been most instructive speaking with you."

Hrrestan rose and bowed deeply. "I am always glad to be of service."

Hrrto left the Government House and made his way to the grid in the heart of the First Village. The mist obscured his vision for a moment, matching the muzziness of his thoughts. Hrrestan had always appeared such a sensible Stripe, even if he seemed to have wasted his opportunities, choosing to be a mere co-leader on an agricultural planet. Furthermore, nothing Hrrto had seen or heard of the Gringg, even the unfortunate hrrss accident, contradicted their contention of pacific nature. The horrific tape shown to him by Spacedep seemed more and more of a fantasy. And they had purralinium.

Throughout the weeks since the Gringg had arrived, Mllaba harped at him that revealing the Gringg's inherent evil would serve to propel him into his world's highest honor. Yet he continually temporized and did not reveal the existence of that damning tape. At this moment, he too had difficulty seeing them as evil. And yet, if he was wrong, he was risking the destruction of a Hrruban colony. He had almost told Hrrestan about the tape. Would that omission cost lives?

Few people of any species were in the corridor of the Federation Center. Hrrto walked soft-footed into the Council Chamber and took the same seat he had occupied the day of the trade negotiations. The chamber was empty, for which he was grateful. He wanted solitude to mull over the conversation with Hrrestan.

In the final analysis, Hrruba had to have whatever purralinium the Gringg had! He could even use that as his excuse for withholding vital evidence.

"But why, Tom?" Todd asked, puzzled and unhappy. The emigration request Tom Prafuli had just handed him was possibly the worst document to cross his desk. A totally unexpected and unwelcome surprise.

Tom Prafuli pushed the sheets toward Todd. His solemn, dark brown eyes were mournful. "Just sign the emigration order, will you, Todd? Don't take it personal. Get it over with."

The colony co-administrator took the pages in both hands and met the other man's gaze. "Tom, we've been friends for more than twenty years. We grew up together; we suffered through university exams together. I don't want to see you take off on an impulse like this."

"It's no impulse," Prafuli said, straightening his thin shoulders. "Sigrid and I talked it out all night, but a month of nights arguing won't change our minds. We want to get off Rraladoon. We don't like the change the neighborhood is taking." The colonist made a meaningful gesture with one hand, holding it high above the ground beside his head.

"The Gringg?" Todd asked, astonished. "Tom, you're one of the greatest proponents of diversity I know. The Gringg will make great friends and allies. They're harmless."

"Oh, yeah!" the rancher said, bitterly, and Todd could almost see tears starting across the man's shiny dark eyes. "Ask Crystal Dingo how harmless they are."

"Crystal Dingo?"

"My mare. My prize brood mare that was. She's the one who's going to be cheval steaks and a tanned hide today. But my mare is just the beginning, isn't she? I hear you're giving a big prime chunk of Rraladoon to those Gringg."

Todd stared. "What? Who told you that?"

"There's a Hrruban going around saying that you're going to plant those bruin-monsters right in the middle of town, taking our land away for them, and fardle anyone who protests. I'm not one for racial or species solidarity, Todd—you know that—but I think these Gringg are plain dangerous. Just like that Hrruban said. A lot of people are listening close to him, and what he says makes sense. I've been hearing worse, too. They're killers."

"That's bull," Todd replied staunchly, suppressing the rise of anger at such ridiculous gossip, "and you know it, Tom. Even if one of them wanted to settle right here, they'd have to take unclaimed land. That's in both the Decision and the Treaty. You know how I feel about them, don't you?" Todd put a little heat in his words because Tom had been pro-spaceport.

"Well, there's those that say you're thinking of them before your own folk, Hayuman or Hrruban."

Todd eyed him. "If you weren't hurting, I'd take exception to a crack like that, Tom."

"You can take what you like, so far as I'm concerned. You can give them my ranch when I'm gone. I don't want to be anywhere near them. Let me go, Todd," Prafuli begged. "I heard through the bulletin board that they're taking applications for homesteaders on Parnassus. We're already booked on a ship heading in that direction next week."

"I wish you'd reconsider," Todd said, sensing even as he spoke that his attempt was going to fall flat. "Snake Hunt is only a week away. We'd miss you if you left before it started."

Prafuli shook his head. "Thank God, because that's how we can get out of here *now*, when we want to. I'm not the only one who feels this way, Todd. I'm just the only one who's going right now. You ought to get out there and listen to your friends."

Without further protest, Todd signed and affixed his seal to the form and handed it back to the rancher, who left the room without saying another word.

When the sound of Prafuli's retreating footsteps died away, Todd got up from his desk and stared out the window for a moment. Usually the view relaxed him enough so he could think. The vast garden, changing with the season and overlooked by the grand presence of Saddle Ridge, was a most soothing view. This morning, though, the garden was flooded by a gathering crowd. Among them he could pick out the probable dissidents by their pallid complexions, somewhat scorched across noses and cheeks by the sun. All this past month there had been a steady stream of agitators swelling the original numbers, troublemakers Todd was sure Barnstable had gridded in.

He really hadn't thought they'd have much effect on dedicated Rraladoonans, but Tom Prafuli had proved him wrong. Unfortunately Rraladoon had never seen the need for any exclusion policy for "undesirable" visitors, much less professional agitators. Whoever had the money—or the interest—to come to Rraladoon was made welcome. Right now, with so many arriving for New Home Week and the Snake Hunt, and every Rraladoonan involved in those affairs, there wasn't a spare someone to screen the spurious from the serious. Wryly Todd thought that those who took in paying guests for the New Home Week festival would be making good money.

He vowed that once New Home Week and the Snake Hunt Festival, which was its finale, were over, he'd start weeding out the agitators on the grounds they were disturbing the peace. Which they were.

As he watched, in full view of the crowd, some of these new "activists" unfurled banners and stapled them to poles of green rla wood. Todd squinted to read the badly printed messages snapping in the light breeze: *Gringg Go Home, Two's Company—Three's a Crowd*! . . . *Doona for Doonans*.

That last slogan was obviously contrived by Earth-dwellers, since they didn't even use the current name for the planet. Todd recognized many neighbors and people he knew from all six villages. No one seemed to protest the waving banners, and that saddened him.

Once the banners were erected, the group hoisted the poles and began to march in a large oval, obstructing the pedestrian walkways to the building. Todd forced himself to watch several circuits, listened to them chanting their slogans, then turned back to his desk.

His mail was full of messages of complaint: the Gringg were an unwelcome and threatening presence. He erased most of them as soon as he saw their content, stunned by the depth of ill-feeling. A half-dozen suggested that he step down from office immediately and allow a "responsible, right-thinking Terran" to take over before disaster struck. Where had his wits been all these weeks? He'd been so convinced that the best possible outcome for all Human-and Hrrubankind was to form a partnership with the new species that he'd ardently pursued that goal. Had he been so wrong to inflict his world-view on the rest of his people? Was his idea of galactic unity so unwelcome to the majority?

Hrriss slipped into the office. "Arre you ready to go yet, Zodd? My father would like to take a few moments to talk wiz you befrrr ze conference begins. What is ze mazzer?"

Todd looked up at him, his blue eyes wide with confusion and hurt like those of a lost child.

"The first real test of my government, and I don't know if I've failed my responsibilities or not." He told Hrriss about Prafuli's visit. "I've forced my judgment on others, without caring what happened to anyone, or what anyone else thought." He threw up his hands, paced fitfully to the end of the room, and spun self-accusingly on his heel.

"You have not failed," Hrriss assured him. "Hrrestan has had such messages, too, and he is paying no heed zo zem. Zere is bound zo be malcontents who will not wait frr all to come out right. How many of zose messages were signed by villagers?"

"More than I like to count." Todd felt suddenly unworthy of the office Hu Shih had ceded to him.

"You always assume zat you are ze one who is wrong," Hrriss said with a gentle grin as he opened the door. "Let me suggest a little experiment. Ask zese folk what zey zink."

Todd's personal staff consisted of two Hrrubans and a Human, whose workstations were in the outer office. They looked up as Todd and Hrriss came out. The office manager, Kathy Hills, fluttered her long blond lashes at him in a demi-flirt, then stopped when she noticed his expression. Her large blue eyes filled with concern.

"Todd, what's wrong?"

He wasn't very sure how to frame the question. Anyway, these people were loyal to him personally. It was those who had no connection to him that he had to reassure.

"Er, Kath, are you comfortable with the idea of allying with the Gringg?"

"That's a funny question," she said, a little puzzled. "Sure. Why?"

"Well, I . . . would it trouble you to have them as permanent trading partners? Neighbors? Friends?"

Kathy laughed. "Well, I can't imagine being closer to anyone than I am to my two best Hrruban friends. It'll be a shade difficult," she added with a giggle, "to be on the same level as a Gringg, but every one of them I've met so far has been polite and curious and really rather interesting. Need you ask?"

"Well, yes," Todd said. "It seems I do need to ask. I should have done it before."

Mrrowan, at the desk across the room, exchanged pitying glances with Kathy and Hrriss, and shook her head.

"Zodd, you can be so blind sometimes. We zrust yrrr judgment. We sure wouldn't work so hard for you if we didn't!"

Barrough, beside her, his jaw halfway to the floor in amusement, nodded agreement.

"We can't be considered a good cross section in a random poll," he said. "But we get out and about when you haven't got us slaving over hot consoles here. So we do know that the majority will follow you and Hrrestan. We elected you to succeed Hu Shih, didn't we? And most of the people I know"—he turned to get emphatic nods from the two females—"think you're handling a difficult situation very well. Any fainthearts don't know how good they've got it here."

"Thank you," Todd said, his shoulders relaxing somewhat, though the tight knot in his gut remained. "I needed to hear that. I was half-convinced that I've been ignoring what's been going on right around me. I'm not going to bull it through without the approval of the people who live here."

"And you are not," Mrrowan insisted. "Rraladoon exists as it does because we've always helped each other. You have had help from many people zese long weeks of zeaching ze Gringg to speak our language. Zose are not disapproving. It has been a prrject we have all shared. And enjoyed."

"Tom Prafuli's emigrating," Todd said, still ashamed of that disappointment.

"So?" Barrough demanded with a shrug. "He was never really a Rraladoonan. He only came here to hunt Snake. We can do without his kind."

"And you're letting that upset you?" Kathy demanded, screwing her face up in disgust. "You amaze me, Todd! Let it run off your back, the way you did the other stupidities that have been perpetrated. You're on the right track. Don't you doubt it!" Her expression turned fierce.

"I second that!" Barrough and Mrrowan chorused. "But it is nice of you zo ask," Mrrowan added, dropping her jaw in a big grin.

"I zold him he was mad," Hrriss said, his eyes alight.

"No, they're not exactly disinterested parties," Admiral Sumitral said when Todd consulted him on the matter, "but loyal enough to you to warn you if the matter was getting out of hand. So why are you letting one emigration give you second thoughts?"

"It just made me realize that not everyone agrees with the policy Hrrestan and I have been following. I mean, bringing the Gringg along as quickly as we can, opening our homes, our businesses, our lives, to them is good for interspecies relations, but are we doing the right thing for the greatest good of the people on the planet we administer?" Todd asked, and paused.

Hrriss grunted low in his throat, but it was Sumitral who answered.

"Would I"—the diplomat touched his chest—"have backed you so solidly if I felt you were *not* acting in the best interests of a planet which is very dear to my heart?"

That rhetorical query wrung a wry smile from Todd. "You'd be the first to set me straight, I guess."

"If I hadn't firrrst," Hrriss said, twitching his nose and whiskers.

"I admit that it can be unnerving to see people carrying such unflattering banners round and round your office," Sumitral agreed, "but surely you saw how many of them are not even residents?"

"It's the ones who were that upset me. There were letters demanding that I step down. Kelly's reported rumors all over the complaint board."

"Pay no azzention to zem," Hrriss said. "Zey do not speak for ze majrrity."

"Do you, in your mind and heart, doubt the merits of what you're doing?" Sumitral asked, leaning forward over his folded arms.

"No! Not for a moment," Todd said. "Not for myself! But I'm not acting for myself anymore—or alone."

Sumitral smiled. "You are acting for the good of Rraladoon and that has always been an instinct with you, and with Hrriss. Remember that. Ignore the dross. Myself, I have trusted very few in my life . . . a survival technique. But I trust you, and Hrriss, and certainly Hrrestan. And oddly enough, I also trust the Gringg. Call it professional instinct. That's why I'm backing you. And, to give you a little encouragement"—Sumitral pulled up a file on his desk computer and swung the screen around for the two friends to see—"I'll give you the straight facts from homeworld newsprints. Here's the result of an opinion poll circulated by the Amalgamated Worlds Council on Earth. You see, in the beginning when the first data about the Gringg's arrival began to circulate, a general poll showed seventy-five percent were against getting involved with them. But look at the demographics: most of them are oldtimers, who grew up when there weren't even Hrrubans on the horizon, when settling space meant hardship and terror. The young people, between sixteen and twenty-five, were ninety-two point seven in favor of getting to know the Gringg better.

"Now, after the initial reports"—Sumitral allowed a tiny smile to touch his lips—"and I might add, after a little judicious salting of news programs with tapes of you two and other Rraladoonans interacting in friendly, nonthreatening activities with the Gringg, teaching them Middle Hrruban and playing with them, there's a forty percent swing in the oldest demographics, and anyone under sixty is ninety percent or better in favor of forming a Treaty with the Gringg. This is what I based my platform on when approaching the Council, and that's how I won approval to offer them both diplomatic immunity and a trade agreement." Sumitral tapped the screen with a stylus. "Don't doubt yourself,

Todd Reeve. You've the backing you need. And an interstellar reputation as a fine example of Hayumankind and a role model for aspiring youngsters."

"Zere, you see?" Hrriss asked, whacking Todd solidly on the upper arm with the back of his hand.

With such reassurances, Todd was finding it hard to hold on to his gloomy mood. Hrriss was grinning widely, his jaw dropped almost all the way to his breastbone.

"I'm not sure I like having an interstellar reputation," Todd said in a low grumble.

"You should have thought of that when you were six," Sumitral said, with the ghost of memory liming a smile on his face. "Now, come, take your optimism into the negotiating room with you. You can deal with the rumormongers when the job is done."

In their dress uniforms, Sumitral, Todd, and Hrriss shouldered their way out of the building past the protesters and walked quickly to the transport grid. Ignoring the cries at their backs, Hrriss set the controls. The mist rose around the three of them, obscuring the ring of dissident Hayumans and Hrrubans. Todd was never more grateful to see the plain white walls of the Federation Center. He nodded a greeting to the grid operator, a young Hrruban male with a very pointed face and narrow-striped tail.

"We'll meet the Gringg on the landing pad," Sumitral said.

As they emerged from the grid facility, they were surprised to see the crowds on the Treaty Center grounds. A handful of Alreldep regulars in their maroon uniforms stood guard on the concrete apron attached to the building, around a grand table with three pens and inkwells but only two seats, for the public signing of the Treaty between Terra, Hrruba, and Gringg.

Most of the Hayumans and Hrrubans waiting near the landing pad were Rraladoonans, waiting eagerly to view the signing. Many had brought seating, while others had spread blankets on the ground. There was a buzz of pleasant talk which stilled as the official escort arrived. To one side, however, Todd was dismayed to see yet another cluster of protesters. This bunch suddenly pushed their way through the scattered onlookers, right up to the boxy Gringg shuttle, waving their posters. These featured caricatures of Gringg, ill-drawn as well as defamatory. One showed a Gringg tearing apart a small body, obviously a Hrruban cub.

Another featured a mass of Gringg, wearing extravagant collars and harnesses, trampling down both Hayumans and Hrrubans, exaggerated paws reaching toward a table heaped with food stuffs.

Ken Reeve, Jilamey Landreau, and Ali Kiachif immediately stepped up to the shuttle hatch, daring the mob to start something. A phalanx of the commercial space crews emerged from behind the shuttle, their hand weapons still holstered but ready, and formed a sort of barrier.

Jilamey waved to Todd and Hrriss and gave one of his outrageously cocky grins.

"Damn!" Todd muttered under his breath.

"Well, I didn't expect this!" Sumitral muttered under his breath.

"I did, after the crowd around my office. Kiachif and Horstmann dragooned their crews into guard duty," Todd replied out of the side of his mouth. "I'd hoped it was just talk. Damn 'em for using pictorial insults."

"Since it's all too well known that the Gringg have concentrated on spoken, not written language, that's one way for them to make their points."

"And Eonneh's in the shuttle and has probably faithfully drawn what's on the posters for posterity," Todd said, his tone savage with frustration. Even as he'd been speaking, he'd been surveying the faces of the orderly Rraladoonans, estimating the numbers. "Wait a sec!"

He held up his hand to delay the others in the formal escort. Then he took a step toward the dissidents.

"You're not citizens of this planet," he said, rapidly scanning the protest group to find the leader. "You have no right of protest here." Then he turned to the friendlier faces, and raising his voice, added, "I recognize a lot of you from previous Snake Hunts. How about removing the vipers in our midst? I think they need to go back to whatever hole they emerged from. Quietly! Out of respect for the rules of hospitality!"

Before the protesters could rally effectively to defend themselves, their posters were confiscated and their persons bodily removed by willing hands. Some loud and outraged cries drifted back. Todd waited a bit, grinning at Sumitral.

"All right, that's out of the way. Let's proceed with the scheduled formalities."

• • •

As soon as Todd, Sumitral, and Hrrestan approached the Gringg shuttle, the door slid open. A buzz started, this time a welcoming one.

Waving cheerfully and with a pleasant smile showing all her fangs, Grizz alighted, her powerful legs making the long step easily. Todd sighed, hoping that the Gringg had not been there very long.

Honey and Kodiak followed Grizz, turning to help Teddy down the tall steps.

A hearty cheer rose from the crowd and some laughter. Grizz twitched her ears and seemed to scan the gathering, but her fanged smile remained in place—the same fanged smile that had been caricatured on one of the posters. Todd hoped that the Gringg might just dismiss those as bad Rraladoonan art. The Gringg and officials had taken no more than a few steps, when suddenly a fist-sized rock winged past Todd's head, ricocheting off the side of the shuttle. A clatter of pebbles hit the ground around them.

Todd swung immediately in the direction of the assault. A man, tawny-skinned but with the sallow complexion that spoke of limited exposure to the sun, threw another rock straight at Grizz.

Anticipating its trajectory, Todd jumped up with one hand high and caught the rock. He swore as it stung his fingers. Teddy squealed with fear. The Gringg immediately closed about the cub, hiding him from any further attack.

There were cries of "Shame! Shame on you!" from most of the onlookers, and agitated movements in the crowd as a number of them chased after the assailant.

By all that's holy, Todd resolved, *I'll find some punishment to fit this crime, all quite within my authority as co-leader*. A glance at Hrrestan told Todd that the Hrruban had the same uncompromising opinion. The sharp chunk of granite he'd had caught would have done some damage had it reached its target, no matter how tough Gringg hide was.

"I'll want to see that man when you catch him," Todd said aloud and gestured to two of the crewmen to follow through.

Todd dropped the stone to the ground and, with his boot, ground it into the dirt.

"My sincere apologies, Captain," he said in a ringing voice. "Let us proceed with the order of business."

Then, flexing his stinging fingers, he raised his arms and gestured for the crowd to give way. A respectful aisle immediately opened up, wide enough for the Gringg and escort to proceed.

That such an incident had occurred at all rankled deeply in Todd, marring what should have been a great occasion.

With Kiachif, Jilamey, Ken, and Hrriss flanking the aliens, they marched toward the Center, the space crews forming a guard behind them.

The Treaty Chamber door swung wide to admit Hrrto's erstwhile allies, the Hayumans from Spacedep. Of those expected at the noon hour, they were the first to arrive. Barnstable, in his dress blues, nodded sharply to Hrrto as he slid into the chair opposite, and surveyed the room. The only other occupant was Mllaba, who sat discreetly against the wall, allowing her senior to mull over his thoughts by himself. Greene waited patiently as Barnstable seated himself, then escorted Castleton to her chair on the other side of their senior commander.

"Well, Speaker Hrrto?" Barnstable asked. "Anything to report?"

"I have spoken to Hrrestan. Ze conference goes on unhindered, and a Zreaty seems imminent whether we will or will not apprrove," Hrrto said, but his voice was distant. "If we are right, zis means zere are only hours left. I can do nothing more. Despite all advice to the contrary, the High Council wants to trade with zese Gringg."

That was true enough, for once Hrrto had mentioned the existence of purralinium, the High Council would hear of nothing but an agreement—any agreement—that would augment the dwindling supplies.

Mllaba, in her chair by the wall, glared at the floor with glowing yellow eyes, but said nothing. Hrrto had not requested her presence at that High Council meeting and he knew she was certain that he had mishandled that meeting. No matter. His conversation with Hrrestan had caused him to alter more than one long-held opinion. He had even altered his desire to win the upcoming election: such crushing responsibility for all sorts of unexpected incidents had lost any appeal.

"Withhold your approval," Greene said. "The Treaty will require signatures from all three governments."

"I am not sure zat will be possible," Hrrto replied. "Nor zat it will mazzer."

"But it can," Barnstable said urgently, his eyes glittering. "Think of it: the Gringg have given us a map of their systems. They have claimed hundreds of planets. If you don't sign, all the provisions *and* the safeguards become null and void. Hrruba could take over valuable mining planets—even habitable worlds. Considering what they did on Fingal, the Gringg don't deserve to colonize more worlds."

"No," Second said wearily. "I am too old for war. Nor am I one to take anozzer's worlds. We Hrrubans, too, have put such greed behind us. But ze others will sign ze Zreaty anyhow. It will not matter if I sign or not."

"It will matter, Speaker," Greene assured him. He held out a small datacube. "I have the tape from our exploration ship. It proves that the Gringg ship did fire on Fingal Three, destroying at least one of the cities on the surface and several of the satellites. The weapons we have suspected all along must be hidden somewhere aboard that leviathan. Our combined fleets are hours away. They must not hesitate to attack."

"Is zis wise?" asked Hrrto. "It is not us who will die." *And,* he thought, *we are so close to gaining new supplies of purralinium.* He closed his eyes in despair.

"Too many will die if we don't act. You saw that tape," said Greene through gritted teeth. "These Gringg are deceivers and vicious killers. I can sense it every time I'm close to one of them."

Grace Castleton, sitting by Greene, angled her body away from him. As close as they had been the night before, she felt uneasy about contact with him just now. She was weary of trying to argue with Jon. He kept on the same theme and would see no other logic. For the first time since she'd received her own commission, she found her command onerous, as her private opinions could not interfere with her obedience to orders from the Admiral. Barnstable was as rabid against the Gringg as Jon, wholeheartedly willing to believe evidence she found spurious.

"We need more time," Mllaba said. "Just a few hours and ze fleets will be here to support our views. We need a diversion. Now is ze time to show Rrev and Hrrestan zat tape!"

"And Admiral Sumitral," Castleton added.

"Those confounded, optimistic hand-in-friendship fanatics won't believe it," said Barnstable, dismissing the leaders of Rraladoon with a gesture. "Alreldep is full of fools who can't see a real threat when it weighs half a ton and has claws."

"Yes," Greene said promptly, "but showing them the tape buys us time. They'll demand proof of its authenticity and we can drag that out as long as we want to. Let 'em rant and rave a while. That'd be to our benefit. And I've arranged one more delaying tactic. Those should eat up the hours we need for the fleet to get into position."

Everyone nodded in agreement, and nervously settled back to wait.

As soon as they were safely past the crowd, Teddy started to whimper, having managed to control his terror until the safety of the Treaty Center was in sight.

"Here, Teddy," Jilamey said, stroking his shoulder, handing the cub a handful of peppermint humbugs he happened to have in his pocket. "Can't imagine how those layabouts got here! Must be some fringe nuts."

Far more reassured by something to put in his mouth, Teddy stuffed in as many candies as he could and so forgot his earlier fright.

Having emerged unscathed from that incident, Todd was dismayed to find an even more substantial number of onlookers surrounding the meeting hall. But this time there were neither placards nor stones. Disconcertingly there were people, carrying tri-d cameras and flashing seemingly legitimate reporter idents, who wanted to ask the Gringg questions—a tiresome but necessary interview. Todd tried to appeal to them to wait until after the formal signing, but the protests were so loud that he relented. Voders were passed over to the reporters, which Todd hoped would prove so irksome to use that the news-gatherers would depart. Instead there was a barrage of inane questions, the kind of tripe that made Todd's innards roil.

"Captain Gringg, how did you feel discovering not one but two sentient races inhabiting this planet?" "Do we differ from other species you've encountered?" "How long was your journey here?" "From what part of space do you originate?" "What's your homeworld like?" "How many cubs would you have in a life span and doesn't it interfere with your professional duties?" "Why was Middle Hrruban used as the bridge language?"

"I wasn't informed that news-gatherers had landed here," Todd murmured to Hrrestan.

"Nor was I, but it is never wise to annoy zose who broadcast news," Hrrestan said.

"If such broadcast is ever aired on Earth and Hrruba," Todd said, feeling uneasy about the unexpected delay. He glanced down at his wrist chrono. They were already late for the scheduled arrival time, but he agreed with Hrrestan that it wasn't politic to irritate news-gatherers. How many of those quickly flashed credentials might prove bogus? And *how* did so many arrive so propitiously? As if he needed to go far to find an answer to that question. What did Barnstable and his crowd think they'd achieve by these delaying tactics?

However, when he and Hrrestan suggested that the interview had gone on long enough, there was immediate protest.

"This isn't half enough of an interview, Reeve," protested one of the more aggressive Human interrogators.

"Our people, too, need to know ze facts," a Hrruban of very narrow Stripe chimed in.

"What news channel do you represent?" Todd asked, holding out his hand for their credentials. "My office was *not* informed of your arrival, and any interview should have been cleared first with me or Hrrestan. We could then have allotted sufficient time for a proper interview. Now, we've given you as much as we can. After the ceremony's over, I'll arrange a longer session for you with Captain Grizz and her crew."

Todd cast a significant look at the commander of the Alredep honor guard, and immediately his troops moved in to form a barrier between the Gringg and the news-gatherers. Then Todd and the others politely herded their guests into the building.

"I know who planned that little diversion," Todd muttered to his father. "I just don't know why!"

"The 'why' worries me, too," Ken said.

"I must check the records of ze grrrid operrators," Hrrestan said. "Zere have been too many unauzorized uses of zat facility!" He twitched muzzle and whiskers, and his tail lashed angrily.

When they reached their destination, Todd sighed with relief, thinking as he did so that maybe such relief was premature.

"Who was so kind as to arrange a press interview?" he said, glancing around those already seated at the table.

"There were no news-gatherers when we entered," Barnstable said, glancing up casually from his personal clipboard. "Just the usual bunch of onlookers one would expect."

"Surely"—Greene grinned smugly—"you want as much publicity as you can get on such a momentous occasion? Surely you don't wish to keep any of these negotiations secret?"

"Surely you don't expect me to believe you didn't arrange it, Greene," Todd countered with an insincere smile.

"Please, let us put aside rancor," Hrrestan said in Middle Hrruban, hand raised for silence. "Will you not all sit down?

This is the final phase of our negotiations. I have here three copies of the Treaty worked out between Admiral Sumitral, Captain Grzzeearoghh, Second Speaker Hrrto, Admiral Barnstable, myself, and Zodd Rrev. The suggestions and input come from many quarters and have taken days to compile. I ask you all to glance over this document to ensure that all the salient points discussed have been included to your individual satisfaction."

It was only when Hrrestan sat down that he realized half the room was more interested in the ornate timepiece at one end of the room—admittedly a fine piece of engineering, since it registered the precise time in the administrative centers on Hrruba, Earth, and Rraladoon. He had the distinct sense that only the Gringg and Rraladoonans had paid any attention to his brief words. While he was not of a Stripe that took offense at minor snubs and slurs, he was decidedly uneasy about the atmosphere in the chamber. He glanced at Speaker Hrrto, who had his eyes carefully averted.

To Hrrestan's surprise, the Spacedep commander asked to be recognized. He nodded to Greene, and the Hayuman rose.

"The agenda of this meeting does not allow sufficient time to read every clause of this weighty document," Greene said, making a show of the effort it took for him to raise the weight of the thick document. "There were many points that had to be discussed in great detail. We will need more time for a thorough reading than you have allowed."

"I must point out, Commander, that you are not an official member of the Trade Treaty Committee," Hrrestan said in Middle Hrruban for the voder to translate. "You were present only as an observer for the Admiral, who was involved in another discussion."

"However, as the Admiral's appointed representative, surely I may speak to that point?"

There was the slightest edge of smug superiority about Greene's manner that irritated Todd. The commander was obviously initiating yet another delaying strategem. *Why*? The question was beginning to obsess Todd.

"You attended all the meetings, that is true," Hrrestan said, replying with dignity. "You had ample opportunity to bring up any points then for clarification. Read!"

As Greene quickly riffled a few pages, and then held the document open, it was clear to Todd that the man was totally familiar with the contents.

"On page fourteen, clause five, subsection twelve, there is an ambiguity in wording that I feel ought to be clarified," and he read it out.

"I hear no such ambiguity," Hrrestan said. "And furthermore"—he tapped the keys on the terminal nearest him—"here is a transcript of that particular discussion. You will note that the wording is exactly as it was decided upon at that meeting."

"Ah, I see that you are correct," Greene said, all affability even as he turned pages again to a new section. "Would you also check paragraph nine, clause three, Honored co-leader? Now is *that* as it was decided? I really do feel there's been an error in the quantity of lithium with respect to trade weights."

Todd began to fidget, but a glance from Hrrestan suggested to him that his colleague would allow only so much of Greene's disputation.

"No," Jilamey said bluntly. "That's written as decided upon, Commander. And you know it!" He pointed an accusing finger at Greene.

"I do, Mr. Landreau?" Greene asked, all innocence.

"You forget, Greene, that I have an eidetic memory," Jilamey said.

Captain Grizz raised her brow at the new word, and Jilamey leaned across the table to clarify the term.

"Ev," Sumitral said, turning to Barnstable, "what is all this in aid of?"

"Well, you can't expect me to sign a faulty or error-strewn Trade Agreement, now can you?" Barnstable said, raising his eyebrows at Sumitral. "And I never approve of a document I haven't read thoroughly."

"Your approval of this document is not required," Todd said bluntly. "This is Alreldep business. You are here as an observer, Admiral, and on our sufferance."

Barnstable raised his eyebrows in placid amusement at the warning.

"But I," Hrrto said firmly, "wish to read the text before it is signed." Second Speaker glanced round the table. "I would be failing in my duty to my Stripe and my position were I to dispense with such a formality"—he bowed courteously to Hrrestan—"for such a momentous document."

Todd had to stifle his impatience. The conspiracy of delay which he had suspected was now proven. Spacedep and Second Speaker were clearly working together to slow the proceedings down to a crawl. Fortunately the Gringg seemed unconcerned by the delay. So Todd offered the oval mass of the Gringg-language copy to Eonneh, who brought it to Grizz. She flipped to the first page of the document and began to read.

Most of the Hayumans crowded around Admiral Barnstable, who had pulled the Basic-language copy over in front of him. Kiachif put a pair of spectacles on his nose and peered down them at the pages, scanning as Barnstable read to himself.

Just then, the first quiet, decorous intrusion of Spacedep aides began, the first with just a whispered message for Greene, the second and the third bringing him message cubes, which he read before passing them to Barnstable for his perusal.

Mllaba stood behind Second Speaker as he read slowly. She hissed, startled as Jilamey Landreau sidled up to look over Hrrto's other shoulder.

"Too much of a crowd over there," he said, smiling at her winsomely. "Just as well I can read formal High Hrruban as easily as Basic."

"Provisions for trade, galactic court, common currency based on table of values . . ." Barnstable muttered to himself after spending several minutes thumbing through the pristine pages. "Wait just a nanosecond, here—what is this?" he demanded, planting an indignant finger in the middle of one page. "What is this about a panel for scientific interchange to be chaired by the Gringg?"

"At my humble suggestion," Honey replied. "The Gringg see that Hrruba and Terra require an arbiter of scientific matters to ensure most efficient development of important technology. We will do this for you, in exchange for a place among you."

"Never!" cried Barnstable. "Ridiculous! Afroza, you can't sign this," he boomed at Sumitral.

"I can, Ev, and I shall," Sumitral said. "I have the permission of the Amalgamated Worlds Council to do so."

"But a seat on the Joint Supervisory Council overseeing trade!" Barnstable's face turned bright red with aggravation.

"If the Gringg trade with you," Grizz asked, "is it not fair to allow us a small say in the laws and privileges? We will agree to abide by them. If we governed, would you not expect such a courtesy?"

For that Barnstable had no objection. "I . . . suppose so."

"We keep faith," Grizz replied. "Even as you have asked us, we have kept our ship in the same orbit you recommended many weeks ago."

Greene was surprised to have that fact raised. Could the Gringg suspect? Had they instrumentation powerful enough to see through the large Rraladoon moon which was obscuring the approach of the fleets?

For another half hour everyone read quietly while Todd and Hrriss became more uneasy. Todd drummed his fingers on the tabletop. Every legitimate signatory for this Trade Agreement had been intimately involved and had approved each day's finished negotiations. *Why* delay the inevitable? Or did those messengers mean the Spacedep contingent were waiting for something more?

Greene had edged forward and was perched on the edge of his seat, turning an occasional worried glance at Captain Castleton, who responded with small shakes of her head.

"And what is this?" Mllaba asked a few minutes later, pointing over her senior's arm at a statement near the end of the document. "A section of Treaty Island to be designated as an Embassy of the Gringg?"

"Of course," Todd said. "As we discussed at length last Tuesday afternoon, they will have ambassadorial status to Rraladoon. It's an acceptable compromise, since they are not actually members of our Hayuman-Hrruban alliance. No, change that to 'federation.' An alliance suggests there is an enemy to ally against."

To Todd's surprise and concern, Castleton visibly winced at his wording. She looked almost guilty, but he continued with his explanation. "They are entitled to have a base for their trading houses and a diplomatic compound. I'm still not at all happy to see the Hrrunatan inhabited, but that part of the continent's useless for anything else, so it might as well be a spaceport, and the Gringg are to have their own quarters there as well as here in the Treaty Center." He looked around the table at the troubled expressions. "Look, you'll have to accept that the universe isn't composed of only two sentient races anymore"—he stared significantly at Greene—"or just one. We've been sought out by a third. One day there may even be more." He kept his grin at their dismay to himself. "That portion of the text was agreed on yesterday morning."

"And you agreed to this?" Barnstable demanded of Hrrto. "When? After I left? How could you?"

Suddenly stung by the Hayuman's presumption, Hrrto struck back.

"Hrruba does not answer to Earth for its actions," he replied.

"It sounded quite reasonable to me when I discovered how much that would benefit Hrruba you Hayumans would deny us."

"Now, wait!" Barnstable roared. "*We* deny *you*? What about you and your precious grids?"

"Just a moment, Admiral," Kiachif said soothingly. "To be just, judicious, and nonjudgmental, there are processes we deny the Hrrubans and could very well offer without any loss to ourselves, if you understand me. Our new cryogenic techniques for one thing."

"That's top secret, military only!" Greene said, narrowing his eyes at the Codep captain.

"As if we have a constant call for frozen soldiers," replied Kiachif with a snort.

"If we may be allowed to mediate this point—" Grizz began pleasantly, with her paws folded over her belly. "The function of trading is to sell to others what they do not themselves have. Both parties should gain in the exchange."

"So let's exchange," Jilamey said eagerly. "Let's exchange spaceships for grid systems. Amalgamated Worlds would gain what they need and Hrruba would be able to explore more efficiently. That'd be the greatest trade—and the greatest gain—possible." He beamed around the table, apparently unaware of the frozen, outraged silence.

"And, under special auspices, that might very well be possible," Hrrto said. Mllaba nearly choked and jumped from her seat to whisper urgently in Second Speaker's ear. After only a few words, he pushed her from him.

"D'you mean that, Second Speaker?" Jilamey asked, incredulous.

Just then two ensigns hurried quietly into the meeting room and placed a communications unit on the floor next to Barnstable. Todd noticed that the unit was operational.

"Now just a moment, Barnstable," Todd said, rising from his chair. "This is a closed session and that thing is on broadcast. You two"—he pointed to the ensigns—"get that out of here, on the double."

Hrriss indicated his distaste with a swish of his tail. Hrrto, usually a stickler for protocol, glanced up and seemed to draw in on himself.

Todd's order was ignored as, hard on the heels of the Spacedep technicians, uniformed Hrrubans brought a similar unit for Hrrrv.

"Just what is going on here?" Todd demanded, glaring at

Barnstable and Hrrrv. Neither answered him. "I want an answer, or, by all that's holy, you'll leave this meeting!"

"Not until you've seen what we can now show you, Reeve," Greene said, pitching his voice louder, his eyes fixed on Todd. "You've lost this one, Reeve. You and your all-for-one, one-for-all!" He sneered. "You've lousy judgment, Reeve."

"In what respect, Greene? or by the powers of the office Hrrestan and I hold, you'll be off this planet and you'll never get back on it!"

Out of the corner of his eye, Todd saw the smug grin on Barnstable's face. He nodded at Greene, an obvious signal to continue.

"Yes, you've erred catastrophically in the matter of the Gringg. These great, peace-loving creatures you're so eager to invite everywhere! That you're stupid enough to trust."

Sumitral and Hrrestan both leaped to their feet.

"If you fault Reeve's judgment, then you fault ours, too," Sumitral said in a cold, hard voice.

"You're obviously getting a little too old to practice basic common sense, Sumitral," Barnstable said. "If you resign now, we can probably see that your long service is suitably rewarded."

"My what?" Sumitral's face was expressionless, but his tone was unforgiving.

"You've all made the mistake of taking the Gringg at face value," Barnstable said. "And it is a mistake! Which Spacedep and the Hrruban Arm can at least control."

"You had better explain yourself, Admiral," Todd said, anger rising to a barely controllable pitch.

"Indeed you better, and immediately," added Sumitral.

"Now!" Hrrestan's single word held overtones of threat, causing the Gringg to respond by standing taller.

"Before those naval ships coming in behind the moon get into a position to cause both us and our Gringg friends considerable discomfort," Ali Kiachif said, his black eyes flashing with warning. He removed from under the table a small but powerful receiver which he had obviously been monitoring.

"What?" Todd said, thunderstruck. "Space fleets? Ali, why didn't you tell us?"

"Just got the confirmation I've been waiting for. I thought this laddie buck"—he jerked a thumb in Greene's direction—"was up to no good, so I've kept an eye and ear pricked until he overstepped himself. You, too, Admiral."

Todd turned on Barnstable. "I demand to know on what grounds you have brought armed ships into Rraladoonan space!"

Sumitral drew himself up in regal dignity. "If you have data you've been concealing from us during these negotiations, you must now reveal why you are obstructing the progress of these peace talks."

"The data was *classified*"—Greene stressed the verb—"until it could be confirmed. It is now. I contend that in your naive and ingenuous fashion, you have put all of Humanity and Hrrubanity at risk."

"And that you, in your usual warlike and suspicious nature, have arbitrarily decided we need to be defended by two space fleets. Humpf." Kiachif's black eyes sparkled with outrage and indignation.

"Ev, what have you done?" Sumitral asked, distress and disbelief spread across his face. "How could you supersede my authority in this matter?"

"I have rectified—and not arbitrarily—a serious error of the current civilian government—" Barnstable turned toward Todd, levelling a finger at him. "You have negligently placed the civilians of this planet in grave mortal danger. Therefore I declare martial law on this planet. I am taking over here. Two cruisers are approaching the Gringg ship and have orders to fire if it moves or they detect any unusual emissions. Furthermore, the entire fleet will take action in one hour if I do not cancel the mission with a code word known only to myself." The Spacedep Admiral glared at Grizz as he finished speaking and Todd realized just how frightened the man really was.

At this point a squad of heavily armed Human marines and another of even more heavily armed Hrruban soldiers entered the Chamber. Mllaba smiled with intense relief.

"Guards will be here in minutes to take these Gringg into protective custody until we can search their ship." Greene pointed at Grizz and Honey as he spoke, signalling the marines. One immediately tried to remove Grizz's collar. Honey attempted to prevent it, but withdrew when a laser rifle was thrust in his face.

"How dare you?" Todd said furiously, rushing over to place himself between the marines and the Gringg. "We're on the verge of making lasting peace with these people. We've already begun commercial transactions!"

"You are so naive, Hayuman," Mllaba said, her voice coldly insulting, "opening the way to the Gringg domination of

Hayumankind and Hrrubankind. Because that's the climate you were preparing—or did they make it worth your while?"

The marines had removed the collars of all the Gringg now, even Teddy's, though he had tried to resist. His dam had given one shake of her head. Sniffling, he had allowed it to be removed, though he kept his eye on the side table where it lay. Then marines took up positions behind the now-shocked Gringg, their rifles pointed at the large aliens' backs. At that, Teddy slipped from his chair and nestled under his dam's arm. Eyes straight ahead, she cuddled him.

Todd ignored Mllaba's snide insult. "Domination?" he asked, wanting to guffaw out loud as he glanced at the passive Gringg. If she had chosen to, Grizz by herself could have overcome both squads, without requiring the help of Honey or Kodiak, but she remained quiescent—almost amused, Todd thought. (Or were the loud and conflicting exchanges jamming her voder with meaningless sounds?)

Barnstable continued. "Spacedep is in possession of data that proves a Gringg ship destroyed a planetary civilization in the Fingal system."

Sumitral sat bolt upright. "I have received no information on such an incident!"

"The matter was classified but we have the tape of the exploration group, tape showing the devastated planet, *with a dead Gringg ship orbiting it.*" Barnstable enunciated that phrase with intense satisfaction at its effect on the Rraladoonans. Almost patronizingly, he continued. "Further examination proves that the weapons that killed the population and destroyed the cities came from that ship."

"What proof is there the Gringg actually were the aggressors?" Todd demanded.

"Quite enough, Reeve. More than enough," Greene observed drily. "We missed the shot, but can see the smoking gun."

"Then the evidence is circumstantial?" Hrrestan asked, stiffening his shoulders under his formal attire.

"They *were* there!" Barnstable said defensively. "The remains of their ship are still in orbit. The race they wiped out did inflict mortal damage on the ship, which is why we have proof of their infamy."

"And when did this happen?" asked Kiachif. "How many eons ago?"

"That hasn't been ascertained yet," Grace Castleton said, speaking for the first time. Greene gave her an odd look, then hurriedly took over the explanation.

"What we have is from a scout ship . . ."

"Which only has limited scientific capacity," Sumitral said in a crisp tone.

Greene glared at the Alreldep official. "The fully equipped naval team sent to conduct a thorough investigation of the system hasn't had time to reach Fingal yet."

"And for this you want to put Rraladoon under martial law?" Todd protested.

"It is for your own protection," Greene answered, looking pleased at Todd's dismay, "since you aren't showing the sense to protect yourselves. Spacedep is doing its job, risking lives to rescue you from your folly."

Todd spun to confront Barnstable. "As the representative of Rraladoon, I order you to end this nonsense. There is no clear threat and you have no basis for the illegal actions you've taken, including letting an unauthorized war party into Rraladoonan space."

The Gringg were now looking around nervously, their subsonic rumbles adding to everyone's agitation.

"He's right," Kiachif agreed. "These are bears, not bombs or brigades."

"They aren't bears," Barnstable said. "They're an alien race—strangers."

"I have always made myself personally responsible for Grizz and the others," Todd added. "Send those guards out. I know these people, and they are a threat to no one."

"Gone native again," Greene said to Todd with such repugnance the room was completely silent for several seconds.

"I have evidence of a clear threat, as I've told you all along," Barnstable said. "Sit down, Reeve."

"If you're accusing me of being a closet Gringg, then this won't surprise you, either."

With lightning fingers, Todd reached out and wrenched the corner of Greene's collar away from the body of his tunic. There was an audible gasp from Grizz and the rest of the Gringg. Greene recoiled, wondering if Todd was about to strike him, then sat very still. He had been present for Honey's explanation of the Gringg custom, and knew precisely what the gesture meant. Second Speaker and his aide looked puzzled, and glanced at Todd for enlightenment.

Todd spoke intensely, to Greene alone. "I challenge you to personal combat. I resent your interference. I deplore your attempt to embroil me and my world in your petty, secret bureaucratic games. You have tried and condemned an entire race on the basis of an isolated incident and no evidence. Do you realize that if they weren't so peaceful, you might have just given them cause for retaliation? You've insulted the captain, scared her cub, and have they moved a muscle?"

"How could they?" Greene demanded with a sneer, "with lasers aimed at them?"

Todd laughed again. "Haven't you seen how fast the Gringg can move when they want to? Have you any genuine notion of their physical strength? Grizz alone could account for every marine in this room and bend those laser barrels into pretzels. But I've a quarrel with you, Greene. And I mean to get it settled right now!" He poked a hard finger into Greene's sternum. "Knives or bare hands?"

Greene hesitated, shocked at Todd's wrath. "Knives or bare hands? That's barbaric . . . that's—"

"Barbarians have a keen sense of honor, you stupid button jabber." Todd cut him off with a ferocious smile on his face that made him look not unlike a hairless Gringg. "I do, too, and there are many on Earth who have considered me an arrogant barbarian. But I'm willing to fight for what I believe in. Whereas you are preparing to initiate a bloody and unnecessary war, and turn a very profitable colony on its ears with martial law! Well, I'm willing to fight for self-determination. Are you as willing to fight for your beliefs, Greene? Is individual combat too immediate, too undignified for you? In your hearing, the Gringg said that 'tearing the collar' has long been considered unacceptable. Or didn't you understand that?"

Greene was stunned by the onslaught of Reeve's tirade. He glanced down at his torn collar and up again at the relentless glare of Reeve's hard eyes. He'd never been challenged before; not since he'd been a very young boy. He hadn't won that fight either. Physical training as an officer had always been isometric. For the first time, he was aware of Todd as a man who was physically fit and was known to have wrestled with and killed a large Doonan snake.

The two men stood facing each other for long moments. Castleton moved her hand to her side arm, only to be answered by a threatening growl from Hrriss.

"Zis is between the two of zem," he said.

"Enough!" the Admiral said in a thundering voice. "Jon, Reeve, sit down! The very idea of a physical contest between the two of you is repellent."

The two men remained eye to eye for a moment; then Greene spoke.

"I . . . decline your challenge, Reeve."

"There speaks a really brave man," Ken Reeve said. Greene eyed him, looking for sarcasm, but the colonist's face was as sincere as his voice. "Maybe we can all have the courage to refuse to fight when there are alternatives."

"Admiral Barnstable, you will show us that incriminating tape, *now*!" Sumitral demanded, so forcefully that he had the instant attention of everyone in the room. Then he turned to Hrrto. "I count on your support, Second Speaker," he said to him. "An individual, as well as a species, is innocent until proven guilty. The Gringg are here to speak for themselves. The tape, please—" He held his hand out to Greene. "Somehow I feel certain that you have it to hand." As if in a trance, Greene fumbled at a tunic pocket and drew out a tape, laden with security seals. "Thank you. But—" Sumitral raised his hand—"no matter what transpires here, this Gringg and her crew are to be allowed to proceed out of this system without hindrance. Do I make myself clear?" His cold gaze fell on the Spacedep officers. "Or by all the powers and the favors I can call in in the Amalgamated Worlds, you'll be sorry!"

The silence was profound.

"Grurghgle . . ." Eonneh's voder began, "I have not completely understood all that was said, but I did hear you mention a destroyed Gringg ship, did I not? I would very much like to see this tape you speak of."

Barnstable and Greene exchanged cynical glances, but Second Speaker looked decidedly uneasy. When Mllaba wanted to whisper in his ear, he pushed her away.

"Well?" Todd asked pointedly.

With quick deft fingers, Sumitral slipped the tape into the appropriate slot and keyed it to play on the table projection. Todd was not the only one in the chamber who watched in horror as the camera skimmed over the dead surface of the planet, then followed a searchlight through the heart of a cold, dark ship. The faces of the dead Gringg swam out of the blackness and disappeared again. Eonneh and Grizz were still, watching, their mobile faces for once devoid of expression.

"Hold that image," Grizz said suddenly, pointing an unsheathed claw as the recorder skimmed along the hulk's battered exterior. She peered closely at the picture, then leaned back in her chair, her face saddened. She gave Eonneh a brief nod.

"We can identify this sad ship," Eonneh said in a slow, solemn tone. "It is the *Searcher* and was commanded by Captain Vrrayagh, an ancestor of our captain. It left the motherworld many long Revolutions ago. We had only two brief reports from Vrrayagh. The first when the *Searcher* arrived at that system and discovered the planet was torn by a massive war, its peoples fighting against one another. When the Gringg attempted to make contact and sent a shuttle to land in the largest remaining city, it was immediately attacked and destroyed." Eonneh bowed his head briefly. "Then, even as the two armies still fought each other, they turned their weapons also against the *Searcher.* Whatever armament was used was immensely powerful, and the *Searcher's* engines were destroyed. The second and last message told us this, and that the crew would defend themselves as well as they could, but, if no further message came from the *Searcher*, this planet was not to be approached again." Honey bowed his great head, and Grizz put a sympathetic hand on his back. "It was a long time ago, and for some considerable Revolutions, we worried that these hostile people might trace the *Searcher* to our motherworld. But no one came. A brave captain, Zeeorogh, volunteered to make a solo mission to that system in case our people had survived but were without communication. She found the world—and the *Searcher*—lifeless. Perhaps if the *Searcher* had not returned the attack, it might have been allowed to depart in peace. Perhaps, our people might even have mediated the quarrel that started such total conflict. But in those early days of our exploration program, our ships were armed. No longer. Better the loss of one ship than encourage retaliation or indulge in lethal exchanges which require so much expenditure of energy."

"How wise of you!" Sumitral said softly. "So we are the first life forms—and with the events of the day I am not sure I can say either of our species are as intelligent as they should be." He shot an almost malevolent glance at Greene and another at Mllaba. "We are the first life forms you have encountered face-to-face. I deeply regret this misunderstanding. Though to be perfectly fair, the evidence would give a military mind cause to make exhaustive inquiries." He glanced briefly again at the Spacedep contingent.

"Reh," Grizz said, nodding solemnly. "It would cause concern when similar strangers appear in your skies. Vrrayagh's ship was left where it had died, and it is our custom to take those cubs who would arm our ships to see what this can cost. Gringg cubs learn that lesson at once."

"How tragic to encounter a race bent on self-extermination," Kiachif said in a sympathetic voice.

"Reh. It became a great sadness to all Gringg," Honey said. He bowed his large head in deference, but then lifted it again and smiled at Kiachif. "It is why we were so happy to meet the Rraladoonans and that they came to welcome us, without loss of life."

Sumitral looked at Todd with a wry expression. "Their experience is not so far from ours in the Siwannah Tragedy."

"Gringg, Hayuman, and Hrruban have a great deal in common," Todd said. He breathed a deep sigh of relief that his faith in the Gringg had not been misplaced, that he had not been mistaken to trust his gut feelings about them. He felt a tremendous surge of elation.

"So, zey are trrruly friendly," Second Speaker said to Hrrestan, respect in his eyes. "You were right to trust."

"Trust is worth more than any other treasure of spirit, mind and heart," Hrrestan said, nodding sagely.

"But what about those parts of the ship you would not let me enter?" Greene asked. "What's hidden in that mass of water at the center of your ship? Why did you pull me away when I went to investigate?"

"You did not ask to go," Honey replied, surprised. "It is our custom to ask permission before viewing another's domicile. What do you wish to see? The bottom of our swimming pool?" He broke into a loud, grunting laugh, joined by his mate and cub. "Most certainly, if you can swim, you are welcome to come see that or any part of our ship, any time. Come now!"

Greene flushed, but said nothing.

"But why do you want such trivia as food and clothes from us?" Barnstable asked the Gringg, breaking the uncomfortable silence. He was still looking for reasons to doubt.

"With all due respect, Admiral," Kiachif said with a huge grin, "you stick to running spaceships and leave this to us trade captains. Whatever the customer wants, if he's willing to pay for it, I'll convey it to him. Trade is important for more than just the items we transport. Trade opens minds as well as credit sources.

It brings new customers together and circulates goods, which means more goods get made, and more gets traded to satisfied customers, anywhere in this galaxy that we can navigate to."

"Reh," Eonneh said, showing his teeth in a brilliant white grin. "No misleading was meant. It is not the items themselves which are important to the Gringg, but the act of exchange, leading up to the exchange of all things: goods, then techniques, then ideas. We understand the confusion, and we forgive without grudge."

"I was misled by another's enthusiasm," Barnstable said, glaring at Greene. "There are some who always see the downside of situations."

"Sir—" There was a humble tone to Greene's voice. "I thought that, based on the information I had, I was acting in the best interests of us all."

Castleton turned to look at him with a surprised but pleased expression, her eyes glowing.

"Look, Greene," Todd said, facing the chastened officer, "It's your job to err on the side of caution. Just stick to that, avoid explosives, and leave us planetary types to do ours."

Greene's face flushed, and his lips were pressed tight. He turned to Barnstable. "Sir, I wish to tender my resignation and accept full responsibility for my actions, authorized and unauthorized."

"You acted under my authority, so I bear the responsibility, too, which is to safeguard this colony as I would our homeworld. I did as I thought advisable under the very . . . unusual circumstances. And that's that!" He turned toward Hrrto and Hrrestan, then muttered brief, crisp orders into the communicator. "Red Alert's cancelled and my units are returning to previous duties."

"I have done ze zame," Captain Hrrrv said with an impassive expression and dulled eyes.

Barnstable exchanged a glance with the Hrruban captain and cleared his throat. "With your permission, Captain Grizz—" he said, and she nodded, lowering her eyelids briefly. He cleared his throat again. "I would welcome a full tour of your ship and its facilities. I believe Captain Hrrrv would, too." He even attempted a smile at the Gringg.

At a gesture from Castleton, the marines returned the Gringg's collars, shouldered their weapons, and filed out of the room. Hrrrv's squad followed.

Barnstable swivelled his chair to face Greene.

"In view of the unauthorized actions you personally initiated which put civilians in danger, I accept your resignation, Jon. What may serve a combat officer well is simply no good in an aide. Perhaps you're more suited for other duties."

"If I may suggest an alternative for Commander Greene, Admiral," Captain Castleton said, her manner devoid of emotion, "the *Hamilton* has an opening for an executive officer. Commander Fletcher's tour of duty is over in two weeks' time. I would certainly accept Commander Greene as a replacement."

Barnstable's snowy eyebrows rose high on his forehead, and he favored her with a paternal smile. "Whatever you say, Grace. It looks like someone has to keep a leash on him."

"I won't let him out of my sight for long, sir," Castleton said. Her eyes met Greene's, his expression changing from stern endurance of disgrace to surprise. He pushed back his chair and stood up.

"Request permission to be excused for a moment, sir?" he said, saluting both Barnstable and Castleton. Grace looked queryingly at the Admiral, and he flicked his fingers for her to answer.

"Granted, mister," Castleton said. Without another word Greene stalked from the room.

Todd leaned sideways to Hrriss. "Whaddya want to bet there won't be any protesters awaiting our departure?"

"I never bet on a sure thing!" Hrriss wrinkled his nose. "Hope no one will need ze grid for ze next few hours."

"Admirrrral," Hrrestan said severely to Barnstable. "In all this confrontation, I have seen that Spacedep has been closely involved. Why should it be necessary to start trouble where there isn't any?"

Barnstable glared at the tabletop. "You have to admit that that tape was pretty damning. What else was I to do to protect the colony?"

"You could have informed ze colony leaders of your suspicions," Hrrestan said fiercely. Then he turned to Second Speaker.

"And for you, a Speaker of the High Council, to go along with such machinations!" Hrrestan said. Todd heard the hurt and suppressed anger in his colleague's voice and trembled as he had when he and Hrriss were small, caught by his friend's father, doing something they knew they shouldn't. "We must learn to see all beings as potential friends, for we are terribly alone in the void of space. No offer of friendship should be rejected out of hand. See what you nearly did, destroying the peace both our species have enjoyed. For the sake of Hayumankind, for the sake of all Hrruba, for our hopes for the future, we must never come this close again to disaster!"

Hrrto gazed at him thoughtfully. No one spoke, for Hrrestan's words struck home in every heart.

Sumitral broke the silence. "Well, gentlefolks, we do have some business to conclude here. Are there *now* any changes to be made to the Trade Agreement?"

Silently, Barnstable shook his head. Second Speaker glanced up and blinked.

"No."

Grizz spoke for the first time, smiling. She had been watching and listening to the whole interchange with the greatest of interest, and now beamed upon Todd. "I find all to be very well."

"Then let nothing delay the signing," Sumitral said urgently. "Shall we make this official?"

"All in favor?" Todd said. The vote was unanimous. A moment later, he sent a clerk running to the Duplication Office with the approved copies of the Tripartite Trade Agreement.

The party went outside to the prepared table. The Alreldep guard withdrew to each corner and stood proudly flanking the officials, obviously relieved to be back on ceremonial duty. It was such a momentous occasion that Todd felt quite six years old again. He could almost feel Hrruna's reassuring presence as that six-year-old helped to formulate the Decision at Doona.

As they neared the table, Todd could see that the news-gatherers were gone and those that remained were smiling with friendliness, eager to be present at an auspicious occasion. Grizz, accompanied by her two scribes and her son, took her place at the end of the table and rolled her haunches gracefully onto the pad provided. Sumitral took his place opposite her and waited until Second had seated himself at the center of the table.

Todd, Hrriss, and Hrrestan opened the copies of the Trade Treaty Agreement and placed one before each of the signatories. Ken Reeve dipped the archaic pens into the inkwells and handed them ceremoniously to each delegate.

"Hayumans, Hrrubans, and Gringg," Sumitral said, turning to the crowd. "I welcome all of you to witness the signing of this historic trade agreement between our three peoples. This is only the beginning of what I hope will be a long and fruitful alliance."

There was a wild cheer. The deep voices of the Gringg boomed louder and lower than the rest of the crowd. Flowers, brought along specially for the occasion by Rraladoonans, were thrown into the air like confetti. A handful of fragrant stephanotis landed on the treaty table in front of Second Speaker Hrrto.

"An omen, Speaker?" Mllaba whispered the question in his ear.

"I believe so, Mllaba," Hrrto said, nodding.

When the Trade Agreement was placed before him with the page open to the complex and beautiful seal of Hrruba, ready for his signature, Hrrto took up the pen and signed. He felt relieved, strangely at ease, as if more had been settled that day than the peaceful accord of three diverse and independent races.

" . . . For our hopes for the future, this must not be!"

The tape ended, and the lights came on in the High Council Room. Hrrto glanced around at his fellow High Council members. Sixth Speaker was looking irritated, Fifth thoughtful. The sergeant-at-arms was smiling slightly. At a glance from Hrrto, he snapped his jaw closed and assumed a properly blank expression.

Second Speaker rose and placed his hands on the desk. "This concludes the file I have been assembling on Hrrestan, son of Hrrindan. You have had copies for your personal review, and heard personal witnesses testify to his wisdom and devotion to Hrruba. I nominate him for the seat of First Speaker of the High Council, and withdraw my own candidacy in his favor."

Gasps and muttering from the rest of the council. Mllaba looked absolutely livid, but suppressed her anger as best she could even if she couldn't control the twitching of her tail.

Hrrto did not entirely regret that he was unable to help her advance further, but he no longer envied anyone who must sit in the First Speaker's chair. The power—which old Hrruna had rarely invoked—was simply not worth the attendant responsibility. Younger, stronger shoulders would bear the burdens better. He would be remembered, however, perhaps as often as Hrruna, as the Stripe who had secured unlimited quantities of purralinium from the Gringg. It would be enough.

"He is a younger, stronger person, impartial and possessed of great patience and wisdom. With all humility, I would serve the Council and Hrruba best by remaining as Second Speaker. In that capacity, I can cement the relationships with the Gringg which I have already begun. Therefore, as temporary Council leader, I direct the sergeant to commence the voting for the First Speakership."

Each member placed his hands on the hidden panel below the level of the table. The blind monitor at the head of the table would tally the votes without revealing who had cast them. The sergeant stood up.

"The nominees for the position of First Speaker are Fifth Speaker for Health and Medicine, Sixth Speaker for Production, Carrdmarr, an industrialist and philantropist of Hrruba, and Hrrestan, Village and Colony Leader of Rraladoona and Chief Liaison Officer to Hrruba," the sergeant intoned. "For Fifth Speaker?"

One light went on at the tally board.

As tradition dictated on Doona-Rraladoon, the construction of new quarters—in this case the Gringg Embassy—became a community affair.

The site chosen for the Gringg compound was a woody area near the northern sea on the banks of the Treaty River, the major artery on the small continent.

From all over Rraladoon, trunks of the fast-growing rla trees were brought in and cut to size according to the blueprints drawn up by a team of indigenous architects and the Gringg. Vats of strong smelling rlba bubbled in several places on the site. Hayumans and Hrrubans in respirators with brushes full of the sticky sap treated the timbers, which became strong as iron and rigid in their newly cut shapes, yet still light enough to be hauled about by two sturdy workers or one Gringg. Other teams carried the finished beams and wall sections to the builders. It was all going by the numbers.

While those workers prepared the building materials, heavy loading equipment that had been used to build the Center and the Councillors' Residences had been rolled down, and were now in use excavating a deep swimming hole, with dams at each end to keep the level suitably high.

In the spirit of cooperation, artists from every village worked alongside the Gringg scribes to stencil and paint handsome, colorful designs as soon as the walls were ready.

When Todd arrived that morning on the site, he estimated that there must have been five hundred people pitching in to help. He was inordinately pleased by that—another subtle vote of confidence in himself and Hrrestan. When he and Hrriss had put out the word that volunteers were needed, the response had been so overwhelmingly enthusiastic that they'd had to set up two shifts. Feeding the large crew presented no problem; over a hundred households had offered to supply meals.

"At this rate, it could be finished in two days," Todd told Hrrestan, who was sitting at a safe distance from the sawyers, going over the blueprints. Amid loud cries to keep clear of danger, workers raised the pylons for the foundation. Gringg, using mighty hammers, almost casually pounded them into the ground. From where they sat, Todd could see how enormous the finished complex would be. But then, the Gringg liked a lot of space. The curved archways were a lot like the halls on their ship.

"As quickly as the rlba sets," Hrrestan agreed cheerfully in Low Hrruban. "It is hot enough to dry the sap, but not too hot. Donations of furnishings have also been coming in. Have you noticed them? I asked Kelly and Nrrna to take careful notes so the donors can be thanked."

The generosity of the Rraladoonans was indeed impressive. Piles of tapestries, cushions, carefully boxed works of art, even some electronic entertainment equipment, lay upon outspread tarps under a vast expanse of waterproof canvas. The period of settled weather had been chosen intentionally, but with such fine gifts, no chance was being taken. Kelly and Nrrna climbed around the heap of goods, compiling a rough inventory.

"Hey, the pickings are great! The Gringg'll be able to furnish several embassies with what's come in," Kelly called to Todd, waving her clipboard.

Todd grinned, and held up a hand, still slightly yellowed from last week's bruising rock. Hrrestan glanced at it.

"Kiachif tracked the culprit down."

"He did?" Todd was surprised. "Is he still breathing?" he asked, knowing Kiachif's penchant for making the punishment fit the crime.

Hrrestan grinned. "Kiachif *is* careful to keep his customers. The man is from a trading company which does a lot of business with Spacedep. With all the false rumors being circulated, he evidently believed that the Gringg were going to be allowed sanctions that would ruin his business."

"So, what punishment fit his crime?" Todd asked, seeing Hrrestan was amused.

"Tell, tell, tell!" Kelly cried, coming over to join them.

"Kiachif demanded a cut-rate for all merchandise he is now empowered to supply at the spaceport." Hrrestan's dropped jaw indicated how well he approved of the solution, and Todd's smile was just as big.

Kelly turned wide eyes on her husband. "You've given up fighting the spaceport?"

"Well," Todd said, dragging out the word and the suspense, "a triangle is a much more stable construction than a two-sided affair." He heaved a sigh. "And with the Gringg mediating, I don't foresee the problems that obsessed me when the project was first suggested."

"The Gringg have done us many favors," Hrrestan said, and answered a hail from a group of workers, leaving the two Reeves together.

"That's a tremendous relief, darling," Kelly said, giving him a firm hug and a long kiss. "You don't know how Nrrna and I have worried . . ."

"Oh, yes, I do," Todd said, and held her tightly for a long moment more when she would have disengaged. "Yes, I know," he added more softly, "and I've blessed you for letting me make up my own mind."

"Humph," she said, struggling out of his embrace. "As if *any* agency but you will make up *your* mind!" Todd followed her as she went back to inventory-taking. "So when will that start?"

"Right after Snake Hunt," Todd replied, with a broad sweep of his arm. "Which will be soon. Ben Adjei predicts it'll start in two days at the most."

Kelly gave a groan of dismay. "Oh, lordy, will we have time to finish the Gringg house?"

Todd laughed, waving his hand at the hustling workers. "I don't see why not. At least they'll have a roof over their heads. They're as eager to join the Hunt as anyone else on Rraladoona right now." He grinned broadly. "That'll be some sight! Gringg tackling Big Momma Snakes."

Nrrna looked up from note-taking. "Hrriss says to tell you zat ze Sighters say ze snakes are gazzering on ze sea marshes. Some are even heading for ze dunes."

"Good, good!" Todd said, nodding.

Nrrna grinned. "Ze children have talked of nozzing else all day. Zey arre eager to show Zeddy what a G.B.M.S. looks like."

"From a safe distance, I hope." Todd looked around. There were numerous children on the site, but he couldn't spot his twins. "That reminds me: where are they?"

Kelly glanced up. "Hmm? They were around here just a minute ago, with Teddy in tow. Together with Nrrna's two, they're so inseparable I'm starting to think of them as the Fearless Five." She stood up and called out the twins' names.

"Over here, Dad," Alec's unhappy voice came from around the back of the tarpaulins.

Todd found the five youngsters sitting together in a heap. Hrrana had her tail wound firmly around Teddy's leg, and Hrrunival was sandwiched between the Alley Cats with his head on Alison's lap. All of them wore glum expressions.

"So what's wrong here, Cats?" Todd asked.

"Daddy, couldn't Teddy stay here with us?" the twins asked in hopeful unison. "We're afraid if he goes away, we'll never see him ever."

"Well, since his mother's a starship captain as well as a fully accredited consul to Rraladoona, she might be spending a lot of time either in the embassy or running cargoes between our world and his," Todd explained. "So you might get to see him as often as you do Ali Kiachif."

"That'd be okay," Alec said. He had screwed his face up under his mop of red hair, hardly daring to let hope show.

"You may be absolutely certain that we will be staying in touch with our Gringg friends," Kelly promised, sitting down on the tarp's edge beside them.

"How?" Alison asked.

"How?" Todd echoed, beating Alec's identical query.

Kelly smiled. "Oh, Grizz has signed on my computer bulletin board. Her engineer and that marvellous Cardiff worked out a conversion program. Her entries will be holographic or audio/video for a time, but the Gringg have all the parameters to create a congruent written-language program. I gave them a lot of read-and-listen books to help them connect the spoken to the written word."

"What kind of books?" Todd asked, eyebrows raised, seeing the mischievous gleam in his wife's eyes.

Kelly affected innocence. "Very simple ones to start with. Children's books, like *The Three Bears*, and *Winnie the Pooh*."

Todd laughed and hugged her close. "Thank you, love."

"But of course! I don't want to lose touch with them either," Kelly said, and reassured the children with her smile. "So you can message to Teddy as often as you want."

"I'm glad," Alison said, seizing Teddy's paw. "I like him."

Teddy blinked at her shyly. "I like you too, Alison."

"And me?" Hrrunival demanded, determined not to be left out.

"And you. All of you." The young Gringg bestowed rib-cracking hugs on each of his dear friends, which left them gasping for the breath to giggle.

"Teddy is going to be able to ride out on Hunt with us tomorrow, isn't he, Dad?" Alec asked, his tone demanding an affirmative. "Hrriss said he could have that old plodder of his."

Todd scowled. "It may not be tomorrow. And it might not be safe. Have you considered what Captain Grizz thinks of all this?"

"Oh, she wants to go, too," Hrrana said. "She is very interested in snake eggs. Teddy told her about his lunch that day."

"Please, Dad?" "Please?" "Please, Uncle Zodd?"

"We will stay back where it is safe," Hrrana promised, opening large green eyes at him. Todd sighed.

"Let's talk it over with your parents later."

"Oh, there you are!" Ken Reeve said, peering in under the makeshift tent flap. He held up his camcorder. "Part of the frame is up, and they're setting the braces for one wall. I thought I'd immortalize this historic moment of galactic cooperation. I'm looking for models to show the scale of the building," he said, glancing meaningfully at the children. "Any volunteers?"

"Oh, yes!" exclaimed both Alley Cats at once, springing to their feet.

They dragged the rest of the Fearless Five behind them, although no one required much urging. Kelly and Todd, holding hands, followed more slowly.

With the same Hrruban and Hayuman skills that had raised the Friendship Bridge, a mighty, cavelike building—translated from an architectural design by Honey—was already starting to take shape. Part of the first level, which would support a solidly buttressed terrace, was cantilevered over the river, so that the water-loving Gringg could dive into the warm, tropical water from their dwelling. Todd admired its handsome lines as much as he did its symbolism.

"Gosh, your own swimming hole, right inside your house!" Alec said, catching the gist of the design immediately. "Hey, Dad, this is a great idea! Can we run a walkway right to the swimming hole? It would be terrific!"

"You wouldn't say that in no-see-um season," Todd said with a mock grumble.

"Aw, Dad!" the twins chorused.

Hrriss and Eonneh pulled themselves away from their conference with the senior builder, a heavy-set Gringg with a graying mane and muzzle.

"Are you pleased with what you have wrought, friend Zodd?" Hrriss asked.

"More and more," Todd said, waving a hand at the building framework. "That's a grand design, Honey, functional and impressive."

The architect sighed. "It is not often such an opportunity is given. I am sorry I shall never live in it." But he eyed his design with evident satisfaction. "Others shall stay as the permanent residents. I and my mate and offspring will only be occasional visitors."

"Well, you'll be welcome whenever you part space to come here," Todd said. "We've certainly enjoyed your visit."

"I contemplate with great sorrow the ending, and I thank you for the invitation to join in the Hunt festivities."

"Couldn't, and wouldn't, leave you out of them," Todd said instantly. "It's just too bad we don't have horses strong enough for you to take part in the Hunt itself."

"Zat is so," Hrriss added, dropping his jaw in a broad grin. "You make even a Big Momma Snake zink twice about attacking."

"I will enjoy what is possible," Eonneh said, with the usual equanimity of the Gringg, "from the shuttle."

"Well, then, Fate protect any snake that gets in your way. In any case, you'll be more than welcome, if only to keep our assorted offspring from haring away to find big snakes by themselves," Todd said with a laugh. "This is the time to see Rraladoon at its best, during New Home Week. Every Rraladoonan who can scrape up the fare from Earth or one of the colonies comes home. We'll introduce you to as many as you can tolerate meeting. They'll spread the word about our new trade allies with no need for tall tales and embroideries. That I can promise!"

CHAPTER 12

TWO MORNINGS LATER, SIGHTERS LANDED THEIR light helicraft outside Todd's bedroom window just after dawn to inform him that the hundreds of female snakes were nearly finished with their egg-laying in sandy dunes. Between one breath and another, Todd roused out of a sound sleep to full organizational mode. As he dressed, he reviewed one or two points that he wanted Robin to check out, but despite the overlapping problems with Spacedep and the Gringg, long familiarity with Snake Hunts assured him that they were ready for the snakes. Robin was a good organizer and meticulous with details, so Todd anticipated few problems. But then, the snakes might not cooperate. They could create glitches almost as if they were testing the Hayumans and Hrrubans who had invaded their traditional routes. Years of coping had provided ample experience to handle anything that could possibly happen. He hoped!

Fortified by a good breakfast, he and Hrriss reined their Hunt horses in the middle of the village square in front of the Assembly Hall. The peripheral support personnel—Sighters, Beaters, Lures, Wranglers, and First-Aid crews—as important as the Teams who herded the snakes along the way, were all accounted for. The complements of the individual Teams were still assembling, their Team leaders checking each person to ensure that gear was in proper order and appearance. The Aids were well supplied with traditional medical gear, plus big tubes of the healing salve vrrela, good for any general wound, but a sovereign remedy for rroamal poisoning. The mere touch of the toxic vines was enough to raise large welts even on furred skin. Team members carried tubes of the salve as well, but it wasn't just Team riders who blundered into the poisonous weed.

Experienced Hayuman and Hrruban hunters wore "chaps and

straps" to protect them against rroamal and the thin whips of young branches that scored flesh on a hell ride through the forest. Hardhats were buckled across chins and inspected for soundness. Where a Team had green riders, one member was assigned as "wrangler" to assist those who might have trouble controlling their horses in the excitement of the Hunt.

The square was crowded with double the indigenous population of Rraladoon, included many who got vicarious thrills from observing those who were qualified to participate in the Hunt, as well as visiting dignitaries from planetary governments all over Hrruban and Hayuman space.

Not only did the Hunt provide a real boost to the treasury of the colony, it attracted enough competent people to help the resident conservationists drive the snakes safely back to their natural preserve with a minimum of loss. Even when there had been few riders to control the thousands of reptiles moving, wholesale killing had been prohibited; the most ardent ProLife fanatic admitted to the necessity for discreet culling of a species whose females each laid hundreds of eggs, a large proportion of which survived natural disasters.

The decision of a safety kill or capture of a certain number of snakes was the prerogative of the Hunt Masters, requiring split-second decisions during the high excitement of the Hunt. Fresh snake meat was a delicacy, generally only available during Hunt season or when marauding young males attacked outlying farms.

Todd and Hrriss checked with each Team leader that all riders had snake sacks and operational handsets. Someone always forgot these essentials. As usual, there was one young rider who protested having to wear a poxy belt unit which he was certain would hamper him. Hrriss gave him the cold-eyed stare of a person who did not wish to argue.

"No handset, no Hunt, young man," Hrriss said firmly. Grumbling gracelessly, the Hayuman took the unit and retreated out of sight of the Masters of the Hunt.

The onlookers framed the main square, keeping a judicious distance from the heels of excited horses cavorting and showing off. Old hands at this Hunt, like Todd's Gypsy, Hrriss' Rrhee, and the old mares that Errala and Hrrin used, calmly circulated, miraculously avoiding a kick or a bite.

"Sappers?" Todd asked, checking his pad.

"I have hrrrd from Hrrol," Hrriss confirmed, pointing a sharp claw at his pad to underscore that entry. "She says zey have finished laying mine charges under bridges, and blockading with fences, zorns, and razor wire over all other accesses leading to vulnerable targets. Zey are spread out along ze route for stragglers, particularly the old Space Center." Hrriss was not above grinning at Todd over that. "Lures are ranged along the route, and zere are relief and backup riders ready to accompany the Teams."

The Lures, mounted on dirt bikes, were trained in their function—to attract renegade snakes of any size and "lure" them back to the main drive. Their bikes and persons were liberally smeared with bacon fat, redolent and irresistible to snakes.

"Great," Todd said. "We've got about half an hour before we have to ride out. I'd better let the guests get into position." He informed the heli pilots.

The excited clamor, mostly from first-time Hunters—duffers in Rraladoonan parlance—vied with the hacking sound of copter blades beating the air, the impatient whinny of the occasional horse, and the general babble among old friends reuniting after long separation as Rraladoon prepared for its annual event. While duffers were permitted to accompany hunting teams, they could not participate in the more difficult and dangerous occupations of Beater or Lure, though over the years, some off-world Hunters who showed the proper amount of care and skill could be "promoted" to Hunter status. Few had the patience to be accorded that honor. Many of the duffers who joined in only wanted to have a crack at "one of the big ones," a Great Big Momma Snake, reptiles that reached up to sixteen meters in length. For the ardent predator, the Rraladoon snake provided a sufficiently dangerous prey, and there were many who wanted the accolades that came with bringing in either two live snakes or twelve intact eggs. For a Rraladoonan, it was a Coming of Age Ritual but Hunter-mentalities of all ages vied to meet that challenge.

Pet ocelots, who hunted alongside their masters and mistresses, now huddled underneath horses' bellies or sat on pillions behind their owners' saddles. Hrriss was running a new ocelot this year, Gerrh; a cub of his two beloved pets, Prem and Mehh, who were getting too fat and lazy to run beside horses. The spotted cat sat bolt upright on back of the shifting mare, his tail curled around his haunches much as his master's was. Most Hrrubans tucked their long tails down inside chaps or bandaged them to one leg to prevent accidents.

As one of the Masters of the Hunt, Todd stood up in his stirrups, one hand on Gypsy's neck to steady him. In a stentorian voice, he ran through his usual caveat.

"We are not here to decimate the snake population. If that's your intention, you can stay right here in this square when we move out," he announced, eyeing the crowd. "The Hunt is for the purpose of controlling the flow of the snakes, driving them back into the salt marshes after they've spawned. When those females come off the dunes, they're hungry! There is plenty of food for them in their regular habitat. Our task is to prevent them from stopping off for a snack on the way." There was appreciative laughter from the crowd.

A timid hand went up among the riders. "But what if a snake attacks me?" a young Human visitor asked. Her riding coat was so new Todd fancied he could see the mark on the cuff where the bar code had been.

"If you should be so unlucky as to have a snake attack you, call in your position and then get out of the way as fast as your horse can carry you; and a snake-chased horse really moves! If flight's not an option, shoot as straight as you know how," Todd said. "That one's for the stewpot. If a snake attacks and gets a taste of blood, it'll go for any hunter near it next year. We call them 'renegades' and they're killed to prevent real trouble later. The snakes that proceed peaceably back into the marshes are to be left alone. Don't provoke them! You don't know what they're capable of. Do not mingle in the main swarm; just flank it. You don't want a snake running up your horse's leg to get a chunk of you!" He grinned then. "I assure you Rraladoonan horses will do their best to keep you clear all by themselves. If you hot-dog, endangering yourself, your mount, or anyone else, the leader of your Team has full right and responsibility to sideline you for the duration. If you don't want to spend the rest of the day in a snake blind, listen to your leader and obey any orders. He or she knows how to save your life. Any questions?"

There were a lot of brash mutters as the inexperienced Hunters mulled over Todd's remarks. It got louder and more intense as the Gringg, led by Kodiak, appeared on foot over the span of the Friendship Bridge.

Fifteen or twenty of the huge aliens had elected to join the Teams, to the amazement and enthusiasm of some of the returning Rraladoonans, and the nervousness of others. Todd was unhappy to see that there was still some distrust among his folk for their newest allies, but he hoped the Gringg performance in the Hunt might alter die-hard notions.

Since there were no horses up to the weight of an adult Gringg, they had agreed to work as assistants to the Beater Teams, whose task was to make enough noise to scare an escaping snake back into the mass. The job was by no means a sinecure. Since the Beaters drove tractors and other light farm machinery fitted with heavy snake-bars, the crews were equipped with noisemakers, flails, and, for use as a last resort, heavy-caliber handguns, anything that could persuade a snake to return to the stream heading south toward their natural habitat.

Todd had Kodiak brief the other Gringg on the safety procedures and then pointed out which driver each Gringg would accompany. Beater Teams One and Two, stationed nearest the spawning sands, got two Gringg apiece.

"Heavy artillery," said a grinning Mark Dautrish, the wheelman for Beater One. He reached down to give Big Paws and Koala a hand up into the cab of the wide-bucket heavy-duty tractor, one of the largest on the planet. It was effective in blocking snakes' escape routes among the marsh grasses, and Mark was wizard in the things he could make his rig do, should push come to shove.

"Move 'em out!" Todd cried as he saw all the Gringg on board their designated vehicles. He pumped a fist in the air. With a roar of engines, the Beaters departed to take up their positions, followed by the Lures, mounted on nippy dirt bikes that looked all too flimsy for the work they had to do.

With Grizz and Eonneh riding in the farm hover truck, Kelly drove slowly enough for the five children to follow on their horses. She also didn't want to bottom the truck with all the weight it currently carried. With her huge arms folded neatly across her belly, Grizz sat with the utmost dignity in the front seat, her bulk crushing Kelly up against the door—rolling the window down gave Kelly the opportunity to lean her upper torso outside. Honey, filling the rear seat, was armed with his ubiquitous pad and stylus. The youngsters were leading Kelly's mare, Calypso, and Alison had a lead rein on Teddy, who was mounted on Rock, the calmest horse in Hrriss' stable. This time the young Gringg sat on a much more professionally modified pack saddle, cushioned by deep fleeces and surrounded by rolls of canvas that acted like a safety belt, preventing him from falling out of the saddle. As the truck reached the square, Kelly hooted the horn to clear a space for her to maneuver the truck inside the crowd, and waved furiously to get Todd's attention. Hrriss noticed her and trotted over.

"Nrrna and the farm managers are lined up at the ranch fences with heavy guns and dynamite in case of tiddlers! Where do you want us?" she called over the din.

"You and ze children go wiz Llewellyn Carn's Beaters toward Boncyks' farm," Hrriss said, checking them on his list, "wherrre the woods end."

"Right you are!" Kelly saluted cheerfully and set the hover truck moving in the right direction. In her rearview mirror, she could see the youngsters urging their horses after her, east toward the river, disappearing among the houses and trees at the edge of town.

"Four Zeams filled and dispatched, twenzy-seven to go," Hrriss informed Todd.

"There you are!" Jilamey exclaimed, forcing his horse through the crowd. The entrepreneur was clad in new and flamboyant riding gear that had nevertheless been chosen with the perils of the Hunt in mind. His hand-unit radio and voder were clipped to crossed bandoliers in the center of his chest where they wouldn't interfere with free movement. After Todd's initial reproof, Jilamey always wore every bit of the compulsory Hunt safety gear, even adding a few pieces of equipment that he considered necessary. His saddlebow was hung with quivers, one full of short spears, another of crossbow quarrels to fit his custom-made, fast-reload weapon, including some marked with the red seal for high explosive. The sedately clad Barrington followed closely behind his master in the small, but very speedy flittercar. Responding to an over-the-shoulder nod from Jilamey, he parked the vehicle beside the Assembly Hall, and disappeared inside.

"Old Overprotective's going to help cook this time!" Jilamey said with an impish grin that made him look like a balding faun. "Out of my way at last. I'm ready, able, and oh-so-willing! Bring on the snakes!"

"Good to see you," Todd said, chuckling. "Now that you've arrived, our Team is present and accounted for. Take a position next to Hrrin and Errala." Jilamey nudged his horse until it edged in between the two Hrrubans.

"We musst all move to our assigned places," Hrriss said,

"Then, my old friend, let us go!" Todd's grin was as much for the memories of past Hunts as it was for the present one. The stresses and problems of the recent past were all behind them. This Hunt was *now!*

A Sighter flew in overhead. The copter swooped low, facing the Hunt Masters. Through the open hatch, Dar Kendrath waved wildly to get Todd's attention. He pointed to his wrist and held up one finger, then five more. The main swarm would reach the dunes in about fifteen minutes.

"That's cutting it close," Todd said to Hrriss, giving Dar the thumbs-up sign that he understood the message. He stood in his stirrups, twisting around at his waist. "At the trrrrrot, forward!" he yelled, swinging his arm over his head in an age-old gesture.

Dar veered his craft out of the way of the oncoming horses. The second Sighter chopper, a good distance from the throng, followed a moment later.

Hrrula, at the head of Team Two, with Robin Reeve as his second riding behind him, wheeled his horse around. His Team was full of visiting duffers, some of whom were reasonably good riders, but Hrrula was competent at keeping Team members from coming to grief.

"Moving out," the Hrruban said, his sharp teeth flashing brightly in a wide smile. "See you at ze salt mrrrshes!"

Jilamey paired off with Hrrin as Team One moved out. As Todd and Hrriss led them along the well-worn river trail, they could hear the two of them shouting excitedly to each other about grids and ships. That left the one recently promoted Hunter, a man named Harris, riding beside Hrrin's mate, Errala, with Jan and Don, Team One's Wrangler and sharpshooter, bringing up the rear. Team One was lighter in personnel than most of the other groups of Hunters, but as the team that took responsibility for steering the lead snakes, they needed to be able to peel away and move faster than any other.

Todd held them to a fast trot until they reached the head of the desert, where the snakes laid their eggs. The weather was slightly overcast, which was a minor blessing. Bright sunshine meant hours of hot riding. Gerrh twitched nervously on his pillion, reacting to the strong odor of snake which a slight breeze wafted down the river path. Errala covered her sensitive nose with a citrus-scented cloth, and coughed. Team One cut along the trail past the other teams in place. As Todd and Hrriss passed, each leader acknowledged their readiness.

The radio crackled on Todd's hip.

"They're swarming!" Leah Kalman's shout came through clearly. "Teams Six and Seven spreading out."

Todd squeezed his legs into Gypsy's sides and lifted him into a gallop, heard his team follow his lead. They arrived at the edge of the marsh in time to see Mark Dautrish rolling up his big tractor with its wide bucket inches above the ground. No snake could squirm through that space.

Several young tiddlers, none more than four meters long, broke in that direction. At the sight of the sharp metal, they thought better of it and cut away toward Todd. Hrrula's team was circling around to the north.

"Yow!" Todd exclaimed, his gaze sweeping the heaving multitude of snakes.

"Numbers have increased beyond estimate," Hrriss called in Low Hrruban. "More must have survived than usual. Good for us that we can trade the excess to the Gringg now they've gotten a taste for the flavor."

"This swarm's going to take real handling, partner," Todd called back and then began shouting orders to the other riders. "Spread out! Contain them. We've got to keep them rolling or they'll stack up here and we'll have the devil's own time!"

Big Paws had his powerful body crouched so low to the ground that he was almost on all fours. But his fangs and claws were bared, and the small snakes that had tried to scoot out past him quickly reversed, and he herded them back to the marked route. When a three-meter tiddler made a hasty break to dive between his legs, he seized it at the back of the neck, and flung it bodily into the main stream of snakes leaving the dunes. He glanced up and waved at Todd.

"Fun!" he cried.

The subsonics in his voice, which tended only to disconcert or annoy the Hayumans and Hrrubans, seemed to cause a violent reaction among the reptiles. At the sound of his rumbling roar, several that were headed in that direction stopped where they were and doubled back on their own lengths.

"Look at zat!" Hrriss said gleefully. "A new deterrent! Zey must dislike Gringg vibrrations!"

Todd, vigorously applying his quarterstaff to curtail breakouts, grinned back. "Keep up the good work, Big Paws!"

"Reh!" the Gringg chortled, flinging another four-meter snake overhand. It struck the ground on its nose and hastily sought refuge among its fellows, slithering away as quickly as it could from the gigantic black-and-white terror.

Todd wheeled to follow the vanguard of the reptiles through the woods. The snakes were relatively placid up near the dunes, in strong contrast to the way they would act later on, when they were tired and the clutching hunger had fully kicked in. Then they became dangerously cunning. The slightest breath of air which carried rumors of a quick meal caused them to take any reasonable chance to avoid the Hunters and find food.

"Ware!" Todd cried, pointing at a pair of very small snakes, probably at the dunes for their first clutches, who zipped around the front of the tractor.

"I'll get the one on the right!" Jilamey shouted, waving his crossbow over his head and spurring his horse through the marsh waters after the snake. He aimed and loosed the bolt, but the quarrel struck mud, missing the tiddler completely. His horse slipped, nearly precipitating him into the fetid waters. Jilamey was improving, but he would never be a match for Kelly, and Todd missed her support on the Team. She certainly wouldn't have missed an easy shot like that, but she had offered to cart the captain around.

A roar sounded from behind the farm machine, and one of the young snakes came sailing over the top of the tractor to land in a heap on the path. Todd jumped. Don swore.

"Fardle it, I didn't think they could fly!"

"Compliments of Koala," Dautrish called to the Team. "She missed the other one, though!"

"I'll call ahead!" Todd said, and thumbed the switch on his handset. "One escapee, heading west from the dunes."

"Got it, Todd," replied Leah Kalman and broke the contact.

The river road became a living, writhing sea of reptilian bodies. Todd kneed Gypsy to the edge of the marsh grasses, loping alongside the leading snakes and keeping the foot of his quarterstaff poised for use. His Team fanned out in single file behind him, riding herd.

A flashgun popped to one side of the path. Todd caught the glare out of the corner of one eye. A margin Hunter, turning back a tiddler that had strayed between the cordon of horses as they entered the woods. The terrain here favored the snakes, who could disappear without trace into the undergrowth by virtue of their natural protective patterning. It took quick eyes to make sure none of the leaders strayed, encouraging others to follow it. Not for the first time, Todd was grateful to the river for bordering one side of the snake run, keeping the Hunters from having to double up Teams along this section.

A low ridge of rock rose up in the middle of his path. Avoiding the obstacle, Todd hugged the opposite side and came out ten feet behind the lead snakes. He urged Gypsy forward. Once they came level again, the experienced horse dropped back to a trot.

From behind him came the raucous snarl that told him that Gerrh had joined the hunt. He risked a quick glance over his shoulder. The young ocelot had leaped from his perch and was after a three-meter-long tiddler that was attempting to go the wrong way around the rocky upthrust. Hrriss cantered by his pet and administered a thwock! to the snake's head with the butt end of his spear. It coiled up and headed into the stream without further hesitation. Gerrh galloped after his master and leaped neatly back onto Rrhee's back.

The ridge had provided one of the few breathers the Hunters got on the trail, where geography did their work for them in keeping the snakes from straying. After that, the long hot ride was made even more dangerous by low branches which knocked against Todd's helmet and shoulders while he tracked the swift-moving snakes along their way.

He passed the first of the snake blinds: one of the small, well-sealed rla-wood cottages smeared with the citrus perfume that kept snakes from smelling the contents. The broad window at trailside was filled with spectators staring out at him through field glasses.

"Todd, I've got a lively one here," Don called through the handset. "Could use your help."

With one hand, he laid the reins along Gypsy's neck and turned him around, while he lifted the small communications unit to his mouth.

"Hrriss, take point. I'm circling back to help Don."

"Rrright!" The friends passed in mid-gallop, Hrriss spurring Rrhee to catch up with the lead snakes.

Far back along the line, Jan was overstretched, herding much more of the cordon of young reptiles than she could really handle as Don went in pursuit. The sharpshooter waved to Todd as he approached, and pointed at the five-and-a-half-meter snake he was pacing. As steady as if he were sitting on still ground, Don's rifle aimed at the back of the reptile's head.

"The damned thing won't go back in line!" he called. He ducked a branch. "I've got a bead on it, but I don't want to kill it if it's just ornery."

"Crank a ground shot next to its head on the right," Todd said, unlimbering his quarterstaff to help prod.

He called for a Lure to come and assist. Nodding, Don squeezed the trigger, and a puff of dust kicked up on the right of the snake's nose. With a violent check, the snake turned a sharp corner and veered toward the stream, but over five meters of body was a lot to maneuver. The tail whipped around and struck Don's galloping horse, knocking it off its feet.

"Wheeee-ee-ee!" the gelding screamed, falling onto its side. Don jumped off and, cursing, rolled into a stand of bushes. He emerged, brushing himself off. Todd raised his flashgun and reined Gypsy to a stop between the fallen horse and rider, standing guard.

The incident attracted the attention of more tiddlers. Todd shot off flash after flash of brain-searing light to divert the predatory snakes while Don helped the gelding to its feet and regained his saddle. Suddenly, a leather-clad Lure on a cycle burst out from among the trees and began riding a serpentine trail between Todd and the mass of snakes. Across her shoulders was a fresh sheep hide, inside out. The heavy scent of blood got the slow-witted attention of the stray snakes, and they followed the Lure, who led them to the main stream. The bike tilted to an angle and roared down the riverbank, out of the snakes' reach.

"Whew!" Don said. "Thank heavens for loaves and little fishes."

"Ow, this thing gets hot," Todd said, letting the flashgun fall on its strap against his chap-covered leg, and airing his gloved hand. Don swung up and leaned over to slap Todd on the shoulder.

"Thanks, friend," he said, reining the horse toward the perimeter of the snake cordon. "I'm not even bruised." Team Two was coming up fast behind them, and Don paced in a couple of beats before Hrrula arrived.

Todd turned Gypsy inland and galloped onward to come level with Hrriss. He passed another group of Beaters with Cinnamon. They were sweeping the snakes back onto the path with brooms, flails, and in the Gringg's case, his own big feet. A jab here, a prod there, and the tiddlers stayed in the boundaries of the swarm. Cinnamon waved and called out happily as he and Hrriss passed.

The day was going well. No injuries or losses had been reported yet from up the line. The most serious problems would probably arise on the Boncyk farm, still some klicks ahead.

Kelly felt as if they'd been waiting for hours in the meadow near the Boncyk farm, but she knew it hadn't been more than one. It just seemed longer, because the children, antsy with anticipation, were on the verge of driving her crazy. She'd known all along the folly of bringing youngsters into the heart of a Snake Hunt. Carn had brought up her horse, so at least she had a chance of chasing them down if necessary. Staying back with a Beater Team was simply the best way for them, and their guests, to see the action without getting hurt. She'd explained the roles of each of the hunting Teams and the auxiliaries. The Gringg listened with careful attention, but the children, who'd heard it repeated for years, were bored.

"Now, if anything goes wrong," Kelly repeated again and again, hoping her instructions stuck in the minds of the excited children, "you pull back! Get out of the way of the Hunters! Immediately! Is that clear?"

"Yes, Mom."

"Yes, Aunt Gelli."

"Yes, Kelly," Teddy promised, wiggling deep into the sheepskins.

Somehow she wasn't totally reassured. In the hour since they'd taken up positions, the five youngsters had made friends with the Beaters, galloped up to take a look at the Boncyk farm, and found the nearest citron-covered snake blind. Alec came galloping back with a report of who was inside it, watching for the snakes to come by.

"That Admiral is in there," her son announced. "The cranky one with white hair."

"Alec!"

"In a blue uniform," Alison said. "Well, he grumbled at us."

"Admiral Barnstable?" Kelly asked. "Huh. Whaddya bet he's here more to keep an eye on the Gringg than the snakes!"

She hadn't her voder on just then, but nevertheless looked over to where Grizz sat at her ease in the soft meadow grass. The captain daintily plucked a tiny yellow flower between two claws and examined it closely. Delicately, she extended it to her mate, sitting with his shaggy golden side pressed against hers.

"See here, Eonneh, the five-petal structure. Most attractive, is it not?" she asked, her red eyes gentle.

"Most attractive," Eonneh replied, accepting the flower. Their claws intertwined.

There's more going on there than a botany lesson, Kelly thought, with a silly smile of approval on her face.

"They're coming," called Llewellyn Carn. Kelly stood up in her stirrups and let out a sharp whistle for the children.

"Come on!" yelled Alec, and headed Tornado uphill.

Seeing his friends respond, Teddy wheeled the lethargic Rock in a wide loop, and at a dignified plod, followed Alec back toward the threshing machine.

Admiral Barnstable, pacing around outside the snake blind, felt unwilling to enter the reeking enclosure until it was absolutely necessary. He noticed that there was some commotion up on the high meadow where Mrs. Reeve and her horde of children were waiting. Hastily hiking up the dusty path, he called out to her.

"What's going on?"

"Please get back to the blind, Admiral," Kelly shouted. "The snakes are coming."

"If you're safe, I'll be safe," Barnstable said, panting a little as he reached the crest of the low hill. The Reeve woman had a small arsenal's worth of primitive weapons arrayed on her sheepskin-padded saddle. There was a strong smell of animal sweat and excrement coming from across the lea to the right. Looking down the hill toward the farm buildings, Barnstable saw a thin, dour-faced farmer and his family waiting on horseback, behind an odd assortment of heavy farm machinery that had been rolled up to the low fence. What a ridiculous barricade, he thought. He turned back to eye the two adult Gringg, seated on the grass nearby, who met his gaze pleasantly.

"Aren't you carrying any defensive weapons?" Barnstable demanded. "These snakes are highly dangerous and excitable."

"Why will you not believe that we have no such tools?" Honey asked, then held up his paws. He flexed his digits, and the sharp claws gleamed in the gray sunlight. "These natural fittings are all we need."

The sounds of galloping, and a curious, terrifying hiss, came from the edge of the woods. Mrs. Reeve tensed, and raised a loaded crossbow. Barnstable turned.

Out of the thin forest came a dappled, tossing, undulating reptilian river. Barnstable's heart started to pound in his chest and his mouth went dry. He sucked his cheeks for saliva. This was like the prelude to a battle. Beside him, the enormous farm machine revved its engine and bucked down the slope toward the snakes.

Two horses, looking amazingly small next to the swarm, cantered along, prodding an occasional snake that tried to break free. What Reeve and Hrriss were doing looked almost easy. For all their admonitions about the dangers involved in the Hunt, it looked like there was nothing more to herding snakes than quick reflexes and concentration. Barnstable was unimpressed.

Then the wind changed to the southwest. Instead of blowing into their faces from the salt marshes, the shift brought a miasma of heavy, stinking air direct from the byres behind them. Barnstable gagged.

"What is that appalling stench?" Barnstable asked, pinching his nostrils shut.

"Pigs," said Kelly amiably. "Boncyks raise China and Poland pigs. No help for it now"—an urgent note crept into her voice—"the snakes have the scent."

The tumbling tide of snake shifted until it was heading directly towards them. Everett Cabot Barnstable had a sudden change of heart regarding the difficulty of managing thousands of snakes as the whole boiling wave of them seemed to come straight at him. For the first time in his life, he experienced gut-twisting terror.

"Llewellyn!" Kelly shouted, angling her steed between Barnstable and the stream. The horses, having caught the snake stink, were dancing frantically about, their riders controlling their antics with unconcerned skill. Teddy bounced up and down like a ball in his high saddle.

"Behind me, Kelly," Carn shouted, raising his hand unit. "Lures! Edge of the Boncyk farm! Now!"

The thresher rolled around the crest of the hill and headed for the outbuildings. The huge machine moved down like an avalanche, pushing the snakes away. A cluster of the reptiles avoided the Beaters by going every which way at once, and looped uphill at speed.

"They're headed to Mr. Boncyk's farmyard!" Alec cried. "Can we go help?"

"No!" Kelly exclaimed. "You stay right here or—!" She left the threat of dire punishment hanging.

Then a three-meter tiddler attempted a fast break around the wheels of the thresher. Carn promptly lowered the boom on it and Kelly shot the crossbow bolt directly into its brainpan. The snake lashed about in muscular spasms, but it was no longer a threat. One of Carn's assistants dismounted and stuffed the writhing corpse into a snake bag.

Todd and Hrriss galloped by, their attention on the fan of stragglers who were enticed by the strong swine smell. Hrriss growled orders into his handset for Don and Jan to keep the rest of the snakes moving down the path to the marshes.

Having learned by bitter experience in the early years of their homesteading just how tempting their stock was to snake, Wayne and Anne Boncyk prepared for the worst. In fact, as individual defenders went, they had more personnel massed on their property than any other farm on the route. As luck would have it, their prize sows tended to farrow every year about the same time as Snake Hunt. But the shrewd and aggressive sows had learned to defend their piglets against these wriggling predators. The females were ruthless and attacked any snake that crossed into their tract, chopping them into squirming pieces with sharp little hooves.

The males were even more aggressive, charging at any snake, no matter what its size, that dared impinge on their territory. Todd had nicknamed the swine herd Wayne's War Boars, euphonious even if there were more sows than boars.

Just to the right of the line of outbuildings, the pigpens were surrounded by high, lightweight but sharp-edged, metal barriers that could rip open the belly of any snake trying to crawl through. Wayne left the spoor of snake blood on them year after year to try and scare off new marauders, though Todd and others warned him that it worked just the opposite way. Snakes happily consumed their own dead. But to get to the barriers, let alone the sties containing the piglets, the snakes had to pass the cordon of angry boars.

Todd counted the boars ranged along the white metal fence, and gave up at thirty, each averaging about 275 kilos. Two black and white Border collies ran up and down the line, using The Look to keep the pigs from wandering away before the battle began.

"C'mon, Reeve! Get these snakes out of here," Wayne cried, hoisting his bow to his shoulder. That was the signal to his crew. They pressed forward to help the Hunters form a strong cordon against the advancing mass of snakes. With hand gestures, Todd directed them to the best points to reinforce the defenses around the byres.

"Where're the rest of the barricades?" Todd demanded, looking at the bare rear edge of the pens.

"Got a stand of new olive trees," Wayne said, pointing beyond the pen to a grove of young saplings with gray-green foliage. "I don't want them snakes mowing them down."

"For life and love, Wayne," Todd said in a groan, slapping himself in the head. "Snakes don't eat olives, they eat meat!"

"The boars'll get 'em," the stockman assured him.

The inrush of stragglers made for a lively few minutes, to the joy of Jilamey Landreau, who'd been somewhat disappointed with the tame atmosphere of this year's Hunt. Once on the Boncyk property, the Hunters and snakes were within a few kilometers of the marshes, the end of the journey, which meant that Jilamey had only a short time in which to secure his second snake to complete his Rite of Passage, or go without for another year. Snake sack in hand, the Human was casting frantically about him for a likely catch.

"Jilamey!" Todd shouted. "Help Anne!"

With a guilty start, the younger man wound the sack around his saddle horn and kicked his horse over to where Mrs. Boncyk and two farmhands were fighting off tiddlers who were slithering around the pen looking for any weakness. The open edge drew the wily squirmers like a magnet. Boars rushed to protect their families, getting underfoot of the horses and squealing fiercely whenever a quarterstaff blow meant for a snake struck one of them in the back. Jilamey prodded escaping snakes until they retreated far enough upwind to lose the pig-redolent air. Most departed hastily for the marshes. One struck back at his quarterstaff. Anne Boncyk raised the crossbow at her knee, and fired.

The quarrel hit the ground under the snake's jaw, missing it by feet. Anne reined her horse away, not quite believing she'd missed.

Hurriedly, Jilamey kicked his horse over and bashed the surprised snake over the head with his quarterstaff, which made it recoil and double away.

"Aim a little higher," he called. "I make that mistake myself."

"My darned sights must be off," Anne swore, fiddling with the cross hairs.

There was a tremendous explosion on the opposite side of the barn. Todd grabbed for his radio.

"Anybody! What was that?"

"Sapper mine," Kelly's voice replied. "A horde of tiddlers was moving in between the house and the granary. The survivors are stopping to eat the carrion. You won't have to worry about this avenue for a while. Team Two's moving up! I just saw Hrrula."

"Thanks, hon," Todd said, replacing the unit on its clip. He gestured to Don to move out to the opposite end of the grounds to check that no small snakes were trying to sneak around the far end of the building.

Hrriss had had his eye on a good-sized Momma Snake that moved up among the ranks of younger reptiles. The smell of delicious fresh meat just beyond the barrier tempted it away from the road home. At present, the huge snake was staying out of range of Hrriss' sharp spear, but still trying to make a break for the pigpens. Gerrh leaped down to join the boars hunting small snakes. The pigs grunted at him, but didn't attack, accepting him tentatively as a fellow predator.

Inside the smelly enclosure, the sows were running round and round their mud patches, screaming challenges to the snakes outside; detailing in Pig—Todd grinned to himself—just exactly what they'd do to any reptiles they got.

The screams of the attacking boars as they stomped tiddlers to death added to the din as the Hunters tried to restore order. Todd's horse slipped slightly on the bloody pieces of one snake. The boar who had killed it was eating some of the flesh with savage grunts of pleasure. Todd held tight with his knees as Gypsy recovered and got to more secure footing. Then he chased four live snakes away from a damaged portion of the fence that lay tilted, leaving a tempting rent through which a small snake would squeeze.

"We are here," Hrrula's voice called through the radio link.

"Good," Todd replied. "I want to split this stream of snakes into two parts, send 'em around the farm and down into the swamps. Can you set up a blockade just below the fence with the Beaters to deflect them?"

"Will do," Hrrula affirmed.

Hrriss' Momma Snake made one more effort to escape before he harried it beyond the farm. Once it was upwind of the pigs, the smell of salt air touched its sensitive tongue and nostrils, reminding it that there were easier meals elsewhere.

"He's down, he's down!" the handsets screeched. With a final swipe at a pair of tiddlers who'd just decided to leave, Todd grabbed for his radio.

"Report! Who is it?"

"Hrrula," wailed the voice, evidently one of Team Two's duffers.

"It's me, Todd," Robin's voice exclaimed, interrupting the hysterical outcry. "Hrrula got spun off when a snake twined a foreleg. He's okay, but there are a couple of Momma Snakes coming around your side of the barn with a flood of tiddlers. I'll join you as soon as I've got him up again. Llewellyn's blocking the path. Five Lures just came out of the woods to help. Hey, it's the Biker Babes!"

"Thanks, Robin," Todd said, smiling grimly. His eyes met Hrriss' over the pigpens. They were in for a tough fight. Momma Snakes were tough and canny, having survived many years of Snake Hunts, and they were *big*.

Another charge exploded noisily, alerting them that more snakes had tried to enter the vulnerable farmyard. Not for the first time, Todd cursed Boncyk, who refused to move his pigs to a more secure location during the farrowing season. The sharp whine and buzz of motorbikes cut through other noises, marking the arrival of the all-female team of Lures Robin had nicknamed the Biker Babes.

Robin had been right to call the mass of snakes a flood. The very ground undulated with a hissing carpet that inexorably flowed toward the sties. The dry grass beneath the snakes sounded as if it were on fire. All the Hunters who were free moved to intercept them.

"Blockade in position, Todd," Llewellyn Carn reported by radio. "Hope you can handle what's up there!"

The smaller reptiles braided in and out between the hooves of the horses, causing even some of the Hunt-hardened mounts to dance nervously. Not even seasoned horses liked a snake twining up their legs, so most were lashing out, fore and hind. The eleven-meter length of the first Momma Snake slithered into view, making directly for the War Boars. She wouldn't be intimidated by their hooves or their cries of defiance, as she could swallow one whole while on the move. Todd fretted that the few Hunters he had on hand might not be equal to her determined challenge.

Then the second of the Momma Snakes appeared around the edge of the barn, pursued by Anne Boncyk and Kelly. They loosed crossbow bolts, hitting it along the back just below the head, which distracted it, but didn't really slow it down. Hrriss and Jan joined the chase.

"Hi!" Kelly called to Todd. "This one's a real trier."

"Where are the children?" Todd asked, looking about him in panic. The ponies would be vulnerable to this Big Momma.

"Back there!" Kelly gestured. "With the Gringg!"

Now the cluster of five young riders and their horses, with their gigantic escort, galloped up the rise. Not allowed to carry more dangerous weapons, the Alley Cats and Hrriss' children did have dart guns and slingshots with which they were uncannily expert. Keeping their horses moving at a good distance and parallel to the snakes, they used darts and sling-propelled rocks to distract them from their intended prey and drive them along.

Teddy threw rocks, too. His pad-fingers were too big to fit inside the trigger-guard of a needler, but the stones he threw had the force of a bullet. He hit one snake broadside with a hand-sized stone that opened a bleeding wound on its back. At the smell of blood, several larger snakes swarmed over their unlucky mate, and it was torn to pieces.

"Good shot, Teddy!" Jilamey called. He was reloading his crossbow. "Look out, someone! Get that one!"

Attracted by the new rich musk from Gringg fur, a four-meter tiddler made for Teddy's horse. No one was nearer than Jilamey. Not stopping to think, he spurred his horse forward until he was nearly on top of the reptile before he struck at it with his quarterstaff. The snake evaded his blow and wound up the shaft onto the saddle before he could drop it. Jilamey went for his knife, but the snake trapped his arm. He let out a roar of pain just as the snake opened its huge maw to engulf his head.

"Morra! Chilmeh!" Teddy cried. The little Gringg leaned over toward Jilamey's saddle and grabbed the hissing snake around the throat with one paw. Hauling its head away from Jilamey's body, he began to batter the snake with his other handpaw, his claws rending the thick scales as if they were no more than cotton. Blood spurted, and the snake hung limply in his grasp. Jilamey, rubbing snake spit from his face, stared down at it. Teddy raised his eyes to the Hayuman, almost surprised as Jilamey at what he had done.

"Thank you," Jilamey said sincerely. As he scrubbed at his face, he could feel his heart hammering in his chest. The muscles of his squeezed arm tingled, and he wiggled the fingers to ease them. "Thank you very much."

"Rehmeh," Teddy replied. "I am sorry I got blood on your coat."

"Think nothing of it," Jilamey said, shaking his head in wonder. "You saved my life. You're a real hero, little bear!" He gave a shaking laugh. "People have always warned me about losing my head over Snake Hunting."

A roar from Grizz attracted their attention. The two adult Gringg had caught the Momma Snake that Hrriss was chasing. Grizz had caught it by the tail and was now working her claws up its back to the head. Meanwhile Eonneh tackled its wide-open jaws, attempting to shut them. The Momma had been all set to swallow the War Boar it had stunned. The immense snake writhed in a furious attempt to dislodge one or the other of its attackers.

"DON'T LET IT GO, GRIZZ!" Robin roared. "It'll be twice as dangerous now it's tasted pork blood."

All the farm Hunters converged upon the scene, peppering the snake with quarrels, while at the same time Eonneh was closing its mouth by the simple expedient of locking his claws right through its tough skull and jaw. Gradually its frenzied thrashing subsided to an occasional twitch. Only then did the two Gringg let go, without noticing the very respectful expressions of the other Hunters.

"Great kill, Gringgs. Thanks. But that's one down and still one to go," Wayne said grimly.

The remaining Momma Snake had turned at bay. It was coiled in a huge knot at the corner of the sty, ready to spring on whatever puny creature dared to attack. Todd estimated the snake at a good twelve meters or he'd lost his eye. In that posture and cornered, it would be a bitch to kill. It could strike out in any direction, and even if all of the Hunters charged, it was capable of inflicting considerable damage.

He and Hrriss signalled to the Team to form a circle around the snake. If there was any way to get it moving, they might be able to drive it downhill into the marshes without killing it.

Just then, Jilamey's horse buckled to its knees and sent him over its head, right into a mass of squirming tiddlers trying to brave the bloodstained barriers around the olive grove. The horse got up and, squealing, fled its immediate danger. Flailing his arms and legs, Jilamey desperately sought to get to his feet. Like living ropes, the snakes impeded his efforts, tripping him until he was up against the light metal blockades. With a cry, he slipped again into the midst of them. Todd spurred Gypsy into the tiddlers, brandishing his quarterstaff from side to side.

That distraction gave the Momma Snake its opportunity. It launched out of its coil at the smallest creatures it could see: the children. Trained in evasive actions, the Alley Cats and Hrriss' cubs scattered their horses in their mad dash, leaving Teddy behind on the old, slow-moving Rock. While Teddy tried to urge Rock to *move,* the powerful snake skimmed the ground toward him, as relentless as lava, as fearsome as lightning. Todd and the others wheeled and hurtled toward the vulnerable pair. Teddy let out a deafening squeal that startled old Rock more than the approaching snake. He reared, adding his own scream of terror, and walked backward on his hind legs right up against the wall of the grain barn. The Gringg cub had learned his lesson about holding on. His legs were locked firmly on the pack saddle, but he didn't know what to do except hang on.

"Mama!" he cried. The voder at his throat made it a weak, high-pitched whimper.

Horses were fast, but Gringg could move with astounding speed when necessary.

"Weddeerogh!" Grizz cried, streaking forward to fall on the snake's back.

It dragged her for yards, then strained to a halt as the Gringg clawed her way, up to its head, repeating the tactic that had been so successful with the other Momma Snake. She threw one massive arm around its neck, wrapped the other one across her wrist, and squeezed. And squeezed. And squeezed.

The snake's long body whipped dangerously from side to side, making it too perilous for anyone to approach to help her. The Gringg hung on, rolled over and over in the dust by the muscled strength of her prey. As Todd and the others watched in astonishment, the serpent's frenzied movements grew weaker and finally ceased. The great coils gave one more convulsion and then lay still. Shakily, Grizz rolled off the dead snake and lay on her back. Eonneh rushed forward to help his mate to her feet. Teddy dismounted and hurried to his parents, dragging the unwilling horse behind him by the reins.

"That," said Robin Reeve, the first to regain his voice, "was the most amazing thing I've ever seen in my life. Ever."

"I warned you how dangerous—" Barnstable began, then stopped, aware of the sudden, almost hostile repudiation of his audience. He cleared his throat and began again. "You are correct. It was an astounding feat of strength. The Gringg make formidable Hunters."

Todd leaned over and slapped the Spacedep man on the back. "Now, that admission has made my day, Admiral!"

"You may be *sure*, Reeve, that I never intended that," Barnstable said, eyeing Todd warily.

"Oh, I'm sure." Todd laughed. "Well done, Grizz," he called. The Gringg, clutching her cub and mate close to her massive chest, beamed at him, showing all her fangs.

"Isn't anyone going to congratulate me?" Jilamey called, rising to his feet from the dust. "I'm going to pass my Coming of Age Ritual at last!" He held up not one, but three snake bags, tightly tied and wriggling.

"You young fool," Boncyk said with a groan, bowing over his saddlehorn in despair. "You've flattened half my new olive trees!"

A beaming Hu Shih took his place of honor on the dais at the Snake Hunt feast that evening in the Assembly Hall. His wife Phyllis, tiny and exquisite, sat beside him in a Hrruban robe of red tissue silk spangled with gems. The presentations for successful Hunters had taken place, with a special round of applause for Jilamey Landreau and his bag of three. But the roar of approval when Grizz was given her medal was deafening.

Then the servers began distributing the dishes which had been tantalizing everyone with their aromas. Jilamey sat at the Reeve family table in the front row below the dais, proudly showing off his Coming of Age medal with its four wiggly ribbons.

Hu tapped his water glass with the side of his fork, and waited for silence.

"Thank you, friends," he said, beaming. "I've been asked to say a few words. This is a triple celebration. Today we celebrate yet another successful Snake Hunt, a festival I have always enjoyed, as it marks the climax of New Home Week, the very first of the traditional Rraladoonan festivals. Rraladoon—the name has passed through many changes over the years: Doona, Rrala, Doonarrala, Rraladoona. It is really time we settled on one designation to be used by everyone. Rraladoon demonstrates our unity as one people, despite our different biologies. 'Wee be of one people, thou and I,' as an ancient poet once said—now and forever.

"The second reason for celebration is the historic Trade Agreement signed with our newest allies, the Gringg. I welcome their captain, Grzzeearoghh—" The name set him coughing. "Dear me," he said when he recovered, "I hope I said that right, and all her crew, and hope they make many more trips here to visit us and enjoy their beautiful new residence on Treaty Island."

"Here, here!" Ken Reeve shouted from his table near the dais. Pat Reeve raised her glass to clink against her husband's. Jilamey, and Commander Frill, seated at Ken's particular request at the Reeve family table, joined them.

Teddy, urged on by his parents, came forward with a heap of tissue-wrapped bundles. He stopped next to Hrriss, waiting with pleading, scared red eyes until the Hrruban took the top bundle.

"Zank you, young Zeddy," Hrrestan said gravely.

The young Gringg sketched a clumsy half bow, made all the more endearing by the roundness of his figure, and moved on to Todd, then one by one to each of the original party visiting the Gringg ship. Commander Frill was delighted to be included, and patted the cub on the shoulder. Teddy's last delivery was to Greene, sitting at one of the front tables with Grace Castleton.

"What is it?" Greene asked, handling the package as if it might explode in his hands.

"It is a collar," Teddy replied shyly, "like mine." He scooted back to his place on the dais beside Grizz and Honey.

"That's sweet," Grace Castleton said, with a warm smile for Teddy, and elbowed the unresponsive commander. "Put it on, Jon!" He reddened, but complied.

"This is in recognition," Grizz announced in Middle Hrruban, the voder raising her voice to a tolerable pitch for the guests "of our first friends here on Rraladoon, and in hopes for the many yet to be made."

She waved graciously, acknowledging the wild applause and cheers. Todd immediately unwrapped his gift and put it on, preening. Gringg-sized, it hung over his shoulders like a shawl. Hrriss donned his. Each collar was beautifully and individually decorated. Grinning at one another at the tableau they made, they leaned over toward the Gringg leaders.

"Beautiful," Todd said fervently. "Thank you."

"It is our pleasure," Honey replied. "You have given us many gifts, most treasured of all being the gift of friendship."

Hu Shih smiled, and put up a hand for attention. "And thirdly, we celebrate, a little prematurely, the fortieth birthday of Todd

Reeve. I know it's two weeks away, Todd, but surely you'll forgive an old man for rushing things a little." The crowd chuckled, and Hu continued. "He is the very calendar of our life here on Rraladoon, and the symbol of our unity, our friendship with our neighbor the Hrrubans. I am proud that he is my successor as Colony Leader. He has secured my safety and my enjoyment in retirement. Let me assure you that I'll continue to vote for him any time he runs for re-election. Happy birthday, Todd, and long life to you." Hu Shih sat down amid applause and cheers.

The Alley Cats left their seats between their two sets of grandparents and mounted the dais, joined by Hrriss' children. Alison pushed Alec, who presented a gift-wrapped box to Todd.

Alec cleared his throat. "We have a special present for you, too, Dad."

"It was our own idea," Alison added.

"Why, thank you," Todd said, really touched by the gravity on their faces. He opened the box.

"It's from us, too," Hrrunival put in. Hrrana, behind him, nodded vigorously.

"What is it?" Hrriss asked, noticing a suspicious hint of moisture in Todd's eyes. Todd held up a rope tail, unmistakably braided together by small, inexpert fingers, but colorful with ribbons interwoven with the sisal.

"It's beautiful, kids," he said, his voice husky with emotion. He tied it around his waist and tugged the knots taut. "What do you know? It fits!"

The children gave him kisses and hugs, made shy by the onlookers, and hurried off to return to their places by their grandparents.

"Speech, speech!" Hrriss cried, clapping his hands together. The cry was taken up by the rest of the room. "Speech!"

"My friends," Todd began as he rose. He pointed at the collar and the rope tail. "If my age is the calendar, then this is the composite picture of the makeup of Rraladoon: part Hrruban, part Hayuman, and now part Gringg, but all very, very happy and grateful. Thank you so much."

"Lions and Hayumans and Bears, oh my!" Kelly chortled. Everyone laughed.

Overwhelmed by a deep feeling of joy, Todd sat down. Kelly, Hrriss, and Nrrna raised their glasses to him. "Happy birthday, my love," Kelly whispered. She was dressed in a glowing, green silk dress that fit her slender form to a degree that was almost illicit. "My present's waiting for you at home." She raised her eyebrows wickedly, and Todd grinned.

Second Speaker Hrrto, seated at the end of the dais, rose. "May I speak, Mr. Hu?" he asked politely.

"But of course, Speaker," Hu Shih said, startled, but in perfect High Formal Hrruban. "We'd be honored by your words."

"It is I who am honored," Hrrto said, bowing. Then he changed to the Middle Hrruban that most of those in the room would understand. "I have a most important announcement to make. I do not wish to diminish the last presentation, but there is a fourth reason for celebration tonight. You are aware that our beloved First Speaker, Hrruna, became one with the Stripes some months ago. We have all mourned his loss, I more than I knew at first. An election was held last night for his successor. The results affect you more"—he dropped his jaw slightly in the equivalent of a Hayuman grin—"than you might think."

"Old Hrrto looks almost happy," Todd whispered to Hrriss. "He must have won the election after all."

"Finally," Hrriss replied, with a grin of relief. "He'd be a better First Speaker than most—not that there was a lot of choice."

Silvery mane gleaming in the lantern-light, Second looked noble and somewhat fragile, except for the totally uncharacteristic gleam in his eye.

"This is a most happy day for me as well," he went on in Middle Hrruban. "I am proud to announce that the Hrruban who will pass into the First Speakership is revered for his wisdom. He is known to have trod a difficult but just path in the best interests of both Hrruba and Rraladoon. He is well known to you all. It is perhaps as well"—again there was that brief, amused drop of the jaw—"that he is not a member of the High Council at present, which I believe is one reason why many of my fellow Councillors felt able to vote unanimously in his favor." His smile broadened as he deliberately tantalized his breathless audience. "By that admission, you know that it is not I who won such an honor. I find myself content to remain Second Speaker and serve First. But I did sincerely believe for some time that I was the only suitable candidate.

"Over the course of the last two months, I have watched and been impressed by another whose achievements I brought to the attention of the High Council. They have seen the merit of my arguments. Consequently, I can announce to you that the duly elected First Speaker of the High Council of Hrruba is"—he paused to turn to the recipient—"Hrrestan, son of Hrrindan."

The surprise was so complete that gasps rippled through the room before yells and cheers broke out and the entire assembly rose to its feet, clapping their hands raw and making the Gringg cringe from the wild whistlings.

A dazed Hrrestan got to his feet, shaking his head at Hrrto as if he could not believe such an honor would fall to him. Then with a snap of his head and a straightening of his lean shoulders, he held up his hands. As silence finally fell in the hall, Hrrestan seemed unable to find words. Into the stillness, tiny Hrrunna, who could have no understanding of the honor just bestowed on her grandsire, purred a childish question. "Rra?"

Hrrto chuckled at the baby's reaction. "It is auspicious that Hrruna's namesake also approves."

Then, with a formal bow of unusual humility, Hrrto presented Hrrestan with a small box. Hrrestan opened it, his eyes widening in surprise. The audience gasped as he held up the great blue sapphire which had been Rraladoon's present to Hrruna.

"Where's Mrrva? She should be here," Todd murmured to Kelly, and started to beckon Alec to him.

"She is here," Hrriss said, drawing his attention to the rear of the dais. The graceful Hrruban woman, her mane whitening slightly around her sweet face, was clad in the most exquisite diaphanous red robe. She joined her mate, looking up at him with great pride as she adorned him with his new badge of office. Another round of cheers and applause followed that little ceremony. Todd was so affected by the tableau that he could feel involuntary tears starting in his eyes. Hrriss wound his tail around Todd's knee and gave him a companionable squeeze. Todd threw his arm over his best friend's shoulders. Kelly and Nrrna joined the hug, insinuating themselves into the embrace and clasping their hands across to one another. The baby sat in the middle, gurgling happily.

"What a splendid tribute! So long deserved," Kelly whispered.

Todd nodded and sniffed surreptitiously. All his life, he'd respected the Hrruban who was, in many ways, a second father to him. Without Hrrestan's guidance, Todd might not have grown up to take over the responsibilities that had been predicted as the fate of the exuberant, disobedient six-year-old colonist. Hrrto was right. There was no one else of all the high-ranking wide Stripes that Todd had met during his nearly forty years who was better suited, or trained, to accept the First Speakership.

He overcame his thickened throat and added his cheers to the prolonged accolade.

"I am honored beyond speech," Hrrestan said when the applause abated enough for him to be heard. "I do not presume to take the place of First Speaker Hrruna, for he was unique in the history of both our worlds, and certainly of this one. But I *will* do my utmost to live up to the honorable principles he endorsed.

"The one regret I have is that my appointment to the position of First Speaker will limit the amount of time I may spend here, among my friends and family on Rraladoon. I will never give up my home here, so it is a good thing that our new friends, the Gringg, have come to us with the materials to make more, and more efficient, grids. So efficient, in fact, that we will be extending this technology to our longtime allies and partners, the Hayumans. And it is the Gringg who have brought us the means to share that technology with Hayumans."

The applause which followed this announcement was thunderous. Hrrestan, beaming, resumed his seat.

"Couldn't think of a better cat for the job," Ali Kiachif said, toasting him with mlada and draining the glass dry. He beckoned to one of the young Hrrubans helping to serve at the feast. "Give me another shot of liquid headache, son."

Todd had one more announcement to make, and stood, raising his hands for quiet.

"The spaceport planning committee will meet tomorrow—tomorrow afternoon," he said with a grin, "giving the delegates some chance to recover from the party tonight." He held up a hand-sized holographic projector. "I have something else that should be public knowledge now. May I have the lights off, please?"

The lights dimmed as Todd triggered the holograph, and a map appeared on the dais before the head table. Each species' claimed systems showed in a different color: amber for Hrruba, red for Gringg, and green for Amalgamated Worlds. "Now, the moment of truth!" He touched the relevant key, and three spots began glowing in the heart of each nebulous blob. The crowd let out a collective gasp.

"Reeve, that's classified!" Barnstable roared in protest, jumping to his feet at his place on the opposite end of the dais.

"Not really," Todd said. "Not for years. It's long been possible to extrapolate the location of the home systems from radiotelescope transmissions. I tried it myself. There is Earth, there is

Hrruba, and there is the Gringg homeworld. We're going to be open and aboveboard now. We've agreed that the homeworlds will be off-limits to the uninvited, but who knows what the future will bring? Oh, and there," Todd said, pointing to a small blue spot glowing gently in the center of the map, "there's Rraladoon."

"Like the nucleus of a molecule," one of the Hayuman scientists observed aloud. "I hope it's a stable one."

"Oh, I doubt it," Todd said, shaking his head, to the shock of the scientist and the assembled guests. "A stable molecule is a closed system. We have to be open." He gestured at his fellow Humans. "It all started with one race of sentient beings. Then there were two, and now there are three. It's only a matter of time before there are four, then ten, then fifty. . . ."

"Stop!" Barnstable protested, his face flushed. Then he took a deep breath and managed a weak grin. "Take it easy, Reeve. Some of us can take only so much . . . incredible news at a time."

"Then let us become a homogenous whole," Hrriss said, his eyes sparking merrily. "Let the party begin!"

The "Doona/Rrala Ad Hoc Band" had a guest instrumentalist among their number: Artos, the Gringg lutanist. He confessed to having learned the Rraladoonan system of musical notation only recently.

"But I can play harmony if required," he added.

"You'll play solos, if I have anything to say about it," said Sally Lawrence, smiling at him winningly. "Ready, everyone? A-one, a-two, a-three!"

They struck up dance music. After listening carefully for a handful of bars, Artos added a delicate but intricate descant to the melody. Everyone listening smiled and started snapping fingers or stamping to the tempo.

"C'mon, Koala," Lieutenant Cardiff said, urging the Gringg engineer out onto the dance floor. "Show us how you do it."

The rangy technician and his giant friend were soon the center of a dozen or so couples merrily stepping along. The children joined hands with grandparents and danced in a circle around them. Teddy spun into the circle holding hands with Ken, and Hrrunival coaxed Kodiak to join with him and Hrrana.

Off to one side away from the musicians, a couple of Hunters who'd started their party not long after dismounting from the ride had adopted Cinnamon, and were telling him tales of being misunderstood in their lives.

"I broke my mother's heirloom teapot when I was a child," one of them said sadly. "Was an accident. Coulda happened to anybody. Have some mlada. You don't have to worry about a hangover, do you? Your eyes are already red."

"My eyes are always red," Cinnamon said, puzzled. "Is this another joke on me?"

The Hunters grinned. "Yeah, Br'er Bear, but a harmless one. Have a drink."

Tentatively Cinnamon accepted their hospitality, sipping, and then, liking the taste, upending his glass.

"Thassa good bruin!"

Ben Adjei collected the pool as the winner for the thirtieth year running, having made the most accurate guess of the onset of snake migration. First-time visitors paid off with groans. Mike Solinari was among the losers, but he anteed up with good grace.

"I don't know," he said, shaking his head at the senior veterinarian. "I think you have some arcane set of motivators to know just when they'll come, because it's never the same hour any two years in a row."

"I've spent a lot of time studying my subject, lad," Ben said, clapping the younger man on the back. "Live, learn, and one day you might guess, too."

On the dance floor, Robin Reeve tapped Grace Castleton on the shoulder. She and Jon Greene executed a gliding turn and stopped.

"Can I help you, young man?" she asked.

"You're a ship's captain," Robin said, his words slightly slurred. He had his arm firmly tucked around Nita Taylor's waist. "Could you marry us?"

"Oh, Robin," Nita said, blushing. "That's an ancient custom."

"But still a valid one, I'm pleased to inform you," Grace said, smiling fondly at the two young people. "I can see that you're both of an age to know your minds. So if you wish, I'd be delighted to officiate. But it'd have to be done aboard my ship. You don't want to leave the party so soon, do you? We certainly don't." Greene whispered in her ear, and she blushed. "Perhaps later, Exec."

A few steps away, Barnstable was recounting the events of the Snake Hunt to a circle of listeners. "Never seen anything like it in my life. Snake comes up and tries to eat a rider, slithers right up the horse's a—" he glanced at his wife beside him and she gave him a long-suffering look—"er, rump. The beggar—I mean, Gringg—just yanked it off by the tail and battered that reptile about the head with her paws until it was dead as a mat! Nothing but her paws! Now I believe they don't need any personal armament."

"Ah, young Reeve," Ali Kiachif said, shouting at Todd and Kelly above the raucous music of the Doona/Rrala Ad Hoc Band. "Congratulations to you and greetings to you, lovely Kelly. My glass must have a hole in it, if you understand the problem. The mlada's all gone."

"I'll find you some," Todd said, laughing. Spotting one of the servers, he directed the girl toward Ali. Arm in arm, he and Kelly wriggled through the crowd to the dance floor. Hrriss and Nrrna were already there, gracefully gliding to the music.

"Todd Rreev," Grizz called. The Gringg captain towered head and shoulders above everyone else in the room. "Todd Rreev, Hrriss? A moment of your attention?"

Todd and Hrriss rose from the table where, over a glass or two, they and Hrrestan, Sumitral, Fred Horstmann, Jilamey, Barnstable, and Kiachif had been having an unofficial roundtable about the spaceport facilities. Kelly glanced at Nrrna.

"Should we go?" she asked Grizz.

"Morra," the Gringg replied. Several of the other Gringg filed in around them, surrounding the table like an impromptu forest. "It is a most interesting thing to tell you. You will like to hear it. Rrawrum, my communications officer, has just called me." She tapped her collar with a foreclaw. "Another species has just attained an orbit around our homeworld. They are so unlike us that they cannot communicate anything except that like us, they arrive in peace." She shot Todd a knowing glance. "And yes, our people have determined that their ship has no weapons, although they do have meteor shields."

"*Another* race?" Kiachif demanded. "Another kind of alien? Not like us, or them, or you?"

"Reh." Grizz smiled, her rubbery black lips peeling back to show all the sharp white fangs in her mouth. "Since you Rraladoonans seem to be able to master new languages with little trouble . . ." She glanced at Todd when he groaned. "That is a proven ability, Zodd, so our leaders, who have been vastly impressed by the voder and all your courtesies to us, have managed to convey the spatial coordinates of Rraladoon to these new creatures."

"Your leaders did what?" Todd asked, half-appalled but also finding himself ready to accept a new challenge. After all, with Hrrestan as First Speaker, there would be harmony with that world.

"They are proceeding with all dispatch here to this Treaty Planet," Grizz said. "It is the sensible solution to a problem we Gringg are not capable of solving."

"Look, Grizz, we can only do so much," Todd began, temporizing only because he didn't want to appear eager.

"But you did so well in greeting us, putting us at our ease, showing us how two species can live in harmony."

"But we treated you badly," Barnstable said, joining them. "We distrusted you."

"You only acted with caution, as a Gringg would," Grizz assured him. She nodded her big head in approval.

"Great stars," Barnstable exclaimed involuntarily, and then looked around him, as if embarrassed to be complimented so publicly by someone he had, until just recently, held in great suspicion.

"I wonder what kind of joy juice they might bring with them," Kiachif mused, sloshing the thick amber liquid which Eonneh suggested he try. "I mean, every civilized species has something or other to ease the pains to which flesh—of any kind—is susceptible."

"What do zey look like?" Nrrna asked.

"We do not know," Grizz said. "A description and other details will follow."

Todd's mind boggled at the hundreds of possible shapes an alien species could have. Kelly nudged him with her elbow.

"I wonder if they have young," she said, assuming a most innocent expression.

"And if zeir young will play with ours," Hrriss added, enjoying the bemused expression on his best friend's face.

Admiral Sumitral of Alreldep grinned broadly at Todd. "Prime your children, Reeve and Hrriss. Alreldep can't seem to get anything done without their assistance."